UnCatholic Conduct

UnCatholic Conduct

by

Stevie Mikayne

2014

UNCATHOLIC CONDUCT

ISBN 13: 978-1-62639-304-2

This Trade Paperback Original Is Published By
Bold Strokes Books, Inc.
P.O. Box 249
Valley Falls, NY 12185

First Edition: December 2014

Credits
Editor: Cindy Cresap
Production Design: Susan Ramundo
Cover Design By Gabrielle Pendergrast

Acknowledgments

The birth of a novel is similar to the birth of a child. If you're lucky, as I've been, a community stands around cheering and handing out champagne, and saying "It's about freaking time!"

This novel required particular patience from my community because I literally lost the plot about 50% of the way through, and had to shelve the novel for three years so I could decide who the bad guy was…

Thanks go to my tutor from Lancaster University, Sara Maitland, who didn't scold me for handing in chapters of this book in lieu of the creative nonfiction novel I was supposed to be working on for my MA thesis.

To my wife and daughter, who have spent a lot of time at the park while I've finished rewrites and edits.

To my supportive and keenly observant beta readers: Pavarti, Jo Ellen, Roxie and Jessica, and the team of experts who received two a.m. e-mails with random what-if questions and answered without ever asking, "Why do you want to know?"

And to the fantastic ladies involved in the final step of this process: my meticulous editor Cindy and the rest of the BSB team who has worked behind the scenes to bring this manuscript into book form.

Dedication

To Nancy,

It's about time I dedicated a book to you…even if you'll probably never read it. Even if you're so shocked by the sex scenes that you blush scarlet and slam the laptop shut, wondering out loud what will happen when our daughter grows up and realizes that when her mother "goes to work," she's actually writing about murder, sex and scandal…

All my love.

Prologue

1999

At ten o'clock in the morning, Megan and Reggie slipped up the musty old stairwell that had lain vacant ever since the new wing had been built. Long ago, the spiders had made cities out of cobwebs in this abandoned part of the school. Dusty light filtered in through narrow windows, disturbed by the movement on the creaking wooden stairs.

The girls darted past the third floor, up to the landing where the door stood shut tight. A green tie hung on a hook by the wall, and Reggie grabbed it, her young girlfriend pushing her into the doorway, kissing her hard.

Reggie slipped the green tie over the door, giggling a little as they pushed the door open.

The smell of old dust and petrified sweat still lingered among the gym equipment, decades old.

Megan laughed as Reggie tucked an old chair under the rusty door handle. "Nobody even remembers this place exists."

"Just in case."

Megan drew her close and kissed her deeply, running her hands along Reggie's shoulders, down her back to her pockets.

"Damn your buttons," Reggie said as she struggled with each tiny disc and hole on Megan's fitted blouse.

Soon, they both stood topless, giggling and shivering.

Behind the wall, someone stepped away from the crack in the wood, and crept down the outward scaffolding.

Chapter One

Jillienne Kidd stood behind her long wooden desk trying to gather piles of reports, folders, and scraps of paper into some semblance of order. A short rap sounded on her door, and she spun around, sending a precariously balanced folder skidding to the floor.

"Hey," she said as she ducked to retrieve it. "What's up?"

"Assignment," said her boss, Padraig O'Hanagan.

Jil's heart sped up. "Yeah?"

Padraig didn't wait for an invitation, just stepped right over the mess on the floor and settled himself on the window seat.

Jil eased herself into her office chair, her back still feeling the effects of the last assignment.

"This one should be easy, Kidd." Padraig smiled a little through his gruff beard.

"Easy? Who said I wanted easy?"

"Your back said it for you. That last one really knocked you out—literally."

"Not my fault!"

"Who said anything about fault? I'm not punishing you, Kidd. I'm promoting you. Comes with a pay raise and everything."

"Yeah, right. We can't afford a pay raise, Padraig, and you know it."

The old PI sighed and knitted his bushy brows. "Why don't you let me worry about the books, and focus on keeping yourself on the stable side of balconies, got it?"

She gritted her teeth but nodded.

"Listen, this assignment is a little unusual."

Jil leaned forward, interested in spite of suspecting Padraig of sticking her somewhere safe just to get her out of harm's way.

"What is it?"

Padraig rubbed the back of his neck. "Now before I tell you, I just want to be very clear…you're the only one who can believably do this assignment, and that's why you're going. If I could send Chet or Rick, I would, but they'd make lousy covers." He squinted.

Jil crossed her arms. That squint was Padraig's tell. He swore he had a poker face, but she'd known him long enough to see trouble coming. "What's my cover?"

Padraig's gaze darted to the door, and a bead of sweat formed between his thick brows. "You'll have your phone and access to e-mail. You'll also be able to go home at the end of the day, and to check in here if you need to. It's a local job."

"Am I getting a disguise?"

Padraig exhaled. "Doubt you'd need it. Don't think you'd run into anybody you know there."

"Where, Padraig?"

He sighed. "St. Marguerite's."

"The high school?" Jil said incredulously. "You want me to go undercover as a teacher? Are you serious? What the hell for? Someone's going over their limit on the photocopy machine?"

Padraig frowned as he handed her a folder.

"What? We need to root out the person who's raiding the cafeteria at midnight?" Jil was enjoying herself now. This had to be a joke. Still, Padraig remained silent.

"C'mon. Don't tell me this is an actual assignment."

"Somehow I knew you'd say that." Padraig stepped back. "But believe me, it's no laughing matter. Superintendent Giovanni DiTullio visited me today. He's very concerned about that particular location."

"And he's seriously willing to pay for a PI undercover?"

Padraig stopped. "A paycheck is always serious. Especially these days."

"Sure it is."

Jil knew their agency, Padraig O'Hanagan Investigators, had hit some hard times lately. People just didn't have the money to spend on private investigations with the global economy tanking. Padraig had been forced to cut a few jobs at the agency in the last few months, and the bills continued to pile up.

If things kept going this way, the PI firm would close, she'd be out of a job, and then…

She stopped as shivers ran down her arm. She was not going to think about that possibility.

What if…the insidious whisper started. What if you lose your job and you can't get another one? What if you can't pay the mortgage and you lose your house? You have nobody. Nobody to count on. You'd be living on the street again.

She clenched her jaw. At the age of sixteen, she'd slept in her last cardboard box. That was before Elise.

Elise would always let her come home…wouldn't she?

"I apologize in advance that it's going to be hard on you."

She flipped open the folder and scanned it quickly to find out what the hell could be so difficult. Her incredulity rose as Padraig actually got up to leave before she could read the pretext.

"Are you serious?" Jil raised her eyebrows. "You're really going to sneak out of here?"

Padraig chuckled. "I'll be in my office. And when you're about to ask me to take you off this case, please try to imagine Chet or Rick going undercover as a first-year teacher in a high school."

He stepped back over the piles in front of the door.

"Okay."

Chet and Rick were brothers, both pushing fifty, and although they were fantastic investigators, they'd be completely unbelievable. Whatever this assignment entailed, clearly, she was the woman for the job.

"And before you go, see if you can't get the GotJunk boys in here to haul some of this stuff away."

Jil shot him a withering look as he left. This office, running from an old 1920s house in the ritzier area of Rockford, suited her well. She had the attic space—sloping ceilings, beaten leather furniture, an old desk that could have belonged to Elizabeth Barrett Browning. And a window seat she'd upholstered herself. And which Padraig had wrinkled. Again. She might not have cared about piles of paper, but she hated her window seat to be disorganized.

Frowning, she got up and straightened the cushions. Then she settled herself in the spot Padraig had just vacated and opened the folder. On top of the pile sat a letter from Giovanni DiTullio, sent on letterhead from the Rockford Catholic School Board. What on earth could the superintendent possibly need a PI for?

Mr. O'Hanagan,

I would like to retain your services for a private investigation regarding uncatholic conduct in several members of staff at St. Marguerite's Catholic High School. This is an ongoing and increasingly serious matter in our board.

Staff members in the Catholic School Board are *required* to uphold Catholic standards in their *personal* as well as their *professional* lives while teaching in the Board. This comes in the form of a morality clause. They sign a contract to this effect before being hired. They require a signed note by a priest saying they are a practicing member of a parish before they can officially become employees of the board. Unless they can meet these conditions (and meet them willingly), they are not hired or retained.

Catholic conduct must be a priority for staff members working in a Catholic school. Without it, we are in danger of hypocrisy, and subject to public scrutiny from Catholic parents and families who send their children to us for a Catholic education. Accusing a staff member of uncatholic conduct is a serious matter, as it could result in termination of a teacher's position. As one of the superintendents of the board, it is my duty to uphold the Catholic Standards set for the staff and the principals. Deliberate breach of contract is a serious problem for me, for the board, and for the community.

In recent years, this issue has been allowed to lapse. The result has been flagrant disregard for Catholic conduct in the community and a don't ask, don't tell policy adopted by many principals. This is unacceptable. Worse, I am now experiencing pressure from various parents' associations whose fundraising efforts we depend upon to fund many of our co-curricular programs.

We have never taken a decision to "look the other way" when staff members are flouting their Catholic responsibilities, and we must not begin now.

Unfortunately, this system works on an honor basis. We operate over eighty schools within Rockford Board alone. St. Marguerite's has over ninety-five staff members. And this particular school is under heavy scrutiny. We have a serious problem there, which warrants investigation. These teachers are in violation of their contracts. The principal is ignoring the problem. Students are being influenced. Parents are angry, and we cannot afford bad press at a time when amalgamation is an ever-looming threat. *We need to do something.*

Please let me know at your earliest convenience if you would be willing to dispense an investigator for this purpose—if possible, for the purposes of credibility, a younger female would be best. I will provide all necessary documentation for her to begin her "employment" with the board.

Thank you for your prompt attention to this matter.

Sincerely,

Giovanni DiTullio,

Superintendent

Jil put down the file, exhaling as if she'd just walked away from a heated argument—no doubt how the writer had felt by the time he'd finished the note—and walked over to the phone.

A younger female, eh? Why not just go to the meat counter at the butcher and select the side of pork you'd like, Mr. DiTullio? Perhaps you'd prefer to go to the Investigator Fair, and pick out your PI for a date night on the town.

"You're hilarious," she said when Padraig answered.

"Why so funny?"

"Uncatholic conduct? That's what I'm investigating? There's no such thing."

Padraig said nothing.

"C'mon!" Jil exploded. "How twelfth century can we get here? At the very least, I'm sure it goes against the Charter!"

"Believe me, if it wasn't paying the bills, I'd be laughing too. But this is a real assignment, and we're not exactly in the position to be turning away work right now."

Jil managed—with effort—to hold her tongue.

"Listen." Padraig sighed. "If you decline, I understand. This was never supposed to be a full-time gig for you, and I know that."

"Padraig…"

"No, listen to me, Jil. I told you I would give you a job and pay you until you finished your schooling and got a real career. And I know you've been sticking around because the cases are interesting and you're young and foolish enough to want to risk your life. But this wasn't for keeps. You've got your papers now and you can go and work a real job if you like."

"Padraig, c'mon. I'm not going to leave you just because things are tough."

"You might be smart to," he said. "I don't think I'm doing you any favors, keeping you around this sinking ship."

"Hey."

"What?"

"I'm not cut out for desk work, and we both know that."

"Yeah, well, you're probably not cut out for this case either."

"It's not a case. Asking people to sign that kind of contract can't be legal. It certainly isn't moral."

"Whether or not the contract is moral is not our problem. The fact is that it exists, it has been signed, and there are people in violation of it. We're private investigators here—not political advocates. Our job is only to investigate whether or not staff members are in violation of their contract. Which, for this period of time, includes uncatholic conduct in a personal or professional capacity. Period. Full stop." It sounded like Padraig had rehearsed for this conversation.

"How can someone ask us to investigate uncatholic conduct? What the hell am I supposed to write? 'So-and-so is living in sin? The secretary has a child out of wedlock'?"

"That's exactly what they're asking."

"And they would fire somebody over it?"

"If they're in violation of their signed agreement, absolutely. You've done this before. Fraud isn't new territory to you."

"Who's committing fraud here? They're afraid they might be open to public scrutiny and accused of hypocrisy? Are they blind? Where have they been living for the past twenty years while the Church has been raked over the coals for one scandal after another?"

"Perhaps that's why they're taking this matter so seriously."

"It's a farce."

"You don't have to agree with it, politically. You just have to understand the dos and don'ts of the contract and write your report. Three months—four months tops."

"I'll never survive in that school for four months!"

"Listen, Kidd. If you think you can investigate ninety-five people in less than four months, be my guest. But it better be a damn thorough job."

Jil swore under her breath. Padraig heard it anyway.

"What amalgamation is he referring to?" she asked, switching the subject.

"I suspect this is the real crux of the issue." She heard the squeak of the hinge as Padraig leaned back in his chair. She pictured his thoughtful look as he stroked his beard with one hand. "The government pays for two separate school boards—the public and the Catholic. Parents opt to send their kids to the Catholic board for a real Catholic education, and their tax money goes with it. Trouble is, if the staff aren't Catholic enough to justify a real parochial experience, why should the government pay for two boards? They'd stand to save a lot of money by combining the two."

"I think I heard something about that in the news."

"The super is probably getting pressure from upstairs to clean up this mess. Because the teachers won't be the first to go in an amalgamation."

"No, of course not. They'd still have the same number of students, so they'd likely need all the teachers."

"Except the religion teachers," Padraig said with a wry smile.

"And the bigwigs would be next," Jil finished.

"Exactly."

"I see. It always comes down to money."

"Well, money and sex. You start Tuesday. First day of school. I'd recommend brushing up on Catechism while you're at it."

"Fine," Jil muttered.

"All right then."

"What am I driving?" she asked as an afterthought.

Padraig sighed and looked down. For a second, she thought he wasn't going to answer, but then he muttered, "Your own vehicle."

"What the hell? I'm undercover in Rockland and you're not even giving me a cover car?"

"If you need one, you can borrow mine."

Jil caught her breath as she realized—

He met her eyes and nodded tiredly. "I sold the last one this week. To pay the overhead."

Jil swallowed. Two agents dismissed, one office at the back of the floor rented out to an accountant, and no more cover cars. Next step, folding up the sidewalk.

"Okay," she said, trying to keep her voice steady.

"And you might want to leave your gun at home."

Years ago, he'd given her his father's old pistol and had made her get a license and target practice. She'd fought him on every single step. "One day you're going to need this, and you'll thank me," he'd said. So far, she hadn't thanked him.

"Remember, school starts at 8:02."

"Of course it does. I'll be there."

Padraig cleared his throat, seeming to decide whether to tell her something else.

"What?" Jil asked impatiently.

"There's one more thing."

"Which is?"

"I wasn't going to mention it because I thought it might distract you, but I figure you'll find out anyway."

Jil waited, heat gathering behind her eyes. She already resented this assignment. Secrecy wasn't going to make her feel any better. She sat back in her chair, resting her feet on the desk.

Padraig sighed. "When you were a teenager, your caseworker wanted to send you there."

"Barbra?"

"No. The other one. Beatrice."

Jil made a face.

"She thought it might benefit you. They have a boarding program for kids in foster care, to give them a competitive advantage, or some other bureaucratic nonsense."

"So why didn't I go?" She hated it when Padraig knew things about her life that she didn't.

"I said no."

"Why?"

"I told your case manager that your mother had been a secular woman, and she wouldn't have approved of her only daughter being put in a Catholic school."

"Mum was Catholic," Jil protested.

"Aye. I lied. But I knew you might have a bit of trouble there, considering…"

Jil felt her cheeks getting hot. Of course Padraig had figured that out as well, before she had. "So I ended up with Elise instead."

"She'd already said she'd take you, and I thought it was probably for the best."

"Her place was definitely better than a boarding school." She made an effort to smile.

"Still call her on Sundays?" Padraig asked gently.

Jil swallowed hard. "I do my best."

"Ah, well. I'll let you get back to work."

She hung up the receiver and picked the folder back up. Usually, she loved getting these. A new identity, a new life to try on for size—make adjustments to—live for a while. Almost like getting to know a new friend. The pretext documents, legal-sized folders in multiple colors—some heavy and thick, some light and nearly empty, like some lives…it didn't matter. She'd never met an assignment she couldn't do, or a personality she couldn't wear. Not to mention a car she couldn't drive. The cars were definitely a perk—or used to be.

But this? A Catholic schoolteacher in the Religion Department? She didn't think she could pull it off. The irony of having to commit fraud—pretend to be someone she wasn't—in order to investigate it, never ceased to twinge her moral sensibilities. She almost reached for the phone again but remembered the look on Padraig's face when he mentioned a paycheck. A four-month job would bring in a hefty sum—particularly if she could unearth something to back the suspicions of the superintendent.

The fact that Padraig all but told her to abandon ship meant that things were pretty dire. She wondered how many weeks had gone by without him drawing a salary. For a brief second, she wondered if she should try to find something else—do something else.

But how could she leave the only person who'd ever been there for her?

Padraig and the agency were more important than any internal dilemmas she might face, so she set back to work, determined to get through this come hell or high water.

"Who am I?" she muttered to herself.

Here it was—her new life. Padraig had put some work into this file. It was more organized than usual, which meant he'd known about this for some time. Which meant he'd been keeping it from her—deliberately.

Gritting her teeth, she opened the cover file.

"Julia Kinness." Well, at least she'd be able to wear her monogrammed shirts. "Nice to meet you, Ms. Kinness."

No new address, which meant she didn't have to vacate her house. Not exactly deep cover, then. Birthday: July 2, 1981. Close enough. False Social Insurance card, driver's license, and credit card—in an envelope. She took out her extra wallet, slipped the cards into it, and put a twenty-dollar bill in the billfold pocket. Julia Kinness now had a purse.

Parents: Michael and Janet Kinness, born in Ireland. Oh, very original, Padraig. No siblings. No grandparents. No husband. Well, at least that wasn't much of a stretch. She didn't have to pretend to be straight and Catholic in one assignment, then.

A copy of her own university degree, doctored to change her name and major. Her own criminology credentials had been swapped for religious studies with a minor in philosophy. The pretext docs failed to include her two-year diploma in police foundations and her advanced certificate in fraud investigation. Instead, they'd forged her a teaching certificate.

Sighing, she put the certificates to one side and plodded through the rest of the folder. A copy of the teachers' contract. A forged note from a priest, attesting to her ongoing Catholic virtue. Now, if that wasn't ironic, she didn't know the meaning of the word. A map of St. Marguerite's. Her timetable. A complete list of the names and addresses of all ninety-five staff members—in alphabetical order.

Feeling about fifteen years old, and without a locker, Jil gave the timetable a glance-over. First period: spare. Second: Grade Twelve World Religion. Okay. The silver lining in all this mess—she only had to teach one course, which gave her the afternoons to herself, and the evenings to check off her targets.

So she was now Julia Kinness—probably the closest cover she'd ever had to her actual identity. For four months, she would be this woman. She'd answer to her name, tell her story, and live her life, which could make dating rather complicated…

The calendar on her desk said Thursday. That gave her exactly four and a half days to review her course material and scour her own extensive bookshelf for a brushup on Catholicism.

"I'm going out," she announced to Mary, the receptionist, as she strode past her to the front door.

She pretended not to notice the small grin that laced the corners of Mary's mouth.

Chapter Two

Tuesday morning dawned gray and rainy. Jil struggled to find her bleeping alarm clock and knocked a box of Kleenex and her reading glasses to the floor.

While the water ran in the shower, Jil took a hard look at herself in the ornate oval mirror in her bathroom: her eyes, shadowed with fatigue, her messy bedhead of hair that wouldn't curl no matter how hard she tried, petite build that was getting curvier by the year. Though she was still on the friendly side of thirty, her hips were crossing the border. Could she pass as a first-year teacher? Would they know, by the way she stood or the way she spoke, that she hadn't set foot in a high school since high school?

The water finally steaming, Jil stepped in, reveling in the hot, pulsing stream. She closed her eyes, ducked her head under, face raised into the rain head. She was never going to get out…never…

She'd almost been able to convince herself that she might be able to step out sometime in the next hour, when the water abruptly turned freezing.

She jumped out of the icy water and into her first day at St. Marguerite's.

❖

The high school didn't look that forbidding from the outside. Three pods of sandstone brick, one wing with five stories, one with three. It was a bit misshapen, actually, with the requisite Canadian flag and Rockford Catholic School Board banner. An outdated placard announcing "St. Marguerite's" hung over the entranceway. The building seemed to have been constructed in pieces, one layer being added upon another, constantly shifting as the old was taken out and replaced by the new.

Jil parked in visitors' parking and hurried into the building just as the bell rang. She'd made it halfway through the atrium—an unfortunate shade of seafoam—when a woman's voice came over the PA. "Good morning, staff and students. Please stand for our national anthem and morning prayer."

Jil proceeded to the main office but was stopped by a glare from a tall, imposing gentleman sporting a loud purple tie and a slightly less loud purple shirt. His raised hand clearly indicated that everyone around him should stop in reflection. Late students, hats in hand, bowed their heads.

Jil looked away from the purple-tied man, to the seafoam floor, as the first triumphant strands of "O Canada" blared from a speaker directly above her head. A woman's voice belted out the lyrics, switching expertly from French to English.

Trying to look patriotic, Jil discreetly checked the place out. The atrium was a huge expanse of space—the central hub from which all three wings originated. A sign on the wall indicated Green building to the left, Red building to the right, and Blue building somewhere halfway in between.

She suppressed a smile. The seafoam tiles continued down all the halls. No blue or red in sight. High ceilings. Lots of light. And lots of crucifixes. And statues. Mary, holding a baby Jesus; Mary in a virtuous pose, serene and loving, Jesus gazing up at her adoringly. Farther down the hall, a painting of St. Marguerite next to a portrait of Pope What's-His-Name. And outside the office, a statue of Jesus, arms outstretched, as if to welcome all the delinquent students to the building.

A loud squeak cut off the end of the anthem, and a different woman's voice began.

"Let us pray."

The students, if possible, bowed further, their hands clasped. Mr. Purple-tie looked as if he belonged in a church pew, his face swathed in prayer.

"In the name of the Father, the Son, and the Holy Spirit."

Jil swore in her head as everyone around her made the sign of the cross—some more reverently than others. She hurriedly followed their example, amazed at how easily it came back.

"Lord, thank you for this day. Let us remember your shining example as we embark upon a new year. Let us remember your generosity and kindness as we, the older students, help the younger students find their way in this new place. Let us remember your lessons as our teachers teach us. Let us see your face in all our neighbors. Help us to do our best each and every day. St. Marguerite, pray for us. In the name of the Father, the Son, and the Holy Spirit."

Jil kept her hands firmly clasped through the final sign of the cross and cursed Padraig once again for sending her here.

"Please be seated for a number of morning announcements," the PA commanded.

Mr. Purple-tie strode off. Jil took this as a sign that she too, was allowed to finally get to the office.

Chaos.

Students filled every chair and bench, and frazzled office staff tried to direct each new and lost soul to where she or he should go. Tripping over two backpacks on her way through the fray, Jil considered the possibility of coming back later. Of course, she had no idea where to go in the meantime, or who to ask.

"Excuse me, Miss?" one tiny, frightened boy whispered. He looked about eleven or twelve—not fourteen.

"Uh, yes?" Jil tried to put on her best teacher face.

"D'you know where G104 is? I missed the orientation. Everyone else got their schedules, and I didn't get mine till this morning. I'm supposed to get my locker number, but it's in my homeroom. And I don't know where G104 is." The boy bit his lip, and Jil saw he was trying hard not to cry.

"Uh…hang on a second." She squinted to see the sign through the leaded glass of the office window. "G104. I'm guessing that's Green building?"

"Maybe," the boy whispered.

"I'm new here too, so we'll just have to figure this out together. What's your name, anyway?"

"Gideon."

"Okay then, Gideon." This kid was starting off high school with enough problems without adding a name like Gideon to the mix.

Jil steered him out of the office and into the atrium. "Green building—this way." They turned left and were immediately confronted by two different staircases—one leading down, the other leading up.

"Let's try down," Jil said.

Gideon followed quickly to the bottom of the stairs, where a classroom door read G108.

Gideon looked up at her hopefully. "Right floor."

"Wrong room, though. Let's try farther on."

They walked down the hall to a T, and Gideon's face lit up. "Hey, Jamie!" he called.

"Hey, Gid! You're in this homeroom? Science?"

"Yeah! Is it G104?"

"Yeah!"

Joyfully, Gideon scampered down the hall toward his friend. "Thanks, Miss," he called over his shoulder.

Jil smiled and headed back to the office, where the din had not subsided one iota.

"Can I help you, Miss?" the tall, genteel woman behind the desk inquired.

"Yes, my name is Julia Kinness. I'll be substituting for Miss Barnes."

"Oh, yes. Such a shame for her." The administrative assistant obviously knew something about Miss. Barnes's absence that she did not. "This is your first day, then?"

"Yes."

"Well, thank you for coming on such short notice. Pity you missed the staff meeting and orientation, but never mind."

"When was that?"

"Last week. You're half-time or full-time?"

"Half-time. Mornings. Spare period one and Religion period two."

"Right then, you already have your schedule. That's a blessing. By the way, dear, teachers call them 'Prep' not 'Spare.' I take it you're first year."

Jil smiled sheepishly. She'd have to pay more attention. She thought of Rick or Chet in her position and smiled more.

"Just have a seat there. I'll let the principal know you're here."

Jil sat in a recently vacated seat and wondered if Mr. Purple-tie was the principal. He looked to be in his mid-fifties and had the requisite bark. She hoped not. In a moment, she saw him stride through the double doors and head directly into an office to the side that read Mark Genovese—Vice-Principal.

"Take off your hat, please," Mr. Genovese boomed to an older boy with low-riding jeans and an oversized baseball hat.

The student rolled his eyes and removed his hat. "Sorry, sir," he said when Mr. Genovese took a step toward him.

The guy was huge. Well over six feet, maybe six four or six five, and built like a football player. He had enormous shoulders, rippled and defined, a head full of graying hair, and clothes that could only have been purchased at Mr. Big & Tall. Though why he chose purple remained a mystery.

From behind him stepped a younger woman, clad in a chic black pantsuit, her intense green eyes focused on Jil. As she approached, Mark Genovese sidestepped out of the way, almost without looking at her. The woman's soft blond strands were cropped stylishly short, and the tousles framed her delicate face.

She strode purposefully through the crowd at the front and came to a stop in front of Jil, hand outstretched. "Ms. Kinness?"

"Hello." Jil got to her feet to shake the proffered hand. It was hot—electric, even. Jil couldn't turn away from her intense gaze, even if she'd wanted to.

"Jessica Blake."

"Oh. Um. Hello." Then, regaining her composure: "You're the principal?"

"Three years running. C'mon in."

Jil followed her back through the maze of desks and chairs to the quiet and spacious office in the corner. As soon as the door closed, the noise level dropped about fifty decibels. Jil felt herself relax.

"Welcome to St. Marguerite's, Julie." Ms. Blake indicated a seat at the round table.

Jil sat, and Ms. Blake did too—one leg tucked up underneath herself on the large, square chair. Quite a feat, in a tailored suit.

"It's Julia, actually." She was determined to redo this first impression. Professional. Detached. Why did she feel like she'd already been made?

"Oh, I'm sorry. Julia." Ms. Blake's speech was clipped and definite—like she had both a word and time crunch. "Welcome all the same. We're glad you could pinch-hit on such short notice." She opened a file and riffled through until she found what she wanted. "Ms. Barnes was in a car accident last week and won't be returning until next semester. At the earliest. We know it's not going to be easy diving in here at the last minute, but you come highly recommended."

"Thank you." Jil wondered what the hell the superintendent could have had to say about a woman he'd never met.

"I'm sorry we didn't have time for a formal interview or orientation, but you're here now, and that's the important thing." She brushed a stray strand of hair away from her forehead and regarded Jil steadily.

Jil tried to smile. Why couldn't she meet Ms. Blake's eyes? "Did Ms. Barnes leave a course outline?" she asked, her voice coming out more of a croak than she'd expected.

"Yes. If you don't want to follow it, you can run the changes by me, and we'll see about making modifications. I'm going to set you up with Buck Weekly. He's head of the Religious Studies Department, and he'll be a good mentor for you. He has some time set aside for you this morning, so he'll be in R200. In the Red building."

"What time do I begin my class?" How much effort would this teaching thing be?

"Buck will be able to answer all your procedural questions. And if he's not available, Mark Genovese will be able to help you. He's the VP for the grade eleven and twelve students, as well as the director of residence."

"Residence?"

"Yes. We have fifty boarders at St. Marguerite's. Many of them come from the Pathways Program, which is for at-risk youth previously living in foster care. Many of them have been kicked out of the regular system and seem to thrive in a more structured environment."

Jil envisioned Mark's six-foot, five-inch frame, and imagined he'd be more than capable of dealing with any student who got out of line.

"I've got to get back to work. Things are a little nuts. But feel free to drop in later in the week if you have any questions."

"Sure. Thanks, Ms. Blake."

"Call me Jess."

"Okay, thanks, Jess."

Jil rose to leave and nearly tripped over the leg of the chair. She smiled sheepishly and ducked quickly out the door before she could embarrass herself further. Her sweaty palms and racing heartbeat were more than the nervousness of starting a new assignment. Undercover was her specialty. She knew how to morph into someone else better than she knew how to breathe. Some days it was the only way she could breathe.

So why did she feel like she was underwater, moving so slowly she could barely surface?

❖

"You must be Julie. Nice to meet you." Buck Weekly appraised Jil as she stood on the threshold of the Religion office.

"Julia Kinness. Pleased to meet you."

His lumbering frame reminded her of a clothed grizzly bear as he ambled toward her, paw outstretched. She shook his hand, and he surprised her by clasping hard and leaning in to kiss her cheek. "Welcome to St. Marguerite's," he said, still holding on.

Jil maneuvered expertly out of his grasp and took a step backward.

"Thank you," she said. Padraig owed her a very expensive lobster dinner after this assignment.

She gave herself a mental check. He'd be lucky to afford a fast-food joint.

Buck bared his teeth in what he obviously considered a welcoming smile and indicated the seat opposite him. His hair, a wavy shock of heavily graying brown, resembled thick beaver fur, arranged expertly on his too-large head. Jil wondered for a moment if it was a rug.

She sat down gingerly at someone else's desk and took out her notepad.

"Can I get you a cup of coffee? Tea?"

"No, thank you." Jil hadn't figured out where the staff room—and therefore the staff bathrooms—were located, and having coffee would require her to find that out sooner rather than later.

"No?" Buck echoed. "Well, I was going to go on down to the cafeteria and get myself something. Maybe we could meet there—a bit friendlier than this office."

"If you like, but I've already had a cup this morning."

"Well, I wish you'd change your mind." A note of impatience crept into his voice. "I'd like to welcome you properly."

Jil sighed inwardly but tried to smile. After all, she didn't want to be rude—or make enemies right from the start. "Tea would be fine," she replied and followed Buck out of the room down the stairs to the cafeteria. He lumbered ahead of her, and Jil noticed his heavily worn shoes, and his misbuttoned, threadbare shirt. She wondered if he was low on funds, or if he just didn't like to buy new clothes. She guessed the latter; he didn't seem like a guy who liked change.

"Two coffees," he told the woman behind the desk.

"Actually, that was one tea," Jil corrected him.

"Oh. Did you change your mind then?" He knitted his bushy eyebrows. "Okay. One coffee and one tea."

Jil took her lukewarm Styrofoam cup and dunked the teabag up and down, deciding that since the water would likely remain that peculiar shade of gray, she might as well leave the bag in. She added a little milk and put the lid back on, noticing a few errant coffee grinds twirling through her cup.

"How's the tea?" Buck asked, leading her to a table in the corner.

"Tastes like coffee."

"Oh. That's too bad. Would you like me to ask her to make you another one?"

"No, thank you." Jil did her best to keep the impatience from her voice as she set her cup aside and looked anxiously at the clock. "I'd rather hear about the school. It's my first year as a teacher here—anywhere, actually—and Jess seems to think you'll have a few pointers."

"Well, Julia…" Buck took a slurp of his coffee. "I'll give you an idea of how this department runs, and if you have any questions, you can ask me at the end. Okay?"

Jil nodded, feeling like she was sitting through a lecture with a particularly arrogant professor.

"The Religion Department is probably the most important department here at St. Marguerite's. Now, I've been asked many times to step out of it—become a religious consultant, or even a principal, but I've always said no, because I love it here." For some reason, Buck seemed to feel the need to bang his fist emphatically on the table as he spoke, which made their Styrofoam cups jiggle and jump precariously.

Jil picked her cup up in an effort to avoid a spill.

"I was a student here," Buck continued. "I've taught here my whole career, and I plan to retire here."

"Wow. That's commitment." Jil struggled to keep the irony out of her voice. Settling in one place and staying there was her idea of hell, not glory. Which is probably why she'd been attracted to investigative work in the first place. "Is it a family tradition?" She feigned interest. She'd once heard that the way to deal with an arrogant person was to make him believe you found him fascinating.

"Yes. My father was a teacher. As was my brother, Charleston."

Jil shook her head. "Afraid I don't know him."

Buck bared his teeth again. "Before your time."

"Did he teach religion as well?"

"Yes. In Africa. We all feel that religion is the cornerstone to Catholic education. It's what sets us apart from the public schools. It's what makes St. Marguerite's such a success. We teach all students, no matter how troubled or backward they are. It doesn't matter if they're mentally retarded or slow. They all come into religion and are taught the Catholic way."

Mentally retarded—now there's a term I'm pretty sure was outlawed back in 1984.

She noticed that students left a respectful distance as they passed the table. None of them even made eye contact or waved. She wondered if they were afraid of Buck, or if an unwritten rule said that students didn't associate with teachers, even in the cafeteria.

She clued in that Buck had asked her about her schedule, just in time to avoid another of his annoyed looks.

"I'm here half-time," she said, as if she'd been paying full attention. "I have one class. Grade Twelve World Religion."

Instead of looking at her, Buck scanned the cafeteria. He nodded, out of sync with her words, as if he were just putting in time before he could speak again. "Yes. Jess and I spoke about that earlier. I'll be sitting in on your class for the first week or so, helping you to get an idea of what you're doing. We tend to stick together, the religion teachers. If you have any problems, you can feel free to see me. I can always help you."

"That's great. Jess said the same thing about herself. Looks like I'll have lots of support."

"Well, now." Buck held Jil's eyes in his piercing blue gaze. "Here at St. Marguerite's we have a chain of command. If you have a problem, you see me, and if I can't solve it, I'll take it to Jessica. Teachers don't normally see the administration about things on their own. And same with the other staff members. If you have a problem with one of them, see me, and we'll work it out together."

"I thought if you had a problem with somebody—not that I expect to—you saw them directly?"

"Yes, well, here we like to work things out as a team," Buck said, a slight edge in his voice. "I promise you that if you trust me with your issues, I'll never lead you astray. You'll be in good hands."

Jil felt her temper flaring, for reasons she couldn't quite put a finger on, and had to take a breath before changing the subject. "So, my class?"

"Yes. World Religions: Buddhism, Sikhism, Christianity, and Hinduism. With an extra unit of Catholicism thrown in too for good measure."

"Is that in the course outline?"

"Not officially." Buck grimaced.

Jil did not smile back.

"We like to remind the students of where their hearts are before the course wraps up."

A moment of silence dragged on a little too long. Buck clenched and unclenched his jaw.

"I'd like to see my office," she said finally. "I need a few minutes to prepare for my first class. And to go over the course outline."

"The secretary at the front desk will have your office keys." Buck waved bizarrely, like a royal dismissal. "It's right down the hall from mine. In R. You're R202."

"Great." Jil rose to leave. "Thank you for your…insights."

As she walked away, she consciously slowed her footsteps, feeling Buck's cold stare at her back. She opened the door to the cafeteria and saw him watching her. No doubt about it: not an hour into her first day, and she was already well on her way to making an enemy.

Chapter Three

By nine fifteen, Jil had keys, a burgundy and ivory lanyard (St. Marguerite's official colors), and a borrowed office full of bookshelves that rivaled her own. No piles of folders, though. Ms. Barnes was clearly a neat and tidy sort.

Jil dumped her stuff on the floor and threw her folders on the desk. She flipped to page one of her instruction manual. Apparently, teachers didn't teach on the first day. They did "ice breaking" exercises and went over the synopsis. Then they gave instructions on how to drop the class in an effort to get smaller numbers, and sent students down to the Student Services mosh pit—apparently the new name for "Guidance."

As she stood over the enormous photocopying machine, trying to navigate her way around the touch screen and various characters, she rediscovered why she'd gone into investigating and not office work. This loathsome piece of machinery. She loaded in her outline once again, and once again, the pages came out blank.

"What did you want to do?" asked an amused voice behind her.

Jil turned around to see a tall woman dressed in shorts and a sweatshirt, an orange flowered lanyard around her neck.

"I'd settle for photocopying."

"You're new?"

"First year. My name is Julia Kinness."

"Hi there. I'm Rosie McMonahan. I teach—"

"Gym?"

"Well, health this unit, but otherwise, yeah, phys ed."

"Brave woman."

Rosie giggled, her chestnut curls bouncing as she turned to point across the room. She looked young, no more than twenty-five or six. A wedding band sparkled on her finger. Looked new.

"Try the one over there. It gives you step-by-step instructions. This thing's a beast."

"Great, thanks." Jil moved over to the smaller, somewhat less intimidating machine.

Rosie loaded the paper in the top for her—blank side up. Jil's face flushed. Of course. Printed side down.

"How do you like it so far?" Rosie asked as the machine started spitting out copies—stapled and double-sided.

"It's a nice facility."

"Nice facility?" Rosie teased her. "Are you from Revenue Canada? Here to do an audit?"

Jil raised her eyebrows. That was all it took to make her stand out? She'd have to be more careful. "Uh, no…I teach religious studies. What about you? How long have you been here?"

"Well, I was on contract here last year, so I feel pretty well at home. It's a little big if you're not used to it, I guess. At least, that's what I remember. Hey, do you play any sports?"

"Not well. Why?"

"We're looking for coaches. After school, mostly. Any chance you'd like to coach a team?"

Jil shook her head. "I'm only here in the mornings." She was glad she had a real excuse. She liked Rosie and didn't want to disappoint her.

"Oh, that's too bad. Maybe next year. I'll have to see if I can con my husband into taking one more."

"Oh. Does he work here? Your husband?" Never miss an opportunity to sleuth. The quicker she eliminated delinquents, the faster she could get out of here.

"Yeah. Mark Ivanhoe. He teaches math. Up in the R building."

"Oh. My room's in R too. What floor is he?"

"Two."

"Huh. We must be neighbors. Ivanhoe, you said?" Not McMonahan? Didn't married people usually change their names? Especially married Catholics?

Rosie must have heard the unasked question, because she looked sheepish. "Yeah. Actually, we're not technically married. We've lived together for five years, but never walked down the aisle. It's just easier to say 'husband' around here, you know?" She pointed ironically to her ring finger. "At least he finally got me a ring."

Jil smiled. *Shit*. Could she just pretend she hadn't heard that?

"Are you married?" Rosie smiled.

Jil shook her head. "Never found the right man for me."

"Don't worry. There's still plenty of time…though teaching's kind of a bum job to find a husband."

Jil liked her smile—bright, genuine.

The machine stopped spitting out paper, and Jil went to collect her pile. "First class." She bit her lip with a nervousness that was only partly for show. "I wonder if they'll like me."

Rosie laughed. "You're hilarious. Good luck." They traded places, Rosie tackling the machine, and Jil going to check her internal mailbox in the alcove beside the staff lunchroom. Some very efficient admin person had already labeled one: Kinness, J.

She found a scroll tucked into the box—a list of teachers, alphabetically by homeroom. Also a class list with phone numbers and addresses of her students, a newsletter, and a copy of that morning's announcements. Wow, they sure didn't waste any time. The school year was starting today—no turning back.

Jil felt a ball of real nervousness settle in her chest. She wasn't a teacher. She'd made a specific point not to talk to teenagers. Ever. Since her own high school experience, the school cafeteria had been on her top five list of most hated places—right below the firing range and slightly above dank, dark basements. Now here she was saddled with a morning break duty every Thursday, and a Bible on her bookshelf for easy access.

As she headed out of the staff room, flipping through her folder of photocopies, she failed to notice the large indoor flower bed in the atrium. She also failed to notice the man in a blue shirt, bending over the flower bed until she almost tumbled over him.

"So sorry!" She caught her balance by laying a hand on the stranger's back.

He looked up from the flower bed with a frown. "Don't worry about it," he muttered and went back to working. His dark hair contrasted oddly with his face, which placed him in his early forties, max.

Jil backed away and headed for her class. These black button-up creased trousers were enough to make her gag. Forget the blouses that required ironing, or the high-heeled pumps she stumbled around in, the dress code at this school was just one more thing to add to the list of things to hold over Padraig's head.

Someday in the future, when they could laugh about what a mess the firm was in, she would drag out these old stories.

The big clock in the atrium chimed nine thirty. Time for the true test of her acting abilities. If anyone could smoke out a fraud, it had to be a senior student—and a class full of them waited upstairs for her. She'd already scoped out her classroom, two floors up, and she headed there now, her heart hammering in her chest as she clutched keys, the course outlines, and a binder full of "break the ice" ideas.

Jil stood in front of her would-be classroom, preparing to meet the incredulous eyes of twenty-nine senior students, none of whom, she was sure, had elected this course.

When the bell rang, the first period class exited in record time, anxious for their eight minutes of unfettered smoking time in the school parking lot.

The classroom smelled of stale donuts and body odor. Worse, the window at the back didn't appear to open any farther than the crack someone had already managed. She set the course outlines down in a pile on the desk and took a few shallow breaths—trying to stop her hands from shaking and avoid the air passing through her sense of smell.

When she went to find a piece of chalk, she noticed white boards and dry-erase markers instead of blackboards and chalk. Grimacing, she uncapped a particularly potent blue and held her breath again while she scrawled her name and the course title on the board.

She heard the bell only seconds before a stampede of feet thundered through the door, and droves of teenagers, hats askew and iPods turned on full-blast, appeared before her, launching themselves into seats, smacking each other in strange and vaguely provocative ways, laughing and making strange noises reminiscent of mating time at the petting zoo. Consciously processing, she knew there must be a test in here somewhere, but for the moment, a strategy completely escaped her.

"Excuse me, ladies and gentlemen," a deep voice hailed them from the corner.

Jil looked up to see Buck Weekly hovering in the doorway.

"I'd like to remind you that there are no electronic devices or hats allowed in the school. You'll need to put them away before coming to class in the future. For now, just take your hats off. Hey—excuse me, what's your name?"

"Uh, Jordan."

"Well, Jordan, I'd appreciate it if you'd look at me when I'm speaking to you. When you look away and talk to your neighbor, what kind of impression do you think I get?"

Jordan looked around, as if he weren't sure he had to answer. Buck's eyes bored into him, and he squirmed in his seat.

"Uh…not good?"

"Not good? In what way, 'not good'?"

"Uh…like, disrespectful?"

"Yes. That's right. It's disrespectful to talk when someone else is speaking. It gives the impression that you're not interested. You might as well say 'shut up—you're not worth listening to.' That's the impression I get when I'm talking to you, and you're looking the other way, talking to your buddy. So next time someone's standing here—myself, or Ms. Kinness—we'd appreciate it if you'd keep your eyes at the front. Now, this is Grade Twelve World Religions. Is there anybody here who isn't supposed to be in this class? Maybe you thought you were coming to Chemistry or English, and you ended up here? Is there anybody who would like to leave now?"

A slender girl in the back eyed Buck coldly. She had short brown hair and a boyish figure, her tight black T-shirt coming just to the waist of her low-riding jeans, which were secured with an alarmingly large belt buckle. She looked from Jil to Buck and raised her hand. "Are you teaching this class, sir?" she asked.

"No, Rebecca, I'm not. Ms Kinness will be teaching this class."

Jil wondered when he would stop talking so she could start.

The girl seemed to decide something and settled back down in her seat.

Just then, Jil noticed a bulky young woman in a baggy sweatshirt gathering up her things. She had a bull's ring in her nose and black hair that had obviously been dyed.

"Now I know you're supposed to be in this class," Buck said. "Please sit back down."

"I don't need a fucking lecture," the girl said. "I signed up for Ms. Barnes, not this. I'm getting the hell out of this fucking class."

She stormed past Buck through the door. They heard her heavy footsteps retreating down the hall.

Silence fell.

"On that note, perhaps we should begin," Jil said before Buck could start up again.

He stood there, glaring at no one in particular, beefy hands on beefier hips—waiting, it seemed, for an opportunity to jump in again.

Jil ignored him and turned to her class. "Good morning, everyone. My name is Ms. Kinness, and I will be your World Religions teacher this term."

"Uh…don't you mean semester?" asked a smirking boy in the front.

"I believe it's the same thing?" Jil looked him directly in the eye.

He shrugged and looked away.

Jil stared at him for a minute longer. Like hell she would be intimidated by a bunch of high school students. Something she knew without having to go to teacher's college was not to give them an inch. No personal information. No age. No middle name. No social media access. And no revelations. Some things held true across every profession in which there were delinquents involved.

"The first thing I'd like to do is take attendance and get to know all of you." She took out a class list and went down alphabetically. The students all confirmed their presence with variations on "yeah," and Jil made a mental note of where each student was sitting.

"Rebecca—"

"It's Bex," the girl interrupted.

"Okay. Thanks for letting me know, Bex."

A small, mousy-looking girl sat at the back, in the row between Bex and the bullringed girl who'd left. She shrank into her desk, chin down, almost trembling with anxiety.

"Alyssa Marco," Jil called. No one answered. "Hon, is that you?" she addressed the shrinking violet. "Are you Alyssa?"

The wallflower stared back, her eyes huge.

Bex shot her a strange glance—at once sympathetic and exasperated.

Suddenly, she seemed to come to her senses. "Yes, Miss," she croaked. "Yes, I'm Alyssa."

"Okay. Are you planning to stay in this course?"

"Yes, Miss."

"Thank you. Theo Ranieri?"

"Yeah, Miss. Here." A tall, muscular boy with quick eyes and a flashy smile raised his hand. A gold chain dangled around his neck.

"Good. Thank you. And lastly, Jeremy Yin?"

"Present."

"Good. You're all here. Minus one. So…I'm going to ask you to retain your seats for the rest of this course. Wherever you're sitting today, that's where you'll sit tomorrow. "

A chorus of groans erupted, and a student named Kyle swore out loud.

Jil glared at him, and he grinned sheepishly.

"Sorry, Miss. Having trouble adjusting…"

"To what? Modern manners?"

He actually smiled. "School, Miss."

Jil picked up her syllabus. "Welcome to the first day of the rest of your life."

She mentally congratulated herself for getting so fully involved in her role. The students seemed to be buying the routine. She wondered how long she could keep this up.

"If you'll all take a look at this outline I'm going to pass around, I think you'll see we're going to have a very full course load this semester." She looked pointedly at the boy in front—Tyler, it turned out—as she began passing around papers.

Buck finally took a seat, and Jil rolled her eyes. Obviously, he wasn't going to leave anytime soon. Pointedly avoiding looking in his direction, she began going over the syllabus, having each student in turn read a paragraph, as educational an experience for her as for them. She began to see why Jess had thought to give her a prep period. With this many kids struggling with basic reading skills, it would take her half a year to mark each assignment.

As students read, she looked around the room. Minus the girl who didn't want a "fucking lecture," she had twenty-eight students.

Bex chewed her bottom lip and stared at the door, as if she expected someone to come through at any second. Jordan, the disrespectful kid, pored over his outline anxiously. Kyle, who was reading, made so many mistakes that Jil wondered how he'd made it to grade twelve at all. She rescued him early and asked the next student to read. Alyssa whispered so softly that Theo stood up from his seat in the back.

"Speak up, yo!" he thundered.

Alyssa cowered.

"That will do." Jil glared at Theo and he sat down.

"Miss, you can barely hear her," he complained.

"Do you not have the information in front of you? Can you not read it?"

Theo hunched back over his desk, sending a hostile glance first at Jil, then at Alyssa.

"Keep going, Alyssa. A little louder."

The girl read the last two sentences at barely a whisper, and Bex promptly took over.

In total, there were ten girls and eighteen boys. According to the information she'd heard in the staff room that morning, at least six of them would drop the course by midterm. She'd just let Buck keep talking next time. Half of them would walk out the door without a second glance.

When the final bell rang, the students sprang up from their seats and stampeded to the door. Lunchtime.

Jil slipped in between the last few retreating backpacks and headed down the stairs, lost in the shuffle. She tried not to think about what Buck would say when he realized she'd given him the slip.

❖

Jil got home late after spending the afternoon in her office at O'Hanagan's, wrapping up details from her last case. She still had a report to write and some loose ends to tie up from the investigation. It felt good to get it off her desk. She could now focus all her attention on St. Marguerite's for the next few months. Tomorrow, she would start digging into the targets' lives—the part she liked best.

She poured herself a glass of wine and took her charting paper from the coffee table. Teacher list in hand, she went upstairs to her office, spread the chart out on the desk, and took a sip of wine. She'd been thinking about how to keep all the information straight during this investigation. There would be a fairly lengthy report to write at the end of this assignment, and a lot of people included.

On the way home, she'd stopped and bought an oversized Bristol board. And now she took out a marker and began creating a chart for St. Marguerite's—a graph, with teachers' names listed alphabetically. Symbols indicated uncatholic transgressions.

First, the Ten Commandments:

-Worshiping another God.
-Worshiping false idols.
-Taking the Lord's name in vain
-Failing to keep the Sabbath day Holy
-Failing to honor one's father and mother
-Committing murder
-Committing adultery
-Stealing
-Bearing False Witness (lying)
-Coveting

And the seven deadly sins:

-Lust
-Gluttony
-Greed
-Sloth
-Wrath
-Envy
-Pride

And the interpreted rules:

-Living in Sin
-Divorce
-Abortion
-Homosexuality
-Birth Control
-Eating Meat on Fridays during Lent

She rolled her eyes. If only she'd been there in the spring. She would be able to eliminate ninety-five percent of the personnel on that last one alone. Investigation over!

She wouldn't be working too hard to find out the gay teachers either.

She stood back to examine her handiwork. Complicated, but beautiful. Obviously, she couldn't keep this chart at work, but every night, she could bring home her notebook and copy the information from there onto the master chart. Her report would be a breeze.

She checked the list against the chart, making sure she hadn't left anyone out. She hesitated over one name for a long minute—Jess Blake. The principal had an intense magnetism that Jil found hard to ignore, a push-pull that drew Jil in while simultaneously keeping her on the other side of a professional boundary.

How and when could she ever investigate her?

Nicole Adamson, the first person on her list, had three social media accounts, all of which were private. "Smart girl," Jil muttered. "But something tells me your friends aren't quite as smart."

She picked the most popular site and clicked through to find Nicole's friends. As she suspected, pictures and status updates were plastered all over the Internet. In ten minutes, Jil ascertained that Nicole, a twenty-four-year-old ninth grade teacher, was a party girl, loved lemon drop shots, and spent most weekends at the bar. She also had an affinity for dancing on tables. One picture caught her eye in particular: her dancing up close and personal in the arms of a shirtless man with rippled abs, unbuttoned jeans, and a cowboy hat . He nuzzled her neck from behind while she threw her head back and downed a long, pink drink.

She saved the photo to her new file on Nicole Adamson and continued down the list. When the clock clicked to two, she turned off the computer, having done a basic search on ten of the staff. Most of the teachers were smart enough not to have any social media accounts at all, but the younger ones were easier.

Chapter Four

On Monday, Jil managed to arrive a full hour early. Time spent in bed was a precious commodity these days—with the investigation, the night stalking, and the teaching during the day, she hadn't been out once. Not that she usually partied hard on the weekend, anyway. Her last relationship hadn't exactly ended well, and she was enjoying a break. Tara would probably be cozying up to her new boyfriend, and it was unlikely she'd see her at any of their usual clubs, but the thought of it made her want to dive under her covers and stay there until Christmas.

Better to focus on the investigating for now and leave the romance for another year.

Investigating in a Catholic school meant sitting unoccupied in the staff room for ten minutes. Rife with gossip.

She had her day planned, beginning with a cup of coffee, a marking binder, and an open ear.

So when she pulled into the parking lot at seven ten, the small group of students already gathered at the door surprised her. She wondered if the custodians had forgotten to unlock the student entrance when they'd come in at six. They usually parked at the side and came in through the service doors, then did a check of the school, and unlocked all the doors from the inside around seven.

Teachers arriving early for clubs knew to use the service doors at the side. Students weren't allowed to use that door, and therefore had to wait for their entrance to be opened. Which, apparently, it hadn't been.

She looked up to see Jessica Blake pulling into the lot beside her.

When Jess saw the crowd, she didn't bother to go around the building to her designated parking space; she just pulled her navy Jeep Liberty next to Jil's black X-Trail and threw it into park.

Jess's face held a wary expression. Students shouldn't be at school this early unless they had a club to get to. They certainly didn't stand at the door like men at the mission, waiting for their lunch. They went to the library, to band, to smoke in the pit by the football field…anything but this.

Jil and Jess opened their doors in synch, their feet hitting the ground, their doors slamming together. "Miss!" a student called—encompassing them both. "Miss, c'mere quick!"

Jil and Jess exchanged the briefest of looks. Something was very wrong. As one, they took off at a run through the parking lot and up the walk to the students' entrance. Despite Jil's training and stamina, Jess matched her pace well. They arrived at the door, and the students parted to let them through.

"Oh my God," Jess breathed, her face blanching as she knelt down. "What happened?"

Lying on the ground, arms outstretched like Jesus on the cross, was a student. Jil immediately recognized Alyssa Marco, the shy girl from her class.

"Call nine one one," Jess ordered a boy standing with a cell phone.

"They're already on their way," he said. "We got here, like, five minutes ago, on the 157 bus. For the band practice. And she was just lying here. We called an ambulance and everything, but she's like, not waking up."

Jil knelt next to Jess. "Get the students away from here," she whispered.

Jil gently guided Jess away from the young girl. Alyssa's lips were blue, and her glassy eyes had been vacant for too many hours to hope they would ever blink again.

"She's dead, Jess. There's no saving her. We have to step away. This is going to be a crime scene."

Jess closed her eyes briefly, then opened them to study Alyssa's ashen face, her rigid limbs.

"Oh my God," she whispered. "Not again."

❖

The ambulance roared into the parking lot, and the attendants unloaded the gurney through the sea of students. As more staff arrived, Jil directed them to restrain the kids—who were gluing themselves to every available window and doorway to watch.

When the medics pulled up to the body, one grumbled, "Nobody told us she was stiff. We need a coroner, not an ambulance. We can't do anything here." He went back to his radio and called it in while the other medic stared down at the body.

"We're going to need some pylons," he said. "Somebody get me something to rope off this area."

Mark Genovese, the vice-principal, brought out pylons from the gym and staked them out around the site, his imposing form doing more to keep the students away than the bright orange cones. Blinking lights hailed the arrival of the police. An officer alighted from a cruiser and wasted no time putting up a barrier of yellow police tape.

"We'll have to wait for Forensics," the officer said.

Genovese frowned. "All students to their homerooms," he commanded, his deep voice resonating through the semi-circular entrance. A pack of younger students scuttled away, leaving Jil standing with Jess by the body.

"Go inside," Jil said to Jess. "Call the girl's parents."

Jess's limbs were slack. "I can't believe this. She was just in the office yesterday—waiting to speak to me. I'd been running late from a meeting with the VPs. By the time I finished, she'd left. I wonder if she would have told me something important. If she was going to confide her plan…"

"C'mon." Jil led her into the school by the side door. They had a few moments in suspended time—not in the crime scene, not in the school, just alone in the little alcove by the door where no one could see.

Jess took a few deep breaths, her iron grip on Jil's wrists almost painful.

Jil squeezed back tightly, trying to physically help Jess reel in her emotions. "They're all watching you."

Jess breathed out and squeezed Jil's hands again. There it was—that electric heat sending a jolt down Jil's entire body.

Jess seemed to feel it too, because she took her hands away and smoothed down her pants. "Thank you, Ms. Kinness."

Jil just smiled, drawing back a little. Had she crossed the line? How could she tell? She didn't even know where the line was.

Jess turned the corner, leading the way into the main atrium.

"Business as usual," Jess muttered, shooting Jil a look as she headed toward the front office where a line of people waited for her to arrive. Jil watched her go, trying very hard to swallow normally.

"Hold everything," Jess told her administrative assistant. "I have a phone call to make."

❖

In the parking lot sat a long white van, its driver slowly going around to the back to unload a gurney.

Jil stood in the atrium, waiting for the young officer at the door to give her a signal. She didn't have to wait long. The side door opened, and the officer beckoned her back outside.

"See anything?" asked the officer, her old school friend, Aidan Morgan.

She shook her head. "Got here just as the kids were coming in. We cleared the scene pretty quickly."

"You on assignment here?" Morgan asked in a low voice. As a professional courtesy, he would never ask her exactly what she was doing.

"Unrelated," she confirmed.

Morgan took out a notepad. "We're waiting on Forensics. And backup. There's only four of us here, and that's not enough to hold thirteen hundred kids."

"Well, most of them are in class now anyway," Jil said. "I wouldn't worry about it. The teachers can help you out."

"What about the principal?" Morgan asked. "Will we have her cooperation?"

"I can pretty much guarantee it. She'll want this done and over with. Which way are you leaning?"

"Well, with the dramatic pose, the location, I'd say suicide. We'll have to do some interviews, wait for a tox screen, and the path report, but…"

Jil exhaled loudly.

"What?" Morgan asked.

Jil hesitated, then relented. "Just something the principal said. It's probably nothing." This wasn't the first death that had occurred on school grounds.

"If it's bothering you, it's probably something."

Jil winked. "What are you up to anyway?"

Morgan smiled. "I've been upgrading at night school. Taking cyber forensics classes, hoping to make detective soon."

Jil gave him a tiny high five. "Computer genius."

"Don't say it too loud. Everyone will want a piece of me."

"Keep me in the loop."

Jil excused herself as the coroner trundled up the path, carting a gurney. She leaned down and examined Alyssa carefully.

"I'm pronouncing."

Morgan leaned down. "When would you say was the time of death?"

"At least five hours ago. I'll be taking her to the lab for further tests, and then I'll let you know. Have the Forensics guys been here yet?"

"Nope."

"Well, tell them to hurry the hell up. I don't want to sit around here all day while they fart around with their photographs."

Jil hid a smile and exchanged a look with Morgan.

"I'll see what I can do," he said politely.

Inside, the final bell rang for the start of period one.

"Would all staff and students please report to the senior cafeteria for an assembly? Students on spare are required to report. All staff and students, please report to the senior cafeteria at this time. Thank you."

Even though she didn't have a first period class, Jil proceeded to the senior caf. Three of her students were waiting outside the doors. Two more were coming down the hall. Three of the girls had tears in their eyes; the boys were sober, looking at the ground. One of the younger girls latched on to her, and Jil hugged her back, awkwardly, whispering soothing words into her bleached-blond hair.

An eerie silence fell as the students filed into the cafeteria and found spots on the floor. Jil took up a position near the wall, where she could see the crowd. They cried and held each other, passed tissues, and exchanged looks. In less than five minutes, all the students had assembled, and Jessica took the stage.

"Ladies and gentlemen, as you have no doubt heard, we have had a tragic event here at St. Marguerite's. One of our students, Alyssa Marco, died this morning. We recognize that this is a great loss for you as it is for her parents and the teachers. We are all mourning together as a community today, asking ourselves questions and grieving." She paused to look at the crowd, seeming to decide what to say.

"The police are still investigating the cause of Alyssa's death, and ask that any staff member or student who has any information come forward and ask to speak to one of the officers. There will be police on our campus today and for the rest of the week, if you think of anything that might help their investigation.

"There will also be grief counselors coming to the school starting tomorrow, for any of you who may wish to speak to someone. This might bring up some questions for some of you, or some feelings that overwhelm you. Don't be afraid to see the counselors. They will be setting up shop in the Student Services office, so just make an appointment and head on down there if you need to.

"Your teachers and the administration are also available, and we'll be doing everything we can to help everybody get through this difficult time. We ask that you try, as much as possible, to go about your daily routine. Go to classes, talk to your teachers, focus on your success as students. We know that this is going to be a very hard road for a few of you—particularly those who were close to Alyssa. But we must stand together as a school community now. Perhaps there is something we can learn here. Something to be gained. We should all try to see God's will in a situation like this. The strength of the church stands behind us now. We can all pray for Alyssa.

"Let us bow our heads as Ms. Reitman leads us in prayer."

A fifty-ish woman with long, white hair bound in a loose braid, replaced Ms. Blake on the stage. Jil stared at her for a brief second, confused. Women couldn't be priests, but apparently they could be chaplains…?

Jil ducked out just as the Hail Mary began. She walked quietly past the entrance to the chapel and up the stairs to her office, wanting to make as much of her time as possible before she had to begin teaching second period. As she unlocked her office door, she wondered how the police investigation was going. Sometimes, she wished she'd gone that route instead of private investigating. Catching the bad guys, making arrests. But then something like this happened, and she remembered why she didn't like to be around death like that.

Homicide, Forensics, beat copping. Forget it. She'd decided against it the year she graduated from the Academy. Basic training was all Padraig had asked of her. Get through school. Get a certificate. Get in shape. Make sure that you're not just doing PI work because it's easy and it's what you know. Get yourself some options, Kidd, then see me if you still want to do this old shit.

She did.

So he'd put her to use in assignments she was good at. Assignments where the landscape of the job changed from day to day, and she was always moving with it. Didn't leave a whole lot of time for sticky things like relationships or holidays, but she never had to worry about putting down too many roots. Offending someone if she couldn't make it home for Christmas.

Just the way she liked it.

What she didn't like was death. Especially deaths of young people. And the fact that one of her students had wound up dead on the doorstep of the place she had to come to work every day creeped her out. Now she would have to worry about the rest of her students too—how they were coping, how they were feeling. All of which would impede her investigation even more, and delay the time when she could leave.

As she passed by the window of the Student Services office, she saw Buck Weekly sitting at a table, pounding his fists emphatically on the surface as he talked to a student. The student stared at his feet, not looking up.

Slowly, he turned his shaggy head toward her, his steel blue eyes holding her to the spot. She felt herself temporarily slow—almost freeze—and she forced herself to look away and continue down the hall.

❖

Blessedly, Buck would not be shadowing her class anymore, which made her free to give her students the time they needed to talk.

A sea of blank faces greeted her. She mentally counted absences. Bex hadn't shown up. Neither had Theo.

"Seriously, Miss?" said the bleach-blond named Joey, her red eyes pooling again. "Do you think she, like, killed herself?"

"I don't know," Jil replied honestly. She sat on top of her desk, cross-legged.

"Yo, I don't understand why people pull that shit." Kyle scuffed his toe against the flecked linoleum floor, his purple suede shoes making an odd shuffling sound. "I mean, yeah, bad shit happens, and it's hard, but it always gets better." He ran a hand through his spiky hair and shook his head.

A few of the kids doodled in their notebooks, heads down, trying not to look at the empty desk in the back of the room.

"Did you guys all know Alyssa well?"

Joey erupted in a shaking sob. The rest of the class ducked their heads, embarrassed, except for Samantha, who sat beside Joey. She jumped up too and took Joey by the hand.

"Why don't you go down to the guidance office?" Jil whispered.

Joey gulped, tears streaming down her face and pooling her mascara in dark puddles under her eyes. Samantha's face drained stark white, and her hands shook as she gripped Joey by the arm, and led her out the door.

Yasmine followed.

A few minutes later, Jordan got up quietly and left.

Jil exhaled a long breath and turned to face her remaining students.

"What are you guys thinking about?"

They spent most of second period talking—about how guilty they all felt for not paying more attention to Alyssa and what they could have done to prevent it. Wanting to know what Jil had seen when the coroner got there—questions which she evaded expertly. Jil privately wished they'd all go down to Student Services and talk with the counselors there.

Not soon enough, the bell rang for the end of the period. When all her students had left, she took her class list and blacked a line through the fifth name up from the bottom.

At lunch, the school emptied, and Jil let herself be carried to the parking lot with the surge. As she hopped into her SUV, she watched Jess Blake and Mark Genovese walk the perimeters of the fields, walkie-talkies in hand. A third woman, slight and small, stood at the entrance to the outdoor education center, watching students smoking. That must be the VP of the juniors, Jil thought. Cynthia.

She turned on the truck and waited for the voice command system to kick in.

"Call Padraig."

"Calling Padraig."

"Hey, Kidd, what's up?" Padraig answered on the first ring.

"Isn't it all over the news?" Jil said.

"What?"

"One of my students died this morning on school grounds."

Padraig let out a low whistle that sounded a bit eerie over the speakers. "I'll be damned."

"She was lying in front of the student entrance this morning when Jess and I got there."

"Who's Jess?"

"Jessica Blake. The principal."

"First-name basis already, huh?"

Jil's heart sped up. "Oh, shut it. Honestly, Padraig. Could we focus on the important things here?"

"Sure. Did the police come?"

"The police, the coroner. The whole shebang. We're waiting on the police report, but it looks like a suicide."

Padraig was quiet for a moment. "You want me to pull you out of there?"

"Why? I'm just getting started."

"Yeah, but—"

"But what?"

"I don't know," Padraig muttered. "I just wonder if it wasn't poor judgment on my part—keeping you away as a teenager, then throwing you to the wolves now..."

Chapter Five

The next morning, while using the staff washroom, Jil overheard two teachers whispering. She kept silent in the stall, hoping they wouldn't notice her. They didn't.

"They came this morning," one woman said. She sounded like she was crying.

"Well, it's not like you weren't expecting them," the other woman said gently.

Jil held her breath over the sound of muffled sobs. "I just know he's hurrying it up because he wants to marry that stupid Cindy," the crier mumbled. "I have a good mind not to sign them."

"Come on, Ivana. You don't want to drag this out, do you? If it's over, it's over. Trust me. Divorce is messy enough when people cooperate. It's hell when they don't."

Ivana sniffed. "Whatever. If he doesn't want me, fine. But if he thinks that little slut is going to be half as good as me, he's in for a big surprise."

The door opened and shut. Jil smiled to herself and made a mental note. She'd just saved herself a stakeout. And she could cross Ivana Ostarak off her list. That made three entries from this week alone.

I.O.—Divorce.
Y.K.—Living in sin.
M.M.—Single mother (Divorce?).

Later, Jil remembered her mailbox. She made her way to the alcove that held all the staff mailboxes. Her little cubby overflowed with two weeks' worth of morning announcements, flyers for bake sales, ticket draws, events—little notes welcoming her to school. She tossed all the flyers and announcements into the recycling bin—conveniently placed along the wall of the alcove for just such a time as this—and scanned each welcome note before tossing it into the blue box.

At the back sat a plain white envelope with her name on it. Instinct told her to wait until she got to her office before opening it. She made her way back to her cramped office and shut the door. She examined the handwriting on the envelope. No one's she recognized.

She slit the top neatly with a letter opener that Ms. Barnes had left her and pulled out a piece of paper. On it were printed ten names—on plain A4 paper, Times New Roman font. Laser printer too—harder to trace. She scanned the names quickly, memorized them, then took the paper over to the shredder to get rid of the evidence. Giovanni must have sent this. Would e-mail not have been easier?

She couldn't help the slight feeling of disappointment as she fed the list through the metallic teeth. The name at the top—presumably the number one priority—was someone she was hoping to avoid for a while. If not forever. Now it seemed she had no choice.

Jess Blake was her prime target.

At home that night, Jil locked herself back in her office and went online again. She'd already determined that Jess wasn't active on any social media sites. Now, she had to dig deeper.

She took out one of a stack of pre-paid credit cards that Padraig had given her for just such circumstances as this—untraceable. The agency had memberships to a lot of paid investigative sites, but plain old government records had to be paid for separately.

She started with moveable property, paid the fee, and found out exactly how much Jessica Blake had paid for her gorgeous Jeep. That didn't help, of course, because the loan was in her name only, which didn't prove a thing. It didn't disprove that she lived with anyone—only that she kept her finances to herself.

On to marriage records next. Another site, another fee, another hit. Jessica Blake (née McIntyre) had married Mitchell Blake ten years ago. So…if she was married, why was she called Ms. Blake?

❖

On Wednesday morning, a memo came down from Mark Genovese, instructing teachers to conduct "business as usual" at St. Marguerite's—the students were there to be educated, and educational activities must still be taking place. Jil tried to elicit a conversation about Buddhism, but the conversation soon wound back to suicide.

Thursday, she was supposed to give a test. She postponed it. No one even cheered. By Friday, word in the staff room said the police report had come in. Officer Morgan was in a meeting with Jess Blake. Jil already knew what they'd found; Morgan had called her that morning.

She watched Morgan leave. He tipped his head subtly in her direction as he strode across the atrium and through the double doors.

Jess's eyes met hers through the crush of students on lunch break. She beckoned Jil inside with a slight movement of her head, and Jil followed her into her office.

Jil noted that the secretaries watched from the corners of their eyes as the door closed. "What did he say?"

"Suicide." Jess sank slowly into her office chair.

Jil perched on the side of her big oak desk. Close. Almost too close. Jess's hand could have brushed her knee if she hadn't carefully placed it in her lap.

"What do you think?"

"I think I should have been more aware." Jess exhaled loudly. "Should have made sure I saw her before she left."

"Did you know her?"

"Not well." Jess leaned back and tucked one leg up. "She came here from St. Matt's, beginning of grade nine like most of the other kids. Stayed out of trouble. Shy, mostly. Not really a social kind of kid. I don't even know if she had any friends. But good God, Julia. What a way to go!"

"Was it drugs?"

"Yep. Lethal cocktail of Xanax and Ativan. Both of which she found in her mother's medicine cabinet."

Jil nodded. It seemed important, for the moment, just to let Jess speak.

"Her parents were in here Tuesday morning, wanting to talk to me, take her things home. Funeral's tomorrow."

"Are we all going?"

Jess shook her head tiredly. "I can't shut down the school. But I can give permission for the teachers to go, and try to find coverage for their classes. Mark Genovese can act for me while I get down to the church. Anyway, I thought you should know first, since you were there."

"How are you doing?"

Jess smiled, her face closed. Finally, she relented a little. "Not great," she admitted. "This is the last thing we need. Given the school's history, we're going to take a lot of flack."

"What history?"

Jess let out a long breath. Creases of fatigue lined her forehead, and her eyes were smudged with dark circles. Her voice, when she spoke, sounded heavy. "We've had a few problems over the years. There was a double suicide in the late seventies—two male students."

Jil frowned. "A double suicide? Like Romeo and Juliet style?"

Jess met her eyes, but didn't say anything more.

"A relationship issue?" she pressed.

Was that a blush on Jess Blake's face?

"Nothing was ever proven." She looked down at her desk "But it looked that way. Society wasn't exactly very accepting back then."

Jil raised her eyebrows. *Back then? What about now?*

"Anyway, apparently, things ended badly. They hanged themselves from the rafters in the old gymnasium. So awful. The building wasn't released for nearly a month. After that, no one wanted to use it, so the school council agreed to build a newer, better facility, and we use the old gym for storage now. Of course, that happened well before my time. I remember my older brothers talking about it, and when I became principal here, they gave me a big fat folder on St. Marguerite's history." She stopped for a moment, caught.

"It's okay," Jil said. "I'll forget I heard that."

"I'm usually a little more discreet," Jess muttered. "I don't know what I was thinking saying that. It's meant to be…"

"A secret?"

Jess smiled wryly. "Confidential."

"Consider it in the vault."

"Thanks. Anyway, in the late nineties, a senior girl named Regina Francis slit her wrists in the bathroom on the third floor."

"You guys have a lot of disturbed people here."

Jess shrugged. "This school has been around for almost sixty years. Some unpleasant things are bound to happen."

"Yeah, but don't you think it's a little odd to have people killing themselves on school grounds? Unless they're trying to make a statement."

Jess regarded her steadily, and Jil felt that peculiar tingle up and down her arms. Jess only shrugged. "I just hope Alyssa's the last one. But it does seem strange to me…"

"What does?"

Jess was holding something back.

"You've already told me half of it, so you might as well finish and get it off your mind," Jil said.

Jess leaned back in her chair but remained silent.

"Do you want a shot of something?"

Jess cracked a small grin.

"C'mon, spill it. I'll even sign a confidentiality agreement if you want."

Jess cocked an eyebrow. "Might not be a bad idea." She sighed, then relented. "High school is a rough time. I get it. Every few years, we lose a student—usually to accidents or illness. I've known about several students who've committed suicide too. It just seems strange to me that they do it here, and not at home. I don't like to think of all the ghosts that haunt this school." She breathed out, hesitating again.

"How many are we talking about?" Jil prompted.

Jess shook her head. "At least five suicides. One accident. At least I think it was an accident…that seems strange too." She stopped again. "I'm sorry. I must be in shock. You shouldn't hear all this."

Jil wanted to reach out and squeeze her hand, but she was afraid of what Jess might do.

She met her eyes instead, and held them. "Jess, you don't have to worry about what you say to me."

Jess bit her lip. "Thank you."

"Lay it all out. It might make you feel better."

She exhaled slowly. "A few years ago, maybe eight or nine, another boy died in the woods off campus."

"In the woods?"

"Behind the track and field pitch, we have an outdoor education facility. That's where the Pathways kids go on the weekend."

"I was living in Rockland at the time. I never heard about that."

"No, you wouldn't have. They kept it very much under wraps."

"What happened?"

Jess blew air into her cheeks, and frowned, like she was struggling to remember the details. "It was February. Subzero temperatures, and he went for a walk by himself, which was against the rules. A blizzard came up and he was caught outdoors, lost. By the time he found the outdoor ed. cabin, he was half frozen."

"So he died there?"

"Yeah."

"Was this in your secret folder?"

Jess looked up sharply.

"Relax, Jess, I'm kidding."

Jess shook her head, allowing a tiny smile. "No. I remember it because I was a student teacher at St. Jo's, around the corner, when it happened. That one, I couldn't do anything about, but this one…"

"There's probably nothing you could have done to stop her, once she'd made up her mind," Jil said, getting back to Alyssa.

Jess smiled ruefully. "Isn't that what principals are supposed to do? Shepherd their herd?"

"You have thirteen hundred students and almost a hundred staff. You can't know us all."

Jess held her gaze for a moment, as if she wanted to say something more. And Jil wondered, once again, how much she saw and never spoke about.

Word about Alyssa spread quickly through the staff, and then through the student body.

"Suicide," kids whispered to each other as they passed in the halls. In less than an hour, every teacher and student at St. Marguerite's knew that Alyssa Marco had overdosed on drugs, lain down outside the doors of the school, and waited for her heart to stop.

What they didn't know was why.

Why was Jil's top priority, most of the time. And this was no exception. She hadn't been assuaged by the official report on Alyssa's death. In fact, her suspicions had only grown stronger. In her gut, she knew there was something strange about the St. Marguerite's ghosts.

❖

When Jil walked in the doors of her industrial loft condo on Friday night, having trailed two math teachers to the movies before giving up on any salacious activity, she caught sight of the milk she'd left on the counter that morning.

Great. No cereal tomorrow for breakfast.

She sighed, then grabbed her stuff and headed back out the door. If she had to go to the grocery store, she might as well stop at the library too. So far, an Internet search had proved fruitless for the 1974 double-hanging incident, so she hoped to find something in print.

She walked into a nearly empty library. A large woman stared at her computer screen and didn't look up as Jil approached the desk.

"Excuse me," she said pointedly.

The woman's gaze flicked upward. The faded remnants of the name Debbie were left on her nametag.

"I'd like to view information from nineteen seventy-four."

"What kind of information?" Debbie's voice seemed too high for her large frame, and the faintest trace of a Scottish accent surrounded her vowels.

"Newspapers, specifically."

"You'll want Periodicals then. That's downtown at Central."

"Downtown? You mean there's nothing here at all?"

Debbie sighed and pointed to the back corner of the library. "You could try the Periodicals section, but really, most of the information from that long ago is at Central."

"Is there any way to have it brought here?"

"No. I'm sorry," Debbie said, her gaze returning to her screen.

Jil gritted her teeth impatiently. "Well then, may I look at the collection here as a start?"

"Please do."

She glanced back down again without so much as a "Let me know if you need any help."

Jil shook her head, and took herself to the Periodicals section. She noticed the microfilm machine and remembered the headache she'd had learning how to use it while in university. Luckily, the headache had forced her to retain the information.

She scanned the shelves for the docket of drawers holding microfilms and spotted it in the far right corner. *Rockford Citizen* lined the top. She scanned and noted that 1974 appeared to be the cutoff for retention of the newspapers. Jil opened the drawer holding January-March and fished out the first few reels.

With minimal cursing, she loaded the microfilm into the machine and sat down, adjusting the lenses. Blurry.

"Christ," she muttered to herself. This was going to take awhile. Particularly if it wasn't front-page news.

She went through seven reels of microfilm before deciding to pack it in for the day. And then, she saw it.

Tragedy at St. Marguerite's Catholic School:
March 27, 1974

> It was a grim morning for staff and students at St. Marguerite's Catholic School in Rockford yesterday as the bodies of Tommy Deloitte and Edward Cartwright were found hanging from the rafters. Cartwright was taken to hospital and later pronounced dead. Deloitte was pronounced dead when paramedics arrived. An investigation into the apparent attempted double suicide is underway.
>
> "It's too bad they didn't have anywhere to go for help," says Rocco DiTullio, a senior student. "They should have said something to someone."
>
> Principal Robert Bourne declined to comment, except to report that St. Marguerite's is a Catholic school and upholds Catholic standards of conduct. A funeral mass will take place for Tommy next Monday at 1:00 p.m. at St. Marguerite's Church. Well-wishers can pay their respects at that time.

Jil sat back in her chair. Rocco DiTullio. Interesting.

She flipped through the last remaining slides from that year, but found nothing more. For a newsworthy story, there seemed to be very little actually recorded.

Fatigue overcame her, and she pulled herself away from the questions elbowing for space inside her already preoccupied brain. Time for home.

❖

She walked slowly up the stairs, peeling off her clothes. In the bathroom, she closed the door to keep the heat in, turned on the heat lamp above the bathtub, and ran herself a hot, deep bubble bath. Before climbing in, she turned on the classical station and lit some candles, then turned off the lights and sank into the bubbly hot depths.

For a moment, she just lay there, letting the hot water permeate her sore muscles, especially her back and shoulders. She imagined fingers working into the knots, squeezing the tension out of her neck.

Whose fingers?

She shook her head. *Not going there.*

Not surprisingly, the fantasy massage had stimulated more than her neck muscles. She let her mind wander, imagining a mouth on her nipples, fingers trailing down her stomach and between her legs. What did surprise her was how quickly she was aroused, an orgasm building almost the moment her own fingers made contact. She breathed hard, fast, until a wave crashed over her, and she moaned quietly.

As she came down, back into the hot bath water lapping against her breasts, the little corner of her mind that she'd been silencing for weeks now began to whisper softly to her subconscious. The part of her she usually kept well hidden, bringing out only when it would advance her assignments—not sabotage her personal life. But it drifted in now, prodding her conscience.

When she was touching herself, she knew exactly who she'd been fantasizing about. And that would make this investigation a hell of a lot more complicated.

Chapter Six

September moved into October with all the frost and fire of Northern Ontario. On the Québec border, Rockford could be beautiful and bitter at once, and this year brought early snow as well as frost that settled on the flaming maple leaves around the campus. The first week of the tenth month, eight centimeters of snow stuck to the pavement, wreaking havoc on the roads as drivers re-acclimated to the slip-and-slide conditions.

Jil eased her truck out of the parking lot and onto the unplowed street. She cursed the frost on her window, the air where she could see her breath. She hated winter, and it had come way too early this year. Muttering obscenities, she searched around in the backseat for her steering wheel cover and slipped it on, grateful for this one small comfort. Still waiting, she blew into her hands, wondering why the red light at the top of the hill got slower every goddamned morning.

Julia Kinness's purse lay on the seat beside her.

Lanyard—check

Notebook—check

Phone—check

Personal life—left at home, as usual.

Her phone began to vibrate. She answered on the vehicle's speakers. "Kidd."

"How go the Catechisms?" Padraig asked, his low rumbling voice still coated with sleep.

"Oh, you know all about the Good Catholics. I'm a little busy teaching, to tell you the truth. That and investigating a dead student.

Not to mention the whole don't ask, don't tell thing. It gets a little tricky to actually get work done when you're in a mosh pit like a high school."

"Yeah, well, you're only a month in," Padraig said. "Don't worry too much, and don't rush things. The last thing you want is to blow your cover over this."

"I'm getting sucked in," Jil said, only half-joking. "The other day, I was driving home and almost collided with another car. When I pulled away, I found myself wanting to make the sign of the cross!"

Padraig chuckled again. "Well, maybe it's a subconscious desire. You were probably fed Catholic guilt in your breast milk."

Jil held her breath, wondering if Padraig would go on. She lived for this kind of information—tidbits about her mother. She hardly remembered her at all. Chestnut hair, arched eyebrows, red lips. The faint scent of apple and vanilla. Laughter like church bells, and a warm white sweater that tickled her nose when she snuggled into her lap. Classical music. The piano. Art. Books. A fierce intelligence behind an even fiercer love. That's all she remembered about her mother.

Except watching her die.

"Just keep doing what you're doing, Kidd. Preliminary report's due by Christmas break, so try not to stay too long after mid-December."

"Believe me, I'm dying to get out of there," Jil said. "It's not like we're getting paid by the hour. I have made some interesting discoveries, though."

"Oh yeah?"

"Apparently, the two students who killed themselves in nineteen seventy-four were gay."

"Really?"

"I came across a report in the newspaper, and Jess Blake confirmed it."

"Jess Blake knows you're looking into this?"

"No, not exactly," Jil backpedalled. "It kind of came up in conversation."

"Must have been a helluva conversation," Padraig returned darkly. "Watch yourself, Kidd."

If only he knew…"Don't worry. I'm as anxious to solve this problem and get out of there as you are to get me back in the line of fire. Oh wait…I mean, back behind a desk where you can keep a good eye on me."

"All right. Okay. Point taken! What's your next step?"

"Well, I've got a list of about twenty staff members for the preliminary report. I have a few more I want to check out today, but then I'm going to investigate the death of that student from the nineties. The one who slit her wrists."

"Of course you want to stick your nose into that."

"C'mon, Padraig."

"Yes, fine. I'm resigned to you by now. Good luck."

"Thanks."

The light had finally turned green, and she sped toward the highway for another day of teaching. She tossed her phone onto the seat beside her and wondered what glorious surprises St. Marguerite's would have for her this frosty Monday morning. Bombings? A science experiment gone wrong? Buck Weekly with an actual smile on his face?

She wasn't sure she really wanted to know.

The last thing she expected was a shiftless group of students. Again. This time, inside the school. Jil's heart leapt into her mouth, and she found herself almost running toward the doors. The students were hushed—eerily so. They let her through without a problem.

Was that blood over the doorway?

"Excuse me, ladies," Jil muttered, and two junior girls moved over quickly to let her through. No, not blood. Red paint. Graffiti. Over the doorway to the chapel, somebody had taken blood-red paint and written An Eye For An Eye. An involuntary chill shivered through Jil's core. She had never pretended to be a religious person (until now), but that particular passage always gave her the creeps.

Jessica and the custodians huddled in conference in front of the mess, which effectively blocked the students from going through the atrium to the R and B buildings. The students looked around, seeming not to know which way to go. Behind them, Mark Genovese blocked off the student entrance in an effort to stop the flow of traffic through the atrium; in front of them stood Jess, whose path they didn't want to cross.

Jil took one look at Jess's face and saw why. She wouldn't want to venture past Jess in that mood either. The students stood, like a herd of lost sheep in the middle of the atrium, staring at the graffiti.

"Through the caf, guys," Jil instructed them, shepherding a few students toward the senior cafeteria door. Relieved to have direction, they scurried down the hall, en masse.

"Go on, get to class," Mark Genovese barked at the few who remained behind.

One older guy snickered while the others just raised their eyebrows.

Mark beckoned to him, and the guy sauntered over slowly. Mark gestured to the paint and said something in a low voice.

The guy dropped the cocky grin and nodded, then looked where Mark pointed and frowned. He then began helping some of the younger students down to the G building. Certainly, nothing like this had ever happened to them at St. Matthew's Elementary school!

One kid looked up at Jil, his eyes wide. She recognized him from the first day of school. "Gideon, how's it going?"

He smiled. "Okay, Miss. How about you?" His voice shook a little.

"Great. Are you guys doing okay? A lot of really weird stuff has happened here since the beginning of the year. Did you go to talk to someone at Student Services?"

His buddy elbowed him, trying to shake his head, but Gideon looked at Jil instead. "Yeah, I did. My homeroom teacher made me."

His buddy shot him a look.

"Hey, I'm Ms. Kinness," she said, extending her hand to the young student.

"Wyatt," he muttered, shaking back. His hand was warm, sweaty. Almost feverish.

Jil resisted the urge to put her hand to his forehead. "You feeling okay, Wyatt?" They moved over as another group of students thundered down the stairs and threatened to topple them over.

"Yeah," Wyatt replied, raising his voice a little to be heard over the noise.

"Did you guys see who did this?"

Both boys looked down at their feet at the same moment.

"No, Miss," they said.

"You're sure?"

"Yes." Wyatt clenched his jaw. Gideon said nothing.

Jil knew when to let a matter drop. If they knew anything, they weren't talking. "If you want to tell me anything, I'm in R202, okay?"

They didn't answer, but as Jil walked away, she caught Gideon's eye, peeking up at her, just barely, as he tried to concentrate on his shoes. She winked.

Jil jogged back up the stairs to the empty atrium.

Jess looked angrily at the mess, radioing somebody on her walkie-talkie as she strode back toward the front office. Apparently, the custodians had already tried the standard paint-removing chemicals, which had done nothing but make the paint run into bloody streaks that looked even worse than before.

"I don't care what the hell you do, but get rid of it. Paint over it," she barked. "I'm not having my school defaced under my nose."

Swearing, Jil noted mentally. She wondered if that would be satisfactory for her chart. Maybe she wouldn't have to probe deeper into Jess's life, where she knew a nest of secrets buzzed. She'd been meaning to get to the courthouse to see if any divorce records existed for Jess and Mitchell, but somehow, something always got in the way.

With the mid-term report due in a few weeks, though, she couldn't put it off forever.

During morning prayers, Ms. Reitman, the female chaplain, made reference to "respecting our school and our property—giving us valuable creative outlets for our anger and helping us express ourselves in constructive, nonviolent ways." This was followed swiftly by more signs of the cross and reverent bowing, and then prayers were over. Thank God.

The students, of course, had all heard about the tagging by now. Most of them had crept into the atrium to see the damage firsthand. The custodians had managed to cover it with three coats of primer, but the bloody streaks still came through. All of the first period prep teachers were assigned to extra duty, so Jil sat for an hour in the atrium, literally watching paint dry.

While she sat there, three senior boys loped down from the front office, intending to use the student entrance, probably to go outside and smoke.

"West door, guys," Jil said, pointing to the side entrance—the only door students had been allowed to use.

The seniors looked at her strangely, then looked at the wall. One student—a tall, athletic kid with a shock of dark hair and an attitude to match—ignored her and headed for the main entrance. She recognized him—the same kid Mark Genovese had been frowning at in the atrium after the tagging. He seemed to be on the student government, so she was surprised when he swaggered right to the door.

"Stop right there," Jil ordered.

The kid froze.

"West door," she said again and pointed, following them with her eyes as they went through the alcove with the snack machines and out the door to the parking lot.

From around the opposite corner, she felt eyes watching her. She turned around slowly, to see Bex—who hadn't reported to her class for five straight days. She beckoned to her, and Bex approached slowly, shoulders slumped.

"What's up?" Jil took note of Bex's pale face. She'd lost weight. "You've been away?"

"Sick."

Jil knew enough to be able to tell when someone was lying, but for the second time this morning, she let it go. Something was obviously wrong with this girl.

Bex put her hands in the pockets of her boys' jeans.

Her rocker belt showed a visible wear line that showed it had been cinched in another two holes.

"Feeling better?"

Bex shrugged. "Not really. Thinking of being away again tomorrow."

"Yeah? Planning to come to class today?"

Bex shrugged again. "Guess so." Her hand shook as she took it out of her pocket to brush a stray strand of short hair from her forehead.

"I can give you what you've missed for the past week. Maybe you could go to the doctor or something this afternoon."

Bex scuffed her foot against the floor. "Can't."

"Oh no?"

"Na. Gotta go to work. 'Sides. It's not that kind of sick."

"I see. Maybe it's the kind of sick that only gets better if you talk it over?"

Bex didn't say anything.

"Like, with me, over coffee sometime?"

Again, a long silence. "We'll see," said Bex, finally, and she ambled away.

Jil watched her go, a frown knitting her eyebrows. Something strange was brewing at this school. Something very strange. She was going to get to the bottom of it—the out-of-wedlock children and the teachers living in sin would just have to wait.

Later that morning, Mark Genovese paged her to his office. The gold "Vice-Principal" plaque was bolted to the door at a perfect 180-degree angle.

"Ms. Kinness." He gripped her hand in an iron clasp. Up close, he was even larger than he appeared in the hallway. He towered over her by at least ten inches, and when he sat down, he had to fold himself into the chair to fit behind his standard-sized desk.

Jil slipped into a chair opposite him while he shuffled through some paperwork. She noticed the degrees and awards on his walls—some framed photographs of a dog, a family Christmas portrait from twenty years ago, and one of a group of boys in camping gear.

"Those your sons?" she asked.

He looked up. "No, that's me. Outdoor education trip as a twelfth grade student." He picked it up off the desk and handed it to her. "Recognize that kid there?"

Jil looked hard. Bushy eyebrows, beefy arms. "That can't be…"

"Buck Weekly." Mark chuckled. "Pain in the ass even when we were in high school. That's his twin brother, Charleston."

Jil examined it more closely. "They're not identical."

"No. Though they do look a lot alike, don't they?"

"Yeah. But Charleston's cuter."

Genovese chuckled. "He was," he agreed.

"Was?"

Mark's face closed. "He died in a car crash about ten years after this picture was taken. I like to keep this picture to remember our merrye bande."

"So you went here as a student as well?"

"Grew up in these halls, did a student teaching position here, and then got hired as a teacher."

Jil heard echoes of her previous conversation with Buck.

"A few of your students won't be moving on, though," Mark said, abruptly changing the subject, "if they don't pull up their socks."

She frowned.

"It's my job to weed out the seniors who are struggling before they crash and burn."

"A lot of my students are struggling, but most of them are passing."

"Well, that's a treat," Mark said sarcastically. "At one time, failure was rare. Now, a C is considered a decent grade. Can you get me a list of everyone with a sixty-five percent or below?"

"Sure."

"Final year. This is the biggie."

"Well, if they want to go to college, it is."

Mark snorted. "They'll be working at the fast food chains unless they wake up."

"What do you do with them?"

"Enroll them in a computer skills class." A grin formed on Mark's face as he steepled his fingers. "Literacy and technology training all in one. Saturday mornings nine to noon if you ever care to join us."

"You teach social media in those lessons?"

He looked up over his screen. "Smart teachers don't use social media at all."

She already knew his views. He'd passed the first round of her investigations: married for thirty years, with two sons, regular church attendance, and no social media accounts.

He turned to his computer, and Jil felt the dismissal.

"See you around," she said.

He smiled without looking up and she let herself out.

Chapter Seven

Next day, while Jil sat in the empty atrium—most of the students having gotten the message to stay in the library or caf—one of the custodians approached.

"Hey, Bean," he said easily. He was short with a head shaved bald, but had deep blue eyes, almost navy in color, and his muscled arms stood out, well-defined beneath his short-sleeved shirt, a tan line where a wedding band should have been, and tattoos around his wrists.

She turned around, surprised at hearing her childhood nickname. For a moment, she didn't recognize her high school chum Brian, but he grinned easily and she remembered what he'd looked like fifteen years ago—with hair.

"Hey, yourself."

"Always knew you'd be a success," he said. "Never thought you'd go in for teaching, though."

And this is why PIs were not supposed to go undercover in their own districts.

She smiled disarmingly, her mind racing. She liked Brian, but she couldn't afford to blow her cover. Lie. "Thanks," she replied.

"So how'd you end up here? What are you teaching?"

"Religion," she answered, smirking a little.

"You're kidding."

"No. Really am."

"Never would have believed it." He shook his head. "The Jillienne Kidd I knew would have bucked that system all the way to the gate."

She looked around quickly to see if anyone had overheard him, and dropped her voice to a whisper. "Actually…"

He leaned in. "Yeah?"

"I hope you can keep my little secret?"

He frowned. "Sure. What is it?"

"Well, I changed my name."

"Your last name?"

"My whole name. I go by Julia Kinness now."

"You married?"

She smiled. "Not exactly. I wanted a fresh start—you know—after I got out of the system."

Brian gave a low whistle. "That's right. I forgot you were in those foster homes."

She bit her lip. Always dangerous to let too many emotions through. "Anyway…"

"Yeah, of course. I get it. So Julia Kinness you said?"

"Yeah."

"No more Jilly-Bean?"

She laughed. "Sorry."

"Hey, whatever. I can adapt—Jules." He grinned, and she cuffed him lightly on the shoulder.

"So this tagging is pretty brutal, eh?"

He leaned beside her on the railing, looking up at the graffiti.

"We've tried everything," he sighed, frustrated. "Turpentine, paint thinner. Nuthin' works."

"You going to have to paint it over then?"

"Yeah, but that means we'll have to paint the whole wall. Maybe the whole atrium. That paint's old, man."

"Can't get a match?"

"For this?" He laughed and gestured to the hideous seafoam walls.

Jil laughed back. "I suggest chartreuse for the next coat."

"Yeah, I'm going with white. Plain old white. That's all they deserve if they're going to mess the place up like this. Besides, I think that's the only paint we've got that's thick enough to cover it."

"Who would have picked this color?"

"All part of the grand remodeling," Brian said, holding his nose in the air. "After that incident with the two dead kids, the whole school got a facelift. New paint, new gym, new everything. Turning over a new leaf. Forty years ago!"

"Well, this leaf is one ugly green. Who do you think did it?"

Brian shook his head. "Just some punks."

"Do you know who they are?"

Brian shook his head again. "Don't like to say nuthin'. Them wall's got ears. But I'd bet money it was those damn residence kids."

"Residence kids?"

"Yeah. The kids who live on campus. Those foster kids they try to turn into model students."

"Are they all foster kids, living here?"

"Mostly. They call them 'at risk,' but what they really mean is 'pain in the ass.'"

Jil considered that for a moment. Jess had said about fifty kids lived in the residence buildings. They would have easy access to the school and could have snuck in over the weekend to tag the atrium.

"Hey, can I ask you something?"

Brian's eyes smiled just as brightly as his teeth did. "Sure."

"Who unlocks the school in the morning?"

"That'd be Marcel."

"Your boss?"

"Ha! He'd like to think so. Jess is my boss, but Marcel's the head custodian. Why you asking?"

"Well, you know about the girl who died, obviously."

"Yeah. Of course."

"I just wondered why, if a custodian was here at six a.m., he never noticed Alyssa's body."

Brian nodded slowly. "Doors don't open til seven. Marcel woulda used our own entrance off the back parking lot to come in at six. But you're right. He shoulda found her before the students did. Unless he was busy."

The way he said busy made Jil narrow her eyes. Doing something he shouldn't have been doing?

Jil saw the tall, dark-haired custodian approaching. He was thin and lank, with an insincere smile in his weathered face. Jil recognized the guy she'd almost tripped over while he tended the indoor flower beds.

"Marcel," Brian sighed under his breath. "Guess I'd better shove off." He eyed Marcel warily, then moved quickly in the opposite direction, nodding and smiling to everyone as he passed.

Jil felt eyes on her and turned her head slowly in the other direction, just in time to see Buck Weekly look away.

❖

When the bell rang for period two, Jil was already waiting outside her classroom. The other teacher cleared out quickly, which gave her enough time to slip to the back of the room and take up a spot behind a display, partly concealed in the far corner. She felt like she'd been walking through a minefield of secrets. This wasn't what she thought teaching would be like. Instead of preparing for a lecture, she was setting herself up to spy on students as they came in.

Bex entered first, trailed closely by Theo—who towered over her. He gripped her tightly by the arm, leading her to her desk, which he shoved her into. She pulled away, shooting him a fierce look.

"You'd better watch it," he whispered, tightening his hold. "Or you know what happens next."

"Fuck you," she spat.

Jil emerged from the corner, carting a globe that she didn't really need.

"Good morning," she said coolly and squeezed between them on her way to her desk. They both looked up, surprised. Her movements forced Theo back several paces, and Jil held her position. "Put this on the desk for me, please, Bex," she said.

Bex scooted to her feet, snatching the globe from Jil, without meeting her gaze.

Jil held Theo's eyes for a long moment. He looked away and backed toward his desk. Bex loitered by Jil's desk, as far away from her own seat as possible.

More students began arriving, and they stormed in boisterously.

"I need you to switch seats with Jordan," Jil said, under the cover of student chatter.

Bex didn't reply. She just ducked into the seat right in front of Jil's desk and flipped open her textbook.

Jordan looked at her in confusion as he came in, almost late. He was about to tell her off when Jil held up a finger and pointed to Bex's vacant desk. Shrugging, Jordan ducked into his new seat.

Theo's eyes shot daggers at Jil, which she pointedly ignored. She wanted to put as much space between him and Bex as possible.

"That was sick yesterday, Miss," Kyle said as he dropped his book bag on the floor and slumped into his desk. "An eye for an eye, yo. In blood!"

"It wasn't blood! It was just paint," Jordan said scornfully.

"Looked like blood to me," Kyle crowed.

"Does the Bible actually mean an eye for an eye, Miss?" Joey stared incredulously at her classmate. "I mean, isn't that kind of stupid? The Bible is supposed to teach love!" She stuck her tongue out at Kyle, who shot forward in his seat. Joey ducked.

"Sit," Jil said, and the students dropped into their desks. "We're already late."

"Oh, c'mon, Miss, aren't we supposed to study like current affairs and shit?"

"And stuff?" Jil corrected him. "Yes, I guess so. But vandalism isn't exactly my idea of a choice discussion."

"Well, there must be a reason that they're putting that sh—stuff up there," Kyle countered. "Maybe the students are sick of some of what's going down. Maybe someone thinks it's time to get even."

"In what way?" Jil perched on the side of her desk. If the students opened up, maybe she'd get some clues.

"Like maybe they're sick of the teachers ragging on them."

"Yeah, or maybe they're pissed about the caf food." Joey laughed loudly.

"Yo, that shit is disgusting," Jordan agreed from the back of the room. Jil looked at him, and he put his head back down again. Bex picked at her fingernails and didn't say anything.

"What do you think it means, Miss?" asked Yasmine, a petite girl with a heavy Columbian accent.

"No idea. Maybe someone was bored on Sunday night and decided to come into school and play a prank. Maybe someone likes knowing that people are on edge. Or maybe, as you said, someone really is offended by an injustice, and this is the way they're choosing to express it."

"Yeah," said Kyle, "and maybe someone wants revenge."

"Revenge on what?"

Bex rolled her eyes. "If it were easy to talk about, people wouldn't need to tag."

Theo banged his textbook down on his desk, his eyes blazing. "Cowards."

Before things could go any further, Jil took out her own textbook. She'd have to sleuth around later. "Page twenty-five. We're going to start learning something today or you'll be with me in August!"

The chatter stopped.

When the bell rang for end of period, she was surprised to see Jessica Blake outside her door. Her heart clenched, then resumed its normal rhythm at double-speed. The students thundered out the door, quieting immediately when they saw Jess standing there.

"Morning, Miss," they said as they ducked their heads and hurried past her out the door to lunch.

"Hello. Save your iPod till you get outside, please. Jordan, take that hood down."

"Hey, Ms. Blake."

"Good morning, Rebecca. How are things?"

"Fine, Miss."

"Great. Off to lunch?"

Bex shot a glance over her shoulder at Jil. "Can I, Miss?"

Jil nodded permission. "We'll catch up another time."

Bex ducked her head and left.

"Does Rebecca have detention?" Jess asked. The room had cleared, and her voice in the silence sounded incredulous.

"No, no. She's just been absent for a while and needs some help to catch up on work." She briefly considered telling Jess about the odd dynamic between Theo and Bex, but decided against it. Now wasn't the time. She needed to wait until she had more to go on than a hunch.

"Ah. I see. It's unlike her to miss school."

"I think she and Alyssa were close," Jil replied.

Jess's face took on a distant and worried look at the mention of Alyssa's name. "Oh. Did you send her to Student Services?"

"Tried. I don't think she's the kind of kid to go for help."

"Hmm. Maybe I'll pull her in for a talk."

"Might not be a bad idea. How are Alyssa's parents?

Jess sighed, and seemed to slump a little against the doorway. "They're suing the school."

"What for?"

"Not sure yet. Everything's in closed-door meetings. Giovanni DiTullio's handling it."

"Really? You're not even in the loop?"

Jess looked over her shoulder, and Jil read her fears. The hallway seemed clear, but this wasn't really the place to be having this type of discussion. If she asked how Jess was doing, would she be crossing that line again? That line that was as unclear as a highway line in a blizzard?

"Do you want to come in?" she whispered.

Jess met her eyes and hesitated, then stepped inside and closed the door. "I shouldn't have involved you in this," she said, as soon as the knob clicked. "It's not your problem."

If it's your problem, I want to help. But of course she couldn't say that. "When will you have an idea of the outcome?"

"Next week? If they even decide to go through with it. The board might just settle to keep it out of the papers." She leaned against the door and closed her eyes for a second.

Jil almost reached out to touch her arm, but Jess's eyes opened, as if she'd suddenly remembered the reason for her visit.

"Payroll called." She shifted a clipboard from one hand to the other, absently stretching and flexing her fingers like they were stiff. Probably too many hours filling out paperwork.

Jil raised her eyebrows. "Problems?"

"Yes. Apparently, you're not on the list. Have you been getting a paycheck?"

"Trust me, I wouldn't be here if I wasn't," Jil replied.

Jess grinned. "Going that well, eh?"

"Well, I can't say this semester has been the smoothest period of my life."

"You can say that again. I'm sorry this has to be your first teaching experience. Things aren't exactly uneventful around here, but this semester is really taking the cake."

"It's all right. I'm only here til December anyway, right?"

Jess stopped. "Yes," she said, as if that hadn't occurred to her before. "You're right. We'll have to see if we can find somewhere else to put you. It'll be quite a loss for us."

"Thanks." She meant it. No way she would ever consider staying, but it meant a lot to her that Jess valued her, at least.

"Anyway," Jess went on. "I called and left a message for the HR person. Can you come down to the office today and get that straightened out with Mary?"

"Sure." Of course she wasn't on the list. She was on assignment, being paid out of the investigation's budget. The school was getting a free teacher in exchange for the privilege of being surreptitiously scrutinized. She'd have to call Padraig and get that particular detail ironed out. It didn't seem like Mary was the type of admin assistant to let things slide. She'd want a reconciliation. Pronto.

As Jess left, Jil found herself wondering why Jess had chosen to deliver the message personally. Surely she could have paged her to the office, or had a note dropped in her box.

Buck Weekly cornered her in the hallway on her way down to her office.

"Julia, I was wondering if you could give me a hand?"

Jil didn't respond. Saying yes before knowing the request would probably get her involved in something lengthy and tedious, but she didn't want to appear unfriendly or rude by saying no right off the bat.

"What is it, Buck?" she asked politely.

"I'm putting together the Thanksgiving Mass. Would you have time to look over the program?"

Jil shrugged. "Sure," she replied, not knowing what else to say. Why not collaborate on a Mass? It would give the illusion of professional rapport—something they sorely lacked at the moment.

Buck led the way to his office, gesturing for her to sit at his desk. She perched gingerly on the side of his chair while he rumbled around the room, looking for something. She didn't like the closed door, or the smell of his stale shirt as he leaned over the desk, reaching for a pen.

"Excuse me," he said, a trace of annoyance in his voice. She scootched back. Why did he make her feel like she was in the way, when he'd asked her to come here in the first place?

He found the program and handed it to her, standing over her shoulder as she read.

Her heart flipped. She had no idea what would be appropriate at a Mass of Thanksgiving. If this was a test, she would surely fail.

"Would you excuse me?" Buck asked. "I need to see Jessica for a minute."

Jil nodded. "Sure." Anything to get him out of her space.

As soon as the door closed, she stuffed the program into her purse and grabbed a Post-it. "Forgot an appointment. Have to go. Took this copy home to give it some more thought. See you tomorrow."

When she got back to her office to collect her things, she found the light on. She grabbed her bag and coat, flicked off the light switch, and locked the door. It seemed that she'd repeated this action once already this morning. Hadn't she already turned the light out? Didn't she always turn the light out when she left?

"Ms. Kinness." Jil whipped around as she passed the chapel—a place that always made her faintly nervous. The chaplain stood in the doorway, a tentative smile on her face, her long white braid slung over her shoulder.

On closer look, Jil realized the chaplain wasn't at all old. In fact, she was quite young. It was just the color of her hair that gave the impression of age. The Coke-bottle glasses didn't help either. Her irises were a very light gray, and a permanent frown line creased her delicate forehead—as if she spent a great deal of time squinting. In fact, Jil realized, the chaplain had no pigment in her eyes at all.

Albinism.

"Hi." Jil stopped.

"I was wondering if you had a moment to talk?"

Jil hesitated. She didn't really want to go inside the chapel. That seemed to be a very likely place to get struck by lightning.

Ms. Reitman seemed to sense her feelings. "I have an office," she said gently.

Jil exhaled. "Okay. Sure."

She stepped into the chaplain's rather small quarters—just enough room for a desk, a chair, and a bookshelf.

"Have a seat. My name is Maggie, by the way."

"Julia," said Jil.

"So how are you settling into St. Marguerite's?" Maggie offered her a chair.

Jil sat, a little awkwardly, and tried not to stare at the huge tile mosaic portrait of Jesus starting down at her. "Fine, thanks. Have you been here long?"

"This is my second year." Maggie took the lid off a jar on her desk and unwrapped a Werther's. She offered the jar to Jil, but she shook her head.

"No, thanks."

"My first few weeks were a little difficult, as I remember," Maggie continued. She rolled up the sleeve of her denim shirt that looked like it had been hanging in her closet since the 1970s. It even had an embroidered cat on it, for God's sake. Apparently, she was not exactly Ms. Fashion Conscious, which might explain why she always sat alone in the staff room. It was high school after all, and the cliques in the cafeteria only graduated to become the cliques in the staffroom. High school never changed.

"Why's that?"

"Oh, because I'm a woman, I guess." Maggie smiled ruefully and tapped a pen against her desk. "The chaplain before me had been here for well over thirty years. He was very…traditional…from what I understand. Some of the staff weren't particularly thrilled with a female recruit."

"Too bad."

Maggie smiled.

"I didn't know women could be chaplains."

"Sure they can. My job is mostly to write the morning prayers and liaise with the Religion Department to organize events. Sometimes be a guest teacher in a class."

As part of the Religion Department, maybe that would have been nice to know.

"I just can't bless a sacrament or perform Mass."

"So basically, nothing a priest can do."

"That's right. But neither could a male chaplain."

Jil thought for a second. "But a male chaplain could study for the priesthood if he wanted."

"Yes. He could. And then he could come back and perform Mass here at the school, if he wanted. But that still doesn't make him any better a chaplain than I am."

Jil smiled. This wasn't at all what she had expected. She didn't know why she suddenly felt like saying, "I'm a bit removed from the church," but she said it.

"Interesting, for a religion teacher. What drew you away from the church?"

She stared past Maggie, at a portrait of Mary, under which hung a pearl rosary. That's what she remembered most about church as a child. The rosary, slipping between her fingers as she counted out the prayers. She could still say it out loud.

Hail Mary, full of grace
The Lord is with thee.
Blessed art thou among women
And blessed is the fruit of thy womb, Jesus.

Fruit of thy womb. The most Catholic of virtues—life. Love, between a man and a woman, which created life.

Jil just looked at Maggie's earnest face. For once, she couldn't think of any lie to tell. She looked down at her hands. "Because I'm no longer welcome."

Maggie tilted her head. "God always welcomes us back. When we're ready."

The sound of Buck Weekly's voice echoed down the hall, and Jil remembered the program.

"I'm helping put together the Thanksgiving Mass," she whispered.

"Oh?"

"Buck asked me."

"Yes. Father MacEvoy called this morning to confirm the time. We'll all head to the church down the road."

"I get the feeling Buck's testing me."

Maggie chuckled. "That could very well be."

Jil took out the program from her purse and handed it to Maggie, who read it carefully. "Well, this would be fine if it were Easter," she said, a small smile playing at her lips. "Let's make a few adjustments, shall we?"

She took out her Sunday missal and handed back the program. "Best be in your handwriting."

Jil smiled and grabbed a pen while Maggie read out suggestions. In ten minutes, the program was unrecognizable, but peppered with Thanksgiving hymns, prayers, and readings, and they were both grinning.

"Thank you," Jil said as she got up to leave.

"Anytime. The ladies must stick together."

❖

"Julia!" Buck called from a classroom down the hall.

She turned around in time to see him approaching.

"I left the program on your desk this morning," she said. "I'm sorry, but I'm late for class."

"Oh." Buck looked at his watch. "I was wondering if you might be free this Saturday?"

She froze. "Excuse me?"

"For a field trip," Buck said impatiently. "The residence students are supposed to have a session in the Outdoor Education Center on Saturday, but Rosie McMonahan's out with the flu, and I need another female teacher with me."

Jil considered this briefly. Buck supervised the residence students? Something about this required more investigation.

"Sure," she said brightly. "What time?"

"Eight."

"A.M?"

"Yes," Buck said, a vague hint of annoyance tracing his words. "Is that a problem?"

"Not at all. I'll be here."

Chapter Eight

Saturday morning, Jil bundled into her freezing SUV with her mittened hands wrapped tightly around a large mug of coffee. Perhaps she should have thought to ask what this field trip would entail.

Buck had mentioned something about survival skills and a high ropes course, so she'd donned her hiking boots and sports clothes with layers. In her knapsack, she'd packed snacks, water, and a Swiss Army knife, though now she wondered if she should have left that at home.

"Better safe," she muttered as she checked her bag one last time, then headed for St. Marguerite's.

A school bus waited in the parking lot, its exhaust streaming blue clouds of steam into the crisp morning air. As she alighted from her vehicle, her feet made crunching indents in the frost-covered gravel.

Buck ambled toward her, grimacing. "Good morning. Glad you could join us. I was beginning to wonder."

Jil looked at her watch: seven forty-five. "You told me eight."

Buck stopped. "No, I said it started at eight. We still have a half-hour bus ride."

Jil rolled her eyes inwardly, but outwardly smiled an apology. "I misunderstood. Hope you haven't been waiting long."

"As a general rule, Julia, I find it best to arrive early when I'm not sure of the schedule."

Jil bit her tongue. "Ready whenever you are."

She climbed on board the bus, where Mark Genovese took up the entire second row—his hulking torso packed into one double-seat, while his massive legs extended over the aisle to the other.

Jil saw the empty seat right behind the driver and scooted inside. "Good morning, Mark."

"Hello, Julia."

Buck was saying something to the driver, so Jil leaned in. "Did he tell you to get here for eight too?" she whispered.

Mark grunted. "That man is constantly confused. Must be all the medication."

Jil pressed her lips together to avoid a snort, then sat down. Interesting.

From the back of the bus came a cheer, followed by some foot stomping and whistling.

Mark barely turned his head. "Quiet in the back," he bellowed. An instant hush descended. A moment later, the bus pulled out.

Buck stood and took the microphone.

Oh, you've got to be kidding me. She snuck a look back at Mark, but he was staring straight ahead, his mouth pressed into a thin line.

"Good morning, senior Pathways students."

"Good morning, Mr. Weekly," they chorused, some more smart-assed than others.

"Today we have the privilege of attending the Outdoor Education Center to participate in their High Ropes Course. This is intended for credit toward your physical education requirements."

"Yo, Mr. Weekly, I don't take no phys ed," called a boy from the back. His hair was gelled into a perfect fauxhawk, and he smirked at his buddies.

"Well, James, first of all, I'd appreciate if you raised your hand before making a comment. I was in the middle of speaking. How do you think I perceive your interrupting?"

James shrugged.

"Well, let me tell you, I perceive it as rude. Like you don't have respect for the fact that I have information to give to everyone, not just you."

"Sorry," James muttered.

"Thank you. As I was saying, some of you are participating for credit toward phys ed. Some of you are participating for other reasons, for example, as part of your rehabilitation requirements from the juvenile detention centers where you spent time before coming to

Pathways. Some of you are here instead of your computer skills training course. And some of you have requested to participate for recreation."

"Yeah, right," Jil heard a student mutter. She looked back, but couldn't identify the speaker.

"We are very lucky to be going on this trip today, so I hope we can show our hosts that we are the best examples St. Marguerite's has to offer. This opportunity is not given to all students. It isn't part of the regular curriculum anymore, like it used to be," Buck went on. "Both Mr. Genovese and I had the privilege of participating in something very similar when we were in high school. Isn't that right, Mr. Genovese?"

Mark grunted.

"Ms. Kinness has also volunteered her time for you today, as Ms. McMonahan couldn't be with us due to illness. Let's show our appreciation for Ms. Kinness by a round of applause."

Some half-hearted clapping followed.

Oh, for God's sake, could you sit down and let the kids ride the bus in peace?

"We will be arriving at the OEC in about twenty-five minutes, so to prepare, I have divided you already into groups…"

Jil leaned against the window and took a long sip of her coffee, doing her best to drown out Buck's constant drawling.

Finally, he sat down and busied himself with papers and equipment in his own backpack. Behind her, Mark Genovese snored.

❖

"Student council, a brief meeting," Mark barked as he stood against the tree line, arms crossed over his barrel chest.

Students broke away from the pack of kids unloading gear from the bottom of the bus, and strode over to where Mark waited.

A couple of younger kids scampered to grab their packs. "Hi, Miss!" called Gideon, grinning widely.

His friend Wyatt shoved him.

"Hi, boys," Jil called back. She looked down at her list and schedule. When she looked up, a group of students had already begun to encircle her. "Good morning," she said, consciously deciding not to take a step back.

"Hi, Miss."

"Oh, hi, Bex."

"How'd they rope you in to supervising a residence out-trip?"

Jil grinned. "Well, Mr. Weekly found me sitting alone and unprotected in the staff room. Then he hog-tied me and dragged me out here on a Saturday morning in the freezing cold to go swing through old tires in the trees."

Bex stifled a smile.

"Wish I'd stayed in your class, Miss," said the girl standing next to her.

Jil looked up and saw the girl with the bullring nose piercing who had left her class on the first day. "Yeah?"

"I ended up in Law, and it's frickin' brutal."

"We get some fireworks in World Religions…and way too much homework," Bex said, the corners of her mouth lifting a little.

"Has to be better than studying precedent and a-priority."

"*A priori*?" said Jil.

"Whatever. Yeah, that."

Jil smiled. "Okay, so who have we got here today?"

Bex looked around. "They put all the girls with you, Miss."

Jil looked down at the pile of equipment a guide had just dumped beside them and understood why. No male teacher was going to be caught dead helping senior girls into harnesses.

Fabulous.

Jil handed her schedule to Bex and asked for introductions.

"I'm Teegan," said the girl with the bull ring. "Grade twelve."

"Nikki," said a small girl with mousy blond hair and huge eyes. "Grade nine."

"Yeah for the minors." Teegan cuffed the girl on the shoulder. Nikki giggled.

"I'm here, Miss," called a familiar voice. Jil turned around to see Joey running up behind her.

"Did you come on the bus?"

"Well, yeah. I was just, you know…"

"Visiting the facilities?" Teagan joked.

"Shut up. I had a lot of coffee this morning."

"Coffee? They serve coffee in residence?" Jil frowned.

"Yeah, Miss. The dons get the first cup, but after that, it's kind of a free-for-all."

"It's okay if you add lotsa sugar," said Nikki, giggling again.

"What—you drink coffee?" Jil poked the girl in the arm.

"Not all the time."

"Great. This should be a fun day." She scanned her list. "Where's Rachel?"

Bex gestured toward the student council group. "She's in a meeting."

Teegan hit her and frowned.

"I don't suppose you'd like to elaborate?"

Bex shook her head.

Just then, Rachel strode over, her backpack cinched neatly across her waist and chest, her white student council shirt glowing through the green trees.

"Hi, you must be Ms. Kinness." She smiled widely and extended her hand, which Jil shook.

"Nice to meet you."

Before Jil could say another word, Rachel had clapped her hands and turned to the group—a grinning trail guide. "Okay, ladies, Mr. Genovese has asked me to go over a few points of safety."

Jil leaned back and watched, amused, as Rachel read the rules from a pamphlet: no wandering off alone, keep in sight of your staff guide, stay on the ropes course, always wear a helmet and a harness, one at a time on the ropes, wait until the guide gives you the go-ahead…

The list went on for ten minutes, and by the time Rachel had finished, the other two teams were heading for the trail.

Buck ambled over with a small woman in climbing gear dashing behind him. "Good morning, everyone."

Jil smiled tightly.

"We're in three different groups, but we'll all be working together today."

Of course we will.

"This is your climbing guide, Marcy. Can we all say good morning to Marcy?"

"Good morning, Marcy," chorused the girls.

Marcy raised her thick eyebrows. "Um, hello."

"Thanks, Mr. Weekly," said Jil before he could launch into another speech. "We'll meet you and the rest of the squad over by the course."

Buck frowned a little and ambled away.

Marcy looked slightly relieved.

"So, where are we going to start?" Rachel beamed.

"We'll start by putting on our safety gear," said Marcy. She picked up a harness and demonstrated how to put it on.

Jil frowned, something bothering her. "Bex, why is student council here?"

Bex snorted. "Peer support, Miss. They help the wayward Pathways student stay on a righteous path."

"But they don't live in residence?"

Bex shook her head. "Most Pathways kids aren't leadership material."

Ten minutes passed while the students giggled and cursed, trying to wiggle into the restrictive straps. Finally, they had all passed a safety check and donned helmets.

They met the other two groups by the first course. Mark's students were already up the first obstacle. One student waited on the platform, forty feet in the air, while another student walked across vertical logs that hung from ropes. Every time he moved from one small surface to the other, Jil gasped.

"Going up, Miss?" Buck said.

"Not likely. You?" She imagined Buck hanging off the giant net at the end of the obstacle.

"Oh, no. Mark and I have had our fill of these courses. When we were lads, this was a five-day-long adventure trip. Now, it's five hours."

"Do they still do a camp here?"

"Yes, survival camp. St. Marguerite's doesn't have the money anymore. It's mostly private schools that come. The kids do canoeing, camping, and high ropes. It's a great experience." He stopped as Mark approached. "Going up, sir?"

Mark frowned. "Not today."

From beside Jil, Teegan whistled. "That's fucking high," she muttered.

Mark's face turned red, and he opened his mouth to say something, but Buck interrupted.

"Teegan, how do you think it makes St. Marguerite's look when you use language like that on a school trip?"

Teegan rolled her eyes. "Sorry, sir."

"I accept your apology. What would be a better word to use?"

"Very," Teegan sighed. "That course is very high."

"Yes, it is. And it will take a lot of courage and stamina to get through it. Are you courageous? Do you have stamina?"

"Yes, sir."

Mark snorted, and Teegan looked at the ground, her cheeks flushed.

"Well then, let's see you. Your turn next."

Jil shoved her forward by her helmet, and she smiled.

"C'mon, team," Mark bellowed. His group of strapping senior boys shoved off to the next course, their white shirts glinting.

Teegan watched them for a moment, then looked up at the course.

"Ready?" said Marcy.

"Guess so."

"Belay on."

She chose the netting to ascend and didn't look back.

Buck nodded at Jil, who grimaced back, and waved as he took his students to a third course.

This was going to be a very long day.

In the truck on the way home, she dialed Padraig's number. He answered on the first ring.

"Thank you," she said.

"For what, Kidd?"

"For not sending me to that fucking Pathways program."

Padraig laughed loud and hard. "Ah, see. This old man does know what's best for you sometimes."

The second tagging came two weeks later on a Tuesday morning. This time, it appeared above the statue of Jesus outside the main office.

VENGEANCE IS MINE! SAYETH THE LORD.

Same red paint. Same slanted block letters. Same indelible quality. Unfortunately, this tagging was even more difficult to remove than the last.

"Who the hell could possibly get up here?" Rosie McMonahan complained to Jil as she watched from the atrium. "You'd have to be a monkey to climb those columns."

Two custodians on ladders scrubbed at the mess. Past them, Jil spotted Jess sitting at her desk, intently watching streams of video from the school's security cameras. The camera outside the office had been blanked out.

Jess shoved away from her desk and came quickly through the doors to the front office, almost sideswiping Jil.

"Sorry," she muttered.

"No harm. What's wrong?"

"We need increased surveillance."

"Seriously?"

Jess's eyes shot daggers. "This can't keep happening."

The heat from Jess's body made Jil swallow hard. Twice. She held her gaze, just barely, and saw something shift.

Jess took a deep breath and let her shoulders relax. "I don't know what we're going to do," she muttered. "This is going to be very expensive."

"Yeah, well, they're going to find a way to do it even if you amp up security to the hilt."

Jess looked up abruptly. "Do you know something?"

Jil stared back calmly, and this seemed to have a steadying effect on Jess as well. She let out a long breath and looked down. "Sorry."

"I wish I did know something." Jil resisted the temptation to lay a hand on Jess's arm. "I'm just as stumped as you are. But maybe I can help you find out." *Why would you say that? You're supposed to be disguising your sleuthing capabilities, not flaunting them!*

If this offer surprised Jessica at all, she didn't show it. "Consider yourself appointed," she said dryly.

Jil hid a nervous smile.

Jess ordered the school cameras to be fixed, protected, and run round the clock. The adjustments were made. Vigilance was increased. The wall around the office entrance received a new coat of white paint to match the wall around the chapel. The atrium was fast losing its seafoam façade, though no one seemed sorry.

Students walked past, discreetly touching their fingers into the wet paint to leave behind their fingerprints. Later, they would come back and write “Johannes was here” and “Vicky + Peter 4ever.” Jess ordered the wall repainted a second time and teachers posted on duty.

“Do not touch the walls,” she commanded over the PA system. “If there is any more vandalism to our new paint, we will use the budget for the prom to cover the expenses of repainting.” She was on the warpath, and she meant business. The students knew better than to argue.

After the second coat of paint had been applied, Mark Genovese pulled student council members out of class and posted them in groups of two or three, at various points in the large entryway.

“Take care of this,” he barked to the oldest students.

“Yes, sir,” said two older youths in jeans and white student council T-shirts.

If a backpack or a sweater got too close to the wall, they’d yell. “Hey! Watch it!” Students stopped, the younger students especially—looks of surprise and awe on their faces. Senior students were talking to them. Reprimanding them.

One young boy dashed away, red-faced. He hadn’t done it on purpose. His backpack was just way too big for his spindly legs.

❖

At seven thirty a.m., Jil came through the front door, cheeks cold from the weather, snow dusting her black hat and wool coat. “Hey,” she said to Jess.

Jess merely nodded.

“What’s wrong?” Jil’s face fell. “Oh, don’t tell me. Where?”

“The chapel.”

Jil opened one side of the French doors to find Maggie crying silently next to the altar. Emblazoned across the stained-glass panel behind the altar was the third tagging. Bloodred block letters ruined the beautiful window.

HATE IS THE ABOMINATION.

“Julia, good morning.” She tried to smile.

“I’m so sorry, Maggie.” Jil stared up at the dripping paint. “We’ll get it cleaned up.”

“Not in time for prayers this morning, I don’t think.”

“We’ll have an assembly instead.” Jess stood in the doorway. “Julia, can you help me in the caf?”

Jil followed her.

Very few students had arrived at school, which meant a small pool of prime suspects.

Jess Blake strode back to the office, picked up the microphone, and made a command over the PA. "All students report to the senior cafeteria immediately."

She stood at the door to the office, watching students emerge from all corners of the school. She made no comment about backpacks or iPods or hats; she just watched their faces.

Jil stepped back as a group of students in hockey uniforms almost trampled her. They were senior girls—tall, strapping young women—annoyed that their practice had been interrupted the morning before a big game.

"Watch where you're going, ladies," their coach barked.

Jil looked up, startled to see that voice belonged to the delicate Rosie McMonahan. "What's going on?" she whispered to Jil as she passed.

"Spot check," Jil replied dryly.

Jil waved students in ahead of her. She peered down the hall, but no one else was coming.

When Jess got up on stage and surveyed the crowd, fewer than one hundred students were present. The stage band, the boys' basketball team, the girls' hockey team, the set painters for the play, and the debate club were all there.

The usual early morning bunch were enjoying breakfast sandwiches at a table in the corner. A few junior students whose parents dropped them off this early so they could get to work straggled through the halls as well. The perpetrator of the graffiti had probably not responded to the PA announcement, but a small possibility was better than nothing.

"I want everyone to form a line in front of me, and put your backpacks on the floor in front of you," Jess demanded.

The basketball team shrugged. They didn't have backpacks. Seeing the younger students shuffle uncertainly, and some of the other kids rolling their eyes, the captain of the boys' basketball team stepped forward. He was not only captain of the team; he was also the head boy.

"C'mon, guys," he said loudly, stepping to the front of the line. The team lined up quickly behind him, and the rest of the students, seeing him cooperating, followed suit—some with better attitudes than others.

Jess came down off the stage and stood at the front of the line. "Palms up, please," she said to the captain.

He turned his hands over, not asking any questions. Clean.

Jess patted him on the shoulder. "Thanks. You can go."

The next boy in line stepped forward and showed his palms. They were clean too. No one on the basketball team had any red paint anywhere visible. Neither did any of the stage band or the debate team.

Jil started at the back of the line and quickly eliminated the entire girls' hockey team.

"Good luck tomorrow," she said to Rosie.

She smiled. "They're really good," she confided.

Jil grinned. "They'd better be. We need some positive news around here!"

The hockey team filed out, and Jil recommenced her search.

"Open your backpack, please," she said to the next student.

"Hi, Miss."

"Oh. Hi, Teegan." Jil's eyes zeroed in on the bullring dangling from her nose. "What are you doing here so early?"

"Breakfast program. The residence breakfast bites."

"I guess."

"I'm not opening my bag for some fucking inspection."

"Language?"

"Sorry, Miss, but sometimes I get really sick of having no fucking privacy anywhere around here."

"I understand that, but this is an equal-opportunity request. And I think it's in your best interest to do this with me rather than force me to confiscate that bag and take it to the officer who's waiting in the front office."

Teegan's nostrils flared, and she stood there for a full minute, staring Jil down. "I might hate Pathways, but I hated foster care a hell of a lot more. I don't want to be kicked out."

Jil held her gaze, not flinching.

Finally, Teegan exhaled angrily and yanked her backpack open, almost breaking the zipper. Out spilled a maroon sweatshirt, musty with cigarette smoke, a half-eaten sandwich in a Ziploc bag, two binders, a pencil case, a pair of black mitts, a baggie full of cigarettes, four different lighters, rolling paper, and half a gram of marijuana.

Jil picked up the pot and the rolling paper and wordlessly laid them on the table behind her. She looked back at Teegan, who stood staring at the floor, her cheeks red.

"Anything else?"

She shook her head.

"Go on then. I'll probably see so many backpacks today that I'll forget whose this came from."

Teegan looked up, a faint glimmer of hope pricking her eyes.

"No more drugs," Jil growled. "They're bad for your brain."

"Yeah, but they're good for my mood," Teegan whispered back. She grabbed her backpack and stormed out.

Jess looked up, saw who the student was, and rolled her eyes, but she was already on to the next student.

Clean hands, clear bag.

"Next."

Nothing.

Jil and Jess both arrived in the middle of the group of students at the same time. Gideon looked up at her and grinned. "Hi, Miss."

"Hi." She looked at his hands, his arms, and the hands and arms of the gaggle of grade seven students surrounding him. They were all covered in paint from fingers to elbows. The drama teacher, Mr. Phelps, was fruitlessly directing them to keep their hands straight out and not to get any smudges on the cafeteria tables.

"What are you painting?" Jess asked.

"The barn and forest for *Once Upon a Time*," Mr. Phelps replied. "Why?"

"Because all of your students are covered in red paint," Jess said grimly.

"It comes off. I wouldn't let them use something that would damage their clothes."

Jess sighed. "Go have them wash up and come back."

Before Jil could even ask Jess what she planned to do next, a loud, grating buzz sounded. The fire alarm. Insistent humming hammered through the walls of the cafeteria, which, incidentally, had the best acoustics in the entire school.

Jess swore under her breath and jumped up. "Outside, everyone," she ordered, opening the doors wide and ushering the students through. "Straight out into the quad. Go, go, go."

Jil pried open the other set of doors and beckoned the students through. They sighed and got to their feet, shuffling out slowly. Jil grabbed her coat and hat and followed them out. "Good thing I held on to these," she said cheerfully.

Jess just shot her a dark look and stepped outside without benefit of either boots or coat. "This has to stop," she said seriously.

"Agreed."

But they had nothing left to say when, upon returning inside, they found another message scrawled on the office door.

WHOSOEVER HATETH HIS BROTHER IS A MURDERER

Chapter Nine

The tone of the messages had everyone on edge, especially Jess. In the wake of Columbine, Virginia Tech, and every other incident of school violence that had occurred in the last ten years, Jessica Blake wasn't taking any chances. She called a meeting of the parent council, the administration, and Superintendent Giovanni DiTullio.

The last thing anyone wanted was the blame after the incident: If only we'd done more beforehand…Cameras and a lockdown system seemed like a small price to pay for the absolution they'd need after the fact. They gave her the money she requested, almost without comment.

The next week, a lockdown alarm system was on order, cameras had been increased three fold, and students were required to keep all personal effects in lockers.

"Put your bags in your lockers. Don't bring them to class," was the phrase overheard hundreds of times a day. Students grumbled and groaned, not used to stashing their belongings and trying to balance two classes' worth of books, binders, pens, and other items with them every day. "Miss, my locker's all the way in G400," her students complained daily. "I don't have time to get there."

"Get to school earlier," Jil said flatly. She had no sympathy for this particular issue. She didn't think kids should have been able to bring their bags into class in the first place. Too many risks. Bombs. Guns. Knives. Explosive powders. Drugs. Forget it.

"Go get rid of your bags and bring me a late slip," she said. After four days of that routine, no one brought their book bags to her class anymore. She didn't want to waste any more time with this crap. It was halfway through October, and rather than getting any closer to finishing her investigation, she'd developed nothing but complications. The only person she spent any time with was Buck Weekly, and if he were any purer, he could have scribed for Jesus himself. That didn't mean he still didn't give her the creeps, though.

"When are the metal detectors coming?" Jil joked as she met Jess in the hallway.

Jess barely slowed her walk. "By the end of November, if we're lucky. You'd think we were in Harlem, for God's sake, not Rockford."

"Better safe," Jil said, walking with her en route to the library. She was a little surprised at how seriously these taggings were being taken.

"It's not just that," Jess replied to her unspoken thought. "It's that whole incident with Alyssa. Scared people—parents especially. I don't know how many phone calls we've had this year from parents wondering what we're doing to 'protect our students.' They feel better with things. Cameras. Increased security. I've even had to hire another guidance counselor, which makes four for a school of thirteen hundred. That's a lot. We're doing anti-suicide workshops next semester. I mean, students used to come to school for education. Now they're coming for everything but, it seems. Teachers don't even spend their time teaching half the day!"

"I know what you mean."

Jess looked at her—the look that made Jil feel like she could see right through her. "Why do I get the feeling I don't know half of what's going on in my own school?" she asked, stopping at the doors to the library. Her eyes probed Jil, and Jil could feel every inch of skin on her arm—the arm that was almost, but not quite, touching…

"Because you probably don't," she replied, trying to keep her voice steady. Which wasn't easy when Jess was this close. Too close. "How can you? Every year, you get hundreds of strangers walking through the doors and into your classrooms. It's not like they get an interview."

"I don't even know half the staff here," Jess replied impatiently. "They're transferred based on seniority from other schools, or recommended to me from other principals. I must admit, this is the first year I've been handed a staff member from the superintendent."

Jil chuckled.

"What did you do before you were a teacher?" Jess asked, as if it had just occurred to her that Jil had had a life before St. Marguerite's.

"That's the kind of thing you'll want to ask your staff in an interview next time." Jil winked. It relieved the tension. Popped the bubble.

Jess smiled wanly. "Thanks for the tip. Believe me, if I got to handpick all my staff myself, I would. Sometimes you just take what comes. No regrets though." She touched Jil's wrist lightly and turned away.

Jil watched her walk away, her attention drawn to the way one of her hips rose higher than the other. She just had time to wonder if Jess was actually limping when a group of students traveled past, obscuring her line of sight.

Back to the staff room to collect more gossip. This investigation seemed even more ridiculous than before. Except for the fact that Padraig had called last night and reported that Giovanni DiTullio's most recent check had paid for the back-rent that was due on their building. For the past four months.

She took out her notebook and scribbled in her own cryptic shorthand.

K.N. has purchased a new home in South River. Whose salary is paying for that? Divorced last spring. No new wedding ring.

R. J. Has a membership to Adult Only Video Store XXX. Frequent flyer.

O. P.—Gay.

G.B.—Also gay.

T.T. is 29 years old and has a 13-year-old girl. Married at 16?

As she looked at her master chart, Jil realized that inside two months, she'd gleaned information on nearly half the staff members, and she'd only actually followed three of them home. She might get out of St. Marguerite's faster than December if she kept this up.

That afternoon, she drove to O'Hanagan's, traded in her loaner X-Trail for a black Jimmy, and programmed the next address into her GPS. William Follett. Math teacher. No one at school seemed to know him too well, and in the three weeks she'd been trying to dig up dirt on him, nothing had come up. No online social media accounts and no close friends at school. He was married with two kids and had a dog. That was all anyone really knew. But before she gave him a tick for Catholic conduct, she needed to do a home visit.

At dusk, she pulled into the quiet residential neighborhood where Mr. Follett lived and parked on the side of the road near his house. She turned off her lights, got out her monocular, and settled in with a thermos of coffee and some peanut butter crackers. Luckily for her, no one had thought to close the curtains yet. She lowered herself in her seat, even though the front windows of the truck were tinted.

There was no car in the Folletts's driveway. But the lights were on, and from the street, Jil had a clear view of the kitchen. She thought she saw William moving around in there, so she peered through her monocular.

"You guys might think about closing the curtains if you're going to go around half-dressed," she muttered to herself. "A little quickie after the kiddies are in bed?"

Suddenly, William seemed to realize he was in sight of the neighborhood, because he yanked the curtains shut.

"Shit," Jil muttered.

She was just packing up to go when a woman exited William's house. It wasn't what she was wearing that caught Jil's attention as much as what she wasn't wearing. No nylons, socks, or tights—though the weather was getting cooler now. She wore three-inch platform heels, a ripped mini-skirt that had a slit right up to the hip, and a belly-top that displayed a gaudy gold navel ring. Her hair was bleached and looked like it had been cut with a hacksaw, and her cleavage practically spilled out of her top.

"I don't think that's Mrs. Follett." Jil lowered herself even further as the woman passed right by her parked Jimmy and got into the beat-up blue Honda behind her.

Fifteen minutes later, a van pulled into the driveway. Two kids leaped out, running up the footpath in matching martial arts uniforms. The driver put the van in the garage.

"*That* is Mrs. Follett."

Jil took out her notebook and found today's date. W.F., she shorthanded, Adultery.

With that, she closed her notebook and drove away.

By Friday morning, the students were beginning to show some interest in Buddhism.

"Miss, do you think that people can be Enlightened for real?" asked Joey, her shining face half-hidden by her bleached-blond hair.

Impatiently, she pushed it behind her ears, searching once again for the hair band she had lost. Jil was growing used to answering questions for students who were clearly distracted by other things: love, crushes, lost lunch money, forgotten locker codes…life.

"Buddha seemed to have achieved it," she replied, flipping on an overhead. On it, there was a Buddha seated beneath a tree.

"Yeah, but Buddha was Buddhist," Joey insisted. We're Catholic. Can Catholics be Enlightened?"

"No, yo!" Kyle interrupted. "You've gotta like—convert—to Budda-ism. Then you can be Enlightened."

Wiley stretched languidly in his front row seat, his purple hoodie riding up just enough to show the rest of his boxer shorts that weren't visible from the back. "Catholics can be Enlightened," he said as he yawned. "Enlightenment means finding God. Catholics already found God. He came to Earth, remember? Jesus?"

"It's not the same," Theo insisted. "That was the real God. Buddhists are Pagan. Enlightenment is not the same as finding Jesus. It's false worship. Jesus and God are the only way to heaven. Do you think Buddhists are going to heaven? No way."

"Maybe heaven is a myth," Jil said, and the class all looked at her. She still wasn't getting used to that—how much weight her words held as a teacher. "Different from sect to sect. Catholics visualize it as an eternal glorious afterlife. Buddhists view it as Enlightenment, and knowledge for the next incarnation. Pagans think of it as the Summerland—a place to rest. Heaven existed long before Christianity did. Even the Vikings believed in Valhalla."

"So, what, Miss, it doesn't matter what religion you are, you still get to go to heaven? You can be a total heathen, and it doesn't matter?"

"That depends on your definition of heaven, Theo," Jil answered calmly. "Is your heaven exclusive? Who wouldn't be let in?"

"All the sinners," Theo answered promptly. "Sinners aren't going to heaven. They go to hell."

"Who do you think of as sinners?" Jil asked. She knew she was approaching dangerous territory, but she didn't stop.

"Well, you know…people who live their lives wrong. People who don't abide by the Ten Commandments."

"Like murderers?" Joey piped up.

"Yeah, and hookers—unless they repent and are forgiven. Anyone who doesn't believe in God. Anyone who isn't Christian. Terrorists. Rapists. Thieves. And gays, too."

"Being gay is against a Commandment?" Jil asked, feigning surprise. "I don't recall any Commandment that says 'Thou shalt be straight.'"

Theo's face tightened. "Everyone knows gays go to hell, Miss," he said. "It's in the Bible."

Jil knew she should end this discussion. It wasn't going to get her anywhere. The students around her fell silent, watching the exchange, wondering who would get the upper hand. Usually teachers argued for Scripture and students against. This wasn't the way things were supposed to go.

"Where?" Jil said instead. She couldn't help it.

Theo's jaw tightened further. "Homosexuality is an abomination," he said, pronouncing each syllable carefully. "It goes against the laws of nature."

"So does wearing polyester, according to the passage you're quoting," Jil returned easily.

A long minute passed. Jil held Theo's intent gaze. He didn't back down well, but eventually, her status and seniority seemed to wear him out, and he glanced away, clenching and unclenching his fist.

"Jesus lunched with lepers and tax collectors, did he not?" Jil asked in a low voice. "Who thinks he also had lunch with homosexuals?"

Every hand in the room went up, except for Theo. Bex purposely did not look back, but bit her lip and kept her hand up.

"Yes, Bex?" Jil asked.

"Jesus associated with everyone," she said clearly. "He associated with all sinners. But it doesn't say anything about him having lunch with homosexuals…" she paused and took a deep breath, staring straight ahead at Jil as she spoke, "because gays weren't sinners. A long time ago, like in Roman times, gay people were just part of the community. The intolerance came later. When the communities were suffering and they needed everyone to reproduce. Then they decided that being gay was a sin—because back then there wasn't fertility treatment, and two men or two women couldn't have babies."

"Interesting," Jil murmured. "Bex wants to challenge Scripture because she believes it was written with an ulterior motive. Is that possible?"

"Of course," said Brianna, a usually quiet girl who must have had an IQ of 180, but rarely chose to open her mouth. "There's absolutely nothing written purely from God's mouth."

"Cynics, are we?" Jil teased her. "Nothing at all?"

"The Bible is the word of God!" Theo thundered, surprising everyone. He jumped to his feet, knocking over his empty chair. Joey ducked, and Bex's face went white as he tramped down the aisle. "You're all blasphemers!"

The door slammed.

Jil raised her eyebrows. "Guess he doesn't like a little friendly debate," she said, trying to lighten the mood.

"He takes religion pretty seriously, Miss," Joey whispered. "I think he wants to be like, a priest or something."

"I've never met a priest who was that staunch in his beliefs," Jil said flatly. "Usually people who are deeply spiritual are also deeply contemplative." She received blank looks. "Willing to consider multiple points of view and examine an issue from all sides to see if there might be some truth to it."

Bex raised her hand at the back. "Are gays going to hell?" she asked bluntly.

"I doubt it," Jil responded dryly. "If they are, then so is everyone else."

Soon after, the bell went, and a sober lot of students gathered up their textbooks and headed to lunch.

"Bex?" Jil said as the girl passed her desk. Bex slowed down. "Are you really worried about going to hell?"

Bex looked startled, then nervously fingered her necklace. "Guess not," she said, staring at the floor.

"Bex, do you want to—"

"What? Talk about the joy of being a lesbian in a Catholic school? Yeah, Miss, it's a blast. Totally accepting community we've got here."

Jil grimaced. "That's kind of what I was asking."

Bex smiled wryly, looking a little apologetic. "Sorry," she said. "I just feel like everyone's looking at me all the time. It'll be even worse after today's class. I shouldn't have opened my mouth. I'll really get shit now."

"From who?"

"I dunno."

"Theo?"

Bex's look confirmed Jil's suspicions.

"You guys aren't friends, are you?" she said, a little incredulously.

Bex shook her head. "Not at all."

"Then why do you care what he thinks?"

Bex exhaled slowly and scuffed her toe along the floor. "It's complicated."

"What? Are you afraid he's going to out you? Is he bullying you?"

"Nothing I can't handle."

"If he's bothering you, you should talk to Ms. Blake."

"You don't understand."

"No?"

Jil heard footsteps coming down the hall. With an instinct she couldn't quite identify, she knew to stop talking.

"I'd like you to keep that in mind," she said, raising her eyebrows to signal Bex. "The more classes you miss, the more detentions you're going to have."

Bex snuck a look at the door and saw what Jil had already guessed: Theo lurked outside.

"Yeah, okay, Miss," she said, looking at the floor again. "I'll try not to miss anymore class. When do I have to come for detention?"

"Tomorrow. During lunch."

Bex smiled a little, her back to the door. "I'll be here."

The next morning, Jil had barely come in the door at school when her name was paged over the PA system. "Ms. Kinness, please come to the office. Ms. Kinness."

Jil sighed and turned toward the front office, knowing as she did that she was headed straight for Jess's closed door.

Jess waved her in, as she hung up the phone. "Have a seat," she said, standing up from her desk and joining Jil at the small round table. "Sorry to pull you in so early."

"Sorry I have to be pulled in at all."

Jess gave her a sympathetic smile, belying the gravity on her face.

"You have some idea why you're here?"

"I can guess."

"Theodore Ranieri has decided to file a formal complaint against you."

"That sounds more serious than is warranted," Jil replied mildly. "He's in a World Religions class. We were discussing religions of the world, and the possibility of an ulterior motive existing behind Scripture."

"Did you tell him that homosexuals aren't sinners?"

Jil pursed her lips. "I don't think those were my exact words, no."

Jess sighed deeply and leaned back in her chair.

"I can't in good conscience tell a student that gays and lesbians are going to hell," Jil said. Her temper flared, but Jess didn't take the bait. Nor did she agree with Theo. "Nowhere in the Bible does it say that," Jil pressed. "And even if it did, I wouldn't teach that."

"Okay."

"Are you going to tell me I have to?"

Jess sighed again. "This is a little complicated," she said. "Seeing as it's a senior class, and seeing that it's a World Religions course, I think there's a lot of room to debate. But, Julia, I think you need to remember that this is a Catholic school, and there are some fundamentalists in the room that you're going to have to deal with. Ideally, we're all supposed to be good Catholics. Which means that in the course of your class, you can't be perceived as advocating for homosexuality."

Jil snorted. "I'm hardly running a recruitment center. I'm simply arguing that the students should think critically about what they're reading and what they believe. Don't you think?" There was so much more she wanted to ask her. So much more she wanted to hear. But Jess only nodded and sighed.

"Wouldn't it be nice if we could have more of that?" she said. "Listen, I'm not going to tell you what to teach. I'm also not going to tell you what you can and cannot say in front of your students. However…"

Jil watched Jess's face flicker from slight amusement to fatigue. "Julia, Theo Ranieri is suggesting that you're a lesbian." She paused for a moment to give Jil an opportunity to jump in.

She said nothing. She was too angry. Too outraged that in this day and age, she would even be having this conversation. The investigation taking a backseat to her emotions, she let her eyes settle on Jess, daring her to say something.

"Oh, boy," she muttered.

Jil said nothing. Jess was the principal. She'd obviously asked for this job. Let her handle it.

"Don't ask, don't tell, right?"

"I'm not asking," Jess snapped. "It's none of my business. I'm not interested."

Jil swallowed hard. Her words stung.

"With regards to Theo," Jess said tightly. "I told him, of course, that his suggestion was serious and inappropriate, and that I didn't think it was a worthwhile use of his time to speculate about his teachers' personal lives."

Jil remained silent.

Jess exhaled, seeming to collect herself a little. "However, in this board, teachers sign a contract which holds them responsible for living a Catholic lifestyle." Her voice was tense, and she couldn't quite meet Jil's eyes. Was it because she knew this conversation was ridiculous—backward, and wrong? Or because she felt like a hypocrite?

Jil snorted. "C'mon, Jess."

"I didn't invent the rules."

"But you live by them, right?"

For the first time, Jess's face registered real fear. A tense silence hung between them. Jil's insides writhed, her indignation about this assignment and all the implications boiling over until she was sure she'd say something she'd regret. She tried to rein herself in. Jess wasn't responsible for the hypocrisy of an entire school board.

"I have the Parents' Association breathing down my neck," Jess finally said, changing the subject. "DiTullio's in here every second Friday wondering what I'm doing about promoting Catholic education. I'm sure you see why this…issue…would be a problem for me."

Jil dropped her gaze to her lap and took a deep breath. "I signed no such contract," she said flatly. "Nor would I."

Jess recovered quickly. "No, because you're a contracted employee. You technically don't have to even be Catholic to work here for a semester. However, I would ask you to consider the climate of the school you're working in. This is a very conservative community. Your relationship status is nobody else's business, and it's doubtful anyone would ask you about it. But it would probably be in your best interests to act as if you abided by the Catholic code of conduct."

Jil had to look away. It was just too ironic. "I understand," she said.

"There are ways to redirect people's questions," Jess continued gently. "I think you're a skilled teacher. Your students seem to have respect for you; attendance in your class is good, considering incidences earlier in the year; Buck has no problems with you that he's identified to me. What you teach is largely your own business, but unfortunately, the repercussions land on my desk, and I prefer that they don't. If it's possible to steer clear of these issues, maybe you could consider it."

Jil let that sink in. She didn't understand why this riled her so much. Jess was entitled to her own opinion—her own methods. She was the one who had to do this job and live this life, day by day. What did she want her to do? Go blaring up to World Religions to tell that idiot Theo to stop being so goddamned homophobic? To publicly condemn Christianity and all the various ways people twisted it for their own purposes? She couldn't do that. She couldn't do that and keep her job; that was for damn sure.

Even if Jess did seem to agree with her on a fundamental level, why would she risk her job over an incident like this? She'd worked hard to get here.

Just shut up and do your assignment, then get the hell out of here, she told herself.

Still, she realized it had gotten personal now. Theo irked her. The entire Catholic code of conduct irked her. Who the hell were they to tell her that homosexuality was punishable by an eternity at a burning stake?

"What would you like me to do?"

Jess shook her head. "I'd like you to use your best judgment," she said, emphasizing "best." "I think you'll make the right choices."

The phone rang, interrupting. Thank God.

"We can talk again next week," Jess said as she went to answer it.

Jil quietly closed the door and kept her chin held high as she walked through the main office to the atrium. Everyone pretended not to stare.

During second period, Buck Weekly unexpectedly showed up in her class. "Just here to observe," he said as he took a seat in the back. Theo had returned again and made no eye contact as he slipped into his chair.

Jil had no intention of playing "excuse me for interrupting" with Buck, or of capitulating to Theo. This class was taking up way too much of her time. Having no patience for any of Buck's lectures today, she turned out the lights and turned on a video. A video that Buck, in fact, had given her. Seeing that nothing exciting was going to happen, he rose quietly and left the room, glaring at her as he passed.

She let another five minutes pass and switched the film off. The class groaned.

"I'm sorry," Jil said. "Were you all enjoying the wisdom of the Dalai Lama?"

"Yes!" Joey answered, wiping crumbs from the corner of her mouth as she yawned.

"Yeah, whatever," Kyle said. "You were just enjoying your nap."

"I thought his point of view on violence was interesting," Brianna said. Two participation points in two days. It was a new record.

"Actually, I wanted to talk to you about your upcoming test."

"Test! What test? You never told us about a test!" A chorus of protests erupted.

"If you'll refer to your syllabus," Jil said calmly, leafing through her binder to find her own copy. "You'll notice the test is scheduled for one week from today. That gives you plenty of time to study. Now, what I'd like to do for the rest of the period is to discuss the topics that will be covered."

For the next half hour, that's what they did—Jil keeping a close eye on the door in case Buck made another surprise visit.

When the bell rang, Bex stayed in her seat. Theo also lingered as the rest of the students left. "Bex, don't forget your detention with me," Jil said, keeping her face grave.

Bex nodded soberly. "'Kay, Miss," she said. "Do I really have to do three days in a row?"

"Well, if you missed three days in a row, don't you think it's fair?" Jil countered, seriously.

Bex shrugged. "Guess I don't have a say anyway. Is it here?"

"No, I think we'd better go down to my office. I've got my extra work assignment for you there."

Bex said nothing, but the way she followed closely behind Jil told her that Bex's fear was physical as well as emotional. Jil knew she would talk when she was ready, and in the meantime, if she preferred detention to whatever she faced in between classes, so be it. She didn't mind staying an extra forty-five minutes every day to help out a kid. Gave her extra time to investigate, anyway.

When she'd closed the door, Bex relaxed into a chair, exhaling audibly. "So what's the extra work?" she asked, smiling shyly.

Jil smiled back. It was nice to see a lighter look on Bex's face. She always looked so serious. Way too grave for such a young kid.

"Well, I guess you might as well use the time to catch up on what you've missed," she said. "A few chapters, some homework assignments. I've made you a folder."

Bex opened the blue folder on the table. "This isn't so bad," she said. "Maybe I'll even finish early."

"Oh yeah? You're that good, eh?"

"Sure, when I put my mind to it. When I'm not distracted."

"By what?"

"I like Wii," Bex said, running a hand through her cropped dark hair. "I play it almost every night. I love the ski jumps."

"Are you kidding?"

"No. I'm dead serious. We have it on in the residence common room. Gideon and I play almost every night."

"Gideon? Little Gideon?"

"My little brother Gideon?"

"Little brother? Gideon's your little brother?"

"Yeah, Miss. He's the whole reason I'm in this hole to begin with. No offense."

"Don't worry about it. What do you mean, though?"

"We're in the Pathways program because our case manager couldn't find a decent foster home for us both to be in. She said she might be able to get us into the program here, even though Gideon is technically a bit young, and I'm technically a bit gay."

Jil smiled. "Well, I guess it worked."

"Yeah. And practically the only time I get to see him is when we're both sitting in front of the TV screen. Mr. Weekly has him marching around on Outdoor Education trips every weekend, and in some study program during the week."

"And that's the reason you don't do your homework?"

"Umm…well, yeah. Not a lot of spare time, you know? Well, maybe you don't know."

"I do."

Bex looked up at her, surprised. "You do?"

Jil nodded. "I was almost in this program myself, but I got placed in my fourth foster home instead. At eighteen, I left there and moved straight into a dorm room. Not a lot of privacy there either."

"Wow," said Bex. "We only had two homes before this one. Our parents are addicts."

Jil bit her lip. "That's tough." She looked up at the clock, and when she looked back, Bex had her head bent over her textbook. Jil smiled and opened her own book—a fundamentalist Catholic view on life. She lost no time in skimming through it, trying to figure out if she'd missed a rule. So far, she figured she had the basics: no adultery, no sex, no homosexuality, no sex, no theft, coveting or murder, and no sex. Lots of rules…and lots of guilty staff members. She wouldn't have any difficulty writing this report at all. If she left her conscience out of it.

Talking to Bex reminded her how long it had been since she'd talked to Elise. If Padraig knew, he'd say she was deliberately avoiding bad news.

She took out her notebook and made a few jots. For the moment, she left out her conversation with Jessica Blake. That, she wasn't quite ready to put in.

Chapter Ten

Her stupid trouser socks had left a dent around her left calf, as usual, and the mud on the bottom of her pants meant they'd have to be washed—and ironed—again. Five for five this week, she thought.

Standing topless behind the curtain, her backlit profile probably visible for everybody in the street below to see, she hurriedly rooted through her drawers for the cami and long-sleeved T-shirt she wanted.

Ducking low, she hurried out of the closet and through the bedroom to the side hall where she'd left a basket of clean laundry for the past three days. At the bottom was her pajama top. And another open window. And two neighborhood geriatrics out walking their dog.

Jil ducked back into her bedroom, on her knees behind the bed, and quickly put on the shirts. Then she ran around, shutting every set of drapes in the loft before heading into the kitchen for some peanut butter crackers.

She arranged the saltines in a circle on the plate, took out some strawberry jam from the cupboard, and searched for the peanut butter. Of course it wasn't where it was supposed to be. She'd been so distracted lately she'd probably put it in the freezer—or the car.

When she opened the fridge for some jam, she saw it, staring at her from beside the milk.

Grumpily, Jil took down the soft plastic jar and carried it over to the counter. She turned the lid, expecting it to come off smoothly in her hand. Nothing happened. She turned it again, harder. It was stuck.

Very stuck. Stuck as tight as Theo Raneri's Christian Fundamentalist convictions.

How the hell could the peanut butter lid be impossible to open? It was plastic, for God's sake. On a plastic jar. This never happened. Tomato sauce? Occasionally. Pickles? Often. But peanut butter? With determination, she turned the lid again, grunting with the effort. The ridge left a long red dent in her left hand.

She took the jar and ran it under hot water—because that's the only thing she could think of to do. And it didn't work. She banged it with a spoon. Which made her feel marginally better, but did nothing for the jar.

Her frustration was mounting. How the fuck can you not open a goddamned jar? Surely it can't be that difficult! Is it the underlying gene of sinners? Everything you touch goes to hell? She had visions of herself on *Just for Laughs*, a camera hidden in her pantry while she struggled with this trick jar, and that made her angrier.

With a grunt, she banged the lid of the jar against the counter. Over and over. It dented the faux wood, but did not release. She threw the jar hard against the tile. The lid shattered. Peanut butter sprayed upward onto the table and chairs, streaking across the floor.

Gingerly, Jil picked up the unharmed plastic jar and fished out bits of green lid. Then she mopped up the peanut butter on the table legs and the little puddles on the floor.

Then, when the mess was cleaned up, she very calmly put her knife into the jar, scooped out some peanut butter, and methodically covered each cracker with the thick brown spread.

There. She'd managed. She wasn't a complete loser. Even if she never would understand why that lid hadn't come off. Once her tantrum had faded, she felt sheepish. She smiled ruefully to herself as she licked her fingers.

"Very good for you," she chastised herself, speaking specifically to her hips. "No wonder you don't have a girlfriend..."

Upstairs, she pored back through her notes, making adjustments to the master chart. This was her new Friday night ritual—transferring all the scribbled cryptic data from her journal to the master chart. J.B. still stood blank—as blank as Buck Weekly—though Jil was sure she wasn't half as virtuous.

"Divorced" at least should have been checked off. "Taking the Lord's name in vain" too. But Jil couldn't bring herself to foul Jess's character. She couldn't believe Jess had done anything to warrant losing her job. Her livelihood. The respect of the community.

So she put the chart away and took her laptop downstairs to the couch. She opened the obituaries, scanning back to 1999.

Just as she had found the right date, her phone rang. ELISE, her phone announced. She sighed. Padraig would have been right—she had been avoiding her. Avoiding what she knew was coming.

She swiped to answer. "I'm so sorry."

A low chuckle answered her apology. "I don't want to hear about it. You have better things to do than check up on an old woman."

"You're hardly old, Elise." She turned to the window and watched the snow cascade in a light procession to the sill. A clear white moon hovered in view—a perfect night.

"Well, I'm about as old as I'm going to get."

The sinking feeling in her chest thudded to the bottom of her stomach. She'd known all along it wouldn't be good news. Elise had been to more specialists in the past six months than Jil knew existed in the city.

"How much time do we have?" She concentrated on making her words come out normally.

"Not a lot," Elise answered. "But enough. A few more months of Sunday dinners, at least. And time to find you someone special so you stop staying home on Friday nights!"

"I'm working," Jil protested.

"That's the problem. Try a little romance in your life before you get handed your walking papers for the next realm."

Jil smiled despite herself. Elise always had a way of turning the tables so Jil became the topic of discussion. "I'll come to see you tomorrow."

"Nevermind. You're in the middle of something important, I can tell. We'll see each other soon."

"Sometime this week, then."

"I'll be glad to see you. Good night, darling."

"Goodnight. Sleep well." Jil hung up.

She stood and paced between the window and the desk, her heart thudding quickly and painfully.

Elise had been her parent for the past fifteen years. Before her, there had been a string of foster homes, and staff and case workers—but Elise had replaced them all and never let Jil go back.

What would she do when she was gone?

Where would she go home to, when Elise's home was no longer hers?

❖

"Rough weekend?" Jess asked as Jil walked into the staffroom kitchen on Monday morning. She was just pouring a steaming cup of coffee, which she relinquished to Jil.

Jil accepted the coffee with a murmur of thanks, and turned to leave.

"Hey." Jess laid a hand on her arm. Electric heat.

The touch made her nose prick with tears, and she turned away to get milk from the fridge—something she didn't usually bother with.

"Are you okay?" Jess frowned.

Jil shook her head, trying to stuff the horrible choking feeling back down her throat. "Can't talk about it."

"Not here or not at all?"

"It's personal, Jess. We agreed not to get personal, didn't we?"

"Okay," Jess moved toward the door, a frown of concern lining her forehead. "Come see me if you change your mind."

Jil walked away, back to her office, and shut the door before anyone in the hall could see her crying. She took out her notebook and stuffed it into her top drawer, as usual. She locked up her purse in the filing cabinet, stuck her snack in the mini-fridge, and flipped on her computer.

She was going to get to the bottom of that kid's suicide if it was the last thing she accomplished before she had a meltdown. She clicked on the Obituaries section of the archives she had subscribed to and entered Regina Francis into the search term.

FRANCIS, REGINA JANE, 1981–1999

Suddenly, in her eighteenth year. Regina is survived by her parents, Russell and Mary Francis; sister Margaret; and brother James. Regina was a promising student at St. Marguerite's Catholic School in Rockford. She will be missed by her many friends, teachers, and coaches of both the girls' basketball and girls' ringette teams. Her favorite phrase was "When God closes a door, somewhere He opens a window." A funeral service will be held on Friday at St. Marguerite's Catholic Church, 1:00 pm. Donations to the Rockford Athletic Club for Underprivileged Children are requested in lieu of flowers.

Jil saved the obituary in her favorites and closed the browser. Something struck her as odd about that message. Sports teams? Many friends? That didn't sound like a girl who wanted to take her own life. On a hunch, Jil locked her office door and headed to the library upstairs.

"Hello, Ms. Kinness." The librarian greeted her with a smile. "I have been looking forward to meeting you."

Jil shook the warm hand offered. "A pleasure," she said. "You must be Ms. Olson. I'm lucky to run into you. You're only here part-time, right?"

"Yes, same as you. How are you settling in?"

"Well, thank you. I'm enjoying the school. I was hoping to get to know a bit more of its history."

"Oh, a history buff," Ms. Olson enthused. "Considering another teachable?"

Jil merely smiled. "No. Religion is quite enough for me. I'm wondering if I could have a look at some of the old school yearbooks?"

"Certainly," Ms. Olson said. "They're right over there."

Jil walked over to the shelf Ms. Olson had indicated and searched out the yearbook from 1999. She flipped through the worn black-and-white pages until she came to the senior class. There she was—Reggie Francis, captain of the girls' basketball team, VIP of the girls' ringette team. Drama club. Student council. Her arm thrown around another girl, both of them laughing.

Jil looked closely at the staged graduation photos—always taken months before the actual graduation day. Regina's hat was perched awkwardly over her short hair; the roses looked like inconvenient accoutrements in her athletic arms. Jil flipped back again to the photo of Regina and the other girl. Arms slung casually—maybe too casually.

She wondered…

The bell rang, and Jil hurriedly shoved the yearbook back on the shelf and rushed out of the library. She had five minutes to run to her office, collect her pile of tests, and get to class. At least if the students were occupied with writing, they wouldn't expect her to speak. Tomorrow they could watch the second in the series of Dalai Lama films, and that would buy her another day. By Wednesday, she'd probably be all right.

Just as she reached her office door, her phone buzzed.

"Hey, Padraig," she answered, letting herself in.

"What's up, Kidd?"

"Not much."

"Oh no? Heard you had some bad news this weekend."

Jil didn't even bother asking him how he knew. He and Elise had been friends for years. Padraig had gotten Jil placed with Elise in the first place—another debt of gratitude she owed him.

"I don't know what I'm going to do without her, Padraig."

"It'll be a loss for all of us." His deep voice resonated with sadness. "Can your old man take you out for dinner?"

Jil smiled wanly, though he couldn't see it. "Thanks. Maybe another time. Later in the week, when I don't feel like I'm going to melt into the floor every time someone asks me a question."

"Okay, Kidd. I'll just keep calling you until you make good on that. In the meantime, you'll be sure to go home for Sunday dinner?"

"Wouldn't miss it."

A minute later, Buck Weekly knocked on her door. "Hello, Julia," he said, baring his teeth in greeting.

Jil returned the gesture with a normal smile. "Good morning, Buck." Usually, she would at least pretend to maintain civility, but today she really couldn't muster the "how was your weekend" and "oh, that sounds nice" that they usually traded on a Monday morning.

"I was wondering if you'd had the chance to do your preliminary report cards this weekend?"

Jil reminded herself to breathe deeply. "You know I don't take my work home with me, Buck."

"Yes, so you mentioned on your first day," Buck replied, annoyance bulging his steely eyes.

"Besides, my calendar says they're not due for another two weeks."

"Well, that's if you're handing them directly in to the administration. But I need time to review them."

"I think I can probably manage on my own."

"Still," Buck insisted. "You're new and I'm responsible for mentoring you. As part of the mentoring process, I would like to review your report cards. Please have them on my desk by tomorrow."

Jil sighed. She didn't feel like arguing with him today. She'd figure it out later. "Friday," she said and turned to grab her stack of tests. Buck nodded curtly to her profile, his eyes boring into her as she turned away. Since it was clear she wasn't paying attention, he had no choice but to back out and close the door.

Second period, he appeared again to "observe" her class.

Jil couldn't help a small smirk of satisfaction as he realized that once again there was nothing to observe. In five minutes, her students were bent over their desks, silently scribbling their tests. She nodded pleasantly to him as he exited.

Chapter Eleven

Jil really didn't feel like staying to chat in the staff room that day. It was enough that she'd even reported to work. Besides, this whole investigation was just ridiculous. Everything was a fucking breach of contract. Catholic conduct was absolutely impossible to enforce. Every staff member in the school had made her list for one reason or another. And who was to draw the line? Should you be fired for living in sin, but forgiven for wearing polyester? Was having a baby subject to investigation? Did you have to provide proof of your marriage certificate if you showed up to school pregnant, or was it all right to simply put on a gold band and refer to your boyfriend as your husband? Who was to say?

Too many conflicts to sort through. Easier to go out and distract herself. She agreed to meet Padraig for lunch. That would get him to stop worrying about her, and scratch another item off her to-do list.

"It's not your job to judge," Padraig reminded her as the waiter refilled her wine glass. "All you have to do is collect the facts and write a report. The rest isn't our concern."

"It's wrong," Jil complained bitterly. "It's wrong to investigate people's personal lives."

"Oh?" Padraig said, amused. "You've decided your entire profession is immoral?"

"Maybe I have," Jil countered, stabbing erratically at a piece of steak.

Padraig raised his eyebrows. "Don't throw away everything you've worked for because of a loss you didn't expect."

"How could I not have noticed?" Jil muttered. "She must have been sick for weeks—months even—if it's as bad as it is."

"Too close," Padraig said, his mouth full of roasted potatoes. "You can't be objective with friends and family. Has nothing to do with your professional skill."

"I still should have seen it."

"Maybe so, maybe not."

"What does that mean?"

"Maybe your subconscious was protecting you. Maybe you're distracted."

"By what?"

"By this investigation?"

"How much money are we pulling in, anyway?"

"Enough. We're clearing a good overhead on money from DiTullio. You'll get a nice paycheck out of this. And so will I."

"Enough to keep things floating?"

"Aye. If that first installment was any indication, we'll be good for the rest of the year."

"Did you clear up that payroll issue?"

Padraig just smiled. "Worked my charm, yes. With a little help from the superintendent himself. You'll start to get a check soon on top of everything else."

Jil grinned. "How did you manage that?"

Padraig just laughed. "I have my ways. Seems it's much more convincing if you're actually getting paid for your job."

"Good. Now you can keep the money from DiTullio and I'll take my check from the school board."

"It's meant to be a bonus, Kidd."

"Well, I don't need a bonus. I need a job. So, keep the money and put it back into the firm."

Padraig sighed heavily. "You're not supposed to be lookin' after me."

She felt tears swell in her eyes and ducked her head. "Consider it a little payback for what I've owed you since I was sixteen."

The snow had started to pile up outside the cardboard box she sat in, behind the train station. She saw his boots, and her heart stopped. She didn't know how to defend herself. She'd only been living on the street for a week.

When she looked up, Padraig's face, half-concealed by a woolen toque, stared down at her. "Jillienne Kidd, it's the first of November. What in blazes d'ya think you're doing outside without a proper coat?"

"How did you find me?"

He chuckled. "Just like yer mam. No child of Aimee's is going to be living in a cardboard box. Now let's go."

He cleared his throat. "I'll make it up to you when we get back on our feet."

"Do you have a case?" she changed the subject.

"Two. Chet's got one and Rick's been on assignment for the past three weeks. We're doin' all right, Kidd. We're going to pull out of this."

Good.

"What do you think the board is going to do with my report?"

Padraig shrugged. "Hard to say," he said. "Can't have employees bucking the system. Otherwise the system breaks down."

"But you know as well as I do that they'd never get away with firing an entire staff," Jil pressed. "Someone would sue, and the whole thing would be blown to bits."

"They signed a contract." Padraig shrugged. "It's not like they can argue duress."

"They could argue something, I'd bet. The contract goes against the Canadian Charter of Rights and Freedoms. Someone could challenge that."

"But nobody ever has."

"And that's why they're getting away with this."

Padraig sighed. "Jillienne."

Uh-oh. She knew she'd gone too far when he started calling her that. "I promise that when this investigation is over, and we've got our money in our hot little hands, I will give you two weeks off to go and lead a rally on Parliament Hill, protesting this entire issue and bringing it personally to the prime minister's attention. But until then…"

"Until then," Jil said, "I promise to shut up and do the job I'm being paid to do."

"You're doing a fine job," Padraig said quietly. "I know it's hard for you. I know you're working through it the best you can. Now all you have to do is figure out whether the principal is willfully turning a blind eye, or if she's just not very bright."

"Oh, she's not dim. She's bright enough to have kept her staff together this long."

"Well, be that as it may, she's still in violation of her own contract if she lets her staff get away with breaching theirs."

"Padraig…" Jil twisted her napkin in her lap, gazing thoughtfully at her plate.

"What is it, Kidd?"

"Something I can't quite put my finger on," she answered slowly. "I just…I get the feeling that there's way more to this than either of us knows."

"In what way?"

"In every way. Every time I peel back a layer of something simple, something else creeps up. First, all of those kids who died were gay."

"How do you know?"

"I've been sleuthing."

"Oh, really?"

"Yes. I found a yearbook from nineteen ninety-nine. It showed Reggie Francis was an outgoing, talented girl with lots of friends."

"She killed herself?"

"Apparently."

"You don't think so?"

"I think there's more to it."

"Hm. What else?"

"So many things. It's just the atmosphere."

"You can't persecute people for creating a toxic atmosphere." Padraig swallowed the last sip of his drink.

"No, but it sure gives me the creeps. There's something else I'm missing, I'm sure of it."

"What's your next move?"

"There's someone I have to talk to."

"Anyone I know?"

"No. She's one of my students. Another piece of this irritating puzzle. Every time I think she's ready to open up, she backs off. She's scared."

"Of what?"

"I don't know."

Padraig wiped his mouth and pushed his chair back from the table. "Well, Kidd, where there's a blocked storm drain…"

"There's a flood," Jil finished. And she smiled for the first time in a week.

❖

By Thursday, Jil had stopped hiding in her office during prep periods and had gathered a host of interesting information in the staff room, bringing her list to seventy-four out of ninety-five. Two of the teachers in the math wing were apparently carrying on an extramarital affair. He was married; she was divorced, and his wife taught at the elementary school down the block. Two checks for the chart!

She felt pretty close to smiling by the time she got back to her office at lunch and rooted around in her desk for her notebook.

It wasn't there.

She took the whole drawer out to see if it had become lodged in the back, as it had once before. No luck. Frowning, Jil thought back to her Monday morning. It had been such a blur, but she was pretty sure she'd put the notebook in there. She must have, because she'd made some half-hearted scribblings on Tuesday. But she hadn't touched it since then. Where the hell was it? And who would have had access to her office besides her?

Her thoughts went back to the day she had returned to her office to find her lights on. She'd been certain she'd turned them off. What if reviewing that mass program had been an excuse to know where she was while someone investigated her space? Someone with a habit of overstepping personal boundaries?

Buck had keys to every office, she was sure of it. He was such a goddamned control freak that if he didn't have them, he'd get them. Reminding herself not to let her personal feelings cloud her investigative progress, she made a quick mental list:

Bex had been in her office, but not alone. She would never have access to keys after hours anyway.

Jess would have a master key, but why would she snoop? She could just come to the door and ask for anything and Jil would give it to her. It wasn't in her nature to do something underhanded. She was far too direct.

The custodians—any of them—could have got into her office anytime they'd wanted. But why would they want to get in here? Who would know what they were looking for? She couldn't imagine Brian snooping through her things. Marcel maybe, but whatever for?

She found Jess in the hallway, monitoring students during break. Luckily, the bell went just as they saw each other. Jess beckoned Jil with a tilt of her head and Jil followed her around to the side door in an abandoned corridor. When she unlocked it and pushed through, Jil was surprised to find them standing in Jess's office.

"I didn't realize there was a door here," Jil said, making another mental note of things she hadn't investigated properly. But why would you, the rational part of her mind argued. When would you ever need an alternate entrance to the principal's office?

"Neither did I," Jess replied. "There was a bookshelf in front of it, and of course, no one ever uses this hallway. It's a dead end since the new wing was added off the atrium. But when the fire inspector was here last week, he noticed the blocked entrance and asked that it be opened. I guess two doorways are better than one. It's nice. Gives me a new view on the world. Hope you don't mind. I wanted to try out this key."

"Who made it for you?"

"Mary has all the keys in the front office. I guess when she looked, she found one labeled 'Principal' that was older than the others. Strange that I never knew it was here."

It was strange, entering Jessica's office from the other side. The enormous bookshelf had been moved down several feet to allow access to the door, and now that Jil looked at it, she realized it would have been impossible to see the door from inside.

"This is the old part of the building, then?" she asked.

"Yes. It was constructed in the nineteen thirties, just before the war. The R building was added in the seventies when the school de-privatized, and later, when we started getting more flow than we could handle, they added the G building. Before that, there was a hallway of classrooms outside this office. They took those out to put in the new building, but that hallway was just left as an emergency exit, I guess."

Jil nodded.

Jess sat at her desk, putting her whistle away in the top drawer. "So, are you feeling better?" She flipped open her laptop.

Jil sank slowly into a chair at the meeting table. "A little." She was too tired to try to keep professional distance. It was like fighting a polarized magnet, being drawn to metal.

"Feel like talking about it?"

"No."

Jess turned away a little. "Because I'm the principal or because I'm me?"

"Because we agreed. You won't ask, and I won't tell."

Jess sighed. "I thought about what you said. It's not fair and I agree. But since I already know, I guess it won't hurt for you to tell me. Might make you feel better."

Jil hid a smile.

"So is it girlfriend trouble?" said Jess, teasing a little.

"No. Family trouble."

"Oh. Something serious?"

Jil found it hard to meet her eyes. Bad enough that Jess had seen her looking such a mess in the staff room. She cleared her throat. "Terminal illness."

Jess reached over and squeezed Jil's hand. "I'm so sorry." Her eyes were mysteriously intense, like her emotions were so overwhelming, they had to come out through her irises.

Jil squeezed back, then retracted her hand, half-afraid Jess could use the connection to read her mind.

Jess sat back and cleared her throat. "I'm sorry," she whispered again, though for what, Jil wasn't entirely sure. For touching her? For crossing that invisible line she could never quite place? She wondered again how much of a compromise Jess had to make to do this job.

"It's my foster mother," she said, to fill the awkward silence.

Jess started in surprise. "I didn't know you were in foster care."

"It's not something you put on a job application, I guess." Jil attempted a smile, but felt hot tears pricking the back of her eyes. Anger. Sadness. Mostly sadness.

"Do you—" Jess stopped herself.

"What?"

"Well, I was going to ask 'Do you have anyone else?' but that seemed too personal."

Jil shrugged. "I don't care, Jess. I'm not cut out for a closeted life in any way, and keeping secrets from you only makes it worse."

If Jess read anything into her statement, she didn't back away. In fact, she seemed to lean in closer. "Tell me, then."

Jil tucked her legs up. "I don't have parents or siblings. I'm used to being alone. Elise came into the picture when I really thought I'd be bounced forever, and I really—I can't imagine life without her."

Jess reached out again, laying her hand on Jil's shoulder. "I'm so very sorry. Is there anything I can do?"

Jil registered the heat of Jess's hand, the closeness of her knee, almost pressing against her own. A faint scent of raspberries wafted from her hair. For a split second, Jil imagined cupping Jess's head in her hand, and pressing her lips—

"No," she said, moving back in her chair, subtly taking herself out of reach. "But thank you."

"Why don't you go home for the day?" Jess stood to let Jil out.

Jil moved toward the door. "I don't know what I'd do at home," she protested.

Jess shrugged. "Make some tea. Put on some nice music. Have a bubble bath."

Were her cheeks as pink as they felt? The last time she'd had a bubble bath, she'd closed her eyes and imagined Jess naked beside her…

She swallowed quickly to mask whatever her face might betray, and smiled as Jess opened the door. "Thank you. But it's probably better I keep busy. See you later."

Back in her office, Jil heated up leftover spaghetti and sat down with a pile of tests. She'd promised her students that by Friday they'd be graded, which meant she'd stay until they were finished. No time for sitting in the staff room today. The way her mind was reeling, she would have spilled everything, like marbles cascading from their loose-netted bag, rolling across the staff room floor. She was lucky she hadn't said anything confidential to Jess.

She had managed to grade two tests when a rap sounded at her door. "Come in." She realized, as her concentration was broken, that her spaghetti still sat in the microwave.

"Hi, Miss." Bex looked nervously around the door.

"C'mon in. Close the door behind you, if you don't mind. I'm grading tests."

"Oh."

Any other student would have asked if hers had been graded yet, but Bex didn't even seem to register what she'd said.

"What's up?" Jil indicated the seat opposite her. A day of confessions, she thought. Bex might as well come clean too.

"Not much." Her chin quivered.

"Yeah?"

"Well…"

"What's going on, Bex? Is something bothering you?"

She shook her head. "Sorry," she whispered. "I shouldn't have come."

"Tell me. You can. Is it about Theo?"

Bex shook her head.

"Alyssa?"

Bex's shoulders stiffened. Tears streamed down her pale cheeks. "I miss her so much," she choked. "I don't know what I'm going to do without her."

At that, Bex burst into tears—great, wrenching sobs that pulled Jil in like a tow rope. She put her arms around Bex and held her tightly as she cried and cried. Jil kept silent, waiting for Bex to speak.

"She was finally going to tell her parents," Bex sobbed. "But she couldn't do it. It was killing her—the lying. But she was afraid."

Jil exhaled. "You guys were together?" she asked gently.

"She didn't want anyone to know. But she couldn't keep it inside anymore."

"Is that why she killed herself?"

"I don't know," Bex whispered. "I think there was something else. Something she wouldn't even tell me."

"Like what?"

"I don't know. One day, she'd be fine. The next day, she'd be quiet and scared and not want to go out. I thought it had something to do with coming out, you know, like going back and forth between deciding whether she wanted to tell people or not."

"Did anyone know?"

"Not really. I mean, my good friends knew, and they were pretty accepting and everything. Every once in a while we'd get a snide comment from someone. We were pretty discreet about it. It's not like we flaunted it or anything. But still, it can be hard."

Jil had to clamp her mouth shut to prevent herself from telling this poor young girl how very well she understood.

"How long had you guys been together for?"

"Six months. I was her first…you know."

"Girlfriend?"

Bex blushed a little. "Yeah."

"And was she yours?"

"No. I was more, you know, comfortable with it. She wasn't really sure how to handle it yet."

"And you think that had something to do with what she did?"

Bex ground her teeth together tightly and pounded her fist against her leg. "I wish I knew. I keep going over it and over it in my mind, trying to figure it out. Why didn't she come to me? Why did she just go and do it? I mean, God!"

"Maybe she was afraid. Maybe something was bothering her and she thought sharing it would cause you problems."

Bex looked at her strangely. "I've kind of been thinking the same thing." She leaned closer and looking over her shoulder.

"Why?"

Slowly, Bex reached into her pocket and uncrumpled a note. On the back, where the letter would have been folded and sealed, remnants of red wax remained. On the inside, in block letters, the warning WATCH YOUR BACK.

A rap on the door startled them both. Operating on instinct, Jil pointed silently to the alcove. Bex crept into the space and crouched down, hidden behind the old armchair. Jil quickly clicked on a movie icon on her laptop.

"Come in," she called, looking intently at the screen as Buck Weekly barged through the door. "Hello, Buck." She made a show of turning down the volume on her speakers. "What can I do for you?"

"Oh, I thought perhaps you had a student in here."

"Nope. Just me and my video."

"Why haven't you gone home?"

"Busy prepping for tomorrow," Jil lied. "I wanted to review this film before showing it to the class."

"Hmm," Buck said. "I thought maybe you'd be finishing those report cards."

Jil pretended to be thoughtful. "You know, I've been giving that some thought. I'd really like this last test to be reflected on the students' report cards. Given how many delays they've had during this term, I really don't think I have enough information to grade them fairly without this test. I'm going to hold off doing the report cards until I've graded them all."

Buck's face hardened. "I was really expecting them to be done this week."

Jil smiled politely. "Well, I understand, Buck. But I think this is what's best for the students. It's a difficult class, and I want to encourage them as much as possible."

"And when do you expect to have the grades?"

"Oh, Tuesday or Wednesday at the latest. I have one or two who still need to write the test." Absolute crap. There hadn't been a single student absent the day of the test.

"When are they writing?"

"Well, it'll have to be Monday now." Jil smiled again. "Was there anything in particular you needed?"

"No," Buck grumbled. "I just saw your light on and thought I'd stop in."

"Well, thanks," Jil said, turning back to her video. "I'll just get back to work then."

Buck said nothing, but the vigor with which the door closed behind him said it all.

As soon as the room was clear, Bex crept out from behind the chair. She didn't ask why Jil had thought to make her hide. They were operating purely on instinct, not logic. Because logically, they didn't know anything for sure except that there were people in the school who made them both extremely uncomfortable.

"Miss," Bex whispered, in case there was anyone listening. "What should I do?"

Jil shook her head. "Business as usual," she said, borrowing Jess's motto. "There's nothing we can do until we have more proof. But I'll work on it if you will."

"There's something I just thought of."

"Which is?"

Bex shuffled her feet. "Alyssa's parents were pretty religious, and I think that was part of the reason she had so much trouble, you know, accepting herself. But she found this chat room online…like for kids to get together and talk about how to come out, and what to do when you went to a Catholic school, or had parents who didn't believe in it…"

"Did she spend a lot of time on it?"

"Yeah. She said it helped. That she found a few good friends on it. There was this one girl on there she really connected with. I think she was a little older, like college age."

"Do you know her name?"

Bex scowled. "Clarisse."

"You didn't like her?"

Bex shook her head. "It seems stupid now," she muttered. "I shouldn't have said anything to her about it. I should have just left her alone if Clarisse was helping her, but…"

"You were jealous?" Jil asked gently.

Bex looked at the floor. "She just spent so much time talking to her…I was okay with it at first, when I thought it was helping, but then Alyssa started, you know, pulling away, and…"

"So you thought it stopped helping, or you thought maybe Clarisse was helping too much and taking her away from you?"

"I don't really know. We fought about it. And then we stopped spending time together almost completely. We didn't break up as much as…kind of go our separate ways. And then she killed herself."

"Was there anyone else on there that she talked to?"

"Some guy. I think he was a youth leader or something."

"Young? Old?"

"Young. And good-looking too."

"Do you remember what this website was called?"

Bex frowned. "Faith Connects or Connections in Faith or something."

Jil scribbled down the words.

Bex stood and looked toward the door. "Do you think the coast is clear yet?"

Jil peeked through the blinds on her window. "Go on," she said, and Bex opened the door, ducking her head and hurrying into the atrium before anyone saw her.

Just as Bex disappeared around the corner, Jil thought she saw a flash of white in the opposite doorway. When she turned to look, it had disappeared.

Chapter Twelve

Jil got out of the car and stared at the small white house for a few moments. The red door looked a little chipped, and one of the eaves troughs had come loose at the corner of the roof. She wondered if Jack the handyman still paid monthly visits to the home, of if he'd stopped since Elise no longer took in kids.

She walked up the wide stone steps and rapped three times on the brass knocker.

Silence followed, and she looked at her watch. She'd waited until the afternoon, knowing Elise got up later these days. She peeked in the sidelight and tried the handle. It opened.

"Elise?" she called, stepping inside. The house smelled of baked muffins and rose potpourri—exactly how it had smelled for the fifteen years since she'd moved in. But there was something else lurking under the homey odors. A sweet, pungent smoke. She shook her head, recognizing it.

Elise stepped around a corner at the end of the hallway. She had a head of curly white hair, but smooth, tanned skin, and a spry gait. Recently, she'd turned sixty, a fact that Jil hadn't forgotten.

"I bought you some special brownies for your birthday," she joked.

Elise grinned sideways. "Can you smell it?"

"Only if you ignore the fresh baked goods."

Elise's eyes twinkled. "That's what I use to distract visitors. Give them a cranberry muffin, and they forget what they're sniffing. Staying for dinner?"

Jil shrugged. "I should have called first, but…"

"Nonsense. I'm not busy."

"How are you feeling?"

Elise smiled wanly. "Alive."

"Did the doctor say anything more?"

"Nope. Only that I'm allowed to smoke Mary Jane."

Jil grinned. Hearing "Mary Jane" in Elise's faint Irish lilt was funny, even though her smoking it probably wasn't.

Elise slipped her arm through Jil's. "Help me with the roast chicken. Tell me all about your new case."

"How do you know I've got a new case? Has Padraig been talking to you?"

Elise ignored her. "I've been to the market this morning. Bought some fresh rosemary and thyme for the potatoes."

"You knew I was coming today! He told you, didn't he? I wanted to drop by unannounced so you didn't have time to make a fuss."

Elise just smiled. "Carrots?"

"I'll kill him, the asshole."

"He loves you," Elise said softly. "And so do I."

Jil just shook her head. "What if I hadn't shown up? Then you'd be eating my favorite dinner alone."

"Nah. We know you better than that."

"Will you let me make the lemon pie, at least? I haven't brought anything for the table."

"Already made."

Jil followed her foster mother into the kitchen where a fresh bouquet of short pink roses sat on the table in a glass bowl, their full blooms lending another heady scent to the kitchen. Absently, she picked up the lighter and touched a flame to the floating candles that surrounded the roses.

"Tea?"

"Yes, thanks. I'll make it."

Elise reached for a tin of cookies to put on the table while Jil ran water into the old steel kettle and set it on the stove. She took down mugs and a teapot, then rooted around in the tea cupboard for her old standby: Irish breakfast.

"You have any good tea at home yet, or are you still drinking that American sludge?"

Jil shook her head. "I'm an investigator. Coffee is a job requirement."

"No kidding. Especially the hours you keep. How's work at the school?"

"It's taking a different direction than I thought," Jil said as the kettle began steaming.

Elise leaned against the head chair, propping her leg up against one knee in a yoga pose. "I'm sorry to laugh, but it seems like that school is part of your destiny."

"I know," Jil said ruefully. "If not as a student, then as an investigator pretending to be a teacher."

Elise didn't ask what she was investigating. She knew Jil couldn't say anything until the investigation was over.

The kettle began to scream, so Jil took it off the stove and poured the hot water into the pot of leaves. Elise had laid out chocolate chip cookies on the table next to the mugs, and Jil sank into her old spot at the small round glass-top, staring out the window for a moment. This foster home was different from any other one she'd been in. No bench seating, no melamine plates or plastic tablecloths. No bunk beds or rec rooms.

The house was quiet, neat, and filled with nice things that Elise loved and treasured. Jil had never broken a single knick-knack when she lived there, and, except once, she'd never gone into Elise's grand study without her permission. Permission she'd never asked for—until today.

"Elise, I've been to the library, and they don't have what I'm looking for."

Elise looked up. "The library doesn't have what you're looking for?" she said incredulously. During her tenure as professor at the University of Rockford, Elise had maintained at least one shift a week at the local library and steadfastly believed in its ability to impart all relevant information.

"It's on microfilm."

"Oh, that's a pain. Digital is much better."

"They only digitized nineteen eighty-five and beyond for the *Rockford Citizen*."

"And you want what? Nineteen eighty-four?"

"Well, yes, actually, and the seventies as well."

Elise frowned. "I have volumes of papers. Every year, I get them bound."

Jil smiled. "I know. I'm looking forward to inheriting your hoard."

"This is not a hoard; it's a collection. Hoards are messy and disorganized and they smell bad. These papers are leather-bound and gorgeous. They're arranged according to the Dewey Decimal System and—"

"Color-coded?"

"Of course not! Arranged by size."

Jil laughed. "Noted."

"And you will be inheriting them, if only so you can drop them off at the nearest reference library."

"I don't want to hear about it," Jil said. Elise dying had been far too much on her mind lately.

"Well, that's too bad, because now you've reminded me…"

Elise strode past her down the hall—not quite as quickly as usual—and Jil frowned as she followed.

When the door opened before her, she felt like Aladdin entering the forbidden cave. For a moment, she stood at the entrance, just staring at Elise's double-story, floor-to-ceiling bookshelves. "Can I climb the ladder?"

Elise laughed. "Not a chance. Wait til I'm dead. Now, pay attention. This is important." She walked around the side of the enormous mahogany desk and felt under the wide round edge, then pulled a hidden drawer out from the back corner.

"Seriously? What are you, Nancy Drew?"

"The desk came with this. From my father's study."

Mr. Fitzgerald had been a criminal lawyer in the 1920s, and had clearly had an interesting job.

Jil peered into the empty drawer and laughed when Elise popped out a false bottom and set it on the desk. The space below contained a folder.

"My will," she said. "And some other things. Just so you know where to look when I kick the bucket."

"We're not talking about that."

Elise sighed. "You know eventually we'll have to. Since you'll have to take me back to Ireland and all."

"Seriously?"

Elise laughed. "Of course not! I want to be in an urn on your fireplace in that beautiful loft of yours."

Jil shot her a withering look. "Standard burial plot it is then."

Elise nodded. "Thank you."

"Seriously, Elise, how bad is it?"

Her foster mother lifted her chin and gave her a small smile. "We've still got time, darling. Now, I'll leave you in here to find whatever it is you're looking for."

When Elise left, Jil took a moment just to look around. Even though she was now an adult, Elise's study still felt magical and mysterious. Elise's love for research had been a compelling part of Jil's becoming a PI.

After an hour, she had a stack of materials piled on the chaise by the door and had filled out a card to let Elise know what she'd taken. Nothing about that boy in the woods, though. Jess had been right about that.

"Supper!" came the familiar call.

"Coming!"

Before ducking out of the study, she punched in Morgan's number. Maybe he could find the police report…

Monday morning, Buck appeared, as expected, in Jil's second period class. She was waiting for him. She'd had enough of these games and was about to put a stop to them once and for all, but in order for that to work, she'd have to play one more round.

"Oh, Buck, I'm glad you're here," she said, speaking faintly on purpose. "I was wondering if you'd mind taking my class this morning? I think I'm coming down with something."

"Sure, Julia," Buck said, nodding his great grizzly head. "I don't mind helping you out."

As long as you get publicly recognized and praised. She could just hear him in the staff room afterward, telling everyone who would listen (confidentially, of course) how he'd stepped in at the last minute to help out a senior class with a new teacher who was really feeling the pressure. Oh, it was nothing. He'd just have to stay late tonight to finish his own work, but it was no problem.

Outwardly, she just smiled—weakly. "Thanks a lot, Buck. There's a video if you don't feel like lecturing."

Fat chance. He'd get going on a moral lesson, punctuated with thrilling stories from his childhood, and there would be no stopping him. She shot Bex an apologetic glance as she ducked out of the room, and Bex shrugged in response—albeit, with a flick of her chin that told Jil on no uncertain terms that she wasn't pleased. Mr. Weekly was annoying, but spending a class hearing stories wasn't the worst way to spend her time.

Jil hurried down the stairs and headed straight for Buck's office. It turned out that it was easy to get keys to alternate rooms in the school. All you had to do was ask for a legitimate key from the secretary, whose ample midsection made her mobility a problem. She waved in the general direction of the key box, and instructed you to help yourself.

Jil had asked for a key to the staff washroom that very morning, and had helped herself to the spare labeled R200. Buck's office. While she was in there, she'd lifted the spare for her own office.

That way, the temptation for someone else to break into her space was thwarted a little. Though who knew how many spare keys were floating around the school? A master key seemed to be common amongst department heads, gym teachers, and everyone else who felt they had the right to access every room in the building.

Now that Buck was safely occupied, Jil strode purposefully into his room. Hiding in plain sight was one of her specialties. If you acted like you had business somewhere, people believed you did. She opened the door quickly. Buck never turned out the lights. He was not environmentally conscious by nature, so it would not seem strange to anyone in the hallway that his lights were on and nobody was home.

She began with the slush pile at his desk, knowing even as she searched that her notebook was unlikely to be there. Still, why not begin with the obvious? Nothing on the desk but piles of tests and informative brochures. Nothing in the desk—the top drawer of which had been carefully locked, the key sitting in the organizer on top.

She searched his bookshelf, his bag, and his coat pocket before a knock on the door interrupted her. She ignored it, hoping the person would go away. Another, more insistent rap sounded. She grabbed the first pile she saw and went to the door.

Brian the custodian stood there. "Oh, hey, Julia."

"Hey, Brian," Jil replied, relaxing.

"Buck asked for another dolly. D'you know where he is?"

"Yeah, actually, he's up teaching my class."

"Why? Don't you want to teach it?"

"Not feeling well," Jil lied. "I just stopped in to get some materials to take home with me, then I'm leaving."

"Hey, if you're not feeling good, there's ginger ale in the office fridge."

"Oh yeah?"

"Might make you better. Want me to get you some?"

"Sure."

Brian hurried off toward the fridge. She searched the rest of the office with no luck, and was just about to leave when she saw an errant page sticking out from under the leg of Buck's desk. She bent down and pried loose a pile of blue watermarked paper.

She didn't have to see the words WATCH YOUR BACK to know that it was the same letterhead Bex's note had been printed on.

"Bastard," she muttered.

She slipped the paper into the waist of her pants, her short jacket barely covering it. Then she quietly locked the door, and headed to the staff room. She had planned to return the key. Now, she thought better of it. Probably a handy thing to hold on to if he was going to raid her office on a regular basis.

But a tiny little glow in the pit of her stomach tipped her off to her true non-objective feelings. She was secretly pleased to have an excuse to investigate Buck Weekly. Somehow, she felt, he was the key to this whole case. A case that was getting to be more than she'd bargained for every step of the way.

"Here you go," Brian said, meeting her at the door. "Hope you feel better."

"Thanks." Jil smiled, taking the ginger ale, and turning back around. "Hey, Brian." She dropped her voice.

"Yeah?" He leaned in too, his face wide and questioning.

"Have you ever seen anybody in my office?"

"You mean, when you weren't there, like?"

"Yeah."

Brian looked around, then dropped his voice even lower.

"Now, you didn't hear it from me," he whispered. "But there's a few things goin' on at this school that Jess oughta take notice of and doesn't. Not that she's not good, mind you, but there's some who've got her wrapped, if you know what I mean."

"Marcel?" Jil asked, reading his expression. There was no love lost between Marcel and Brian—common enough knowledge.

"Bastard can get away with whatever he wants, including snooping through people's things. Stealing. 'Borrowing' for his own amusement."

"What has he taken?"

"Stupid stuff. He's always bragging about how he never gets caught. Teachers' pens or jewelry. A textbook. A picture or a candy. Anything. He keeps it all stashed in his little hiding places around the school. Jackass. It's just a control thing. He likes to think he's king shit around here, you know?"

"Why haven't you told Jess?"

Brian snorted. "Yeah, like she'd believe me," he said. "Marcel would pin it on me, and I'd be out on my ass without a job. I've got two kids to support. No way I'm gonna get fired over Marcel's stupid treasure hunting."

Jil nodded again. "Keep him out of my office, would you?"

Brian's face grew serious. "Ya think he's been in there?"

Jil shrugged, smiling again. "Who knows? I just don't want him to try it."

Brian smiled wide. "No problem, Jules."

Jil shook his hand and turned to leave. She wanted to get out of this godforsaken school. Now.

It wasn't until she was safe back inside her own empty house, with a fire going and a glass of wine in hand, that Jil took out the watermarked paper. Other than the watermark, she couldn't see anything else that might help her identify the sender.

She took out her phone and called Padraig. "I need to see you," she said tensely.

"What happened?"

"Someone at work stole my notebook."

Padraig was silent for a long moment. "Did it have any identifying marks on it?"

"No. I always keep them like you taught me. No name, no numbers. Everything in it was in block-letter shorthand and initials. No way it could be traced back to me, except that it was taken from my desk."

"Shit," Padraig grumbled. "Any idea who took it? And why would they take it unless they were on to you?"

"I can't imagine why. But I'm going to find a way to get those damned scribbles back."

Padraig snickered a little. "You always liked to give me a hard time about that, eh? Thought I was going way overboard teaching you shorthand."

"Well, what would anyone want with my notebook? Why would anyone go snooping through my things? Especially where this was hidden. This investigation's getting weirder by the day. Can I just forget everything I'm seeing and get the hell out of here?"

"Do you want to?"

Jil sighed. "I don't know," she confessed. "Part of me just wants to write the damn report and be done with this school."

"And the other part?"

"The other part's telling me that I haven't even begun to scratch the surface. Did I tell you that the latest suicide—Alyssa—was also gay?"

Padraig let out a low whistle. "So that's four then?"

"Yep."

"Seems like a pattern to me."

"That's what I'm thinking. I'm also wondering who knew about these kids, and if someone could frame a murder to look like a suicide."

"That's what's keeping you at the school then?"

"Well, that and my investigation."

"Are you sure that's all?"

Jil blushed, glad Padraig couldn't see over the phone. As much as he'd support her investigative curiosity and her search for answers, she doubted his sympathy would extend to her compromising her investigation for the sake of a woman she barely knew.

"Yes, that's all."

"Good," said Padraig. A warning underlay that statement—which wouldn't be obvious to anyone but Jil.

She purposely did not tell him that she'd agreed to help Jessica investigate the taggings at the school. She didn't know how she would explain that to him. The one advantage, though, was that if ever anyone told Jess that she'd been snooping around, she could just claim that she'd been investigating the vandalism, and Jess would let her off the hook. She smiled, but if the thought gave her temporary elation, it was temporary indeed. She was sobered by the growing mountain of questions facing her.

The next morning as she dumped her stuff on her desk, she noticed the top drawer had been left slightly ajar. She wrenched it open to find her notebook peeking back at her.

"What the fuck?"

She took out the book and sat down heavily in her chair. Not only had someone snuck in here to take it; they'd also snuck back in here to plant it.

Folded between the pages was another watermarked paper. I'M ON TO YOU.

A chill ran down her arms. So, she was a target now.

She replaced the book just as Bex popped her head into the office. "Ready, Miss?"

"Yep."

Jil jumped up and followed Bex out, careful to lock the door behind her—not that locked doors seemed to matter. Bex walked five steps ahead of her to the computer lab, watching subtly for any movement. Jil pretended to read her notes as she traveled along, stopping once to exchange a "good morning" with Rosie McMonahan.

When she caught up to Bex downstairs, Jil turned the light on in the computer lab. "Which one did she use?"

"That one in the corner."

"Okay. Thanks."

Bex ducked out of the room.

Jil took the login information for Alyssa Marco and sat at the computer. She pressed in the ID and password and got a blinking box.

"Shit." Her account had already been disconnected.

She sighed and leaned back in her chair. Someone had been bullying Alyssa online. She'd hoped to find some history in her account, but now she needed another strategy.

Just as she was about to get up, her phone vibrated in her pocket. She looked over her shoulder to see if anyone could listen in, but the hallway outside was deserted.

"It's me. I found the report," Morgan whispered. "It was sealed, but…"

She smiled. "You're the best."

"I know." She could picture the cocky grin on his face, but also knew that behind that, he was a little worried about being caught.

"What did it say?"

"I think you'd better read it for yourself. But you were right. It's definitely weird. Why does a fourteen-year-old kid go for a walk in the woods in minus twenty-five degree weather? Without proper outerwear or boots? The case file says no foul play is suspected, but the kid also didn't have a history of insanity, so I don't buy it."

"Exactly. There has to be more to it. Something drove that kid out to his death that night, and I want to know what it was. Someone has to know something." She hung up and hurried back to her office to log on to her e-mail.

POLICE REPORT

Case No: 623347-98
Date: February 7, 2004
Reporting Officer: Det. David Lane

Incident: Body of 14-yr-old male student found frozen in woods behind St. Marguerite's school.

Reason for Involvement:

Police were dispatched to the Outdoor Education facility of St. Marguerite's Catholic School on Saturday February 7 after a teacher found the body of fourteen-year-old Bobby Hansen, lying in the snow.

Hansen had last been seen the night before after dinner. He left residence without a coat and wearing indoor shoes.

Action:

Police arrived, along with EMTs at 9:55 a.m. and were escorted to the woods by the director of residence. Paramedics pronounced the boy dead.

Residence students and staff were interviewed, but none remembered seeing Bobby after dinner. Nobody knew why he had left in the middle of the night. His roommate did report that Bobby sometimes walked in his sleep.

The door to the outside was found unlocked.

Conclusion:

The medical examiner confirmed that Bobby Hansen froze to death, somewhere between 1:00 and 3:00 a.m. on Saturday, February 7.

She waited until she arrived home that night before calling Morgan back.

"Is it just me, or does it seem like there's way more to that story?" she said.

"I agree. Unfortunately, we're not going to find out."

"Why not?" She'd already been trying to figure out a way to interview Detective Lane without getting Morgan in trouble.

"That was his last case," Morgan said, reading her mind. "He retired the next week."

"So? We can still find him at home, can't we?"

"Sure. If by home you mean Mount Pleasant Cemetery."

Jil felt the wind shoot out of her. "The guy's dead?"

"Sorry, Jil."

"No, don't be. Thanks for everything you've done on this case."

Morgan didn't say anything right away.

"What?" she asked.

"Nothing. I know what you're going to say so I'm not even going to put it out there."

She chuckled. "No."

"You really would make a great cop."

"I tried that, remember? I hated it."

"Yeah, I know."

"But I appreciate having you on the inside."

"For all your theoretical questions," Morgan interjected.

She grinned, even though he couldn't see it. Always theoretically.

Chapter Thirteen

Knowing she had no hope of turning off her brain, and seeing that at least one hour of daylight remained, Jil quickly slipped into running gear, and popped one earphone in. She heard her mother's voice in her head—though Aimee had probably never said this to her. Don't walk alone at night listening to music!

Jil compromised. She'd enjoy her music with one ear, and listen for murderers and rapists with the other.

For a fleeting moment, she considered bringing that gun of Padraig's, but decided she didn't feel comfortable carrying it. It reminded her that danger lurked behind every conceivable cache, and that made her nervous. Not because of the danger, but because of the paranoia that could set in if someone allowed themselves to think that way.

During the first block, she limped along, her unwilling muscles so used to being cramped behind a desk or in a car that they'd forgotten what exercise felt like.

She stopped to prop her leg up on a rock and stretch some blood into it. Heel cord stretches, hamstrings, calves—nothing wanted to work today. After a good five minutes of stretching warm muscles, she began again. This would be so much easier with someone there to pull her along. Someone with four legs, specifically. For months, she'd wanted a dog—a Great Dane—but Tara didn't want more responsibility. Ironic, since she was now engaged and pregnant.

Now, Jil realized, she could get any sort of dog she wanted.

Two more half-running blocks, and something suddenly released in her legs. "Ah," she breathed, relieved, as she was finally able to take off. She visualized Tara, like a ball and chain, dropping from her ankle and rolling down the sidewalk toward an open gutter. That almost made her smile.

If she could finally get over her, might there be room in her life for a hot blond principal?

Who was not only straight but *married* she reminded herself.

What was it with her and out-of-reach women?

Dusk approached quickly these days. Twilight had set in atop the mature trees behind the park, and the lamplights on the neighborhood properties came on. She turned the corner that would set her on the loop back home to her warehouse loft.

Her building in view, she bent down to stretch again. As she walked the last block to the main entrance, she saw a light-colored CUV slowly pull away from the curb, driving away from her. She ducked behind her own truck, peeking out to read the license plate. In the half-dark, she couldn't make out the digits.

She hurried inside and rode the elevator to her loft, glad that her lights came on automatically, and she immediately closed the front curtains. She locked the front door and set the alarm, then went upstairs to shower, keeping the bathroom door open to listen for anything that might disturb her.

By now, the morning page had begun to lose its novelty. "Ms. Kinness, please come to the office. Ms. Kinness."

Jil put down her glasses and made sure to lock the door before heading into Jess's office. This time, she knocked on the side door that came in to where the bookshelf used to be. Jil heard a lock slide back, and Jess opened the door.

"Hi." Jil stepped inside. She looked through the window next to the common door just in time to see Buck Weekly leaving the main office.

Jess pulled down the shade to give them some privacy, and followed Jil's gaze. "Why didn't you tell me?" she asked seriously.

"Tell you what?"

"That you're having a troublesome work relationship?"

"There's nothing troublesome about it," Jil replied. "He's overstepping his boundaries, and I resent it. If he keeps it up, there will be no professional relationship. He's not my boss."

Jess nodded, as if this weren't the first time she'd heard this complaint. Jil wondered how much of her workday Jess spent fielding problems with the staff.

"What did he say?"

"That you refused to hand in your report cards to him. Is that true?"

"No."

"Really? So you have handed them in?"

"No."

Jess tilted her head. "What's up?"

"I'm not finished yet. I wanted my latest test scores to be included. He wanted me to give him the report cards almost two weeks before they were due and I said no."

Jess just looked at her. "And?"

Jil sighed. "And I don't like the guy." She hadn't meant to confess any of this, but for some reason, she couldn't be bothered lying about something else when it already felt like her whole life was one big lie.

"Julia, he's a good mentor for you," Jess said, still adopting the party line. "He's a model citizen. He's taught here for—"

"I know, I know. Thirty years. I've heard it all."

"Maybe he would help you cope with the fundamentalists in your class. You know, he does have some very creative ideas."

"Jess, if he was in my classroom any more, he'd be teaching the course."

Jess looked surprised. "What do you mean?"

"Is it part of his job to sit in?"

"No," she replied, frowning. "Unless he's been invited to participate. I mean, usually teachers do observe for a few days in the first week—perhaps—but they stop coming almost immediately."

"He hasn't."

"How often is he in there?"

"At least twice a week. Lately, almost every day."

"No, no. That's not right."

Jil breathed a sigh of relief. She felt like she was unburdening a huge weight. "He arrives unannounced, sits at the back, and interrupts my class. On Monday, I'd finally had enough. I told him I wasn't feeling well, and asked if he'd take my class."

"Did he?"

"Of course."

"And what did you do?"

"Other work. It's absolutely ridiculous. I feel like I'm in a fishbowl."

"This is very interesting," Jess murmured, tucking her feet up.

"Yeah, interesting is one word for it. Annoying is the word I'd like to choose."

"I wonder why he's doing it."

Jil shrugged and shook her head. "I have no idea. Maybe it's a control issue. I don't know."

Jess exhaled slowly. "I'd say I'm sorry for calling you down, but in light of what you've said, I guess it's good that we had a little chat. I'll have to deal with this. I'm sorry to hear about this problem."

Jil tried to rearrange her face to hide all the roiling emotion that bubbled over. Why did Buck get to her so much? It's not like she was surprised he'd come to see Jess, but she was still indignant about being called up on the carpet for something as innocuous as not wanting to hand him her report cards.

"I can hand in my report cards directly?" Jil asked.

Jess sighed. "If you'd like," she said. "I can understand why you wouldn't want to be scrutinized. Maybe I'd better rethink your mentoring situation."

"Is it mandatory?"

"Not really. Just recommended. We all have teacher-mentors. Giovanni DiTullio was mine when I first started."

"Oh yeah?"

"Mmm hmm. And when I was a VP, Mark Genovese was my mentee. This is a good arrangement. It takes some pressure off you as a teacher."

"Except that it's putting more pressure on me."

"Okay," Jess conceded. "I won't make you pair with Buck anymore. But I'm also not going to be the one to tell him. If you don't want him as a mentor, you have to tell him yourself."

It seemed fair. Reasonable. But also impossible.

She noticed that the furniture in the far side of the room had been rearranged. The small table that normally sat on the opposite wall had been dragged over to the newly-discovered door, almost blocking the entrance.

"Jess? Why is that table so close to the door?" When she'd come in that way, Jess had been standing there, and she hadn't noticed.

"Security," Jess replied, then looked as though she wished she hadn't said anything.

"From what?"

She looked at the door, but didn't answer.

"Is someone coming in here uninvited?"

Jess wavered for a moment. "I think I might be making too much of it," she said finally. "But it seems to me that when I come in in the mornings, some things are not where I've left them at night. I'm usually the last to leave, and the first to arrive, but somehow, things are going missing."

"Anything important?"

Jess sighed. "Yes."

Jil waited.

"It's nothing."

"Well, it's obviously something."

"I can't really tell you."

"Because it's me or because you're the principal?" Jil said, her tone slightly mocking.

Jess tilted her head. "It's one thing for a principal to turn a blind eye," she said quietly. "It's another thing to let our personal lives become public."

"I'm not planning on taking out a news broadcast," Jil returned evenly. "What's missing, Jess?"

"A piece of jewelry," she said. She didn't specify from whom, and Jil didn't ask.

"What does it look like?'

"Why? What are you going to do?"

Jil stared at her. "I'm going to take out a news broadcast."

Jess smiled reluctantly. "It's a ring."

"Diamond?"

Jess pursed her lips. "Yes."

"Gold or silver?"

"Would you like me to draw you a picture?"

Jil waited, and Jess sighed. "White gold. Tension setting. It has my name engraved in it too, in case you were planning on hiring a PI."

Jil willed herself to maintain a straight face. "Why did you leave it here?"

"Too many questions."

Jil said nothing. First trick of investigation—let the suspect fill the silence.

"This is where I…took it off, and this is where it stayed. In my desk. I can't imagine what happened to it—unless I've lost it. I'm probably suspicious over nothing."

Suspicious enough to move your furniture around.

"I'm sorry about what's happening," Jess said, changing the subject abruptly. "I will speak to Buck about visiting your class, if that would improve the situation."

"Thanks." If the line had been blurry before, it was damn well unreadable now. Her head reeled, because she was fairly sure she knew where Jess's ring had gone.

"I've got to run. I have a meeting this afternoon for a charity event, but first thing tomorrow, I'll get to the bottom of this, okay?"

"Sure," Jil said. "Charity awaits. Starving kids in Africa?"

"No, dogs actually." Jess rolled her eyes a little. "An old friend of mine runs the SPCA downtown, and he asked me to pop in to this meeting tonight. Wants to pick my brain."

Jil smiled. "If you see a Great Dane waiting for a home, let me know."

"A Great Dane?" Jess's brows shot up. "You want a dog?"

"Yeah."

"Feeling lonely?"

Such an innocuous question, but there it was again, that damn annoying pricking of her eyes. What the hell was the matter with her?

"Sorry," Jess said gently.

"It's all right. The loft is quiet, you're right. Or maybe I just don't like running alone at night."

Jess looked at her curiously. "Leave me your number, and I'll see what I can do. Henri says the big dogs are hard to get rid of, because no one wants to feed them."

"I'll bet."

"He could probably get you a reasonable rate."

"Yeah, well, it would be nice if I didn't have to eat cat food in order to feed my dog," Jil joked as she wrote down her number.

Jess smiled. "I'll let you know."

"Thanks."

As Jil left the office—the same way she'd come in—she wondered why Buck would bother complaining to Jess now. They hadn't exactly had a warm and fuzzy relationship up until this point. Unless, as Jess said, it hadn't been much at all. Unless, perhaps, he was just looking for an excuse to get into her office. If he was using the meeting as an opportunity to do something else. Something like taking a key, perhaps? Spying? Feeling Jessica out for any information she might have?

Jil went back to her office, concentrating so hard on the what ifs that she almost missed the room. And as she doubled back, she saw it—stuck into the side of the door. A note. Sealed with red wax. Bex's seal hadn't been clear, but this one was. She stared at it, trying to make out the strange initials. The ornate letters stamped into the wax—almost Baroque—might have been SoA, but she couldn't be sure.

Inside, the slanted writing, the texture of the paper; everything about it was the same as the note Bex had shown her. She ducked into her office, closing the door tight before she unfolded the paper.

Watch your back.

She folded it back up slowly and let out a long breath.

Buck did not show up at her second period class. Neither did Theo. Good thing, because the day's topic was Islam, and if he'd objected to Buddhism, she wondered what his reaction would be to the Middle East.

Out of curiosity, she opened her attendance notebook and counted the absences. Theo had missed twenty-three classes. When he'd missed over half the material, she could ask to have him removed from her class, which meant if he missed again tomorrow and Friday, he would be out. She crossed her fingers and hoped. It would certainly make Bex breathe a lot easier, as she would herself. He was a constant axe in her side as she tried to convey at least part of the course information to the students.

She felt guilty about not paying enough attention to the teaching aspect of her job. The students had signed up for a class, and even if it was just a cover job, her students were affected. Was she taking the easy way out? Was she challenging them? Was she doing her job? If she looked at herself seriously, she'd have to conclude that she could do better.

She made a firm resolution to concentrate on teaching—whether or not someone was rifling through her personal items and potentially parking outside her house at night. Whether or not she got cryptic notes under her door and hid students in her office for no apparent reason. Whether or not the principal at the school had reasons to be concerned about her office being pilfered. She would damn well do her job, and stick it out until the end of term. Hell, she might even stay on for next term just to piss off Buck Weekly.

With new determination, she launched into a lively lesson, her students perking up when they saw the enthusiasm on her face.

❖

That afternoon, when the bell rang for lunch, Jil hurried down to the cafeteria to seek out Brian. "I need to know where Marcel is," she whispered.

He looked around furtively. "What for?"

"There's something I have to do, and I want to know that he's safely out of the way."

"What do you have to do?"

"Something."

Brian puffed out his cheeks. "What kind of something?"

"A little look around."

"Wish I wouldn't have said nuthin'." Brian shook his head. "If you go in there, and he finds you, you'll be toast. I mean it."

"Why? What do you think he'd do?"

"You don't know Marcel," Brian said. "He's a mean son of a bitch when he wants to be."

"Yeah, well, anyone who routinely helps themselves to someone else's property isn't exactly a nice guy."

"You think he stole something of yours?" Brian frowned.

"I'm not saying another word. If he catches me, I want you to honestly be able to say you didn't know anything about this."

Brian clenched his jaw. "He's out in the quad. He spends lunch out there smoking with the guys while I clean up in here. The workroom downstairs is usually free until after lunch, and then we all meet here to clean up the mess after these hooligans."

"Downstairs? In the B building?"

"Yeah. But you need a key."

Jil smiled. "Already taken care of."

Brian looked worried. "Jules…" Jil turned around. "Don't get caught."

"I wasn't planning on it."

Chapter Fourteen

Before she could reconsider, Jil ducked out of the cafeteria by the door by the stage. She went quickly through the R building and opened the doors to B. It was eerily quiet there. All the students were in either the R caf or the G caf, with a few loitering outdoors smoking and throwing balls around.

The B building was the oldest on campus, and the chipped sandstone gave rise to a musty, old odor that hinted at secrets and lies. She felt a shiver run through her, which could have had everything, or nothing, to do with the draft coming in from the old windows.

Down the corridor was the high-needs classroom. She could hear the shrieks and gurgles of the severely disabled children. She scurried through the door as one of the kids came down the hall in his wheelchair, being pushed by a tired-looking staff member.

Jil descended the stairs to the basement. This entire building was seldom used, but the basement classrooms were especially vacant, only occupied when no other room was available. Even the portables had higher traffic than this part of the building.

The lower door creaked loudly, like a dying crow. It was heavy and smelled like rusting metal. When she let it go, it slammed behind her, its hinges having died a long time ago. Her heart beat faster and louder in her chest, and she stopped dead for a minute, listening intently. There were no students on this level. She peeked into classrooms as she passed, making sure. Not a soul.

Slowly, she inched her way over to the custodians' lair. As she did, she looked up discreetly. No cameras down here either. She wondered if that was deliberate. She paused outside the door, her ear to the crack, listening. Silence.

When she put the key in the lock, it opened easily. She crept inside, closing the door quietly behind her. She only had a few minutes at most, and the painful thudding of her heart made her regret this almost at once. It was dark and dusty down here. It smelled bad, and it was far too empty and discreet a place for a school. Schools should be lively and bursting with activity. They shouldn't have these tucked-in alcoves and spots where people could go missing. Easily. She made her way to the row of lockers on the far side of the room.

Easy enough for her, the lockers were identified with the custodians' names. She picked up the combination lock on the door that said "Marcel" and spun the dial once around until it hit zero again. Then she put the lock to her ear and slowly turned the dial, making note of each number that produced a tiny click: 10, 21, 46.

She tried the first combination. It didn't work. She reset the dial to zero and tried reversing them. 46, 21, 10. Nothing.

There were six different combinations of this set. Four more to go. On 21, 10, 46, the lock finally burst open. Quickly, Jil scanned the contents. A coat. Some old work boots. Posters of half-naked women. Of course. And on the top shelf, a key. A key to what? A piece of paper fluttered down from the top shelf as she removed the key.

The water stain on it was familiar. Pocketing it for examination later, she scanned the locker one more time. No box. Leaving the locker door open, she prowled around the room, stiffening every time she thought she heard a noise.

No other lockers were open. The room contained a small kitchen—a microwave, a table and plastic chairs, a mini-fridge. There was a couch and a small TV. A table for checkers. A mat with overshoes and boots. Wait, why did Marcel not keep his shoes in his locker? In fact, he kept nothing on the bottom shelf at all.

She went back to the locker, then bent and felt around the bottom. The floor was loose. She grabbed the lifted corner and pulled out the entire bottom shelf. It came out easily, revealing an old tin box, its lid dented at the corners—probably from repeated use.

She fit the key into the lock and opened the lid. "Wow." She mentally catalogued the items, shocked at how many valuables were in there.

"Bastard," she muttered as she retrieved it.

At the bottom, in the right-hand corner, was a blue velvet box. Jil snapped the lid open, and saw a white gold tension-set diamond ring. Bingo. She pocketed the ring and put the empty box back inside. Unless Marcel examined his treasures daily, she should have a short reprieve to distance herself. She frowned. If she only took back those two items, he'd know immediately it was she who had found his treasure.

She rooted through the box and carefully picked out four other articles that looked the most valuable. With luck, he'd be so distracted by the missing rings and tennis bracelets that he wouldn't notice the loss.

A small leather box, dented at the corners, caught her eye, and she pried it out from under the weight of all the other odds and ends Marcel had packed into his box. She opened the lid and found an old-fashioned metal seal, a stick of crimson wax, and a small pile of familiar watermarked paper. She turned the seal over and saw a scripted SoA carved into the metal surface.

Who did these belong to? And what was the SoA?

Well, if the idiots didn't have their precious seal and wax, perhaps they'd send fewer notes. She decided to keep that too. She was just replacing the box and the key when she heard a loud squeak—like a dying crow—followed by a loud bang. Shit. The door down the hall. Someone was coming.

She eased the locker door shut and snapped the lock tight, turning the dial back to zero just as the deadbolt shot back on the door to the custodians' room. She tensed, her heart in her throat.

"Hey, Marcel!" she recognized Brian's Eastern lilt from down the hall. The door stopped opening. In a flash, she ducked behind the door to the bathroom, holding her breath as her pockets bulged with her recovered loot.

Brian and Marcel entered together. "The boss is complaining about the mess in the senior caf," Brian said. Jil heard a locker open and close.

"Yeah, well, tell 'er we've got lots of extra work to do with that damn graffiti. We don't have time to worry about ketchup and mustard spills."

Brian laughed nervously.

Jil leaned back against the wall, as far back from the door as possible, praying Marcel didn't have to use the toilet.

"C'mon, we'd better go," Brian said.

"Hang on. I've got something to do. You go ahead."

"Naw, I'll wait."

"Go ahead!" Marcel growled.

"What? You gotta take a leak again?"

"What's it to you? Wanna listen, faggot?"

Brian laughed again—strained and harsh. There was no help for it. He'd have to leave. "Don't take all day," he said. The door to the hall opened and shut.

Footsteps approached the bathroom. Jil was sure he could hear her heart beating. It felt like it would detach and slip right into the bottom of her abdomen, the way it was thundering. She fully expected him to close the door and find her. But he didn't.

She heard the shifting of a lock and the squeak of the cabinet door opening. A box lid lifted and something dropped inside. The door shut and the lock slid back. Another hiding spot? How many did he have around the school?

Jil bit her lip and waited. Would he find her now? Shut the door to take a leak and get the surprise of his life? She'd have the advantage for a split second. She was pretty sure she could take him.

But he didn't close the door. Didn't see her standing there. He left the bathroom.

She waited until she heard the squeak and bang of the door down the hall before she finally let out the breath she'd been holding and crept out of the bathroom.

She didn't look back as she exited the custodians' room and hurried back up to the part of the school that daylight reached. She purposely detoured to pass by the senior caf, catching Brian's eye through the window. He barely looked up, but she knew he saw her. His slight nod and the relaxing of his shoulders gave him away. Marcel's back was turned to her, and she didn't wait for him to turn around. Instead, she headed toward the staff room to check her mail before bailing for the day.

❖

Once at home and changed into comfortable clothes, Jil tucked the box with the wax and seal safely into the top drawer of her desk.

Then she took the ring out of her jacket pocket and studied it. It was beautiful. Expensive. Could it have been from Jess's husband? She held it up, watching the diamond sparkling in the sunlight that streamed through her bay window. It seemed that the ring was making up for all the time it had spent in a box. She studied the inscription on the inside. L.A. & J.B. Who was L.A.? Her husband's initials were M.B. Which was probably why the ring was in a box and not on her finger.

Jil slipped the ring onto the ring finger of her left hand. Watched the diamond sparkle a little longer. Imagined her own diamond ring being placed there. Someday.

She quickly took it off and placed the ring on the table. Now that she had it, she didn't know what she was going to do with it. Presumably, she was the only one who knew it was missing (besides Jess, and the thief himself). She couldn't very well replace it without explaining where she'd found it. Even if she snuck in to her office to replace it, she was sure Jess had scoured the place looking and would never believe she could have overlooked it. She could leave it in her mailbox, but Jess would know it was her.

She thought hard as she opened her laptop and began the first page of the report that would set her free from St. Marguerite's. And by the time she crawled into bed that night, she'd come up with a solution.

The next day, Jil supervised the atrium. She saw Bex walking through on her way to her first period class. Good. She kept the ring in her pocket for all of her prep period, during which she learned that two of the senior science teachers—neither of whom she had met—were married. Really married. Living together. With seven children. They attended church on Sundays and six of their seven children were enrolled in Sunday school. That ticked two off her list. Finally, some good news.

When the bell rang for second period, she stood outside the hall to her classroom. The students filed in. From down the hall, Jil saw Bex approaching, eyes on the ground, as usual, and alone.

Jil quickly dropped one of Marcel's stolen gold bracelets on the ground next to an empty locker, and retreated into the room. She heard Bex stop. Heard her breathe, "Wow."

She came in, nodded to Jil, and took her seat.

"Hi, guys," Jil said. They smiled back. Some yawned. Jordan put his head down on his desk.

"Miss, this winter is seriously long," Joey complained.

"It's only November."

"It's seriously gray, though. There hasn't been sun for like four days."

Jil looked out the window. They were right. It was cloudy, gray, and snowing for the three-hundredth time. "And just think, we've got four more months to go!"

"Miss, can we have like a party or something?" Kyle asked. His foot jiggled against the foot of the desk, sending a jolting rhythm through the floor.

"To celebrate what?"

The class groaned. Jil noticed that some of them were paler than they should have been. Joey had dark circles under her eyes. Wiley's hair was greasy and hung in limp strands. She could hear a few stomachs growling. They weren't in good shape.

"Okay, listen up. I appreciate that school is long and hard sometimes. But there's still some stuff we have to get through. We have a test on Thursday, don't forget."

The class groaned collectively. Joey looked like she was about to cry.

"But," Jil continued. "I have a proposition."

"Yeah, what is it?" Kyle wondered out loud.

"Shut up, tard, and she'll tell you," snapped Wiley.

"Yo," Kyle said, subdued by Wiley's outburst. "Chill."

"Whatever," Wiley muttered.

"I want every single one of your butts in these seats on Thursday," Jil said. "And if you score over seventy percent as a class, I'll bring in Tim Horton's donuts for breakfast on Monday."

"Yeah!" Kyle yelled, thumping his desk. Joey grinned. Even Wiley cracked a smile.

"Timmie's donuts!"

Jil smiled back at them, a little surprised at how well her simple tactic had worked. She realized that St. Marguerite's was a mixed-background school, but she hadn't expected such a response from a simple sugar fix.

Joey's face dropped. "Miss, I'm dumb. I can't get seventy. I've never got seventy on anything in religion."

"Yo, me too," Kyle said. "I'm not good in this class."

Jil was amazed at the way they flaunted their deficiencies. Basic level religion. She'd thanked her lucky stars that she'd been assigned a basic level, but now she was starting to realize the implications. Her students really were struggling.

"I guess you'll have to study," she said simply. "Partner up. Make study dates. Take this seriously. And let's see what we can do."

For the rest of the class, there wasn't a peep out of them. She reviewed all the information that they had covered in the past unit, promising to do it again tomorrow. The bell rang. The students got up from their desks. As they filed out, she heard Wiley and Kyle talking.

"What's your problem, man?" Kyle said.

"Nothing. Leave me alone."

"Whatever, fag."

And then, a loud metallic thud, like a locker falling over. Jil jumped up from her desk and ran into the hall. Wiley had Kyle pinned to the locker. "Shut up. Do you hear me? Don't talk to me, you fucking moron. Shut up with that shit!"

"Wiley!" Jil said. "Let go of him."

"Yo, get off me, asshole!" Kyle said, his face red. He shoved back and Wiley let him go. Then he took off down the hall before Jil could catch him.

Kyle smoothed out his hoodie and shoved his hands in his pockets. His spiked hair had been flattened a bit at the back, and his skinny jeans were revealing even more of his boxer shorts than ever.

"You might want to look in a mirror," Joey said, then giggled nervously.

Kyle just scowled at her. "What the hell's his problem?"

"You guys need to cool it," Jil said. "If you see Wiley, tell him he needs to come see me in my office."

"Yeah, Miss. Okay. He'll really want to hear that from me."

"Aren't you guys friends?"

"Usually. I don't know who the hell pissed in his cornflakes."

"Language," she said tiredly.

"Sorry."

She squeezed his shoulder. "Joey's right. You should go look in a mirror."

He might have smiled back at her. Just faintly.

When the mob scene had cleared, Jil went back to her desk. Bex was still sitting in the room. She'd almost forgotten about her.

"His dad just got deployed," she said.

"Who? Wiley's?"

"Yeah. He was home for a year, but has to go again next week. "

"Oh," Jil said softly. "That's hard."

"He doesn't want to tell anybody. Plus, let's be honest, nobody wants to be called fag around here. And, Miss? I found this outside." She opened her hand to show Jil a gold bangle.

Jil pretended to be surprised. "Wow. That's nice."

"Who do you think it belongs to?"

She shrugged.

"What do you think I should do with it?"

"Give it to Mr. Weekly. He'll know what to do with it."

Bex made a face, but hurried off. Jil counted five seconds, then followed her down to Buck's office. She watched through the window as Bex handed Buck the bangle. He took it, a quizzical look on his face, and she saw Bex gesturing to the upstairs corridor where she'd found it.

As predicted, Buck got up and strode out of the office. Bex met her eye quickly then ducked down the hallway in the opposite direction. Jil made her move, almost bumping into them. "Oh, Buck. Good, I was just looking for you."

"Hello, Ms. Kinness. I'm sorry. I'm just on an errand. Can we talk later?"

"You look busy."

"Well, a student just turned in something rather valuable. I'd like to have a look at where she found it."

"Was that Bex?"

"Yes."

"She found a bracelet or something outside my classroom upstairs. I suggested she bring it to you." Never waste an opportunity to score points.

"That was good advice."

Jil followed him up to her classroom. The corridors were practically empty—all the students now in class or at lunch.

Buck scanned up and down the hallway, frowning.

"What are you looking for?" Jil probed.

Buck frowned. "This isn't the first time something like this has happened," he muttered vaguely. "We have a magpie in this school." He strode over to Jil's classroom and turned around, retracing the steps Bex would have taken to the exit. He ran his hands along the lockers and found the empty three that stood at the end of one row.

"Was it here she found the bracelet? She said it looked like it had just fallen out of a locker."

"Maybe," said Jil, though she knew perfectly well where it had been found.

Buck opened the first locker and scanned it, then opened the second. He ran his hands along the bottom of the metal box and found the loose flooring. With one short wrench, he'd pulled up the false bottom and stuck his hand inside. "Bingo," he muttered, pulling up the box of tennis bracelets and Jess's ring that Jil had placed inside.

Jil whistled. "Wow, you weren't kidding."

Buck shook his head. "If you'll excuse me, I will take these to the office."

Jil trailed him down to the office, watched him speaking with Mary, the head secretary. Watched as, predictably, he insisted on giving Jessica the box himself. Watched Jess's look of surprise when she lifted the lid and saw what was inside.

Mission accomplished.

Chapter Fifteen

Friday night, at five o'clock, and Jil was already in her pajamas with a glass of wine in hand.

She briefly wondered if she should have considered going out, maybe getting back in the game, but she was too damn tired, and the thought of hooking up with anyone else was just a bit too much at the moment.

With a sigh, she logged onto FaithConnects and scrolled around until she found a place to create an account. If she couldn't get into Alyssa's account, she'd make one as close to hers as possible and hope that whoever she was talking to online would come after her next.

She had a fake picture, bio, and backstory ready, and as each box asked her more information, she felt herself becoming a scared seventeen-year-old girl from St. Marguerite's.

How many identities would she need for this assignment? Today, she was AlleyCat, a timid high school senior. She hovered her mouse over the "Interested In" box. Boys? Girls? On a hunch, she clicked "Both."

Just as she was uploading a composite photograph Morgan had made her, the phone rang.

She hurried from her office, down the stairs to the living room where she'd left Julia Kinness's cell phone. "Hello?"

"Hi, it's Jess Blake." She sounded distant—a little hesitant, maybe?

"Hey." Jil noticed that dusk had fallen. She reached up to close the drapes and went back to shut and lock the balcony door. It was jammed. First sign of winter coming on—everything metal within a fifty-kilometer radius gave her attitude. Heaving all her weight at it, she managed to get the door closed, and the deadbolt shut.

"Do you still want that dog?"

"Yes! Why?"

"My friend Henri, the guy who runs the SPCA? He called back this afternoon. He's got a two-year-old at the downtown location. He weighs something like a hundred and sixty pounds. He says he's blue. I'm not sure what that means."

"It's a type of coloring," Jil replied. "It means he's gray all over."

"Oh. Right. Anyway, he said he'd be happy to waive the adoption fee for him if you wanted to take him. He's too big for the place, and they haven't had anyone ask about him in the three months he's been there. They're really glad someone wants him."

"What's his name?"

"Don't know. Do you want to go see him?"

"Sure. When did you want to go?"

"Oh. Um. Tonight would be fine."

Jil realized that maybe Jess hadn't intended to go with her. Oops. Too late now.

"Okay. I'll meet you there in about an hour."

She showered quickly, towel drying her uncooperative hair, and running a glob of gel through it. She even put on a little makeup before going back to the closet and trying to find something appropriate for the dog pound.

She finally settled on dark jeans, a darted white blouse, and a brown leather jacket. Wow, this fancy clothes thing was really starting to rub off on her. She chose her dark brown leather boots, and gave her hair a final scrunch before heading out the door. On a normal day, she would have thrown her hair into a ponytail, put on a pair of ripped jeans, and not even bothered to look in the mirror. But on a normal day, she wouldn't have been meeting her boss/target in the SPCA. She also wouldn't have been trying to impress her boss/target for reasons she didn't even want to admit out loud to herself.

Jess was sitting in her car waiting when Jil pulled up behind her. They both alighted at the same time, Jil noticing that Jess did, in fact, own a pair of jeans. A nicely fitted pair.

"Hi," she said, suddenly shy.

Jess put a hand to her hair. "Hey. Um. He's waiting inside. I brought dog treats."

Jil realized just how unprepared she was for this beast. No food. No bowls. No leash. What happened if she needed to take him home tonight?

As soon as they got inside, barks and yaps and deep belly woofs greeted them. A tall man with shaggy hair ambled toward them, and as he approached, he smiled, revealing perfect white teeth.

"Hi, you must be Julia," Henri said, extending his hand. Jil shook it and smiled. Henri kissed Jess and hugged her warmly. "How're you doin'?" he murmured.

She nodded, her eyes cast down, hiding the mistiness that clouded them. She seemed lost in his arms—his baggy sweater enveloping her, holding her together. Finally, she pulled away, seeming embarrassed.

What was that about?

"So, where's Big Blue?" she asked, blinking a few times.

Henri laughed. "Not a bad name for him. 'Big Blue' is named Zeus. And he's right down here."

Jil began walking in the direction he pointed, wondering how exactly Henri and Jess had become friends.

He led the way down a row of wire cages, where dogs yapped and wagged and threw themselves against the door. The aisle was narrow, and they had to walk in single file to the end.

Jil found herself face-to-face with a massive canine head.

"Woof!" thundered the dog, leaping up so that its enormous paws thwacked against the wire cage inches from Jil's face. She laughed as Jess jumped back.

"That's no dog. It's a hippo in disguise," Jess said, standing back from the cage as Zeus came crashing down on all fours, his massive tail sweeping back and forth.

"He hasn't been cropped," Jil remarked as Henri opened the cage. Zeus bunted him happily, slurping his hand and looking for biscuits.

Jess handed Jil a handful of treats, maintaining her distance. "They'll be like Tic Tacs to him," she muttered as Jil smiled in thanks and followed Henri into the enclosure.

Zeus immediately turned his attention to Jil, nosing her pocket with his great head. She laughed and fed him three treats from the flat of her hand—obviously these had been intended for a cocker spaniel or a pug—something about one tenth the size of this creature.

"He's a big boy for eighteen months old," said Henri, standing back as Zeus and Jil got acquainted.

She stroked his floppy ears and rubbed under his scruff, a puddle of drool forming in her hand. She wiped it on his gray silky coat. "Keep your spit to yourself."

Zeus made a noise like he was blowing out birthday candles—somewhere between a snuff and a half-hearted sneeze. He seemed to know they were going to be new friends. He was on his very best behavior. He gently licked the crumbs off her hand, and Jil reached for more biscuits. Jess handed them to her, staying well outside the cage.

"Are you afraid of him?"

"Jessie? Are you kidding?" Henri laughed. "She's the biggest suck of them all. Don't know what I woulda done if she and Mick hadn't taken in so many of the sick ones."

Mick? "Did you used to foster?" Jil asked.

Jess nodded, shooting a warning glance at Henri, who seemed not to see.

"They were amazing. They fostered all the little puppies who were born here and caught one thing or another. They even had one Newf for like, a year, before we found a home."

"Nothing quite like this beast, though. And that was when I lived in the country," Jess said. "I don't do that anymore."

"Yeah, whatever," Henri said, scratching Zeus's head. "That's only cuz what's-her-name didn't like dogs."

Jess tensed.

Jil couldn't help the smile that spread across her face.

"Could you just concentrate on Julia?" Jess said sharply.

Henri seemed to realize his error, because he looked at his feet, color high in his cheeks. "Sure, sure. Sorry, Jessie. So what do you think, Julia?"

"I think he's mine," Jil replied, grinning.

By now, Zeus had decided that Jil was his as well. When Henri closed the cage so that they could go sign papers, he whined—a deep, heart-wrenching sound—as his big hazel eyes searched her out. "Woof," he barked dejectedly, then again, more frantically, as he watched one more potential friend walk away.

"I'll be back tomorrow to get you," Jil promised him, reaching through the bars to scratch him again. "Just wait one more night, okay? I've got to get out to the pet store and get my loft ready for you. I'll be back tomorrow. I promise."

"Loft?" Henri said, eyebrows raised.

"I read up on it," Jil replied, shrugging. "Apparently, Danes make great apartment dogs."

"Yeah, sure. They sleep about twenty-two hours a day. But watch out for the two they're awake."

Jil smiled. "I'll get him out. We'll do a nice slow jog."

Zeus came down on all fours again, nuzzling his great head against her hand. He whined again piteously.

"I'll stay with him," Jess offered, reaching through the cage to stroke his head. There was something expert about her movements, and Jil smiled as she followed Henri back to his office. Not an animal lover, huh?

Just as they were getting inside, the phone rang. Henri sprang for the receiver like he'd been expecting the call for hours.

"Hello?" he said. Almost immediately, his shoulders slumped. "Uh huh." Then, even more slowly, "Uh huh. Okay. Thanks then. If that's the best you can do, I'll see you tomorrow."

"Problems?" Jil asked.

"Oh, nothing. My car's not ready, that's all." Henri waved his hand.

"You're not still driving Old Yetta?" Jess asked, coming in as Henri handed Jil a stack of papers.

"Yetta's in the shop." Henri shook his head. "Alternator's kaput. I was hoping to have her by tonight, but the part didn't come in, and they couldn't quite get 'er done. Lucky for me, they're open on Saturdays, so they said they'd get it done tomorrow."

"Do you need a ride?" Jess asked.

"No, no. I'm okay for tonight. It's tomorrow I'm worried about. Rockford Transport is striking at midnight. No buses. No streetcars. No way to come to work."

"Yeah, I heard that on the news tonight," Jil replied. "Contract problems."

"I don't know how I'm gonna get here," Henri sighed. "It's not like I can walk. And just try to get a cab."

"Well, I'd lend you my car, but then I'd have to sleep here with you," Jess laughed.

"Oh, I'll take you home," Jil offered.

Henri's eyes brightened.

Jess hesitated for a minute.

"Oh, hey, don't worry about it," Henri said quickly. "I'll figure it out tomorrow. That's a beaut of a Jeep you've got there anyway, Jessie. I wouldn't feel right about drivin 'er."

"No, it's not that," Jess said quickly. "I'd trust you with my car in a heartbeat. It's just that I live so far east that I don't want to inconvenience Julia. We're supposed to get twenty centimeters of snow."

"Don't worry about it," Jil assured her. "I really don't mind taking you home. You can lend Henri your car and we'll come pick it up—and get Zeus—tomorrow. Okay?" *Why don't you mind your own business? Stop cozying up to the suspects!*

Jess and Henri both smiled. "Great," they said at the same time. Jess handed over her keys and followed Jil out to the car.

Outside, the snow had begun to fall lightly in the downtown core while the nightlife got underway. Fridays in downtown Rockford boomed with music and dancing, live theater and cocktails, restaurants and delicious appetizers at high-end bars.

"It's been forever since I was downtown on a weekend," Jess said, shaking her head as they passed by the waterfront. That's where all the action happened. Rockford had the glamour of Toronto and the beauty of Ottawa, and the nightlife that danced between them both.

"Want a drink?" Jil asked, seeing her favorite restaurant up ahead.

"Why not?" Jess replied. "It's kind of sad to go home alone on a Friday night, isn't it?"

"That's kind of what I was thinking."

Jil circled the block, looking for a parking spot—an art within itself. She got lucky when a young couple walking ahead of them got into a car. She swiftly pulled in as they pulled out, leaving the car behind her to circle the block again.

"Nice work," Jess said.

"Now there's a word I don't want to hear again tonight."

Jess seemed to hesitate.

"Julia..."

"What's up?"

"It's just..."

"You're wondering how unprofessional this is?"

Jess nodded. "Maybe this isn't such a good idea."

"What? Going out for drinks, or hanging out with me?"

"Well...maybe both."

"Listen, I promise I won't tell anyone what your beverage of choice is."

Jess smiled. "Yeah, okay. Though I think there are probably worse things about me you could tell."

Jil pushed her tongue against the inside of her cheek. "Touché."

Bowties was a granite-countered, black-tiled affair with dim pendant lights hanging from the bar and private booths up and down both sides of the restaurant. "For two?" asked the server, a redhead clad in a strapless mini-dress. She grabbed two menus from the stack and held them to her chest. They were large enough to cover her entire dress, so as she stood there waiting, she suddenly looked naked. The same thought seemed to occur to Jess, because she exchanged a look with Jil.

"Right this way, ladies," the server said, smiling.

As she led them to a table near the front of the restaurant, Jil leaned toward her. "Listen, there are some people we're sort of trying to avoid."

"Oh. Well, there's a booth in the back alcove if you like. Usually it's for corporate dinners, but tonight it's empty."

"That'd be great."

She set down menus and signaled to a well-dressed young busboy, who set down a crystal jug of water and some glasses.

"Nice place," Jess commented as she settled into the sheltered booth.

"I used to come here a lot as an undergrad," Jil answered.

"Religious studies, right?"

Careful, Jil reminded herself. Just because she was having a little social time didn't mean she could blow her entire investigation. She was walking a pretty thin line as it was. "And philosophy." That much was true.

"Well, I know you're not twenty-three, so what did you do in between school and teachers' college?"

Jil winked. "How do you know I'm not twenty-three?"

Jess laughed. "Because if you were, we would definitely not be sitting here."

Jil took a drink of her water to stall. Somehow, took a Police Foundations certificate and spent five years at a PI agency didn't seem right. "I traveled," she said. She had. Some. "You?"

"Math," came the unexpected reply.

"You're a number junkie?"

"Yep. I was going to be an engineer."

"What stopped you?"

"My parents. They were traditional. Thought women should teach and men should build things."

"So?"

"So…I graduated from McGill and went to teachers' college."

"Then chucked tradition and became the youngest principal in the board?"

Jess laughed. "Yeah, actually."

"At twenty-three?"

"Um, no. Thirty-two."

Jil shook her head. Another naked server approached. "Can I get you ladies anything to drink?"

"Whisky sour, please," Jil answered.

"Vodka martini, three olives," said Jess.

"Coming right up. Will you be having dinner?"

Jess shook her head. "Not for me, thanks. I ate already."

"In that case," said the server, "I recommend the three-dip bread appetizer. It's light, but really good."

"Okay, sure," Jess agreed.

"Thanks." Secretly, Jil liked this little reversal of roles. She would ignore the conflict of interest for the time being. Pretend she was actually going to investigate Jessica and this was an undercover dinner. She didn't know how she'd figure this out, but she would. All she cared about right now was Jess's intense green eyes following her—alight with secrets she wanted to uncover.

"I still can't believe you're a math whiz."

"Yeah, well, we all have our guilty secrets." At that, her face darkened for a second.

The server returned with their drinks. After a few sips, Jess relaxed into the seat cushion, and sighed. "It's nice to be out."

"You spend too much time alone."

Jess raised her eyebrows.

"So who's what's-her-name?"

Jess didn't answer right away, but her eyes flashed before she turned her attention to her drink. "Henri shouldn't have said that."

Jil knew she should take it back, tell Jess to forget she'd said anything. She shouldn't know the answer to that question. No good could possibly come of it. But somehow she couldn't bring herself to retract the words. She wanted to know everything there was to know about Jess Blake: her past, her inclinations, what made her tick, what made her cry. But in the same breath, she wanted to tell Jess to get up and walk out—not to say another word, because she had a job to do, a job that involved uncovering secrets about this woman for a reason that had nothing to do with simple curiosity. And her job had to come first, no matter what her feelings were.

And yet, even knowing that finding out these answers would put her in a terrible and impossible position, she couldn't resist staying quiet, letting Jess collect her thoughts. Listening, as she spoke.

"Lily."

"That was her name? Was it her ring you lost?"

"Did I tell you someone found it?"

Jil just raised an eyebrow.

"It turned up mysteriously in my office." Jess's eyes probed hers. But Jil wasn't letting anything slip.

"I'm glad."

She let silence fill the space for a moment longer, but Jess didn't change the subject.

"So what happened with Lily?"

Jess flinched—whether it was from the admission she was about to make, or because of the way things had gone with this woman—and Jil had an almost irresistible impulse to reach across the table and hold on to Jess's hand, just to make it easier. But if this wasn't bad enough already—being in a public place—that would make it ten times worse.

"Lily was…an artist," said Jess. "She was absolutely beautiful. She sculpted—amazingly. Very talented."

"What did she sculpt?"

"Nudes, mostly. Men and women. Women and women. Whatever. She had some pieces in the National Art Gallery a few years back. Last year too, actually."

"Lily…Not Lily Anderson?" Jil said, squinting.

"You know her work?"

"Yes, actually. My—" She stopped, realizing she had been about to say "my boss." "Friend," she interrupted herself, "is an art fan. I think he has one of her pieces on his desk. It's a woman cradling a baby."

"Yep. That would be her."

"Wow," Jil said, impressed. She loved that sculpture. Had no idea why Padraig, of all people, would treasure it, but Padraig was nothing if not surprising.

"But you aren't with her anymore."

"No."

Jil waited again, but Jess's face had closed.

"She found someone else," she said simply. "A better partner, a better lover, I don't know. Someone who could dote on her and appreciate her art."

"Didn't you?"

"What? Appreciate her art? As much as I could, but she wanted someone who could go out to functions with her. Who could hang on her arm and…"

"And you couldn't."

"No."

Jil felt like she was pulling a very painful stitch out of Jess's skin, and that any small snag might send her screaming from the room. Still, she knew there was more.

"And what happened?"

"The other shoe dropped. It was just too much weight in our already heavy fairy tale. I turned thirty-five and suddenly developed a problem with my joints."

"Like an arthritis?"

"Sort of. My hips and hands swell and get stiff. Not very attractive when…" She blushed and shook her head. "Anyway, she was younger, of course, so this was like a giant Old Age symbol."

"You are kind of young for that, aren't you?"

"Yeah. Just a bit."

"And she…?"

"She broke it off, changed her number like I was some stalker."

"Jess, I'm really sorry."

Jess swallowed hard and tried to smile. “At least I have my very fulfilling career,” she muttered.

And there it was. Exactly the reason why both of them were in that room, in that booth, in the darkest corner of the restaurant. Because of their very fulfilling careers. Jil couldn’t walk away from her investigation; Jess couldn’t compromise her professional integrity.

“How the hell can you stand working there?”

Jess shrugged. “One day at a time, I guess. Same as you.”

“But why did you go into this, when there are a thousand other jobs you could do that would be easier?”

“Easier? Who said I wanted easier?”

“Yeah, okay. But you could at least settle for honesty. Don’t you hate having to lie?”

“And are you asking me these questions, or yourself?” Jess demanded. “You’re walking the same path I am, Julia, but you don’t have the seniority to protect you.”

“I don’t need that kind of protection,” Jil said. “And I don’t lie, either.”

“There’s no need to lie. People don’t ask, and that’s the whole point. There may be rumors—not that I’ve heard any—but I doubt anyone would ever challenge me directly.” She looked over her shoulder, leaned in farther as if she were afraid the walls were listening.

“What about indirectly?” Jil pressed, everything in her heart making her want to blurt out the one fact that would get Jessica to open her eyes to the situation. Someone was investigating her. Someone sitting at the very same table, nursing an almost-empty whiskey sour.

“You mean, having to come to work every day and preach a system that thinks my relationship with Lily was an abomination?” Jess said, a trace of amusement still around her mouth. “No, you’re right. It is difficult to be surrounded by people who think so.”

“Yes!”

“Julia, it’s not like I deliberately set out to do this. When I first started teaching in the Catholic Board, it wasn’t complicated. I was married.”

“To Mick?”

“We’ve been married for ten years.”

“Wait, you’re not divorced?”

“No.”

No wonder Jil couldn't find any divorce records at the courthouse. "Well, then how were you and Lily…"

Jess sighed, before taking a slow sip of her drink. "I never quite know how to explain this to people."

"What?"

"Our situation."

"Well, I have time."

Jess sighed. "Six years ago, Mick was on a hunting trip with his buddies. It was deer season, and there were a group of them that always liked to go together. It was dark when they left in the morning, and they were excited about the first trip of the season. Of course Mick hadn't ever driven an ATV before…"

"Jess…"

"It's okay. I can tell you. They were almost to the edge of the woods. He was driving pretty fast, and something came loose behind him, so he reached back to grab it before it fell off."

"Oh my God."

Jess exhaled slowly. "His ATV hit a tree stump, and he went flying. His buddies told me he just went sailing into that tree. Hit his head."

"He died?" Jil whispered.

Jess leaned back against the bench and twirled her wine. "No," she said softly. "He didn't die. They got him to the hospital and put him on some machines, just to wait to see if he would eventually come around."

"He was in a coma, you mean?"

"He had a severe concussion, but they wanted to give him a chance. See if they could reduce the swelling and get him back. But he hasn't come out of it yet."

"Are you saying he's still in a coma?"

"Mmm hmm."

"And you're still married?"

"In sickness and in health," Jess whispered. "The September after it happened, I became the VP at St. Catherine's. Nobody knew me there. Nobody knew Mick. They just saw my wedding ring and the picture of him on my desk and assumed…so no one talked to me about my personal life."

"Never?"

"If they did, I switched the topic."

Jil sighed. "But doesn't that drive you crazy? How can you get to know your colleagues, and how can they get to know you if you can't participate in any conversations?"

"I don't need to get up close and personal with my staff."

Jil pressed her tongue into her cheek, and leaned back, deliberately not stating the obvious.

Jess shot her a look, acknowledging the clear exception. "Okay," she said quietly. "I will admit that occasionally it's hard to live my life in a box."

"Occasionally?"

"Well, when I met Lily…"

"Yeah, exactly. How would you explain that?"

"You get used to it, really. The more you learn to just go along every day, talking only about work—speaking vaguely about your weekend, only using 'I,' never 'we.' It's amazing how quickly it becomes routine."

"But it's wrong, Jess. It's wrong that you have to hide who you are in order to keep your job."

She shrugged. "Yes, it's true. But it's the only way I can do what I love to do."

"Why not switch? Why not go over to the public board?"

Jess smiled wanly—looked down at her hands. "I've thought about it," she said quietly. "Really. But there didn't seem to be any reason I should have to. My superiors at the board know about Mick. They say nothing to me, because they don't want to be indelicate. And honestly, even if I were divorced, it probably wouldn't matter that much. Divorce really isn't uncommon. If you don't discuss it openly with your students, no one faults you for it."

"But it's still in the contract, is it not?"

"Yes. Technically, it is. And technically, if someone wanted to make an issue out of it, a divorced teacher could be challenged. But to be perfectly honest, the only thing people really take issue with is 'living in sin,' especially if there's a pregnancy."

"Sure. Or several children and no marriage certificate. I know for a fact that some of the teachers are living together and they're certainly not married."

Jess raised an eyebrow. "And that wouldn't be something I'd want to hear about."

Jil rolled her eyes. "Point taken. But it still happens."

"Of course it does. You think I don't know that there are members of my staff who have kids together and only wear rings because it's convenient? Of course I know. Ninety percent of the staff couldn't explain Advent or Lent or any other religious observation. There are at least three gay teachers, present company excluded. I don't want to know. Living in sin—together but unmarried, or together and gay—that's the biggie. And that's what we don't talk about."

Jil sighed. This was all very interesting, but all way too close to home for her to be comfortable. Still, she had to ask.

"So what about you?"

Jess exhaled a long breath, then tilted her head up, her eyes locking with Jil's, deep with mystery and intelligence. God, she was beautiful.

"Too personal."

"Really?"

Jess just closed her eyes and leaned back a little, her cheek pressed into the bench, like she was trying to physically ward off the impulse to spill everything. "I can't, Julia."

"Tell me."

Jess shook her head. Her lips twisted to one side like she was trying not to cry. "Religious education," she said with a note of irony. "Couldn't you have taught gym or something?"

Jil shrugged. "I'm fascinated with faith. Basketball doesn't do it for me. Neither does calculus. You know, there are plenty of jobs for engineers out in the world. Just saying."

Jess shrugged. "I just can't imagine giving it up. Honestly. I love teaching. I love the school. It's what keeps me going. When Lily left, I thought maybe I could flip the switch back, that maybe it was just her. I know I can't be in a relationship with a woman and work in the Catholic school board, but I also know that I can't change who I am, and that I can't give up my job. So I just keep going, day after day, hoping that something will change."

"Well," Jil said, her analytical mind working out a loophole. "You're technically not a lesbian. Technically, you had a past transgression. I assume you went to Confession?"

"Of course. I was still married. It was an affair, and I had to confess it."

"So, now you're on hiatus."

"Sort of like you?" Jess said, smiling a little.

"Kind of."

"Do you want some advice?" Jess asked frankly.

"Sure."

"Get out now. While you still have time to build a career somewhere else. Go public. It'll be a lot easier."

"What if I don't want easier?"

"Well, then, you're asking for trouble. But then again, I guess I'm playing with fire tonight too."

"How so?"

Jess just stared at her, hard.

Jil felt her breath constrict. "Oh," she muttered. Then, a few moments later, "What makes you think you can trust me?"

Jess cocked her head to the side, her eyes locking on Jil's again in that strange way that sent electricity running from the base of her neck straight down to her knees. "I don't know," she said. "I don't believe you would sell out. And so I don't think you would betray a friend. A confidence."

"But what if someone asked me directly?"

Jess thought for a moment. Perhaps this wasn't something she'd considered. Then she shook her head. "They won't. They don't ask. And we don't tell."

The appetizers came, and Jil asked for a glass of wine. "Just a six-ounce," she said. She still had to drive Jess home.

"What about you?" Jess asked. "What's your story?"

"What do you mean?"

"Were you ever married?"

"Nope. Got a long line of broken hearts to prove it," Jil joked, looking down.

"No one serious?"

"Not really. Not until Tara."

"How long ago—"

"Almost a year. She's engaged to some guy she used to work with, and they're expecting a baby sometime after Christmas."

"You're kidding."

"Nope."

"Does that, um, happen often?"

"That I turn women straight, you mean?"

"No! That women go back to men."

Jil looked at her. She seemed genuinely curious. Maybe she still believed she'd be one of the one-off lesbians. Which was yet another reason Jil should stay as far away from her as possible.

If only she didn't feel like invisible strings connected their every move…

"So Tara was it? There was no one else?"

She shook her head. Keep your distance. "I've never been really good with the whole U-Haul deal. I like my own space. I like to own my own things. Come and go, work when I like, you know?"

Jil's wine arrived, and she twirled it around, watching the dark burgundy liquid leave a clear trace around the sides of her glass as she tipped it delicately back and forth. Suddenly, the lights dimmed. Why do restaurants do that?

"Coming home to one person can be nice too," Jess said.

"If it's the right person."

"Yes. Not like my parents, for example." Jess shook her head. "Good Catholics, right to the end. Even if it meant sleeping in separate rooms and having designated shower and kitchen-use times."

"You're kidding."

Jess laughed. "Nope. Their latest silent match has lasted at least three years. Once, they had one that lasted from the time I was seven to the time I was eleven. I don't know what that one was about, but then one day, they just started talking again, and it was like it had never happened. She said, 'I've made pancakes,' and he said, 'I'll have syrup with that,' and they just picked back up talking again."

"Jess, that's awful!"

"Well, they're just so ridiculous that you have to laugh. All week they don't speak to each other, but Mom still cooks all the meals, and Dad still does all the banking. He gets up in the morning, and she bangs his bacon and eggs down in front of him, then goes into the living room and has her coffee. Then, when he's finished, she makes herself some toast while he goes out. She cleans and he reads. Then, she bangs down his ham sandwich and she watches TV while he eats. The only time they get together is to go to Mass, when they meet in the car and drive in silence all the way to the church. Hey, God! Just so you know, we're mortally unhappy, but we're still hanging on to our vows, come hell or high water!"

"I can't imagine that," Jil said. "Sooner or later, I'd snap."

"No kidding. I almost killed them myself years ago. Funny enough, they both agreed I should be in teachers' college, not in engineering."

"Yeah, well, nothing like a wayward daughter to bring a family closer together. Hey, it's not like you came home pregnant, or anything out of wedlock, right?"

"No," Jess murmured. And there was a sadness around her mouth that made Jil regret her words.

"Sorry," she said, searching Jess's face, "I didn't think."

"No, no. I just…"

"I'm sorry."

"I always wanted a baby, but it just never happened for Mick and me. I still wonder if I could have one, someone to hold and rock and love like crazy. I want a family. I want to buy backpacks and school clothes, and go to parent-teacher interviews, sitting on the other side of the table." The tremble in her voice made Jil chuck inhibitions and reach across the table, folding her warm hand over Jess's. There it was—that electric heat. The jolt. The instant connection.

Jess took her hand away and smiled ruefully. "Sorry," she whispered.

Jil looked down. "Ever think of adoption?"

"The adoption option. Yes, I'm familiar with it. They're dying to give out babies to single mothers who work a seven-day stretch."

"What about an older kid? One who already needs backpacks and parent-teacher interviews?"

Jess smiled. "I might think about it. Hey, if you can get a Great Dane, surely I can get a five-year-old, right?"

"Sure. It's just like online shopping. Click on the picture, add it to your cart."

Jess laughed out loud this time. When the server brought the check, Jess reached for it. Jil gently pried it out of her hands.

It was worth the business expense to have found a technicality that would give Jil a valid excuse to check Jess off her list. Her relationship with Lily had been an indiscretion. A fluke. Not a lifestyle.

Chapter Sixteen

Outside, the snowplows were already out. Five centimeters had fallen, and it was still coming down fast. Jil and Jess picked their way carefully through the snow and ice to where the on-loan Jimmy stood waiting. The sudden wind pushed hard against them. "I can barely see," Jil said as she started the engine and pulled out of the space.

"It's really blizzarding," Jess remarked in surprise, watching the whirling white flakes hurl themselves kamikaze-style at the windshield. The heater still blasted freezing-cold air, and Jil blew on her hands to warm them.

"Gloves?" Jess asked, holding up a black leather pair that were resting, as usual, on the console.

"No, thanks," Jil said. "I like to feel the wheel."

Jil inched her way down the waterfront road, keeping a good distance behind the car in front of her. It was an older model, and she had her doubts about its driver. Icy patches gleamed, black and hostile, and Jil shifted into four-wheel drive, frowning as she watched the road intensely.

Jess sat quietly next to her, staring out the window at the snowdrifts building by the minute. At the first stop sign, the car in front tried to brake, and slid the full length of the intersection before recovering. Luckily, there was no opposing traffic.

Jil stopped, carefully, and waited at the stop sign for a full minute, allowing more distance between herself and that car.

"Good idea," Jess murmured.

When they'd started out only a few minutes ago, she could still see the road. Now, she could barely see past her own front bumper. "It'll be better once we get past the lake," Jil said, trying to comfort Jess, whose cheeks looked drawn. She continued forward, at a crawl, ignoring the blinking lights behind her. If that idiot wanted to pass, he could, but it was his funeral. Suddenly, a little Mazda came barreling up beside both her and the impatient guy behind. The driver swerved right around her car and promptly began fishtailing across the road.

"Moron," Jil muttered as she braked again, preparing for the consequences of his stupidity. The car behind her backed off, seeing the Mazda's frenetic jostling.

The Mazda spun out ten feet in front of her, and with a scrunch, its front bumper collided with a snowdrift, wedging it there. The driver got out, slammed the door, and swore. Jil didn't stop. Neither did the car behind her. If he wanted to drive like an asshole, he could dig himself out of the drift.

On the highway, the ploughs had created a clearer path than on the waterfront road, but it was still icy as hell, and the wind blew strong. Jil normally liked driving an SUV, but these trucks were top-heavy—not the greatest thing to drive in gale-force winds. "How far east are you?" she asked.

"Bates Drive."

Jil exhaled slowly. That was at least twenty kilometers. Probably seven more exits after her own. Then she'd have to double back in this.

Minutes in, freezing rain began to pound the windshield, thicker and heavier than any Jil had ever seen. "What the hell is with this?" She struggled to see the white lines. Cars and tow trucks with flashing lights punctuated the highway lanes like Christmas decorations set out for the occasion.

Suddenly, the traffic stopped dead. Jil saw the brake lights ahead of her just in time to come to a complete stop—praying the car behind her could do the same. She noticed it was the same car that had been behind her at the waterfront. As the traffic ahead inched forward, she crawled over to the next lane—closer to the off-ramp. The car behind her did not move up to take her place. He moved over too.

A police officer rapped on the passenger side window. Jess lowered the glass.

"Road's closed up ahead," he said. "Had a bad accident. We're redirecting traffic off the highway. Are you ladies close to home?"

"I am," Jil replied. "She's not. We still have to get to Bates."

The police officer shook his head. "I'd get inside if I were you. Storm watch is in full swing, and this freezing rain is supposed to continue for the next three hours. Combined with the snow we've already got, driving's getting pretty dangerous out there."

"Where does the road reopen?" Jil asked.

"Not until Bay Street." A three-exit closure. Must have been some accident.

"Oh—here you go. Your lane's next, ladies. Keep to the right and follow the car in front."

Jil inched her car slowly down the off-ramp. The unfortunate thing about Rockford was the dearth of alternative routes. The main six-lane highway was complemented by three or four major streets, and a whole slew of side streets, but very few connected in any logical grid pattern—mostly due to the lake—and it made traveling from one end of the city to another a bit of a problem.

"Sorry," Jess muttered, looking out at the weather. "You can just drop me off at the nearest hotel, and I'll take a cab back to the SPCA tomorrow to pick up my car."

"I guess it's a good thing you lent it to Henri," Jil said. "He'd never get into work tomorrow."

"Yeah. And it's a good thing it's Saturday, and I have all day to try to get downtown in the mess this is going to make."

"Now, now…charity begins at home," Jil teased her.

Jess smiled.

"I have an extra bedroom. Why don't you come home with me?"

"But I don't have anything with me," Jess said.

"Um, last I checked, hotels didn't provide PJs either."

Jess shook her head and sighed. "I don't think…I'm not prepared for…"

"What? Weather in Eastern Ontario?"

"No. Being…without…you know…"

"Control?" Jil ventured.

"Well, I was going to say my stuff."

"You like structure. I get it. But what else are you going to do? I'm pretty sure I can find you something to wear. I might even have an extra toothbrush that I haven't used. Possibly some slippers, though you'd be pushing it."

Jess shook her head.

Jil turned back to the road, though she'd barely moved, and guided the car down the first side street that came available. As she neared the end of the road, she looked in her rearview mirror to see the same car following her. Now she knew she wasn't being paranoid. Her fingers tensing on the wheel, she sped up as the car behind her sped up. She wasn't going to be run off the road by this ass-hat in his little car. She had a truck for a reason. Shifting into higher gear, and thankful for her heavy-duty snow tires, she wound through snow-covered roads, crunching through them like they were gravel. If Jess noticed a change, she didn't comment.

The car behind swished and swerved, but kept pace with her, until one particularly snowy road slowed him down a few yards. Jil brought the truck out to a main road—a road without lights—and waited only a few seconds before darting across in the first available pocket of space. Cars, bumper to bumper, immediately closed the gap. Right away, Jil turned down a short road, and down another one, doubling back on where she'd just come from.

"Miss a turn?" Jess asked.

"Forgot I needed gas," Jil replied. She still had half a tank. She found a gas station anyway and pulled in, glad for a moment's rest, and for the bright light of the station. Her heart was beating quickly, and she felt perspiration creeping down her shirt, under the heaviness of her woolen coat. She brushed her hair away from her face, noticing—at this rather inopportune time—that the weather had made it genuinely curly. For once. She scanned the streets—what she could see of them—and took a look in the backseat of the car, for safe measure. It was empty.

While she pumped, she took out her phone. "Padraig, it's me," she whispered. "Someone's tailing me."

"What does he look like?"

"Four-door sedan. Dark blue. Ford."

"Where are you?"

"I pulled into a service station a few blocks away from the loft."

"What are you doing out in this weather?"

"I'm heading home now."

"See that you do. And try to lose the tail before you get there. I don't like the idea of someone following you to your front door."

"I'll do my best."

"Chet's not far from where you are. Park inside tonight, and I'll get him to sit on your street and keep watch for a few hours."

"Okay. Thanks."

To take a little more time, Jil squeegeed the windshield and mirrors, and added some gas line antifreeze. Even though you're supposed to do it before you pump the gas, she thought, hoping Jess wouldn't notice. She did.

"Don't you usually put that in first?" she asked.

"Yeah. You're supposed to. I forgot it," Jil said, sliding back into the car.

"Distracted?"

Jil didn't answer, just started the engine. She was a whole lot more distracted when, as she pulled out of the gas station, she felt Jess's hand slipping naturally, warmly, into her own. "You're freezing," she whispered.

"Wind chill."

"You should wear gloves."

"Can't."

"Why? You like the dangerous possibility of having your hand freeze to the gas pump?"

Jil grinned. At the stoplight, while the light was interminably red, she kept her eyes very firmly on the road in front of her, but found it impossible not to be drawn into Jess—the very essence of her, so close and so warm in the car beside her. She smelled of lilac and vanilla, and her hand, so delicate and so strong, was resting comfortably there, in Jil's own, which was growing less freezing by the minute.

The light stayed red, and Jess stayed close.

"Julia," she whispered.

Jil turned, her head bowed low, that old unwelcome pricking at the back of her eyes thwarting her efforts to keep her face totally neutral. Jess squeezed her hand lightly and left it there.

Jil didn't pull away.

The light turned.

"Green light," Jess said and Jil pulled forward again.

On her own street, the snow hadn't been plowed, but a car had already come down this way, its tracks making a nice following point for Jil's truck. She crunched through the ice and into the narrow passage to the underground parking garage.

She didn't need to look twice to know that Chet was parked in a car across the street. But still, her heart rate could not decelerate to normal.

"It's nice and warm in here." Jess smiled as she performed the good old Canadian triple-stomp onto the front mat.

"Yeah. Perks of being on the top floor. Do you want something to drink?"

"Um, okay. Maybe some tea."

"Herbal?"

"Yeah. Thanks."

Jil hung up their coats on the antique coat rack Elise had given her, and stood their boots on the mat by the door to dry. Not something she would normally do, but she wasn't quite sure where to put herself. Jess, on the other hand, wandered through the open-concept space into the kitchen.

Jil realized that her chart and notebook were on the living room table. Quickly, she brushed by Jess and veered left, piling the compromising materials together and pushing them far under the couch.

"Hiding your underwear?" Jess called from behind the butcher block island.

Jil laughed nervously. "Yeah, I'm not quite ready to show you all my pretty little thongs."

Jess stood in the doorway and watched as Jil folded a quilt.

"Don't you think it's a bit late for housekeeping?" she said. "I've seen your office at school, remember?"

She smiled. "Yeah, well, I've been a bit busy."

In truth, the house was probably the cleanest it had been since she'd moved in. With her cleansing rampage after Tara left, and the fact that she was hardly ever home to befoul the place, there was hardly even a speck of dust.

"You're neater than I expected, given your work environment."

"How do you know?" she asked.

"Spot check," Jess replied, unfazed, as she tucked her feet up underneath her on Jil's dark suede couch. "I check everything out from the doorway once a week. When things get out of hand, you'll find a blue slip of paper in your mailbox with a friendly reminder to 'keep the workspace clean.'"

Jil sat next to her, leaning on the opposite armrest. "Are you serious?"

"Of course," Jess replied. And she wasn't kidding. "I don't like a slovenly school. We're professionals."

"How come I've never got a blue slip?"

"Just lucky, I guess. You're borderline."

"I'll work on it."

"I expect you will."

They laughed softly. "I forgot to put your kettle on," Jil said, rising to go.

Jess laid a hand on her arm. "It's okay," she said. "I don't need tea anyway."

"Oh, wait." Jil took a remote control from the coffee table and pressed the big red button. A whooshing sound made Jess jump, and a fire roared in the gas fireplace.

"Nice!"

"Enjoy it for a sec. I have to go make up your room."

She bent down behind the couch and extracted her chart and notebook, which she carried upstairs to her office in the loft.

In three clicks, she finished the e-mail she had been composing earlier—the latest status report on the St. Marguerite's staff. Next to Jess's name, she changed the status from Not Yet Investigated to Investigated: No Violations to Report.

She filled in details for three other staff members and hit send. With any luck, they wouldn't ask her to dig deeper. And if they did, well, she'd have to figure it out then.

Just as she was turning off her computer, something bleeped. A message from FaithConnects. She clicked on it and the picture of a good-looking teenage boy smiled at her from the screen.

GunSlinger: Hi AlleyCat. Welcome to the fold.

She stared at it for a moment, trying to place the face, but she didn't recognize him.

It would have to wait until later.

Quietly, she locked her office door and opened the door to the guest room. The bed was made, the sheets were clean, and spare towels were tucked into the closet. She laid them out on the bed and dug around on the shelves for a packaged toothbrush. Bingo.

When she returned to the main level, she sat back down slowly and pulled a brown knit blanket off the back of the couch, opening it to share with Jess, who helped her arrange it.

"Soft," she remarked, fingering the material gently.

"My mother made it. She knit it from this yarn with a weird name."

"Angora?"

"Yeah! How did you know?"

"Lucky guess."

"Liar. Do you have a closet hobby besides calculus you'd like to share?"

"Okay, you'll think I'm a total loser, but yes, I can knit. I also play the bass."

"The bass guitar?"

"No. The giant bass that looks like an overgrown cello. And that's all I'm telling you. I'm finished with the embarrassing secrets."

"That's not embarrassing."

Jess just smiled and looked down at her hands, still fingering the delicate fabric. The silence stretched on, comfortably, as Jess took Jil's hands again, and ran her thumb lightly over her cold knuckles. She tilted her head and leaned forward.

Fuck.

Jil couldn't refuse her. Instead, she closed her eyes and met her halfway, kissing gently, running her fingers through Jess's short hair, stroking her cheek as her lips sought and pressed and found the right place to be. Right. Her lips and her heart knew what to do, even if she'd been battered and bruised and unsure before. She purposely did not think of the investigation or how she was going to explain this to Padraig. She just closed her eyes and jumped.

Jess kissed her back, and she didn't kiss gently. She kissed deeply and passionately and sweetly. "Are you sure?" she whispered.

"It's you I'm more worried about."

"I guess some things are worth going to hell for," Jess said ruefully.

"Oh, I don't think you're going to hell."

"Well, I guess that depends on what we're going to do next."

For a moment, Jil hesitated. She wanted so badly to tell Jess everything—to open the closet on all the lies and all the secrets. But she couldn't. If she did, she wouldn't have a job, and she wouldn't have Jess.

She didn't have to think about it long anyway, because Jessica's fingers were slowly undoing the buttons on her blouse, and she was trying to quell the shivers. Jess's fingers brushed slowly against Jil's skin, and rose goose bumps across her breasts.

"Cold?" she asked, drawing Jil's shirt closed again.

Jil shook her head. "No."

They undressed each other piece by piece, kissing and exploring. "You're, um, more gifted than I thought," Jil remarked.

Jess laughed. She shook her head, and guided Jil's mouth to her breast, her bare pink nipple standing expectantly, waiting for the warmth of lips to embrace it. She gasped when Jil's tongue made contact with her delicate skin, and she ran her hands over her bare back and shoulders, lightly stroking her with three fingertips.

Jess's nipples stood out hard, and she pulled Jil up to her mouth instead. She slid into her lap, straddling her as she kissed down her neck, pushing her into the arm of the couch.

Jil closed her eyes, letting Jess explore her, not minding that she lay naked under the blanket while Jess lay topless beside her.

"It's been a while," Jess whispered. "I hope I don't disappoint you."

Jil found it hard to talk as Jess's fingers traced a line down her chest and stopped. "I don't think it's going to be a problem."

Jess touched her lightly, then more firmly, across her chest and waist, and down her thighs.

Jil lay on her back, propped up on one pillow while Jess's fingers went to places she'd only dreamed they could go.

She probed gently, and then more insistently, and Jil let her legs come apart. Jess touched the soft skin of her inner thigh, and worked her way gently inward. When she made contact with the slick wetness there, Jil moaned and closed her eyes as her clit throbbed under Jess's soft stroking.

"Is it okay?"

"God yes." She hadn't felt so aroused in years. Jess circled her gently, her mouth and fingers touching every part of her, lighting her skin on a slow, smoldering fire.

Then her mouth was back on Jil's mouth, her fingers in one hot place between her legs, propelling her toward the cliff edge.

❖

For a moment, they lay in a tangle of limbs, with the blanket twisted between them.

When Jil opened her eyes, Jess was smiling. "Oh, you think you're so smug? Let me see how you like it."

Jess laughed as Jil pulled her into a straddling position over her hips, naked and exposed. "Are your curtains closed?" she asked, looking over her shoulder to make sure.

"Definitely." She ran her fingers up Jess's delicate rib cage and pinched her nipples lightly. They stiffened immediately.

"Harder," Jess whispered.

She obliged, squeezing the pink pebbles til they turned red, and Jess let out a moan that made her shiver. Jil teased her then raked her fingernails down Jess's sides to her waist. Heat pooled on her stomach where Jess's open thighs made skin-to-skin contact.

She pulled her closer, sliding her hands around the tops of Jess's thighs til her thumbs curved around her hot crease. Gently, she stroked farther and farther inward, teasing the delicate skin and stroking the pink folds.

Jess shuddered, slick juices wetting Jil's thumbs as she groaned. She arched her back and cried out, not in pleasure, but in pain.

Jil froze. "What's wrong? What happened?"

"Fuck," Jess said, leaning forward across her. "I'm so sorry. I have to get down."

Jil helped Jess maneuver herself into a sitting position on the couch, noting her white face. "What's the matter? Are you okay?"

"It's my hip," Jess groaned. "It spasmed." She leaned back against the opposite arm, letting her leg fall open. Her lips were pinched white as she gently straightened and bent her leg.

Jil watched her, frowning. "I guess the straddle doesn't really work for you?"

Jess shook her head. "I'm sorry, Julia."

That name snapped her back to reality. Jil felt guilt close in on her. What the hell were they doing?

"It's okay," she said soothingly. "Just try to relax."

Jess closed her eyes and massaged the top of her thigh, breathing through the pain.

"Sorry," Jil whispered, and laid her hand on top of Jess's, gently kneading the knotted muscles. "I guess this is what you meant by joint problems?"

"Yeah. Pretty damn inconvenient. I was having fun," Jess said, a small smile playing around the edges of her white lips.

"I'll bet." She winked, though Jess couldn't see. "Do you want me to run you a bath or something?"

Jess opened her eyes. "You don't have to take care of me."

"Sure I do. You're a guest in my house."

"Oh. And do you treat all your guests this way?"

"Um, no. Usually I don't invite anyone over in the first place."

Jess cracked a wan grin. "I like bubbles."

Jil laughed. "Coming right up."

When the water had reached halfway to the brim, and bubbles layered the surface in a soft creamy foam, Jil helped Jess climb in the tub. From the next room, her cell phone beeped.

"Enjoy," she said, closing the bathroom door behind her.

Padraig's number flashed across her screen.

"Hey, boss man, what's up?" Jil said, a little too brightly.

"Chet's sat there for an hour and hasn't seen anyone," Padraig said, getting straight to the point. "Except the girl you've got with you."

Jil froze. She'd almost forgotten about their tail, but sobered up when Padraig mentioned it. "I, uh…picked someone up at the bar."

"Don't let me interrupt you."

"Is Chet going home now?"

"As soon as you give the all-clear."

"I'm okay. Well, I will be tomorrow anyway. Got myself a watch dog."

"Seriously?"

"Yeah. I adopted a Great Dane from the shelter downtown."

"You must be joking. You're going to own a pet? Something living? Breathing? That needs to be walked and loved?"

"Shut up, will you? I'm—"

"What? You're not lonely are you?"

Jil swallowed past the lump in her throat. No, I'm not lonely… I've got plenty of company. Company she shouldn't have at all, let alone be having fun with.

"If more people would spay and neuter, there wouldn't be so many dogs in shelters," she said in her best TV voiceover. "But seeing as there are, I'm doing my part."

"By adopting a horse?"

"Yes. By adopting a horse. They happen to make fantastic apartment dogs. Now, is there anything else important?" She was sure Padraig hadn't even heard her over the sound of his own chuckling.

"No, that's all, Saint Kidd. Hope you enjoy your leather shoes tonight. Not to mention your expensive couch."

"Thank you ever so much. You will be the first one to fall in love with him; I guarantee it. Good night."

Chapter Seventeen

From the bathroom, she heard subtle laps of water, and the occasional groan as Jess stretched out her leg. She was suddenly overcome with fatigue. It had been a long week, a long night, and a really good—

"Julia?"

"Yeah?"

"Do you have a towel?"

"Yes, sorry. I'll be right there."

She ran upstairs to get the spares, then ran back down, double-checking her route to make sure no personal information was lying around. She kept everything in her locked office as a force of habit, but every once in a while, she'd toss a bill on the stairs.

Jess stood in the bath, bits of bubbles clinging to her flushed skin, her nipples standing out, soft and pink.

Jil held out the towel, trying not to stare. "You're hot," she said with a small smile.

Jess blushed. "That's why I'm getting out."

"So not what I meant." Jil brushed her teeth as Jess toweled off. "Do you want some pajamas?"

"Not particularly."

Jil laughed, laying out an extra toothbrush on the counter. "Suits me."

They slipped into bed, Jess's head cradled in Jil's arms. "I'm sorry about that," she said softly.

"Why? It's not your fault. I'm sorry you have problems like that. Makes sex a bit…"

"Of a chore?"

"Well, no, I was going to say challenge, but is it a chore for you?"

Jess sighed. "I'd kind of forgotten."

Jil stayed silent, waiting for her to explain. The dark enveloped them, and she ran her fingers lightly through Jess's hair.

After a moment, she went on. "I'd forgotten what it felt like to be really into the moment…and how much pressure it is when my body doesn't…and then going to bed feeling…"

"Disappointed?"

"Yeah, I guess so…like I'm disappointing."

Jil kissed the top of her head. "I'm not disappointed," she whispered.

Jess leaned in closer on her chest. "No?"

"No."

Silence followed, and Jil wondered what else Jess wasn't telling her.

"When I was with Lily, I had issues for a long time before we found out about my arthritis," she said at last. "I kept putting off going to the doctor, thinking I'd just overdone it jogging or gardening or something, so it went on for a year or more before I got treatment, and…"

"Wasn't that painful?"

Jess nodded. "Definitely. Everything hurt all the time, and I felt guilty about being such a drag. Lily wasn't very…she didn't understand, and she was such a fast-paced person."

"Impatient, you mean?"

Jess snorted. "Yeah, you could say that. When I stretched in the morning, or took too long in the shower, she'd get frustrated. I'd encourage her to go out on her own, and she did, but I always felt like I was letting her down. So when she wanted to make love, I'd make her come. Honestly, sometimes it just felt like she was using me as a quick get-off-and-go-to-sleep. We never…or she never…"

"You never worked it out, you mean?" Jil finished gently. "Found a way around it?"

Jess shook her head. "No. I felt like she was already making enough compromises in the relationship by being with someone in the closet, and add to that someone who was sick so often. So when I wasn't able to…do it like we used to, I just…let her think I didn't want…" Her voice trailed off and Jil squeezed her tighter.

"Jess, are you saying that you haven't had sex—like really had sex—since you got sick?"

"Yeah."

"So tonight…"

"When I said it had been a while…"

"You weren't kidding."

Jess sighed. "I should have remembered how hard it was."

"No," Jil said softly. "You should forget how hard it was. It shouldn't be hard, and it's not going to be. You are beautiful and sexy, and we will find a way for us to enjoy each other—not a way for you to please me and go to bed crying. Okay?"

Jess exhaled slowly, not saying anything for a long moment. "I can't believe I just said all that to you. What the hell are we going to do on Monday morning?"

Jil bit her lip. "I'm only there til December," she reminded her.

"Thank God. I don't think I could fake it any longer than that."

In the dark, Jil bit her lip and sighed silently. No fucking joke.

❖

When Jil woke up, the first streaks of dawn were just beginning to paint the sky. She looked over at the pillow next to her and froze. She felt so many things: joy at knowing last night wasn't a dream, panic at how she was going to ever explain her real identity to Jess, fear that she would lose everything she'd worked for because of this reckless decision, and this insistent tugging feeling in the pit of her stomach that drew her closer and closer to this woman sharing her bed.

The sheet had slipped down, exposing one of Jess's generous breasts. Jil felt heat gather between her legs. She'd never had the chance to finish what she'd started the night before. If straddling didn't work for Jess, maybe the good old missionary style would, especially if she were as relaxed as she looked right now.

For a full minute, she lay and watched Jess's deep, even breathing, her breast rising and falling with every inhale. Sex could be so easy. So slow and gentle and sweet. There was no reason at all that Jess shouldn't be able to enjoy it, and come hard.

Slowly, she let her fingers wander across Jess's shoulder and over her exposed throat.

Jess stirred but didn't wake. Her legs were entwined with the sheet. Should she do it? Take advantage of her relaxed, unsuspecting position? All she needed to do was push the sheet up a few inches higher…

She trailed her hand over Jess's thigh, up to her stomach.

Jess sighed in her sleep and turned onto her back. An invitation?

Jil's nipples hardened at the thought of everything she could do. Gently, she pushed the sheet up higher onto Jess's waist and let her fingers probe and stroke every inch of her legs, igniting, teasing.

Jess's legs fell open, but her breathing remained soft and even. She was still asleep. She sighed as Jil kissed along her pale thighs, licking lightly until she came to the slit.

Jil took her time stroking up the crease, into the pink folds that moistened in response to her touch. There, she slipped her tongue gently inside, probing the delicate cherry skin that bloomed open as Jess's thighs fell apart. She went slowly, licking and teasing until she found the hardening nub.

She heard Jess moan softly, felt her fingers pressing on her head. "Oh my God," she breathed. "What are you doing?"

That was all the encouragement Jil needed. She circled Jess's clit with her tongue, backing off the moment she felt her thighs tense. She waited until she had relaxed again, then pushed in gently, tugging lightly with her lips and teeth.

Jess raked her fingers through Jil's hair, moaning and guiding her mouth.

Jil massaged her thighs, relaxing any tense muscles before they had the chance to cramp. Jess's legs melted under her fingers, and she arched into Jil's mouth, sighing as her fingers traveled up to her nipples, tugging and tweaking.

Softly, Jess's hands covered hers, their fingers snaking together as they worked Jess's responsive nipples into hard, pulsing nubs.

"Okay?" Jil whispered.

Jess nodded, her face flushed. She bit her lip as Jil pinched one nipple, then the other one, harder. She gasped, open-mouthed, whimpering.

Jil hesitated.

"Don't stop."

She didn't. Below, she made firm circles with her tongue, flicking away from the most sensitive place, making the zone wider and hotter.

Jess shifted her hips.

"Too much?"

"Getting tense," Jess managed.

"Try putting your legs over my shoulders."

Jess obeyed and her hips relaxed. She gasped as Jil's tongue met her flesh again. "Christ, you're good at this," she groaned.

Jil could feel the tightening of her skin, the rock-hard pulsing of her clit. "You're going to come," she said, barely breaking contact.

"I know."

She licked and sucked until Jess arched her back, moaning softly, then louder. Her head ground into the pillow as her hips lifted to meet Jil's every move. Finally, she groaned deeply, her legs trembling as she collapsed against the pillows.

For a moment, they both lay still, then Jil disengaged herself from Jess's legs, and slid up the bed to lie beside her.

Jess turned away and drew the covers up, her back to Jil.

"Hey," Jil said softly, running her hand down Jess's spine. Jess's ribs shook, and Jil realized she was crying. "What's the matter?" she whispered. She snaked her arm around her smooth waist, holding her tight. "It's okay. You're okay."

"I just didn't…expect that," Jess whispered, her voice shaking.

"What? To come like that, or…"

"To wake up with someone trying to make me feel—"

Jil froze. "I'm sorry," she said. "Did I make you uncomfortable? Did you want some warning?"

"No," Jess broke in. "No, it was perfect. I didn't have time to worry about anything, or tense up. I was practically having an orgasm in my sleep and it just felt…so natural. So good. It was amazing…"

"Yeah? Well, I sort of think that's how things are supposed to go." She squeezed Jess tighter, putting her mouth to her ear. "So why are you crying?"

Jess laughed through her tears. "Because it's been a long time since someone cared about me enough to want to do that, to force me to have fun."

"Oh, that was more than fun," Jil said, kissing her temple. "That was downright hot."

"No kidding." Jess turned around, pulling Jil tight against her, their breasts pressing together as they kissed, deep and slow. "Thank you," she whispered.

Jil touched her face, her neck, her shoulders, letting Jess play with her tongue. "My pleasure."

When Jess dragged her teeth along Jil's lower lip, Jil felt slow fire igniting throughout her entire body.

Jess must have noticed, because she slipped her leg between Jil's, her thigh fitting hot and snug against Jil's pulsing groin.

Jil groaned. "Are you kidding me?"

Jess ran her hands down Jil's back, cupping her ass cheeks and pulling her closer so Jil rode her thigh, the friction between them making her cry out. With a surprising swiftness, Jess flipped onto her back and pulled Jil on top of her. She held her hips tight to steady her while Jil pushed up on her knees, riding Jess's thigh, and arching back.

Jess ran her hands up Jil's belly and chest, massaging her breasts and tweaking her nipples until she moaned. "It's not fair," Jil panted. "You can't do this."

Jess smiled, continuing the skillful use of her hands. "No, but I can watch you."

Jil ground against her leg, her slick juices easing the friction and making her head swim. Jess kept one hand on the small of her back and tweaked her nipples with the other. Occasionally, she'd pull Jil closer, and suck one of her aching breasts into her mouth before releasing her.

When Jil began to see stars, Jess slipped her hand between them and thumbed her screaming clit. Within a few deft strokes, Jil was plunging into a mind-blowing orgasm, arching and riding Jess's hand and leg, barely even noticing the bed frame cracking against the wall. She closed her eyes and threw her head back as the sensation enveloped her, and then she toppled down onto the bed, groaning and laughing.

Jess giggled too—a sweet sound coming from her otherwise serious mouth.

"All right, we need to get a grip," Jil said, flopping down on the pillow. "And maybe a shower."

Jess pushed up on one elbow and trailed a finger down Jil's breastbone, stopping just below her belly button. "I hate to get out of bed, but we have a dog to pick up. Not to mention a car."

Jil smiled, trying not to think too far ahead, purposely not thinking about Padraig and the investigation she had to pick up again on Monday morning.

❖

At the shelter, Zeus recognized them immediately. He whined and stomped, waiting impatiently for Henri to open the door to his enclosure.

"Got everything?" Henri asked as he leashed Zeus for Jil.

"Food, dishes, giant dog bed, a leash, and a few chew toys. Think that's enough to get me started?"

"Don't forget doggie bags." Henri grinned. "Extra-large."

Jess shoved him. "We went shopping this morning," she said. "I brought your list. Stop teasing her, or she might change her mind."

"Ahh," Henri said, a twinkle lighting his eye as he turned around. "Went shopping this morning, eh? Does that mean you never made it home last night, Jessie?"

Jess blushed and bit her lip. "Could be," she muttered.

He put his muscled arm around her and squeezed tight. "Good for you." She smiled when he kissed her cheek and put his lips close to her ear. "I like her a lot better than what's-her-name."

Jil grinned, taking the leash.

Henri winked. "At least this one likes dogs."

Chapter Eighteen

Jil reported to St. Marguerite's on Monday morning, her stomach doing nervous flip-flops and her palms sweating. How was she going to face Jess in the halls? What would they say to each other? How would they act?

Jess was probably reconsidering. She had to be. There was no way she'd ever compromise her job, and dating a teacher (or someone she thought was a teacher) couldn't possibly happen. No way. She had to think this was a mistake too.

It was a mistake. It could never happen again.

She bypassed the office—and that issue—and headed straight for her own space, three boxes of Tim Horton's donuts in tow. What the hell was she doing? This was going to end in disaster—no doubt. She was stupid and irresponsible. She should never have let herself get involved with a woman she was supposed to be investigating, no matter how beautiful or intelligent or captivating or sexy…

Even if she had found a loophole that excused Jess for now. If she was asked to reinvestigate, then turning in her report would end Jess's career—and not turning it in would compromise her own.

"Good Christ," Jil muttered to herself as she flicked on the lights and closed the door, leaning against the frame. Why did she always get herself into these situations? She couldn't tell Jess the truth. She couldn't lie to her anymore. She couldn't make good on her promise to investigate this school, and she couldn't get out of it.

What options did that leave?

Compile the facts, write the report, and duck out of there without ever looking Jess in the eye again? Pretend the feelings weren't there? Pretend she hadn't already fallen for the perfect woman? The perfect woman who was the principal of a Catholic school and who wouldn't abandon that belief system, even if it crushed her? Only to have Giovanni DiTullio pay her a visit and present her with a damning report Jil herself had created? No.

Could she just tell Padraig she wanted off the case and live with his disappointment? The knowledge that she'd single-handedly bankrupted the agency?

God, what a fucking mess.

And on top of that, they were starting a new unit today in World Religions. She was screwing Buck and scrapping the extra unit in Christianity. Instead, they were studying Paganism. Wicca, specifically. There—that was something she could teach. If she hadn't completely self-destructed already, she was certainly going to today.

She opened her bag to take out the folder she'd prepared over the weekend—mostly in an effort to keep her thoughts from straying to Jess. Her hair, her perfume, her touch. Everything about her. The way she giggled a little when she laughed out loud. Her delicate, soft hands. Everything.

It was almost the end of November. She had successfully rooted out information on eighty-two of the ninety-five staff members (including Jess). Of those eighty-two, forty were living in a situation that ran counter to their job descriptions. The infractions ran from divorce (eighteen); to cohabitation without the benefit of marriage (twenty-six); or both of those (ten); having children out of wedlock (three); same-sex relationships (three). Sixty had engaged in more minor infractions such as failing to report to church on Sundays. The only two with a perfect record so far were Buck—because she could not drag up any dirt on him no matter what she looked for—and Jess, because she'd filed her assessment before dragging her into a life of sin.

She had just under a month to scout out the remaining staff. That shouldn't be hard. Rosie McMonahan was a willing talker, and she seemed to have the information on everybody.

Jil set the kettle on and prepared to make a nice cup of tea. That's the only thing she'd been able to stomach all weekend. Not calling Jess made her feel terrible, but calling her would mean more lies, and she just couldn't do that. Not anymore. Again and again, she went over the ways to make this situation all right, but there just weren't any options. She just couldn't see a way out of this.

Someone knocked on the door.

Jil stood. "Come in," she called.

Bex opened the door and quickly shut it behind herself.

"What's the matter?"

Bex's face was flushed, and she was panting. She looked like she was going to pass out. "I ran to school," she said. "They followed me all the way from the dorm across the football fields."

"Who?"

"I don't know. They never get close enough so I can see their faces."

"They've done this before?"

Bex nodded. "Sometimes I see them hanging around outside the school—down the block. Sometimes they're in the mall, or waiting for me after practice. They never come near me. And they're always just out of range, you know?"

"You've never approached them, have you?"

"No," Bex said. "There's like seven or eight of them and only one of me, Miss. I'm not crazy. No matter who they are."

"Do you think they're students?"

"Yeah. One of them's Theo, I'm sure of it. But I don't know who the others are."

"Bex? Why did you run to school today?"

"Because, Miss. They were coming after me. They were walking toward me, real slow. They've never done that before. But then this morning, while I was waiting for Gideon outside the dorm, I saw them by the forest. They started coming. I waited a few seconds to see if they would shove off, but they didn't. They got closer and closer. So I ran."

"Have you told anyone?" Jil asked.

Bex shook her head. "No one to tell, Miss."

"Still. I'd like to get to the bottom of this. You think these are the same people who might have threatened Alyssa?"

"I don't know. But I got another note."

"Did you keep it?"

"No. I flushed it down the toilet."

Jil exhaled slowly, sinking into her armchair. She indicated her office chair, and Bex collapsed into it gladly.

"Are they all boys?"

"I don't think so. Mostly, but there are some girls. Seniors. Maybe some juniors. They're all pretty big. I saw them up closer this morning than I've ever seen them. They were all in white clothes. And jeans, I think."

Jil sighed inwardly. That described half the population of St. Marguerite's. The school colors were white and burgundy, and all the athletic teams wore school colors on game days. The tuck shop also sold long-sleeved white T-shirts to anyone who wanted them, and in the absence of a uniform, a lot of the students actually did purchase school clothes.

"All of them? Could they be members of a team?"

"I don't know, Miss. I didn't really let them get that close, if you know what I mean."

"Probably wise. Okay, listen, Bex. I want you to leave school on time today, with everybody else. Get to your dorm and stay put, okay? Do any of your friends live in residence?"

"Yeah. Joey and Kyle both do."

"Okay. Well, I want you to make plans with those two tonight. Maybe work on your group assignment. Okay?"

"We don't have a group assignment."

"You will by the end of class," Jil said grimly.

That solved two problems. One, how to keep Bex safe. Two, how to evaluate her students on a topic she hadn't thought to cover until this weekend. With Theo out of her class, she could get away with a little more diversity. But she hadn't run this new course direction by Jess yet. Which meant she would have to go and see her.

Which was probably for the best.

Bex stood to leave. "I'm going to grab some breakfast," she said.

"Good idea. See you in class."

"Thanks, Miss."

Jil watched the door close and waited for a few moments to make sure Bex was gone before picking up her phone. She dialed Jess's office.

"I need to talk to you," she said.

Jess's voice sounded a little guarded. "All right. Come on over."

Jil went around to the side door of Jess's office and knocked. She was already waiting, because the door creaked open immediately. The blinds on the windows were already drawn.

"Hi," she said, trying to smile.

Jil shut the door. "Hi."

They stood there for a minute, suspended in time. Jess turned and led Jil to the desk, sitting stiffly in her chair. Jil perched on the side of the desk, as usual.

"I'm sorry I didn't call," Jess said quietly.

Jil just nodded. "I understand why you didn't."

"You do?" Jess seemed surprised. "I thought maybe you'd be…"

"Offended?"

"Yeah."

"No. It's complicated, Jess. This whole thing is…"

Jess looked away, biting her lip. "A bad idea?"

"Yeah."

"I thought you might think that. It was unprofessional of me to go home with you, Julia. Not to mention completely against the rules. All the rules. I shouldn't have done it. I'm sorry. I'll understand if you don't want to talk to me anymore. I've violated your trust as a first-year teacher. You're my staff member—"

"Hey, slow down," Jil said. "I'm not a wandering sheep you've led astray. I'm the one who should apologize."

"For what?"

Jil kicked herself mentally. Shit. Why did she always have to open her big mouth? She should have kept quiet—just let Jess break it off before anyone got hurt any more. But she couldn't. She couldn't stand the idea of Jess beating herself up for something that wasn't her fault.

"Jess, we're two consenting adults. I wanted you to come home with me as much as you wanted to be there."

Was that a blush on Jess Blake's face? Was she embarrassed? God. She was new at this. Still practically a virgin to the women's world. "I'm sorry," she whispered. "I wish I could make this easier."

"It's not your fault either," Jess said. "I think we just got a little carried away. If you want to stop, that's fine with me."

Yes. Yes, that's what they should do. Stop right now and go their separate ways. Forget they ever saw each other. Before they ended up creating a complete mess.

"No," she said. "I don't want that at all."

Back in her office, Jil logged on to her FaithConnects account. She had three more messages from new friends—all of them from the same online group. Clarisse had written: *Nice to meet you, Ally. Join our Bible study!*

Jil wrote back. *Thanks. I'll think about it!* Could this be the same girl who'd sent messages to Alyssa?

The good-looking boy had sent her another message. *Hey AlleyCat. I've added you to our online TeenFaith group. Lots of kids from Rockford Catholic schools are in it. Welcome! What are you into? Music? Fishing? Hope we can be friends. :-)*

This time she responded. *Hey yourself. Would I see you around the halls?*

In a second, a message bleeped back at her.

You might. Would my charm and good looks be enough to hold your full attention? ;-)

So she'd been right to check the "interested in both" box. It had obviously triggered his attention. Some guys just couldn't resist the challenge of turning a wayward girl straight.

She clicked on the button to take her into the TeenFaith chat room. There were hundreds of past topics of conversation. She'd have to come back and investigate later. But Gunslinger seemed to be the leader of many of the forums. Maybe he was the Youth Leader Bex had talked about.

After a few more exchanges, Jil noticed the time. *Gtg. Class.*

Later, wrote GunSlinger.

Jil cursed herself as she gathered up her folders for World Religion. She had been so busy with the relationship conversation that she'd completely forgotten to run her course plan by Jess. Too late. It was time for class. In fact, most of the students had already arrived.

"Hi, guys." Jil dropped her stuff on her desk.

Bex gave her a little wave. She smiled back. Joey and Kyle were having a contest to see who could make the rudest noises. So far, Joey was winning. She flapped her cheeks in and out, creating a noise like wet fish hitting the docks.

"That's pretty good, for a girl." Kyle grinned. Joey stuck out her tongue at him.

"Good morning," Jil said. They looked up and saw the boxes of donuts on the desk, then erupted into cheers.

"We did it, yo!" Kyle shouted.

"What was our average?" Bex asked.

Jil smiled and popped open the first box. "Seventy-two."

"Two points over!" Joey crowed.

"Come and get your rewards, and let's settle down for today. We have a lot to get through."

"Yo, Miss. There's nothing on the syllabus for today. It says TBA. What is that, like Total Body Aerobics?" Jordan grinned at his own joke as he licked powdered sugar off his fingers.

"It means To Be Announced."

"So what's the announcement?" Kyle asked.

"Today we are starting a unit on Paganism."

The class looked at her in awe. "You mean, like heathens?" Jordan bellowed.

"No, scumbag," Brianna said scathingly. "She means Pagans. Like pre-Christian Goddess-worshipping. You know?"

"They think God's a woman?" Kyle said, sitting up. "Yo, that's sick."

"Why not?" Brianna demanded. "Why couldn't God be a woman? Women are responsible for bringing life into the world. Why would anyone assume God was a man?"

"God is not a woman," said Jordan, laughing.

"Yeah, you're right," Joey retorted. "The world's way too screwed up for any woman to have created it. It's gotta have been made by a man."

Jil listened to them bantering for a few more minutes before cutting in. "I thought that since we've studied four major religions this year, all of which focused on the male aspects of the divine, that it was time to look at the female aspects."

A lot of the girls were nodding, faces full of pastry. "All right!" Bex said.

Since Theo had dropped the course, Bex had become much more lively and engaged. It was really nice to see.

"Any of the boys have a problem with that?" Jil asked.

Most of them shook their heads. "Yo, as long as you don't ask us to start praying to God, the Mother, we're fine."

"This class isn't about teaching a belief system. It's about opening your eyes to the way other people view things. I think it's important that you get a good look at what the world thinks."

"Okay, Miss." And nobody made another smart-assed comment for the rest of the period. Not even when she assigned them a group project and read out the pre-assigned groups.

At the bell, she watched Bex approach Joey and Kyle.

"Hey, guys?" she said, not smiling. Her uncertainty made her come off as harsh.

"Hey, Bex," said Joey a little nervously. Bex had a reputation for being a bit tough. Jil knew they weren't friends, but she'd hoped they could maybe start to be friendly.

"So, do you guys want to get together tonight and start?" Her tone indicated "or else."

Kyle looked at Joey.

"Yeah, sure. Might as well get going," Joey said.

Kyle groaned. "Yo, I hate projects. I'm no good at this research shit."

"Yeah, but you sure are good at talking," Bex retorted. "You can do the presentation to the class."

Kyle actually cracked a smile. "You're on. You know I can run my mouth pretty good."

Jil smiled as she watched the three of them leave together for lunch.

Chapter Nineteen

"It's here," Jess said when Jil walked past her in the atrium.

"What's here?"

"The lockdown system."

Jil realized it wasn't delight she saw in Jess's face. It was disbelief. Fear that she actually needed this equipment in her school.

"Are they installing it now?" Jil took note of two men in navy coveralls busily circling the atrium.

"It'll be in by the end of the day," said Jess.

Jil exhaled. "I'm sorry."

"Me too. I can't believe it's come to this."

"Better safe."

Jess watched the workmen closely while she talked.

Jil oriented herself so she could watch the students at the same time. She scanned the crowd for GunSlinger, but the students' faces blended into one another as they passed, crammed into the overstuffed corridors. Maybe this student didn't exist. Maybe he was a catfish too.

"Listen, Jess, there was something about my lesson plan I wanted to run by you yesterday, but didn't get the chance."

"Oh. What was it?"

Just then, Buck Weekly approached. "Julia, good," he said. "Good morning, Ms. Blake."

Jess smiled.

"I wondered if I could have a word with you?" His steely eyes pierced their conversation, even more than his tense tone.

"What is it, Buck?" asked Jil politely.

"I have heard some rumors and I was hoping to dispel them," said Buck, his eyes boring into her. Why did Jess not seem to notice this?

"Rumors of my death have been greatly exaggerated," she quipped.

He didn't smile. "Is it true you're teaching Paganism in World Religions?" he barked.

Jil met his gaze unflinchingly. "I am teaching a unit in pre-Christian faiths, yes."

"Why?"

"Because I feel that it is important for the students in the class to experience a balanced view."

"Paganism is not a World Religion."

"It was before Christianity swept it out."

"You're teaching witchcraft."

"I most certainly am not," Jil snapped. "I am providing the students with information on a widespread religion that existed before Christianity, and still exists. They've studied four patriarchal religions, and I'm introducing the idea of God as a female."

"They burned people at the stake for this," Buck thundered.

"And you'd like to do it again, wouldn't you?" Jil retorted.

"Both of you, in my office," Jessica said quietly. She turned without another word and strode through the main office to her own lair. When the door was shut, she gestured toward the round table. "Have a seat."

Buck slowly lowered himself into a chair, his jaw clenched. Jil sat opposite him, on Jess's right side.

"Buck, I appreciate your concern," Jess said. "And, Julia, I appreciate your enthusiasm."

"Surely you don't agree that she should be allowed to teach this?" Buck spluttered. "It's heathenism. This is a Catholic school!"

"Yes, thank you," Jess said icily. "I am well aware of this school's Catholic roots. I am also well aware of the church's position on Goddess religions. It's the same as its position on Buddhism, Sikhism, Islam, and Judaism. Thou shalt not worship false gods. According to the Bible, all religions are created equal—equally wrong."

"But at least they're all practiced today."

"This isn't a Twenty-first Century World Religions class," Jil exploded. "What's wrong with educating the students about things that were important to the ancient Celts? Things that shaped their own futures as Christians?"

"Christianity does actually have a lot in common with Paganism, Buck," Jess said reasonably. "Isn't it fair to let the students explore those links for themselves?"

"She told them Christ was born in April!" Buck roared. "Where the hell did you get that?" His face was flushed, and he banged his hand down with emphasis on each word.

Jil lifted her head. "Some researchers believe that Christ's actual birthday fell in the spring. Christmas was purposely placed in December to overshadow the Winter Solstice, in order to get the Pagans to convert to Christianity."

"She's been reading the *DaVinci Code*," Buck spat.

Jil sighed. "Paganism was around a long time before Dan Brown."

"You're just going to let her dig this hole?" Buck demanded.

Jess sighed. "Buck, Julia is the teacher of the class. It is up to her to decide what units to teach and how."

"I'm the department head. She's supposed to follow the curriculum! Shouldn't she at least run these 'additions' by me?"

"Perhaps if you were more open-minded, I would!"

Buck rolled his eyes. "So, I hear Satanism is big nowadays. How about having a go at that?"

"Let's not get carried away," Jess interrupted. "Ms. Kinness, I want a unit outline on my desk by noon. Mr. Weekly, I will review the content and let you know my decision."

Buck stood and wrenched open the door. He composed himself, seemingly with effort, and strode through the front office, grimacing at everyone as he passed.

Jil stood up. "Thank you for considering it," she said tensely.

Jess, already standing, reached behind her and closed the door. She faced her squarely, not flinching from her gaze. "Don't ever put me in that position again. I need to know what you're doing in that class every single day. Otherwise Buck Weekly will have every parent in the school calling for your resignation, and there'll be nothing I can do about it."

She wrenched open the door and stood aside.

❖

The next morning, Jil woke to the sound of Zeus puking on her bedroom floor. She leaped out of bed and hauled him down the three flights of stairs to the common backyard, where he finished retching in the snow. She shivered outside in her pajamas while he did his business, then brought him on the elevator back up to her loft. En route to finding a bucket, a shammy, and some pet deodorizer, she stepped in a cold, wet puddle.

"Oh, Christ!" she yelled, lifting her foot from the pile of vomit she'd stepped in. Gagging and holding her foot up so as not to spread the mess, she hobbled to the en suite and lifted her foot into the sink, trying not to topple over as she rinsed the puke off.

By the time she'd cleaned the mess, she was twenty minutes late. She hurriedly shampooed her hair, and managed to cut herself only three times with a razor. Bleeding and stinging, she toweled off and pressed a Kleenex to her nicked skin. No time for contact lenses this morning. She shoved her glasses on, dabbed a little moisturizer on her face, and trekked to the closet. She realized she'd forgotten to do the ironing last night. She had no pressed pants to wear, and it was definitely not dress-down Friday.

"Shit." She had absolutely nothing but jeans, and a black skirt that she reserved for funerals.

Sighing, she wrenched on black lingerie, black pantyhose, and her black skirt. "I look like I'm going to a fucking wake," she muttered to herself. From the kitchen came Zeus's thunderous bark.

Jil abandoned her makeup and dashed through her bedroom door, sure he was alerting her to an intruder. He stood, watching her plaintively, almost smiling. She scratched his head. "Sorry you're sick," she muttered. He whined. And then puked on her feet.

By the time Jil got to school, "O Canada" had been sung and the morning prayer had been prayed. She dumped her stuff in her office and banana-clipped her hair, which, not surprisingly, had chosen this day to be completely unmanageable. Taking one last look in the mirror and discovering poppy seeds in her teeth from her drive-thru bagel, Jil exhaled in disgust. What the hell had happened to her? She used to be so together, so organized. She actually looked like a harried schoolteacher this morning—and not on purpose. What would Padraig think of her?

With determination, she gritted her teeth and mentally started the morning over. She hated skirts of any kind. And more to the point, she hated nylons. But she wasn't going to think about that now. She was going to prepare for this morning's class and then sit in the staff room having coffee. She needed to check three more names off her list this week, and she knew just the person to chat with.

"Hey," she greeted Rosie McMonahan. The gym teacher grinned and brought her power bar over to the couch where Jil was sitting.

"How's it going?" she asked in a hushed voice. Why did she look concerned? Sheepish even?

"Okay. Why?"

"I heard you had a run-in with Buck," Rosie said sympathetically. "I'm so sorry. I know what a hard-ass he can be."

Jil sat up straighter. Usually people acted like Buck was King Midas himself.

"He was certainly in his glory yesterday," Jil replied. She didn't ask how Rosie had heard. News traveled as fast as people's feet in this school. And they had got into it in the middle of the atrium. At least half a dozen students and staff had seen them following Jess into her office.

"Don't take it personally," Rosie said. "He does that to everybody."

"What do you mean?"

"He's a real control freak," Rosie said, her voice dropping to a whisper. "Last semester, Holly wanted to take the kids on a trip to the museum."

"Holly Barnes?"

"Yeah. The one whose classes you have."

"Okay. The museum sounds like fun."

"Yeah, it does. Right? Well, Buck told Holly that it was too risky to take the kids on a field trip in the winter, especially since there was only one of her and about thirty kids. Holly said that she'd ask around and see if anyone wanted to go along. Buck said he didn't think it was a good idea."

"Why not?"

Rosie shrugged and looked over her shoulder before continuing. "Holly didn't know either. But she didn't push it."

"Why does everyone let him get away with that stuff?" Jil asked.

Rosie just smiled and sighed. "I don't know. He's a real prick. I guess people are afraid of him. Anyway, the next week, Buck went to Jess and told her he thought Holly should be doing more with her kids.

He told her he'd suggested a field trip to the museum and that Holly had refused to take them."

"What the hell?"

"Yeah, it gets better. So Buck makes this huge public show of 'helping Holly out.' He organizes the trip, calls the museum, and tells everybody who will listen that he's going on this trip so that Holly doesn't have to take her kids alone. Then, on the day of the trip, the kids are all waiting outside, and the buses don't show up."

"Did he forget to order them?"

"Oh, no. He says, in front of everybody, to Holly, 'Didn't you confirm the buses yesterday?'"

"What?"

"Yeah. And then Holly goes 'I didn't know I was supposed to. You didn't say anything.' So Buck is all polite and respectful, meanwhile making accusations left, right, and center."

"So they didn't get to go?"

"No. And then Buck goes to Jess and tells her that Holly screwed up the buses and Holly's banned from taking field trips for the rest of the year."

"Oh my God." Jil shook her head.

Rosie's eyes glinted, and she nodded slowly. "There's one more thing," she whispered.

Jil leaned in. This was the stuff investigations were made of.

"I didn't know you well enough before, but now I know I can trust you."

"What is it?"

"You know how Holly's off this semester?"

"Yeah?"

"They said she was in a car accident?"

"Yeah."

"She was, but she wasn't hurt."

"What do you mean? Jess said she'd ruptured her spleen and had to be off for medical reasons."

Rosie shook her head. "That's what she told them. But there's not a scratch on her. A bit of whiplash, but that's it. Cleared up almost right away."

"Why is she off?"

They were so close their heads were almost touching. "Stress leave," Rosie whispered. "She was on the verge of a mental breakdown. Her doctor wrote her a note to get her off until after Christmas, but I doubt she'll be back."

"Why stress leave?"

"Wouldn't you go on stress leave working with him?" Rosie asked pointedly.

Jil nodded.

"If everyone weren't so afraid he'd go off the deep end again, someone might actually say something to the guy."

"Go off the deep end again?"

"Yeah, back to the loony bin?"

"He's actually been to the mental hospital?"

Rosie arched her eyebrows. "More than once. Why do you think everyone tiptoes around him?"

Jil exhaled slowly. Wow.

"Oh," Rosie said, looking at her watch. "I've got to go."

"No problem. See you." Jil sat nursing her coffee for a long moment after Rosie had left. Glancing at the clock, she realized she still had half an hour before next period, and a lot more sleuthing to do. Tucking that information about Holly in the back of her mind to revisit later, she walked over to the next table. With her widest smile on, she extended her hand.

"Hi, I'm Julia. I don't believe we've met…"

When Jil saw Jessica in the hallway, they acknowledged each other with a nod and a small wave. That was all for the entire day. And as she proceeded to her office against the thronging crowd, trying to maneuver her way through students with a cup of coffee in her hand, she saw Bex talking to a tall blond guy with a white T-shirt on.

Bex didn't meet her eye. In fact, she seemed to be deliberately avoiding looking at her. She didn't report to class that morning. And later, in the cafeteria, when four strides would have brought them into speaking distance, she deliberately turned and walked out the other door.

❖

The next morning, Jess was standing in the atrium when Jil got to school. She looked like she hadn't slept well. Jil was going to head straight to her office to take off her things, but found she couldn't walk by without at least saying hello. She hadn't slept well herself.

"I'm sorry," Jil said quietly, carefully avoiding any contact.

Dark circles rimmed Jess's eyes. "I know," she said. "I am too. I'm sorry Buck is being so hard on you."

"I'm trying to understand him," Jil said. "Truly I am. But we have such different points of view."

"I know."

Students brushed past and doffed their hats and iPods when they saw her. She nodded good morning then looked away.

"Okay," Jil said, heading off again. "I'll see you later."

"My office. First period?"

Jil smiled. "Sure."

Jess had the side door unlocked, waiting. The blinds were tilted down and the curtain on the glass window beside the door was drawn.

"Jess, we need to stop seeing each other," Jil muttered as the door closed behind her. "This is too hard." She deliberately didn't look her in the face. She didn't want to see the hurt or disappointment or misunderstanding that she always caused when she opened her mouth on the subject of relationships. Deliberately, she concentrated on the steel toe of her black high-heeled pump—the only pair of shoes she'd found that blended her need for professionalism with her own personal style.

If she ever set off a metal detector, she could blame it on her shoes, the toe and stiletto of which gleamed silver in the dullest of lights.

"I thought you would say that," Jess said softly. She perched on the side of her wide oak desk, folding her hands in her lap. "I don't blame you at all. It's too risky. It's not worth it for you. I understand." She smiled wanly, but her eyes revealed how much Jil's words had hurt.

"Jess, you're worth everything," Jil murmured, crossing the space between them in two long strides, and taking Jess's delicate face in her hands. "You're beautiful and perfect, and I would happily be fired for you. But you've worked hard to get to where you are, and being with me could ruin it."

"It could," Jess whispered. "It absolutely could. But I want you. I want you more than I've wanted anyone in my life."

Jil stared at her, more surprised than she'd ever been. Jess wanted her? Even knowing what it could do to her career?

She kissed Jil's palm then rested it against her face.

"You haven't thought this through. You have to consider the consequences."

"I have." Jess pulled Jil in, locking her in a long, slow kiss. She pulled away. "What the hell am I going to do when I'm sixty? Retire with my glass-blown apple to talk to at night? I will have sacrificed my whole life for something and be totally alone in the end."

"Jess, slow down," Jil said gently. "Don't throw away everything you've worked for."

"I'm not." Her tone was completely matter-of-fact. "I'm not taking out a billboard, and I know you aren't either. Let's just take this one day at a time and see what happens."

Jil felt her heart race, her pulse speed up almost to the point where she felt dizzy. Jess had obviously given this a great deal of thought. More than she had herself. Emotions surged through her, and she kissed Jess back, deeply, wanting to taste her lips, her tongue, her soul.

Wrong! Her brain screamed. Stop! But she didn't stop. She didn't even want to stop. No. She wanted to keep going and going and going until she and Jess were on a plane, riding away from this whole fucking mess, never looking back. The kiss went on forever, as Jess wound her hands through Jil's hair, tears streaming down her face. They fell noiselessly against the cement wall next to the hidden door, kissing and touching—reading each other's faces.

Jil closed her eyes to the secret she couldn't share, promising herself that she would find a way out of it, somehow.

Jess traced her finger along Jil's hairline, outlining her eyes, her nose. "I want you," she whispered.

"Here?"

"Please."

"Is the door locked?"

"They both are."

Jil's eyes went to the exit, scoping out the room, even as she reached up and slowly undid the buttons on Jess's shirt. Jess let her, moaning softly from that slight touch, and Jil saw the desire in her eyes. She peeled her shirt open to reveal Jess's hard nipples. "You're not wearing a bra," she said, her jaw dropping.

Jess grinned. "Sometimes I feel a little rebellious in the morning."

"Do you do this often?"

"Often enough."

Jil captured one ripe pebble between her lips and pushed Jess gently back so she was half-sitting on the desk. "You're sure you want to do this now?"

"I want to be fully awake this time," Jess answered.

Jil's mouth worked around Jess's lips, her neck, her breasts. Tiny goose bumps flashed across Jess's collarbone in the wake of her hot breath, and Jess shivered, her legs wrapped around Jil's thighs, holding her close.

In one breathless motion, Jess firmly took Jil's hand and guided it to the waistband of her dress pants, fitting it snugly inside.

Jil took the hint and slid her hand in all the way.

Jess moaned softly, leaning back as Jil's fingers found the place that made her melt.

Jil kissed her to silence the noise and whispered gently in Jess's ear to be quiet, for God's sake.

Jess breathed hard, but quietly, as Jil slid her hand up and down in the slick space. She squeezed her eyes shut and bit her lip, but Jil didn't stop. She stroked Jess's throbbing nub until she bucked upward and clamped her legs shut, letting out a gasp that made Jil's groin throb.

"Good God," Jess said when she'd recovered. She slid down off the desk and pushed Jil into a chair.

Just then, her phone rang. Jess looked at it, then back to Jil.

Jil laughed. "Never mind. We can finish this later." And she slid out the side door as Jess picked up her phone.

"This is Jessica Blake."

Jil found a blue slip of paper in her mailbox that morning. She smiled a little, wondering if perhaps she'd been gifted with her first infraction for an untidy office. She left it folded and gathered up the rest of the mail: a copy of this week's announcements, a flyer advertising a bake sale to support the breakfast program, and a little handwritten card with an envelope.

Back in her office, she threw away the announcements and the flyer and peeled open the card.

Dear Ms. Kinness,

Thank you for our enlightening chat. I enjoyed speaking with you. Please come again anytime.

Maggie Reitman.

Jil smiled and tucked the card back in the envelope, pinning it to her corkboard as a reminder that she had at least one friend in this increasingly disturbing environment. Then she unfolded the blue slip, and the smile vanished from her face.

It was printed in the same block lettering as her warning letter had been—complete with a light watermark on the page. She squinted at the marking, turned the paper around, and held it up to the light. What was that mark? She squinted at it, but it remained vague—something like a cross and sword. She would have to take it out into the daylight to see. Then she turned her attention to the script and analyzed the writing.

We know what you are.

That could mean so many things, Jil thought to herself. Who knew what? They knew she was a PI? They knew she was a lesbian? They knew she was having sex with the principal? Or, more likely, they didn't know anything, but they were trying to scare her.

And clearly, that wasn't going to work.

Chapter Twenty

Jil strapped Zeus to his leash and laced her runners. He galumphed excitedly through the house, sounding like a donkey gone wild. Those two hours they're awake…

"Settle down!" she commanded, and he stopped on the spot, wriggling and whining, his tongue hanging out as he tried to control himself. Filling her pocket with treats and searching out the keys, she noticed that the sun was already beginning to set. The days were getting shorter and shorter, and she was getting less and less time to walk Zeus before she had to leave at night.

He looked at her anxiously, pawing the ground.

"Sorry," she said, realizing he thought he was going to be left behind. Again. "I don't know what I was thinking getting a dog."

She did know what she'd been hoping—that he'd be a companion and a guard dog, maybe even go with her on stakeouts, help get the bad guy. But it seemed he was never going to be a good and staid service dog. Maybe she should have gotten a shepherd or a retriever. A Great Dane was imposing, but apparently, they weren't very bright.

She made him sit as she opened the door. He turned around and pawed the air. "Sit," she tried again. He whined. She sighed and opened the door, not at all surprised when he wrenched her halfway to the elevator before she could convince him to turn around so she could at least lock the door.

For a moment, she considered bringing Padraig's gun along, but decided against it. Zeus would probably set it off, and then she'd have a lot of explaining to do. It was one thing for a PI to own a registered handgun. It was another for her to carry it in a residential area.

"Zeus, for Christ's sake," she sputtered as he took off at Great Dane speed after a whirling maple leaf. He stopped, cocked his enormous head at her, then continued galloping across the open field.

"Come!" she called, not expecting much. But he did come, wagging his long tail, which thwacked against her calves and left little welts on her skin. She grasped hold of his tail. "Watch where you swing that thing." And he backed away, accepting a treat.

The trail Jil wanted to take involved a long tunnel that went under a major road. There was no crosswalk above it, so they had to take the underpass, which led to a wide-open space that Zeus could run in.

"C'mon, boy," she said firmly, setting a brisk pace. Zeus trotted next to her heels, weaving around her a few times in an effort to escape. "No," she said, and the sound of her voice boomed back over and above. Zeus reared back, coming down hard on all fours.

Jil stopped, tightened the leash, and proceeded. Zeus carefully followed, his ears cocked, his head whipping from side to side at every noise. Once she stopped, he started leading the way out of there. She let him, knowing he wasn't happy with the dark, enclosed space or the way the snow crunched under her feet.

At the other end of the tunnel, someone was coming toward them.

Zeus stopped, sniffing the air. He pulled her left then right.

"No," Jil said, stopping.

The man walked slowly, hands in his pockets, a toque down over his ears. Zeus whined and darted left again, trying to get behind Jil. "Come on, you big chicken," she said, walking forward again. Zeus wrapped himself around her, attention on the stranger. He barked then cowered at his own sound.

"Sorry," Jil said.

The man didn't reply, just continued walking. Toward them.

His hand came out of his pocket and, with surprise, Jil saw the glint of a knife blade.

"Back off," she said firmly.

He didn't. He continued toward her slowly.

"I said back off," Jil repeated, her hands coming up in a defensive position.

In the dark, it was hard to tell what he looked like. The toque covered his hair, and his jacket was done up all the way to his chin. He was Caucasian, with gray eyes and stubble, and he wore a black jacket and boots.

He was three feet away. Zeus trembled by her side, whining and barking.

"Shut that dog up," the man rumbled. His voice was raspy, and Jil smelled something on his breath—cigar smoke, maybe. Though he looked way too young to be smoking cigars.

"What the hell do you want?" she demanded. She scanned the trail behind him, looking to see if anyone was coming. It wasn't a well-used path, but it was by no means deserted.

"Pretty little women like you should stay home in the kitchen where you belong," he sneered, then, with movements that belied his slow approach, the man lunged at her, the knife blade inches from her face.

Automatically, Jil's foot found his groin, and he doubled over, shocked.

Zeus, snapping and barking, reared up, his bared teeth glinting in the dark. In one fluid motion, he pinned the man to the ground, his 160 pounds of muscle crushing the supine attacker. His massive head in the stranger's face, he growled and snapped, teeth zoning in on his neck.

In the enclosed tunnel, the sound was terrifying.

The man rolled once, stood up and ran for his life, back the way he'd come.

But he'd dropped his knife. It glinted on the white snow on the floor of the tunnel, silver and unstained. At least there wasn't blood on it, Jil thought sardonically. Shaken, she knelt and kissed the dog's enormous head. Zeus put a paw on her back, almost as if he were giving her a hug. She smiled a little and stroked his long floppy ears. He poked a cold, wet nose into her face, and nuzzled her. "Good boy," she whispered, her voice trembling.

When she went to retrieve the knife, though, Zeus blocked her. "It's okay," she said, bending over with a Kleenex in her hand. He watched, uncertainly, trying to paw the weapon out of her hand. She wrapped it up and stuck it in her pocket.

Hm. Maybe Danes are smart after all.

"Good boy," she told him again. And then she took him to the field where he could run, just so she'd have to come through this tunnel again on the way home. And tomorrow she'd take him again, just so she wouldn't be afraid.

But next time, she would be bringing her gun.

❖

It was past midnight with no moon and a sky too cloudy to show any stars that might have been peeking out. Jil lay awake, listening to the sound of Zeus's even breathing coming from the doggie bed on the floor beside her. She mentally recounted all the doors and windows in the house. She was certain she'd locked them. And set the alarm too.

The phone rang again. She picked it up, waited. Only silence. Again.

"Stop calling," she said sharply to whoever was prank-calling her at this hour. Then she slammed down the phone and unplugged it from the wall.

She hardly slept.

The next morning, she downed two cups of coffee before she even got into the car and stopped at Second Cup for an espresso on the way. Coming in the door, she spotted Jess with a Styrofoam cafeteria cup in her hand. "Rough night?" she asked.

Jess only nodded. She had frown lines between her eyebrows, and her face was a few shades whiter than normal.

"Some idiot kept calling the wrong number," Jess said. "And it's not like I'm sleeping terrifically anyway."

Jil nodded. Coincidence? Not likely.

"Listen, Jess—" She stopped. She felt eyes on her. She shifted her gaze to the left and saw a group of senior students—two boys and a girl—standing silently by the door, watchful, staring at her and Jess.

Jess didn't notice. She was too busy scanning the hallway for drug deals and fistfights. Jil started down the short flight of stairs toward the group. Inconspicuously. Not even looking at them. But by the time she reached the door, they had melted into the crowd, as unobtrusively as they'd been standing.

❖

After school, they met for coffee at the shop near Jil's flat.

"So what are we going to do tonight?" Jess asked.

"I think I'd like to take your clothes off."

"Oh yeah? Well, I might just let you, but first I'd like to cook you something."

"Cook?"

"Yeah, you've heard of it? Heating and mixing ingredients until they're edible?"

Jil laughed. "Yeah, I understand the concept, I just didn't realize you had any more talents that I didn't know about."

"Osso Buco. It's a slow-roasting dish. Plenty of time for the meat to get tender and juicy and delicious while we…entertain ourselves."

Jil watched in fascination as Jess seared the veal shanks and placed them in a roasting pan she'd forgotten she owned. She took item after item out of her magic grocery bag, deftly crushing garlic and peeling whole cloves for the sauce, stirring beef stock and opening a jar of homemade stewed tomatoes.

"Do you have any white beans?" she asked, frowning.

Jil went to the cupboard and rooted around. "I have canned ones. Don't know what from. Tara must have bought them." She stopped and bit her lip. "Sorry. Didn't mean to say that."

Jess's face twisted sympathetically. "Of course you're going to mention her."

"Yeah," Jil said, wrapping her arms around Jess's waist and nuzzling her neck. "But I'd rather talk about you. And me."

Jess turned around and kissed her slowly, open-mouthed and hot.

"Damn," whispered Jil, running her hands through Jess's hair, slightly moist with steam and sweat from the oven.

"Yeah." They kissed again, the jar of tomatoes lying abandoned on the counter as Jil leaned Jess back into the butcher block top.

The oven beeped, interrupting them, and Jess pushed her back gently. "Temp's right."

With fluid precision, Jess dumped the jar of tomatoes and can of beans over the seared chops, put the lid on the roasting pan, and pushed the whole thing into the oven. "We have an hour and a half."

"That's plenty," Jil said, pulling her close again.

Jess wrapped her arms around Jil's neck and kissed her, her hard nipples poking through the borrowed apron.

"You're braless again."

"Yep."

Jil yanked the string that held the apron around Jess's hips, then pulled it over her head, grabbing her waist again and running hot kisses down her neck.

"Oh, you're sneaky." Jess put her hand to the back of Jil's neck and guided her back up for another slow kiss, pulling her shirt out from its waistband, and sliding her hand along the cool, bare skin beneath.

Heat seared Jil's lips where Jess's pressed against hers. "I want to fuck you," she whispered.

"Like…fuck me, fuck me?"

"Yeah."

"Here?"

"No. On the bed where you can hold on to the bedpost."

Jess's jaw dropped and she bit down gently on Jil's lower lip, eliciting a soft groan. "I've…um…never done that before…"

"Oh. Ever?"

"Well, not with a woman."

Jil bit her lip where Jess's teeth had left a tiny spot of blood. "Let me show you."

Back in the bedroom, she pushed Jess down on her back and sank onto the pillows beside her, taking her time removing Jess's clothes piece by piece until she was laid out naked and shivering.

But Jess surprised her by rolling quickly on top and expertly undoing Jil's buttons with her teeth.

"Don't hurt yourself," Jil teased her.

Jess grinned and pinned her hands over her head with one hand, sliding her other hand under the line of Jil's bra and brushing her palm over her hard nipple. Jil gasped in surprise at the bolt that ran from her breast to her groin. Jess pinched her nipple lightly, rolling it between smooth fingertips. She hiked the bra up over Jil's breastbone and bent to circle the sensitive flesh with her tongue.

"Bite it."

Jess obliged, clamping her teeth gently around the shivering bud while Jil moaned and writhed under her. Straddling Jil's hips, she pulled her up to a seated position, quickly wrestling off her shirt and unclasping her bra. Then she pushed her back down and focused her attention back on Jil's aching breasts.

"Oh my God," Jil panted as Jess teased first one, then the other, with her warm, skilled tongue. She opened her mouth to take in as much as she could, biting gently, then harder. "I thought you were new at this."

"Well, I'm new to some things, but not to this."

"What's-her-name liked her tits played with?"

Jess snorted. "Yeah. What's-her-name liked attention, period."

"Well, there we go. We found a positive to that whole mess. You are very talented as a result."

Jess laughed out loud, then slipped her tongue into Jil's mouth, pushing their breasts together and lighting a spark that resulted in a hot and tangled make-out session, where their last articles of clothes were ripped off and discarded. In the end, they lay side-by-side, naked and entwined in each other's arms.

Jess propped herself up on her elbow and ran her hands down Jil's stomach, separating her legs with one firm push. Jil didn't resist, letting Jess's fingers explore as much as they wanted to. "How do you want to fuck me?" she asked as she stroked Jil's slit with one finger.

Jil moaned. "How do you want me to?"

"I want you to tell me." She flicked her finger up one side of her clit, then down the other, sending shivers cascading through Jil's whole body.

"God. Okay. Open my drawer. I have a few ideas." The cool air that rushed over her when Jess took her hand away made her clamp her legs together.

Jess opened the drawer and laid out the selections on the bed.

"They're all new. You can pick whichever one you like."

"How are you going to do it?"

"Well, I have a harness. I could use that."

"Is that what you used with—"

"No," Jil said, blushing. "She wasn't into it."

"Oh. So you bought these all…"

"For us. Or, you know, for me alone, minus the harness."

Jess shoved her. "I don't believe you'll need to fly solo. I think we should give this one a try." She held up a purple silicone dildo with a small add-on at the top. "What's this part for?" she asked, playing with the little piece that faced back toward the base.

"Um, I think that's for the wearer."

"Ohhh," Jess said, understanding at once. "Well then, I definitely think we should try this one."

Jil slipped into the packed harness. Before she could say a word, Jess's tongue was back in her mouth, and they were making out again, this time with hands and arms stroking and fingering every exposed crevice. Jil almost came just from the attention Jess was giving her nipples, but just as her head started swimming, she pushed her away.

"Turn around."

Jess knelt at the top of the bed, facing away from her. "Like this?"

"Just like that." Jil knelt behind her and ran her hands down the length of her front, from her shoulders, over her breasts to the top of her thighs. Gently, she pushed Jess down onto all fours. "You comfortable?"

"Yeah. Not bad at all." The relaxed position would put the least stress on Jess's hips. Plus, Jil got to hold those hips as she moved in slowly from behind.

"Oh, Christ," Jess moaned as Jil cupped her, stroking her clit with one hand, her breast with the other. "Don't do that too long or I'm going to come."

"So come," Jil said.

"I want you to fuck me like you promised."

Jil slowly eased the dildo in, and Jess moaned deeply. Touching her clit and being inside her at the same time made Jil's groin ache. She could only imagine what it was doing to Jess. She took her hands away from the other sensitive places and put them on Jess's hips, drawing out the moment.

Jess gently eased back into Jil's thrusts, rocking back on her hands and knees. "That feels so good," she whispered.

Jil pulled out and pushed in a little deeper. "It's supposed to hit your G-spot."

"Yeah, well, I'd say it's doing its job."

Every time Jess thrust back, the clit stimulator pushed against her, sending shock waves through her whole body. She began to pant, grinding against the silicone piece as she thrust into Jess. She let Jess control the timing until she was moaning so loudly she couldn't keep time any more.

"Harder," Jess panted, burying her face in the pillow between her hands.

She pushed in farther, faster, harder, unable to tell which sounds were hers and which belonged to Jess. Waves began crashing over her and she felt Jess's legs stiffen, her back arch. Knowing she was close, she reached around and stroked her clit again. Jess started gasping, parting her legs to allow Jil's fingers more space.

"Fuck, I'm coming," Jess groaned, her lips pressed into the pillow.

Jil felt Jess's pulsing nub get rock hard, just as the biggest wave crashed over her. She concentrated on keeping a steady rhythm as the orgasm bowled her over, and she thrust into Jess for the last time.

They collapsed on the bed, spent.

After Jess left around eleven o'clock, Jil made some tea and headed upstairs. She glanced in the door of her office but couldn't bring herself to look at her work notes. Not tonight. The smell of Jess's perfume still clung to her skin from where they'd lain pressed together for hours. The secrets and the deception clung even closer.

What was she going to do? She was getting in deep with Jess—a connection that went so far beyond the physical, to the place where trust and commitment could live. But how could she hope that could happen if Jess didn't even know her real name? Something had to give here—either the investigation, or the relationship, but she couldn't have both anymore.

Hiding the truth from Jess at this point was no longer evasive—it was outright lying.

Worse, she couldn't even say she'd tried to avoid this complication. The magnetic pull she felt toward her had been enough to make her close her eyes to the complications. So many complications…but she wasn't a dishonest person at heart. She knew she had to tell her and accept the fallout. Hearing the truth now, from her, had to be better than the betrayal Jess would feel if she found out by accident from someone else.

The situation at St. Marguerite's was getting more intense by the day, and when things got wound up that tight, they had a tendency to snap.

Tomorrow, she would confront it head-on. She would tell Jess the truth about who she was and reveal everything she'd discovered about St. Marguerite's history…and then apologize like hell to Padriag, but explain to him why she'd had to blow her cover to Jess.

Three a.m. came and went while she went back and forth with her decision. The alarm went off at five thirty, before she'd ever fallen asleep.

After dragging herself out of the shower and into the least-wrinkled clothes in her hamper, she hesitated for a moment at her closet before strapping Padraig's gun to her ankle. This job was making her increasingly uneasy, and the gut she relied on so often in this job was telling her to be careful today.

She entered through the staff room where no metal detectors had been installed yet and made a note to scope out other places around the school where someone could sneak in weapons.

Jil traveled slowly through the atrium to the cafeteria. No sign of Jess—not in the hall, not in her office. Just as she was doubling back from the library, she saw her slip into her office by the side door. Shaking out her hands to stop them from trembling, she crossed the space to the door and knocked quietly. Could she really do this? Tell her the truth and expect her to accept it? There was more at stake than just their relationship. Jess could expose her, kick her out of the school and she could be fired. Padraig could lose the contract.

Still, she couldn't lie to her one more minute. She'd just have to trust Jess to understand. Maybe she could help with the other, unofficial investigation she was carrying on. Yes, that's where she'd start. She'd tell Jess everything she'd found out, and then ease into how and why she knew those things.

She knocked on the door.

Jess opened it

"I need to talk to you," Jil said.

Jess hurriedly shut the door, a worried expression on her face. "What? What is it?"

Jil took a tremulous breath and sank into the couch.

Jess leaned forward, brows knitted. "You look like you've seen a ghost."

Jil laughed shortly. "I have. Tommy Deloitte. Edward Cartright. Regina Francis. Bobby Hansen. And Alyssa Marco."

At their names, Jess blanched. "What are you talking about?"

"I've been investigating the deaths at this school," she said quietly. She looked over her shoulder, not able to shake the feeling that they were never completely alone. It seemed sometimes that the walls had ears.

"What do you mean you've been investigating?" Jess sat back. "I thought we agreed you'd forget what I told you." She dropped her voice. "What I *shouldn't* have told you."

"You'll understand everything soon, I promise. But doesn't it strike you odd that all the students who died were gay?"

Jess frowned. "How do you know that? There were only ever rumors."

"Rumors are all it takes sometimes."

"Alyssa?"

"Had a girlfriend," Jil said. She thought about bringing up Bex, but decided against it.

Jess frowned again. "What are you doing? Why are you raising these ghosts?"

"Because the reason behind their deaths is still alive and well in this school. We have to do something about it—expose it—before others get hurt, or worse."

But before Jil could say anything further, a loud, cracking boom made them leap to their feet. Jil grabbed Jess's wrist, instinctively to protect her. And in a second, they were both dashing for the door.

Gunshots.

In the main office, the admin team stood white-faced and trembling, all watching the door as if they expected an armed gunman to come through at any second. Without a moment's hesitation, Jess ran to the lockdown alarm, smashed the glass with her fist, and pushed the button.

Instantly, the school was filled with a whining, buzzing, insistent alarm.

Jil directed all the admin staff into Jessica's office. "Not a word," she said. "Get away from the windows. Get behind the desk and don't talk."

Mark Genovese stormed through the doors to the main office, his jaw set. "What the hell is going on?" he barked.

"We're having a lockdown," Jess replied tightly. "Get in your office."

Mark looked taken aback for a minute, but he grabbed Cynthia, the other VP, and hurried her into his office.

"What about the students?" Cynthia asked, standing in the doorway, bewildered.

"They know what to do. We've had a drill." Jess shut the door firmly. "Get into an office, Julia," she said, casting an eye into the hallway. The atrium was eerily empty. And the alarm buzzed on and on.

Jess grabbed the PA microphone. "Staff and students, this is a lockdown. Proceed to the nearest room and follow lockdown procedures. I repeat, this is a lockdown. Proceed to the nearest room, and follow lockdown procedures."

From the corner of her eye, Jil saw something that made her heart stop. The flash of a contraband green baseball cap. Gideon was standing alone in the atrium, his back to the office. And he was walking into an empty hallway.

Get into a classroom. Go. But when she saw him heading the wrong way, she had to act.

She grabbed her gun from her boot and headed for the door.

Jess stared from her to the gun and back to her again, her face a mixture of shock, fear, and bewilderment. "What the hell are you doing?"

And then she looked past Jil's shoulder and saw the same thing. Her face blanched.

"Stay here and get inside that office," Jil instructed. "Do not come out until I come get you. Do you understand?"

Jess nodded, for once not arguing. Her worst nightmare was coming true.

"And lock the door after me."

Another shot went off.

Jil realized she couldn't see Gideon anymore.

And then she ran.

Gun in hand, scanning up, down, and side-to-side, she streaked through the atrium to the staircase. Every statue and every painting seemed to have eyes that followed her. She passed the door to the cafeteria, seeing through the wired glass that two huge tables had been stacked against the doors from the inside. Smart move.

In the chapel, Maggie stood paralyzed, her back flat against the wall. When she saw Jil's gun, she gasped, her hand going to her throat.

"It's okay," Jil said, and Maggie breathed again.

With her gun, Jil pointed to the altar, and Maggie ducked quickly under the altar cloth into better hiding. Jil closed the chapel door behind her and heard the click of the automatic lock. Then she was on the move again. So many choices. So many routes. For God's sake, she hoped Gideon had ducked into a classroom or a bathroom by now.

She put her back against the wall and crept quietly down the stairs to the basement. Someone was in this school with a gun, and by the time anyone got there, it might be too late. Another shot sounded, not far from her position. And she had to stop to breathe before she could force herself forward. Any second now, she expected to come across a wounded student—bleeding or dead—but so far, nothing.

She didn't have a bulletproof vest on. She hadn't fired a gun in almost five years. But today she was chasing down an armed criminal in closed quarters. Not exactly how she'd anticipated her day going.

The alarm buzzed, hollow and throbbing all at once. It obscured anything else she might have heard, and she whipped around from side to side, counting on her vision to spot danger before it attacked her.

She looked down, under the water fountains in the alcove to see two terrified-looking students, one with her hand clamped tightly over her friend's mouth. Her friend was shaking so hard she was whimpering. They both had streaks of mascara on their faces. Jil put her finger to her lips and pointed at the two girls, beckoning them forward. The braver one crawled out, but the other one was rooted to the spot. It was easy to see why they hadn't made the dash for safety. The little one was too terrified to move.

Jil grabbed her by the arm and pulled her out. "Shh," she said, helping her to her feet. "Let's go."

She covered them with her gun and led them down the hall to the nearest room—which happened to be the boys' washroom. Jil just pushed them both inside. "Lock this door from the inside. Then lock the doors on the stalls, kneel on the toilet seats, and don't move," she whispered.

They just nodded and disappeared. A moment later, the dead bolt on the door slid home, and Jil was on the move again. As she passed a statue of Jesus, she paused. It used to be Jesus. Now it was

Jesus without a head. She wondered if someone had crashed into it on their way past—running without looking. But no. She bent closer and looked. The whole head was blown off. It looked like it had been shot.

A sound like a firecracker made her jump. She sprinted soundlessly to the end of the hall and peered around the corner. The gym was to the left. Another staircase to the right. Briefly, she peeked into the gym. It was empty. If Rosie was smart, she would have put her kids in the supply closet at the back and locked the door.

Rosie was smart.

Jil dashed for the stairs, creaking open the door as quietly as the old metal would let her. Once inside, she stopped dead, listening hard. One landing up, she spotted a door to the outside. Then nothing but stairs all the way up, stopping at every floor. That gunman could be anywhere.

And who the hell was it?

She could hear nothing now except the crunch of gravel outside. The police were arriving. Unfortunately, they would take a while to come inside. A lockdown meant no one entered or exited the building—because there might be bombs triggered to doors, and if they were opened, the whole school could blow up.

That was the theory, at least.

Quietly, Jil started creeping up the stairs.

She peeked through to the second floor and found an empty hallway.

Silently, she turned around and began the ascent to the third floor. The sound of her shoes on the rubber stairs made her cringe, but she kept going. She thought she heard someone breathing, but there was nowhere for them to hide.

On the third-floor landing, she flattened her back against the wall and peered around. A flash of green turned the corner.

Jil opened the door and sprinted down the hall. With four feet to go until the junction, she stopped, then began inching toward the corner. With her gun in front of her, she whipped around, gun ready to face the gunman.

"Jesus fucking Christ," she breathed, lowering her weapon.

Gideon's wide eyes stared at her, like a baby deer caught in the headlights of an enormous truck.

"Gideon, what the hell are you doing?" Jil sputtered. "I could have shot you!"

Gideon breathed deeper, his shoulders shaking. "I wish you would," he said. He raised his hand, and that's when she saw a semiautomatic in his trembling fingers. Instantly, her gun was back in the air, pointing at his chest.

"Drop your weapon!" she barked. Her heart thundering in her chest, Jil stared him down. His eyes full of tears, his lips trembling uncontrollably, he held tight to the gun.

"I can't stop," he said. "I can't stop now. They're going to get me, Miss."

"Who? Who is bothering you?"

"Everyone."

Jil stared at him, trying to figure out if he was high, or paranoid, or just so scared that he couldn't see reason anymore.

"They're everywhere I go," Gideon choked out. "In the locker room, in the cafeteria. Even at the convenience store down the road. When I'm with my sister. Especially when I'm with my sister."

"Why haven't you called the police?"

Gideon laughed and the gun wobbled in his hand. Jil took a step back.

"Sorry, Miss," Gideon said, chagrined.

"Gideon, put down your gun."

"I won't hurt you, Miss."

"You might not mean to, but someone will get hurt here."

"You have a gun too."

"Yeah, and I promise you that I'm a better shot. You can tell anyone you like that I put you in a chokehold and put a gun to your head. You can even pretend I shot you. But I need you to put that gun down."

Gideon clenched his jaw. "I can't," he said through gritted teeth. "They hurt Bex. I can't let them do it again."

"We're going to get you out of this mess," Jil promised.

Gideon just shook his head.

"Gideon, I know it feels like they're everywhere, but they're not. They only want you to think that. The whole world isn't out to get you."

"They are," he sobbed. "They're everywhere I go, and I can't take it anymore."

"Let me help you."

But Gideon just shook his head. He raised his gun again, toward a stained glass window.

So Jil tackled him to the ground. None too gently either. Anyone who happened to be disregarding the lockdown drill and peeking out the classroom window would have seen Ms. Kinness, the religion teacher, tackling a seventh-grade student, and putting him face-first into the ground. At gunpoint.

"How was that?" she whispered into his ear, as she leaned over him.

"Good," he grunted.

"Too hard?"

"Let up a little on the left," Gideon wheezed. And Jil released her grip so that his skin turned back to its normal color.

"Sorry," she muttered. She had the presence of mind to tuck her gun back up into her boot before the sound of footsteps got close enough that eyes could see it.

"S'okay. Are you the police?"

"Not anymore."

It didn't take long for the real police to arrive. They thundered through the hall like Sherman tanks, hauling Gideon to his feet and handcuffing him. He looked terrified, his eyes searching out Jil's. "It's okay," she mouthed to him.

Then Jil spotted Morgan in the brigade. "Hey!"

"Hey," Morgan said. "Still here?"

"Yep."

"Almost done with whatever it is?"

Jil sighed and closed her eyes. It seemed like it was just beginning, actually. She didn't know when the hell she was going to get the rest of the answers.

"He's fourteen," she said instead. "And I know there's a lot more to this. Please do me a favor?"

Morgan nodded. "Sure."

"Get an advocate and a lawyer there pronto?"

Morgan pursed his lips. "Yeah, okay," he said. "I'll see what I can do."

At that moment, Jil spotted Jess at the end of the hallway, staring at her silently, as if she'd never seen her before. From opposite ends of the G building, they watched as the police officers took Gideon away and secured the school. The students emerged from their classes to run down the stairs into the arms of their waiting parents, who were barricaded into the parking lot by police.

One minute, Jess was standing twenty feet away. The next, she was gone. And her voice played out over the PA system—steady and strong, as usual. Through a speaker, you couldn't see the look on her face, the whiteness of her cheeks, the tremble in her lip, or the anger in her eyes, which Jil was certain registered loud and clear up close.

"Staff and students, the lockdown is over. Thank you all for your cooperation. The lockdown is over. It is safe to come out. Please proceed in an orderly fashion to your next class."

How could she even suggest it? Jil shook her head. How could she even think students would proceed quietly to Calculus when, ten minutes ago, a student with a gun had come through the halls?

But of course, most people wouldn't have known what the lockdown was about. Only people in the top floor of the G building would know. Others, in opposite ends of the school, had probably been playing cards and whispering to each other as they crouched low behind desks. This was so common for them. They'd had a drill. They probably took it no more seriously than a fire drill.

Shit.

And what else was she supposed to say? "Please proceed anxiously and wildly to the parking lot to skip the rest of the day?" Not likely.

And Jil realized, in that moment, how much of what Jess said and did was dictated by her job, and not her personal feelings. She was desperate to know the real Jess. The woman behind the suit. Her real thoughts, her real feelings. Everything about her. But that came with a price. She'd have to reveal herself too. She'd have to tell her something—anything—to take that look of shock and betrayal off her face.

Jess was waiting at the front doors to the main office, watching students straggle by. "Off to Biology?" she asked pleasantly. Two junior girls nodded, subdued. "Good for you," she praised them. They lifted their heads a little higher and walked on. "Hello, gentlemen."

"Miss."

"Make sure the younger ones you pass in the halls get on to class, would you?"

"Yes, Miss."

"Good boys."

Jil stopped at the bottom of the short staircase that led to the top of the atrium and met Jess's gaze. Jess just turned and walked away, toward her office, not looking back. Jil knew her well enough to follow, silently, through the cubicles to the back corner.

"Who the hell are you?" Jess demanded, the door to her office slamming shut with such ferocity that Jil actually jumped.

She felt her heart flutter and sink. She knew this day was coming. She'd just never been prepared for the total devastation she'd feel at having to let Jess go.

"My name is Jillienne Kidd."

"Well, Jillienne, it's nice to meet you," said Jess, sarcasm dripping from every word.

"Jess, c'mon."

"C'mon? Are you kidding me? I didn't even know your real name? Does anyone know your real name? Are you responsible for what's been going on here? Are you even a teacher?"

Jil swallowed hard, trying to decide which of her questions to answer first. She took a deep breath. "Why don't we sit down?"

Jess's eyes flashed fire. "Like hell." She looked like she might be able to calm down sometime within the next decade.

"No, I'm not a teacher."

"Not a teacher. Where the hell did you get your credentials?"

"I'm a PI."

"A private investigator?" she seemed confused. Not quite as angry. "Who hired you?"

"I can't say."

"You can't say?"

"I've already compromised my investigation by my actions today."

"Your investigation? What the hell are you investigating?"

Jil shook her head. "I'm sorry, Jess."

Jess just stared, her intense eyes flashing anger and disbelief and confusion and hurt all in one strobe light succession. Her voice dropped almost to a whisper. "You owe me an explanation."

And Jil felt like she'd been hit by a truck. "I know," she answered. "I know I do. But I can't right now."

"You're investigating me," Jess whispered, horrified. "Right?"

"Yes."

"Is this a game to you?" Every inch of her pulled back from Jil—emotionally, physically. "Was I pawn in something?"

And Jil couldn't even find the words to speak. She could only shake her head slowly. "No," she choked.

But Jess was gone. She had retreated into herself so far that Jil doubted she'd ever reach her.

"You need to leave."

Jil stood up slowly on legs that would barely carry her. And this time when she walked through the main office, no one pretended not to stare.

Chapter Twenty-one

Zeus greeted her at the door, for once, not even barking. She dropped her bag and coat and shoes by the front door, walked slowly to the couch, sat, and stared at nothing—nothing—for hours.

At four o'clock, she got back into her car, drove the twenty kilometers to O'Hanagan's, and parked. Padraig's car was there. She felt cold, like icy blood was trickling through her chest and down her arms. How could she ever explain this to Padraig?

With deliberate precision, she unbuckled her seat belt and pushed open the door that suddenly seemed too heavy to move. Every step inside was painful. Slow. Heavy. The knock on Padraig's door was too loud. Too revealing. She looked behind her to see who was watching. No one.

"Hey, Kidd," Padraig said, smiling brightly when he saw her. Then the look on her face registered, and his smile faded. "What is it?"

Jil just stood on the other side of his desk silently and handed him the gun without a word. Then she gave him her keys, her pretext folder, and her ID.

"I'm so sorry," she said.

And she turned and left.

❖

Jil went home to her loft alone. She ran a shower and stayed in until the hot water tank ran cold. Then she wrapped herself in a soft robe, poured a glass of wine, and sat, again, on the couch—staring at nothing.

How had she made such a series of errors? How could she have been this blind and this stupid and this selfish? She had known from the beginning that this could happen—that she could compromise her investigation, compromise Jess's career, and compromise their precarious and forbidden relationship. But she'd never imagined that she could fuck it up this royally.

Now, not only did she not have a job, but she had let Padraig down. She couldn't finish her investigation, and maybe worst of all, Jess would never look at her again. She couldn't remember a worse day. Or a worse night. Or a worse day following.

Friday morning, she woke early. Even before the sun had risen. She lay awake, staring at the ceiling, her stomach nauseated. Zeus was still snoring on the floor beside her. She rolled over and pulled the pillow over her head, trying to drown out the drumming in her skull.

Her phone rang, and she looked at the number—Elise—then declined it.

She lay there for an hour. Turned over. Lay on there for another hour. Got up.

She wondered what was going on at the school. Would Buck Weekly be teaching her class? Would everyone be talking about her? Talking about how she strolled through the halls of the school carrying a gun? Would they be afraid of her?

It killed her that she couldn't get dressed and go into St. Marguerite's to find out. She had spent months trying to find a way to get out of that place, and now all she wanted was to get back in.

And to talk to Jess.

The minutes went by excruciatingly slowly.

She got up, dressed in jogging clothes, and took Zeus for a long, slow run. He panted and leaped beside her, darting into the woods, then darting back, catching a stick. Nothing she did seemed to ease the brick of ice in her chest, or the twisting of her stomach.

Was this the first day of the rest of her life? No career, no lover, no life.

God, she was such an idiot.

She imagined Jess fielding phone call after phone call from parents, from news reporters, holding an assembly, denying interviews, being hauled on the carpet by the superintendent wondering how this had happened with all the extra security measures they had taken.

And who the hell that teacher was who had tackled the young boy at gunpoint.

Jesus.

When the sun finally did set on Friday night, Jil was sitting on the floor, cradling Zeus's enormous head in her lap, and crying soft tears onto his long, silky ears.

When Elise called her again, she didn't even bother to decline it, just let it go straight to voice mail.

At eight o'clock Saturday morning, when Jil had dressed, taken a walk with the dog, and managed to force down some toast, Padraig called. This time, she knew she had to answer.

"Hello?"

"It's me. I'm coming over." Before she could object, he had hung up. She had time for a quick once-over in the living room before he was barging through her front door, without even knocking.

Zeus went crazy. He ran to the front door, barking and howling, his deep woof bouncing off the tile floor and vibrating the walls. Padraig was a little taken aback for a moment, then he put out his large, rough hand for Zeus to sniff. The dog's tail started wagging as Padraig's fingers found an itchy spot behind his long, floppy ears. He melted into him with the famous Great Dane lean, and Padraig almost stumbled over.

"Nice guard dog you've got here," he said sardonically.

"You wouldn't want to meet him in a dark alley," she said quietly. "Can I get you a cup of coffee?"

"That'd be good. Thanks."

Awkwardly, Padraig followed her into the kitchen, seeming not to know quite where to put himself.

"Have a seat," Jil offered, her voice still small. She knew it was hard for him to come here—maybe even as hard as it was for her to see him.

"Heard about what happened Thursday," Padraig said, accepting the cup of coffee and slowly stirring in sugar.

"Figured you would," Jil replied.

"So you're quitting, I guess."

Jil couldn't even look him in the face. "I'm so sorry," she said. "I don't know how I managed to make such a mess of things."

"Sure you do," he said bluntly. "You fell in love with the woman you were investigating."

Jil stared at him. "How the hell do you know?"

Something close to a rueful smile played on the corners of Padraig's lips. "I met her," he said simply. "She's something."

"Did you talk to her about me?"

"Of course not," said Padraig. "Give me more credit than that. I just showed up when the police were still there, investigating every nook and cranny. The teachers thought I was with the police; the police thought I was a teacher. I had a few words with some staff—even said hello to the principal herself. Figured out pretty quick that she was the problem here. Pretty lady, but definitely plays for your team."

Jil shook her head. "It doesn't matter," she said. "I shouldn't have let myself get involved with her."

"What were you thinking?" Padraig asked. He wasn't accusing as much as curious.

"I wasn't thinking at all," Jil replied, turning away from him. God, why were they even having this conversation? "I just kept telling myself I'd figure it out. That I would find a way to do both my investigation and be with her."

"And did you?"

"Would I be in this mess if I had?"

"I wanted to come over yesterday," Padraig said, changing topics. "But you seemed so dead set on something, I thought it was better to leave you alone. And then I heard about the lockdown at St. Marguerite's."

"How?"

"All over the radio, and broadcast live on CNN."

"God," Jil said. After everything that had happened, it had never occurred to her to turn on the news.

"What did they say?"

"Oddly enough, not much," Padraig answered. "All they said was that St. Marguerite's was in a lockdown emergency and that there had been shots fired. Of course, parents panicked and drove like bats out of hell to come pick up their children. They were getting frantic phone calls from their kids saying that some idiot was taking over the school.

But on the news, they couldn't release the name of the student, because he's a minor."

"Did they show anything about him being arrested?"

"No. They didn't show that part. They just said the student was apprehended by police."

"Nothing about me?" Jil asked. She was hopeful and confused at once.

"No," Padraig mused. "Nothing. No one mentioned you at all, actually."

"How is that possible?" Jil demanded. "I took that kid down, Padraig. I had my gun on me, and I pointed it at him. I was going to shoot him if he didn't give me his gun. He's fourteen years old. Fourteen."

Padraig's face clouded doubtfully as he looked at her.

"Fourteen's still old enough to be armed," he said quietly. "If he was a threat, you did the right thing."

Jil shook her head, frustrated. "But that's just it," she said. "I don't know why he was doing it. I don't know how he got that gun into the school. All I know is that there's something much bigger going on here than just an angry kid with a gun. The fact that I'm not even in the news just proves it to me."

"Obviously, someone didn't want your presence to be known," Padraig replied.

"Have you talked to DiTullio?"

"Only briefly. I didn't tell him you'd quit. Thought that might give him a raging aneurysm, and I didn't really want more to cope with, if you follow."

Jil nodded ruefully.

"Whew…" Padraig breathed. "You had to pick that day to change your mind about carrying a gun, did you?"

"Sorry," she said. "And I'm afraid it was your gun I used."

"How did you know what was going to happen?"

"I didn't. I just had a really bad feeling. Things were getting way out of control there. Taggings, threats, knives coming at me. Students afraid to walk alone in the halls. Notes with weird symbols. Everyone's eyes on me all the time. Even Jess, sometimes doesn't seem to be safe. I don't know—"

"I told you that school gave me the creeps."

He stopped stirring his coffee and looked at Jil instead. And like a dam had burst, Jil found herself telling him all the details that, up to this point, had seemed like a jumbled pile of nothing: Alyssa and Bex's relationship, the other students who had died at St. Marguerite's over the years…

"What do you think?" Jil asked, seeing Padraig's eyebrows get higher and higher, as his jaw got tighter and tighter.

He sat back when she was finished, stroking his beard thoughtfully. Then he started stirring his coffee counterclockwise, like he always did when he was deep in thought.

"I think this investigation isn't nearly over."

Just then, the doorbell rang. Jil and Padraig exchanged a quizzical look, and Jil went to answer it. She peeked through the peephole and just about fell down.

Standing on her doorstep, at ten o'clock on a Saturday morning, was Jess Blake.

Chapter Twenty-two

She opened the door slowly, and they stared at each other for a few seconds.

"Just wanted to see if you actually did live here," Jess said tightly.

"Touché," Jil whispered. "I don't usually bring people home with me, given my line of work."

Jess stood, waiting for Jil to say something more, but she didn't. "I can't do my job right now," Jess said, and she sounded angry. At Jil? At herself? "I can't seem to make sense of anything, and if I can't even sort out my own life, how the hell am I supposed to sort out the school?"

"Jess, I'm sorry I made you doubt yourself."

"You made me doubt everything!"

Was her nose red? Were those tears in her eyes? Jil wanted so badly to reach out and comfort her, but she knew that Jess would pull away. She kept her hands under control—crossed them over her chest instead.

"Was I part of the plan?" Jess asked. God, she was really set on that.

And Jil shook her head again. "Not at all. I didn't plan on you at all, Jess. In fact, you made my investigation very, very complicated."

"What were you investigating?"

Jil sighed. The time for deception had long passed. "Everyone."

They stood on the doorstep for a moment longer, trying to settle into something that was familiar, or at least, less strange. "Why don't you come in?" she said at last.

Jess nodded, a mantle of anger dropping away from her shoulders. "Okay."

❖

"If we want her cooperation, we're going to have to tell her the truth," Padraig said simply.

Jil stared at him for a minute. She hadn't expected that. "Okay."

"Have a seat, Ms. Blake." Padraig graciously gestured to Jil's suede couches.

Jess hid a smile, and Jil read her mind. They'd been intimately involved with that couch not too long ago. She felt heat rising in her cheeks.

"My name is Padraig O'Hanagan. I'm the person responsible for placing Jil in your school to begin with."

"Jil," Jess mouthed the word, trying it out. She shook her head. "Okay."

"We were hired by an outside party to investigate—"

"My staff," she finished.

"Yes, I'm afraid that's the truth of it. You and your school. And now this investigation is taking a very sharp turn. And it's our responsibility to carry it through, even if it is uncomfortable—even dangerous."

"Is it? Dangerous?" Jess asked.

"It seems so," replied Jil. "And I think we need to get to the bottom of things right away."

"Who hired you?"

Padraig sighed. "Someone higher up than you."

Jess pursed her lips. "I can guess, so you don't have to tell me. I know the Parents' Association has been breathing down the necks of the board members as much as they've been a pain in my ass for years. So you're investigating the contracts?"

"Well, at least that's what I thought I was investigating." Jil sat on the opposite end of the couch, far enough away that no part of her touched Jess.

"I think we'd better just focus on where we're going, not where we've been," Padraig said.

But Jil just smiled—a tentative olive branch. And Jess returned it.

"Okay," said Jess. "So the board is so interested in my personal life that they'd hire a PI to investigate me. Fine. That doesn't make me at all paranoid."

Padraig grinned. "Great. Then let's get on with it." He grabbed a spare Bristol board from Jil's stack behind the couch and laid it out on the coffee table. "So here's what we know."

Jil and Jess both sat up a little straighter, Jil privately wondering how much he had managed to put together.

"There's Alyssa Marco's death." He put Alyssa in the middle, circled it, and sat back.

Jess's face had gone white. "This is about Alyssa?" she whispered.

"This is barely scratching the surface," Jil warned her. "So put on that battle armor."

Jess swallowed hard.

"We have Marcel," Jil continued, taking the marker from Padraig, and putting MARCEL off to the side, an uncomplimentary THIEF next to his name.

"Really?" said Jess.

Jil just raised her eyebrows. "Your ring?"

"Are you kidding me?"

"More about that later."

"We have Buck," Padraig continued, another point. Jess rolled her eyes, but Jil refused to make eye contact. She took the marker from Padraig and scribbled Buck's name on another section of the board.

"C'mon," Jess interjected. "He's not out to get you."

"I know."

Jess looked surprised. "You do? You don't exactly have any love lost, you two."

Jil sighed. "Well, now I have another theory. At the very least, I think he knows something."

"How are you going to find out?"

Jil flashed her a smile. "I'm going to ask him."

"Moving on," said Padraig dryly.

"We have Bex, who was involved with Alyssa. Gideon, Bex's brother, who was the shooter. We have yet to find out who was responsible for the threats or the tagging," Jil said, getting into it. It felt good to get it all down on paper—not to be mulling through it all in her head. And it felt even better to finally be able to share all of this with Jess—which is all she'd wanted to do from the beginning.

If Jess was shocked by any part of this, she was doing an excellent job of hiding it.

"And the attacks?" Padraig clarified.

"Attacks on who? Julia?" Jess asked, alarmed. "I mean Jil. God. It's going to take me a while to get used to that."

"Don't worry," Jil said, shooting Padraig a warning look, which Jess easily intercepted.

"Is someone out to get you?" she demanded.

Jil sighed.

"You said you'd tell me the truth."

"No, I said I'd tell you more than you knew."

Jess narrowed her eyes. "I'm not four years old. Spill it."

"Remember that night we were coming back here from the restaurant?"

"Yeah. When you missed your turn and we stopped for gas you didn't really need?"

Jil smiled sheepishly. Jess noticed a hell of a lot more than she gave her credit for. "Yeah."

"What about it?"

"Someone was following us that night. I doubled back and stopped so I could call Padraig and have him send someone."

"Who was following us?"

"I never found out. They were gone by the time I pulled out of the gas station."

"Shit," Jess breathed.

"Yeah."

"What else aren't you telling me?"

Padraig was watching this exchange with an unreadable look on his face.

Jil suddenly felt uncomfortable—a little too intimate—even though she wasn't saying anything but facts. Her personal life and her professional life were colliding—eclipsing—and she didn't like it. She was afraid of what would happen if she told Jess about the man with the knife in the tunnel. "Why don't I fill you in later?" she muttered.

"Sure."

Jil took the marker out and began filling in more blank spaces.

-Wax seal with SoA
-Watermarked notes
-Secret club?
-Student Council

From her notebook, she pulled out the watermarked notes, and pinned them to the board.

Jess stared at the list and paled like some long-dormant ghost had tapped her on the shoulder, dripping blood. When she spoke, her voice was barely above a whisper. "SoA. That couldn't be…Sons of Adam?"

Padraig and Jil both looked at her, surprised.

"What the hell is going on in my school?"

"Jess, does that mean something to you?" Jil asked.

Jess stared at her.

"Who are they?" Padraig asked, leaning forward.

Jess struggled to form words, and when she did, they were soft and strangled. "Years ago, at the time of that young boy's death—"

"Bobby Hansen?" Jil interrupted.

Jess blinked, like tears had suddenly pricked her eyes. "Yeah."

"Sorry," Jil muttered. "Go on."

"I was a teacher at St. Joseph's, which is just in the next district to St. Marguerite's. I was brought into St. Marguerite's to talk to students. Another student teacher and I were parked in the guidance office for about a week after the incident.

"Most of the kids talked about other things—not even about the kids who died. But there was this one guy. This one scrawny little bit of a thing. He can't have been more than fifteen. I swear he said the Sons of Adam were responsible."

"And did you ask him what that meant?" Padraig asked.

"I did. But he was pretty tight-lipped. Didn't even look like he wanted to be there. I think he was the one guy who made about three appointments and missed them before he finally came in. And then, when we did sit down, he wanted the door closed, which I wasn't allowed to do. So he whispered really low and kept throwing glances over his shoulder. Anyway, I didn't get a whole lot out of him at that point, but I do remember him saying something about the Sons of Adam."

"Did you tell anyone?"

"Actually, yes," Jess said, her brow furrowed as she remembered incidents from a decade ago. "I remember going back to my own school at the end of the week, still thinking about this boy. I told my mentor what he'd said."

"And what did your mentor tell you?" Padraig pressed.

"He said that he knew this kid from elementary school and that he was very disturbed. He had a history of mental illness, or something to that effect. Not to pay too much attention to what he said. So I dropped it. But now that you bring it up again…I wonder."

Jil remembered something Jess had said a few months back—when she'd been complaining about Buck and the mentorship process. "Jess," she said slowly. "Your mentor when you were a student teacher was—"

"Giovanni DiTullio," Jess finished.

Jil and Padraig exchanged a look.

"What does that have to do with anything?" she asked.

"That," Padraig said gravely, "is what we're going to find out." And then, when Jil looked at him closely, seeing the wheels spinning in his head, she had to ask.

"You mentored Mark Genovese, is that right?"

"That's right."

"Why? He's got to be more than twenty years older than you."

Jess frowned. "I had a master's degree and I climbed the ranks faster. I was a VP before he was, and DiTullio paired us together."

Padraig and Jil exchanged a look.

"When? When was this?"

"The summer after…when everything happened with Mick." She swallowed painfully.

Padraig leaned closer, his voice urgent. "Jil—your investigation."

"I know."

"You were right. It was never a real investigation. It was just a ruse."

Jil breathed out, her thoughts racing.

"More than a ruse," she whispered. "A setup."

Well past lunchtime, Padraig stood up.

"Where are you going?" Jil asked.

"First, I'm meeting with our accountant. Then, I believe I need to see our generous sponsor. And then, I need to clear away the little matter of the gun."

Jil blushed.

"What gun?" Jess asked.

Both Padraig and Jil looked at her.

"The gun I had belonged to Padraig," Jil explained.

But Jess just stared at them poker-faced. "What gun?"

Slowly, like an ember catching flame on paper and blossoming into a fire, it dawned on Jil. Jess was the one responsible for keeping her name out of the media. She was the reason no one had heard about her involvement. Jess knew as well as anyone that civilians weren't allowed to carry weapons—even ex-police officers turned PIs. She had been trying to protect her. But was it possible that she could have convinced the entire rumor mill to stop churning out that one particular piece of information?

"No one saw a gun," Jess said firmly.

They stared at each other for a moment.

"How can you do that?" Jil asked.

"Do what?"

"Pretend that nothing happened? Pretend that I wasn't running through your school with a loaded weapon?"

"No one saw you do that. In fact, no one saw you at all."

Padraig chuckled. Jil just stared at her, baffled.

"We're a Catholic school," said Jess, a small smile twitching at the corners of her mouth. "Denial is our way of life."

Chapter Twenty-three

When Padraig had given Jil instructions to meet him at DiTullio's office later that afternoon and had taken his leave, Jil and Jess were left sitting awkwardly on the couch, carefully avoiding each other's eyes. Jil's mind raced with the puzzle pieces she was beginning to put together.

"Can I get you something to eat?" she asked, heading for the kitchen. Anything to get in the way of having a real conversation. The real topics.

Jess hesitated a moment. "Sure."

Jil took out a container of homemade soup and put it on the stove then unwrapped a pre-made garlic bread and put it in the oven.

"So, Jil," said Jess, taking a seat on the raised barstool and cupping her face in her hand. "What's your plan for next week?"

Jil smiled. "Well, it looks like I'm out of a teaching job," she quipped weakly.

"I should have known you weren't a teacher. No one with your grit decides to go into teaching religion, for God's sake. So, how will you finish your investigation?"

"Not sure yet. I'll have to wait for Padraig on that one."

"You're finished investigating me, then?"

"It was never just you."

"Someone wants me gone. Is that it?"

And in that second, Jil made a decision. In her heart of hearts, she knew what was right to do, and what was wrong to keep secret. This investigation was more than a paycheck, more than politics and morality and biblical teachings. It was about how she was going to live the rest of her life.

She remembered what Padraig had whispered to her, just before he'd left—gone to do something he didn't even want to reveal to Jil. "I don't want you sacrificing who you are for your work. And I sure as hell won't let you do it for me."

Permission to spill her guts.

"Why would Giovanni DiTullio want me gone?"

"That, I haven't yet figured out," Jil replied honestly.

"So you've been investigating me since September? I was your prime target?" Something else lingered behind her words—more than just anger. Jil waited and finally she asked, "Was it part of your job to get involved with me so you could learn my secrets?"

"No. No, Jess. I didn't even get the list of names I was supposed to start with until after I'd already met you—after I—after we…after I figured out I liked you," she finished, blushing furiously.

"And then what? You just thought, 'Hey, this is convenient. I can use her to get what I want?'"

"Jess, I'm so sorry. I don't expect you to understand at all what I was thinking. I don't even understand. I just kept delaying things in my mind. I investigated everyone else before you, telling myself that maybe I could just leave you off the list, claim I couldn't find anything wrong with what you were doing."

Jess smiled wryly, seeming unable to decide which was winning—her overwhelming sense of betrayal, or understanding for Jil's position.

"I can name at least ten acts of uncatholic conduct that I've committed in the past hour. There's no way you could have left me off the list…after…well…" She stared at Jil for a long moment, just digesting the news.

"I have yet to find anywhere in the Bible that states 'thou shalt not be gay,'" said Jil softly.

"You might make a good Catholic after all," Jess replied. "Seems you have a knack for self-denial."

Bolstered by that small gesture of understanding, she went on, turning to the soup on the stove so she wouldn't have to look Jess in the face. "I couldn't let you go, and I'm sorry for that. I should never have gotten involved with you. It was wrong, but I couldn't help it. I was just so drawn to you that…"

"That what?" Jess asked, her voice softer now.

"That I just…I wanted to believe that it was right."

"Right in what sense?"

"In any sense. Not only are you my target—" At that word, Jess's face tensed again. "But even being with you, being anywhere near you, was a conflict of interest. How can I investigate someone for uncatholic conduct when I'm the person causing them to act that way? And how can I investigate the person I care about? And if that wasn't complicated enough, how can I throw away an investigation because of my own feelings, knowing that it would jeopardize Padraig's agency? I've made such a mess, and I'm so sorry. And I hope that you can understand what I was doing, because God knows I can't."

Jess sighed deeply. "No one has ever lied to me like this before," she said tightly. "Jil, I'm falling in love with you, and I have no idea who you are."

Jil stopped stirring the soup to look up at Jess. For a second, they stared at each other over the countertop, silently, no words seeming to be enough to cross the distance between them.

And then Jil walked over to the bar, grasped both Jess's hands in hers, and said, "There have been so many times that I wished I had never met you. But I wouldn't trade you for anything. Not my job. Not normalcy. Nothing. But, Jess, once I move past this case, I can do my job and have you at the same time. You can't. You have way more to lose."

Jess grinned at her, a smart-assed comment clearly playing on her lips. But she kept it to herself, regarding Jil steadily, as if trying to decide how much she could trust her. And then finally, she leaned forward, mouth tilted up, instead. This time, when they kissed, there were no lies between them, and the roadblock removed was palpable.

❖

Padraig parked his car smoothly and waited for Jil to unbuckle her seat belt. "You don't have to say a word at this meeting. Leave it to me."

Jil's palms sweated and she rubbed them against her jeans as Padraig led the way into the white stone building that housed the Rockford Catholic School Board. He didn't pause at the front desk, but walked straight to the elevator, and up to Giovanni DiTullio's corner office.

"Mr. DiTullio, good morning," he said as he opened the door, letting himself in.

DiTullio looked up, surprised. "Hello, Mr. O'Hanagan," he said, rising, a quizzical expression on his face. "How can I help you?"

Padraig stepped aside. "I've brought Ms. Kidd with me."

At this, his face fell. "Ms. Kidd," he faltered. "How nice to meet you."

Jil shook hands but said nothing.

Padraig smiled widely and helped himself to a seat, settling down comfortably. "In light of recent events, I thought I'd best come see you in person."

DiTullio sat down gingerly again, fingers steepled on the desk. "Yes, I understand. I apologize for not calling you sooner, but I've been rather busy with the implications of that incident."

"What implications are those, exactly?" Padraig asked amiably.

"Oh, I won't bore you with the details, but I do hope Ms. Kidd wasn't injured in the process."

"No, no, not at all. In fact, she wasn't even there," Padraig replied.

"No?"

"No," Padraig said. "She was off sick that day."

"Really."

"Yes. In fact, I brought her chicken soup at home. Right around the time when the lockdown alarm went off."

"I see," DiTullio narrowed his eyes at Jil. "Then I suppose there was another person in the school at that time who just happened to look like Julia Kinness."

"No, no. Don't think so," Padraig replied. "Seems everyone agrees that Ms. Kinness was MIA that day."

Giovanni was silent. "Well," he said carefully. "I guess that makes sense. Something tells me she tends to stand out."

"She does. Indeed she does," Padraig replied. "Which is why she's one of my best investigators."

Jil shuffled her feet, trying to figure out why Padraig had dragged her to this uncomfortable meeting.

"The most special thing about her is that she would willingly give her life for someone she thought was in danger. That, she has proved to me over and over again. She'd even bring a contraband weapon into a public place in order to protect young students from a threat."

"Quite the woman you've got working for you." DiTullio met her eye.

"Yes, indeed. I value her. And when someone else willingly puts her in danger, that really bothers me, Mr. DiTullio."

"Now, why would that be the case?"

"No idea. Doesn't seem to make much sense to me at all. Perhaps it's something I'd like to investigate further. Why a young agent would be brought in to do a job, which she does successfully—perhaps a little too successfully—and then suddenly becomes the target of malice. Why do you think that might be?"

"I'm sure I don't know."

"Well, I'm quite bothered by it," Padraig said. "In fact, it bothers me so much that I would, without hesitation, put the person responsible for injuring my agent directly in the line of his own fire, if I knew who he was. Don't know how I'd do it, exactly, but I'd be sure to do something. It could be at night, sometime—walking out of the pub. It could be in broad daylight, on the highway. It could be while he was sleeping, oh so soundly in his bed. But I promise you, it would happen."

DiTullio's face was so tight and his lips were so drawn that he looked like a bad caricature of himself, sitting there. Jil almost felt sorry for him. But then she remembered Gideon's face, and stopped.

"Ms. Kinness filed an absentee form for last Thursday," he said in measured tones. "I understand that she's been off ill for the past few days."

"Is that right?"

"Yes. The paperwork is on Ms. Blake's desk."

"As we speak?"

"As we speak."

"Excellent. I'm glad to hear that's sorted. We'll have our final report to you by week's end."

"Very well, Mr. O'Hanagan. And your final check will be in the mail. Thank you for coming to visit."

"My pleasure, Mr. DiTullio. My pleasure."

As Jil followed Padraig out, she paused to touch a picture standing on a shelf by the door. Four young men—arms slung around each other, grinning in front of a high ropes course.

Something clicked. "Outdoor Education trip?" she asked. She turned around in time to see DiTullio's eyes widen.

"Uh, yes."

"Looks like a great time."

"It was. It was."

Jil turned and strode back to the desk, the picture in hand. She leaned over DiTullio, her face inches from the man's clean-shaven jaw. "Why did you do it?" she whispered. "After all these years, why expose them now?"

DiTullio swallowed hard. "I don't know what you mean."

"You do. You knew I would find out about the Sons of Adam. That's why you hired us. You were part of the club—have been since you were a teenager. Why did you want them exposed?"

DiTullio loosened his tie. "I hired you to investigate contracts," he insisted.

"Like hell. You know those things aren't really enforceable. You hired me to expose the Sons of Adam. You knew Jess Blake wouldn't let this bullshit stand at her school and would go to the wall to protect her students. Why did you want this secret out? Why now?"

DiTullio gasped for breath, hesitating a full minute before leaning forward. "This goes no further," he said in a strangled voice.

"My word," Jil agreed.

"My son," he choked. "I wanted to send him to private school. I thought they'd be more accepting of him there. But what kind of example is that? The superintendent doesn't even send his own children to the Catholic school board? St. Marguerite's is his district school."

"Your son is a student there?"

"Next year," DiTullio said. "Next year, he'd have to go there and…with his…tendencies…I know…"

Jil stopped for a moment to let it all sink in, then stood up. "I understand."

"No. I don't think you do." DiTullio straightened up. "Once they know you, once they target you, it goes on for life."

"That's why these students didn't wait it out until graduation? They realized, somehow, that the SoA would follow them?"

"Into university. Their careers. It's like a stain you can't shake. They appear to be everywhere. The priesthood—"

Jil let out a low whistle. "I'm beginning to see now. Thank you, Mr. DiTullio."

DiTullio collapsed back into his chair, wiping his brow with a clean handkerchief. "Thank you, Ms. Kidd."

❖

Jil thanked Megan Donnelly and headed down the front steps, away from the two-bedroom townhouse Megan now shared with her wife, Frances.

Her mind churned with information, but she couldn't yet make sense of it.

Before she could forget anything valuable, she locked herself inside her car, pulled out her notebook, and scribbled down everything Megan had told her about the late Regina Francis, and their high school days.

Then she started on the four-hour drive home.

Chapter Twenty-four

The alarm buzzed, and a corrections officer showed Jil through the doors of the Rockford Penitentiary, Juvenile Division. "I'm here to see Gideon McPherson."

"This way, ma'am," he said and led her down a dark corridor to the visiting office.

When Gideon saw her, his face went pink, and he hurried to the table.

"Where are my parents?" he said as soon as he sat down.

"Your parents? Were you expecting them?"

"My social worker called them, but they're leaving me here to rot!" Gideon sputtered, his eyes full of tears. "They haven't come once. Not once!"

Jil reached across the table, and squeezed his hand. "Gideon, you need to relax, okay?" His shaking alarmed her.

"Miss, what's going to happen to me?"

Jil squeezed his arm harder. "Breathe, kid," she said. Across the room, a corrections officer moved toward them, and she released Gideon's arm, mouthing "sorry." The CO stepped back.

"I don't know, Gideon. But Ms. Blake and I will work as hard as we can to get something done, okay?"

"Ms. Blake?"

"Yeah."

At this, Gideon exhaled, seeming at last to relax a little. "Ms. Blake. You're sure?"

Jil wasn't at all sure what Jess could do, but since this was the only reassurance that seemed to be working, she put on a poker face and repeated, "I'm sure."

"Okay, Miss."

Jil was moved at how easily Gideon still flocked to her as his teacher—someone who should have been protecting him.

"Can you find out from my social worker what's happening?" Gideon asked. "Even Bex, she hasn't been here once either."

"Bex isn't allowed," Jil said. "But I'll tell her I saw you, and I know she'd want me to tell you to stay strong and hang in there. Okay?"

He nodded, his face flushed.

"Right now, I'm here to ask you some really important questions, okay?"

Okay."

"And it's really important—for you especially—that you don't tell anyone I've been here."

"Why?"

Jil just silenced him with a look. The less he knew the better. If anyone got wind of the fact that she'd elicited a full confession from this kid, and she was ever subpoenaed to his trial, it would be very bad for his case.

"Gideon, you don't know me. Got it?"

He just nodded. "Got it, Miss."

"I need you to tell me everything. Right from the beginning. Can you do that?"

Gideon clenched his jaw.

"Start talking. And start with the Sons of Adam."

Gideon looked at her, wide-eyed. "How do you—"

"Gideon," Jil warned him.

"I can't tell you anything about them," Gideon said, looking away.

"You don't have a choice. Tell me who they are."

"I don't know."

"Gideon, c'mon. I need to know. Things are getting way out of hand at St. Marguerite's. They need help, and you're the only one who can give it. I need to know who these people are."

"They're not just at St. Marguerite's." Gideon leaned forward. "They're all over the place, Miss."

"You mean at the school, or in the community?"

"Everywhere." Gideon looked over his shoulder, like he expected one of them to pop out of the woodwork. "It's like a fraternity. You know, you join in high school, and you're with them for the rest of your life, kind of thing."

Jil swallowed hard. "Okay. Who recruited you?"

Gideon shook his head. "That's the thing," he replied. "I don't even know who they are."

"What do you mean?"

"You're not allowed to meet any of them. Only to hear them."

"Okay. Start from the beginning."

Talking seemed to be helping Gideon to shake off his fear. Even though he was leaning forward, he didn't appear as hunched or hampered as before. His voice was urgent, low.

"They sneak up on you. You don't know who they are, but they always come as a surprise. They come up behind you in the bathroom or in the hall, and they shove you into an empty room. Then they blindfold you and tie you to a chair, or a post, or a desk, or something. And there's always a group of them."

"Guys or girls?"

"Mostly guys. But there are some girls. The girls usually come later. They don't do the kidnapping part, mostly."

Made sense that they wouldn't send in the ladies to do the takedown. They were better at the subverted manipulation.

"How many times has this happened to you?"

"A couple of times," Gideon replied. "After the first time, they said I would get notes in my locker after that, and that I had to follow what it said to do."

"And did you?"

"Yeah."

"And did you follow them?"

Gideon's face fell. "Yeah," he whispered. "At first, I thought it was kind of a game. Then I got scared. The worst part is not knowing who they are. Not knowing who to look out for or who to trust."

"Did they do it to anyone else?"

Gideon nodded.

"Who?"

"Wyatt," he replied. "He was the only one I knew for sure. And I only knew because he came to math one day and his hair was soaking wet from when they'd dunked him in the toilet. I asked him, kind of sneaky-like, you know? And he admitted it. That someone had jumped him in the bathroom."

Jil recalled the day of the first tagging when she had met Gideon and Wyatt in the hall—their terrified expressions, their guarded stances.

"Why did they target him?"

"I don't really know, but they spray-painted 'Bastard' on his locker one day, and another day, gave him a cloth letter A and told him to give it to his mother."

"Is Wyatt's mom single?"

"She never married his dad, if that's what you mean."

"I think that's why he was a target."

"They told him if he did what they said, they'd stop going after him."

When did this start?"

Gideon shrugged. "September. Miss, I have to go to that school until grade twelve. That's six whole years. Do you know how long that is? It's forever. Forever."

To a seventh-grader, absolutely, six years seemed like a life sentence.

"You said you got notes."

"Yeah."

"What did the notes say to do?"

"Mostly it was to just deliver stuff. Like, other envelopes to other people."

"Anything else? Did they ever ask you to do any graffiti?"

Gideon looked genuinely surprised. "No," he said. "Nothing like that."

"Did they ever ask you to hurt anyone? Follow anyone?"

"No. Well, yeah, actually. Once, it was to…follow someone."

"Who?"

"A girl. They said to wait until she went to the bathroom, by herself. Then I was supposed to put this mask on and scare her. Like, jump out at her, and call her names, then run away."

"Did you?"

Gideon shook his head. "No. I could never find her alone. I tried, and when two days went by and I still hadn't done it, some guy in a mask came up on me and dunked my head in a toilet. That's how I knew about Wyatt. Because the same thing happened to him."

"Do you know who it was that dunked you?"

"Some senior," Gideon said, shaking his head. "It's hard to see when someone has a mask on. All I saw was his student council shirt."

"You're sure it was a student council shirt?"

"Of course. They all wear them. White with the St. Mag's crest."

Jil took out a piece of paper from her pocket—the watermarked paper that contained her first warning.

Gideon looked at it, his eyes registering shock, then disbelief, then finally, understanding.

Watch Your Back.

"Was this the symbol?" asked Jil.

"You mean…" he said, "You mean…they were after you too? A teacher?"

"I'm not a teacher, Gideon. I'm an investigator."

"An investigator? Like a real-life undercover private eye?"

Jil smiled. "Sort of like that. And I will get to the bottom of this. But I need you to understand how serious it is."

If he hadn't been on board before, Gideon certainly was now.

"Do you remember what you were supposed to say to the girl you had to follow?"

"Yeah. The first one, I was supposed to call her like 'slut' and 'bitch.' It's because she was pregnant or something. I don't know what happened to her, because she got kicked out of the school."

Jil frowned. She remembered some announcement earlier in the year about a student withdrawing from the eleventh grade. A reason hadn't been given.

"There were more you had to follow?"

"Just one more. I was supposed to put a note in her locker and then wait til she went into the bathroom. Then I had to follow her in there and yell 'dyke' while she was in the stall and couldn't see me."

"Do you remember who it was?"

"Yeah. She lives in residence too. But she got back at them."

"Got back at them how?"

Gideon's eyes twinkled, but he remained silent.

"With a little red paint?" Jil said, connecting the dots.

Gideon remained silent.

"Can you tell me her name?"

The boy shook his head. "I promised."

"Can you describe her?"

"No."

"Can you give me anything, Gideon? I'm trying to help you here."

Gideon thought for a second, then pinched the tip of his nose and tugged.

A ring? A bullring?

Teegan.

Jil frowned. But she'd checked Teegan herself the morning of the fire alarm…and been so distracted with the pot in her bag that she hadn't checked her hands. *Wow. Awesome, PI.*

"Teegan was vandalizing the school? Why?"

Gideon shrugged. "She didn't like those student council kids always breathing down her neck."

"The student council?" She remembered something Teegan and Bex had said at the climbing trip—something about the student council keeping the wayward Pathways students on a righteous path.

Things were beginning to click. The Sons of Adam had a front…

"She thought if she said anything out loud, she'd get kicked out of the program. So she decided to just write her message, you know?"

Jil sighed. Wished she'd thought of that.

"Yeah."

"Dyke is like 'fag,' though, right? It's like, a really bad name," Gideon said, switching the subject.

"Yeah, you shouldn't use that word."

"Bex hates that word," Gideon said quietly. "She says it's discrim—discriminate…"

"Discriminatory. Yes. That's right. She wouldn't like it."

"You know my sister's like, you know. Gay, right?"

"Yep. I know."

"Did she tell you?"

"Uh huh."

"Well, see, the last foster parents we had, they didn't like that she's gay. They kept trying to make her straight. They even sent her to this camp to like pray the gay away. And they wouldn't let her talk about it at home. They thought it was gonna—I don't know what they thought. Before we moved to the Pathways program, I heard Bex arguing with them like a thousand times."

"About you too?"

"Yeah. They thought it'd be harder on me if everyone knew she was gay."

"Do you think it will be?"

"I dunno. But that's why I did what they said with their stupid notes. Because they told me if I didn't, that they would go after Bex, and I was afraid for her, because of what they did to other people."

"And did they leave her alone?"

Gideon shook his head. "No. They started—" He sniffed, and his nose turned red.

"What?"

He gasped, trying to hold back the tears.

"What did they do?" Jil probed.

He wiped the back of his hand across his eyes. "Miss, you have to promise not to tell anyone I told you."

"Is it bad?"

"It's really bad."

"You said they hurt Bex. That day in the hallway when I tackled you."

Gideon nodded. "Yeah."

"What did you mean?"

His chest heaved and he sniffed loudly.

"How did they hurt her?"

"She was with some other kids from her class."

"Joey and Kyle?"

"Yeah. Them. I figured she was okay if she was in a group, so I went off to the rec room to play Wii. But when I saw her later that night, she was acting so weird, Miss. She was all white and she wouldn't look at me. I asked her what happened and she wouldn't tell me. I stayed with her for the whole weekend, but she didn't look me in the eye once."

"Did you find out what happened?"

"Finally. They raped her, Miss. The group of boys."

Jil left the Rockford Penitentiary, her thoughts reeling. She dialed Jess's direct line, all the while keeping half an eye on her GPS to make sure she was on target for her next appointment. Well, calling it an appointment was rather a loose representation of facts. Usually an appointment indicated that both parties knew they were going to be meeting. The Deloittes had no idea she was coming—which made this more of an ambush than a rendezvous.

"Jess, it's me," she said when Jess picked up the phone.

"What did you find out?" she asked.

"He's in the juvenile section. No lawyer. And his parents haven't visited."

"You're kidding me. What about his sister?"

"Nope. Is she even present at school?"

"No. She's been absent since last Thursday."

Thursday—the date of the incident.

"Any idea where she is?" She felt her chest constrict.

"None. But I have the feeling I need to find out."

"You need to find out now. She's in serious trouble, Jess. Go to her dorm room, drag her out if you have to, but she's got to get to the hospital."

"What happened?"

"I'll explain later. Promise me you'll find her."

"I promise. I'm going right now."

"Okay. We'll rendezvous at six."

"Bye, Jil."

Jil smiled. She still hadn't got used to Jess using her real name. It was nice, somehow, to be known.

Chapter Twenty-five

At six p.m., Jil parked half a block from the school and took the long route around the football field to the side entrance where Jess was waiting for her. She felt in her pocket to make sure her tiny technological gift from Morgan was still there. She moved it between her finger and thumb, like a worry stone.

"Stick this in the USB slot," Morgan had said that morning, as he'd slowed down in his car to pass it to her through the window.

She'd known better than to press him for details. It would do the job she needed, and the less she knew the better.

"Will it self-destruct?" she quipped.

He winked at her and pulled out of her loft's parking lot. Now, if only she and Jess could get into Genovese's office, they might actually be able to use it.

Jess ushered her inside.

"Who else is in the building?" Jil asked.

"Custodians mostly. A few stragglers. Buck Weekly is in his office still."

"But the main office staff?"

"Gone home," Jess confirmed. She went first down the hallway, peering around each corner before smuggling Jil along the hall to her office.

Once they closed the door, Jil breathed a sigh of relief. "First, tell me about Bex."

"Right. She's at the hospital now with Rosie McMonahan. Rosie promised to stay with her until her social worker got there, or until she was released. But they're going to provide her a counselor in hospital who will follow her afterward."

"Do you know where she's going?"

"Not back here, that's for damn sure," Jess said. "The poor kid wants a placement as far away from here as possible." Her forehead creased and she looked to be fighting back tears. "I just can't believe any of our students could behave so horribly. Gang-raping a girl? Bullying kids into suicide? What the hell kind of environment is this?"

"One that's been festering for a long time."

"Right under my nose."

Jil shook her head. "They played you. Picked a young, inexperienced principal—"

"Who was distracted by her own life," Jess finished. "Green and relying on her mentors. God. I made it so easy. I let them run that residence program, because that's what the principal before me did. I let student council take an active role because I believed our own press about St. Marguerite's having the brightest and the best students. Blinded by our trophies and our headlines."

"But there's one thing you're forgetting," Jil said gently.

"What?"

"DiTullio. He knew you'd put a stop to this."

Jess shook her head. "Small consolation."

Jil's phone buzzed. A text from Padraig. *All clear outside*.

Jil felt better knowing that Padraig was surveilling the perimeter, but the knot in her stomach would not release until she'd found what she was looking for and vacated.

She put her hand in her pocket again. Morgan, her ever-reliable friend. She could hardly count how many scrapes he'd gotten her out of, and now that he was into cyber forensics, his knowledge apparently knew no bounds. Theoretical knowledge of course. Because there were some lines no good officer would cross.

Jess slipped out the door and crossed the main office to the doors there, which she locked. On her way back, she hit the light panel.

Jil followed her to the office next door and over to Mark Genovese's desk. She peered out the window and caught a glimpse of Padraig's darkened SUV across the road.

She pulled herself up to the desk and flipped on the computer. A popup box prompted her to enter a code. She looked to Jess, who typed in the code that was supposed to override access to any school computer.

A loud ding echoed through the room. Jil punched the sound down with her thumb. "It didn't work."

Jess shook her head.

"Morgan, it's me," Jil spoke into her phone. "That theoretical computer is encrypted."

"Okay, here's what I might try," Morgan said.

Jil followed his instructions, and in a moment, the popup box flashed, and they were in.

"Thanks."

Morgan's low chuckle reverberated in her ear. "I'd say 'anytime,' but I'm afraid of the phone calls I'd get."

After they'd hung up, Jil connected the small device in her pocket to the computer, and began scanning. Every few clicks, she needed to override the system, and as the minutes ticked by and Jess fidgeted behind her, the knot in her stomach tightened.

Her phone buzzed. Padraig. *Black Panther on the prowl.*

Her stomach lurched. "Jess, Genovese is outside."

"What?" She moved to the door and peered out. "What's he doing here?"

"I don't know. Did you say Buck's still here?"

She turned around. "Yeah. Do you think that's important?"

Jil shrugged. "I don't know anymore. I have a feeling the answer might be locked in this computer."

"Okay, if Mark comes this way, I'll head him off. How long do you need?"

"Five minutes. I have to log into his FaithConnects account and get the final piece of this puzzle."

Jess slipped out the office door, and a moment later, Jil heard the main door clink open.

Silence followed as she clicked the keys, searching for the one thing she was sure she would find.

"Bingo." The hairs on her arms stood up as she saw GunSlinger's face flash up on the screen. She scanned through the conversations from last fall—between him and Alyssa. "Wow," she breathed, not quite able to believe what she was reading.

On a hunch, she clicked on the "Linked Accounts" tab at the top. Clarisse's picture popped up. So, Mark was both GunSlinger and Clarisse.

From down the hall, she heard faint voices. She knew she didn't have much time. As quickly as she could, she uploaded the data to the device, streaming it directly to her computer at home. She waited for the green light to flash.

The main office door clinked open. Jil felt bile rise in her throat. She pulled the device out and gently closed the lid on the computer. No time to shut it down.

Footsteps sounded outside, but they didn't come right for the door, as she'd feared. Instead, she heard drawers gently easing open and closed in the main office.

Then Jess's voice rose. "Looking for something to hawk?"

A drawer banged shut.

"Uh…what? I don't know what you're talking about." Marcel's voice sounded panicked.

"The St. Marguerite's magpie," said Jess. "I think I just caught him."

"I was just…cleaning."

"Brian is assigned to this office, not you."

"Well, Brian's slow. This isn't the first time I've had to clean up his areas." Some of the cocky bravado had returned to his voice.

"Save it," said Jess. "Just leave your things and go home."

"But—"

"Now! I have enough to deal with at this school without thieves on top of it all."

Jil heard the main door open and was about to creep out of her hiding place behind the door, when she heard Mark Genovese's voice. "What's going on?"

She froze.

"I caught the magpie," said Jess clearly. "Do me a favor, Mark, and follow him out. Make sure he doesn't take anything valuable with him. And check his locker. See if he's kept anything in there."

"I was just going to grab something from my office." Jil held her breath. "But I'll get it on my way out."

"Okay. I'll leave the main doors open for you. I'm leaving now, just as soon as I file a report about this incident."

The main doors clinked again, and Jil counted to ten before coming out of hiding.

Just then, Jess opened the door. "In my office, quickly."

"Just a second." She crept back to the computer and shut it down properly. Mark could never know she'd been in there. In Jess's large room, she hid against the side door.

"What did you get?"

"I'll have to download it all at home, and read everything again, but I think we got him."

"Really?" Jess's tone was bleak.

"I know."

"Part of me was just hoping…"

"I'm sorry."

"I'm actually afraid to be alone here. Isn't that ridiculous? I never thought I'd say that about my own school. So many secrets, lies…"

Jil looked around, making sure again that the blinds were all drawn. "Padraig's right outside. We'll leave together."

"I actually do have to file this report."

"Okay then. I'm just going to take a trip down the hall and talk to Buck."

"Right now?" Jess's voice rose.

"Can you think of a better time? I can't exactly waltz in while school's in session."

Jess rolled her eyes. "One incident with damage control wasn't enough?"

Jil grinned. "Sorry. I'll meet you by the car." She peeked into the atrium and saw no one, so she dashed across the empty space and down the hall.

Once at Buck's office, she entered without knocking and closed the door firmly behind her.

He looked up, startled. "Ms. Kinness."

"Hi." She quickly switched on the dim desk light and hit the panel for the bright overhead halogens before yanking the blinds closed. From the hallway, the office would look dark. Nobody home.

For a second, she had a fleeting feeling of dread—that she'd just locked herself in a dark cage with a man whose history she still found dubious—but she'd started now and couldn't quit.

"What are you doing here?" Buck asked.

"I've come to talk to you."

"Why now?"

"Because you have valuable information, and I need it."

Buck leaned forward in his chair, seeming to sense her urgency, because he kept his sentences short and his voice low. "You shouldn't be here. People will start to figure out you're not a teacher."

"How many people know that already?"

Buck frowned. "Jess didn't say much after you left. I've been citing the party line."

"What is it?"

"That you had to have emergency surgery and wouldn't be back this term."

Jil snorted. "A lobotomy, more like." She stopped abruptly, wondering if she had just put her foot in her mouth. Had Buck ever had a lobotomy?

He stared at her. Not a good time to ask. "What do you need from me?"

Jil sighed. "How long did you know I wasn't a teacher? From the beginning?"

Buck ran his fingers over his chin. "DiTullio thought you might get into a little trouble."

Jil smiled ruefully. "I did, of course. Teaching religion in a Catholic school. Sorry for being so difficult."

"Well, likewise. But I was tasked with looking after you, and I guess I made an ass of myself."

"Sitting in on my class, wanting my report cards…."

"I was trying to prevent Jessica and everyone else from finding out about you. The students are a lot smarter than you'd give them credit for."

"Well, thank you. I'm sorry I didn't make it easy for you. But tell me something else."

"What?"

"DiTullio admitted to sending me in here to find out about the SoA."

Buck sat back like he'd been smacked. "What?" he choked.

"I know this was a setup. I know I wasn't here to investigate uncatholic conduct."

Buck leaned heavily on the desk. "I didn't know. My God."

"I know you tried to protect me from them as well."

His face took on a haggard look. "He told me you were here to look into contracts. That this was the best way to protect our teachers and students—by making sure they toed the line. He didn't say anything about exposing the…"

Jil gave him a moment to collect himself. "I need to know how long this organization has been here. Who's involved?" she said quietly.

Buck sighed—a hollow sound. "DiTullio?" His voice sounded strangled.

"Yes."

"Why? Why now?"

Jil said nothing. "The SoA. You've known about it for years. Why keep their secret?"

"What else could I do? I'm just a bumbling old man who's lucky to hold on to his job. The one who's been to the loony bin twice. Now I start talking about secret societies and conspiracy theories? They'd lock me up forever. I have no proof."

"No proof and a VP who's in on the whole thing."

Buck glanced at the door, alarm sketched on his face. "You be careful who you're talking to," he muttered. "Mark Genovese is someone you want to keep tabs on at all times. Don't trust him."

"Why?"

"Just…he's dangerous."

"Is that why you've stayed here all these years? To keep an eye on him—on the school?"

"It's all I can do," Buck said helplessly. "Try to keep the kids on the straight and narrow. Lend a hand to the Residence program. Those kids are always a target because they're such easy access. Try to reach any of them before the SoA gets to them. It's difficult when you never know who they are, and who they're going to target."

"But people have still died," Jil whispered.

"Alyssa," choked Buck. "I didn't see it in time. I was too busy with Holly Barnes and her mental breakdown to notice what was going on." He clamped his mouth shut. "That was meant to be a secret."

"It's okay," Jil said. "I already knew."

Buck nodded. "She was going through a divorce. She'd started seeing someone new after finding out her husband had cheated on her for the past decade of their marriage. And then she started getting notes.

People followed her home from work. Eggs were smashed on her door. She was in a car accident. I can't say whether it was related, but she decided to take time off. She told everyone she was injured, but some found out it was stress leave. I told her to blame me. Tell someone in confidence that I was hard to work with. I know it's partly true anyway."

Jil pursed her lips. At least he admitted it. "You were here back when those boys died. Tell me what happened."

Buck lowered his head til his chin almost reached his chest. "I couldn't prove anything," he muttered. "They shut me out. Wouldn't talk. I don't know what happened."

"Who shut you out? Your brother? DiTullio? Genovese?"

Buck put his face in his hands. His fingers trembled in the dim light. He reached for the handle of his top drawer and opened it, gazing at a bottle of pills for a moment before popping one.

Something clicked in Jil's brain. "Your brother, Charleston."

Buck's face blanched ever whiter.

"Mark told me he was in a car accident. You were young then."

"Thirty years ago. Seems like several lifetimes," Buck confessed.

"Why was he targeted? What happened?"

Buck rocked forward in his chair, his breath labored. "He couldn't live with what had happened. Had nightmares, like I did, but didn't ever…you know…"

"He wasn't hospitalized?"

"No. He went traveling instead. Did foreign aid and taught at missionary schools. He never could put it behind him, though, and eventually, he came to me and said he planned to confess and expose the Sons of Adam."

"Confess what?"

But Buck didn't hear her. "He asked me to help him. I told him I'd have to think about it. Next day, he was dead."

"In the car accident."

Buck took in several breaths. "The police said he didn't even try to stop. There were no skid marks. He just plowed right into that tree like he had no brakes."

Jil swallowed hard. Another "accident."

"Buck, what couldn't he live with? What did he need to confess?"

Buck banged his fists on the desk. "I can't betray my brother. I know he only meant to harass them. Not that it's an excuse. He was there when those boys died, but he was no killer. Their deaths couldn't have been his fault, but he still felt responsible."

"What about DiTullio?"

"No," Buck said. "I know they both saw something. But neither of those boys were capable of murder."

"Neither of those two…"

Buck looked into her eyes, and she saw his haunted look.

"But Mark was?" she finished.

He looked at her but didn't say anything.

"Buck, how do you know Charleston was there?"

"That day, I saw the group of them heading up to the loft of the old gym. I figured they were smoking up or something, so I followed. When I walked into the lower gym, Tommy was hanging dead. I was paralyzed. I didn't know what to do. Then I saw that Edward was still… putting up a fight. I…I held him up and screamed for help. Charleston… Charleston came running down from the loft above the gym and cut him down. We called the ambulance. It was too late. He died anyway."

"You found the boys?"

"Yes. Charleston and I."

Jil nodded. "So that's why you're…"

"Disturbed?" he growled.

"Affected," she said gently.

"I'm sorry," he wheezed. "I can't talk about this anymore. You should go. I won't mention you've been here."

Jil watched him a moment longer. There was so much more she wanted to ask him, but he already looked like he might be due for a third stint. She pulled back. "You're going home now?"

"My wife will be wondering where I am."

"I'm sorry I had to bring it all up."

With seeming effort, he met her eyes. "I understand why. But I can't say any more."

Jil got up and peeked out the blinds into the dark, empty hall. "Is that side door unlocked?" she asked, looking down the hall to where the Exit sign glowed red.

"There's a door behind my desk," Buck said. "It leads to the parking lot. Better take that."

Ten seconds later, she sprinted across the parking lot to the street and climbed into her car, where Jess was already waiting. Four places behind them, Padraig started his engine. They watched him blink his lights to say good-bye, and then Jil spun the car around and headed for home.

❖

"Did you get that?" Jil spoke into her phone. She had just viewed the contents of Genovese's computer and streamed it to Padraig.

"Sure did," he said. "But it's still circumstantial. Buck's memories are hearsay at best. It's not enough to get him on any of the other murders."

"I have a plan."

"Does it involve calling Morgan in the morning?"

Jil sighed. "Sure does."

Chapter Twenty-six

Five thirty on a Monday morning, Jess threw the covers off her bare leg and snaked her arms back under her pillow to bury her face. "I don't want to go to work today," she mumbled.

Jil kissed her gently on the temple. "You have to. You're my spy inside."

Jess turned so that she could see Jil under the pillow that covered her head. "Do you really think we can pull this off?"

Jil shrugged, lacing her fingers in Jess's. "We have to."

Jess sighed. "God. I feel like I should sleep there at night. I can't believe Marcel took my ring!"

Jil snorted. "You should see what else he's got stashed around the school. It's like he's some sort of jewel collector. He's obviously been doing it for years."

"It's going to give me great pleasure to ransack that custodian's closet today."

Jil grinned. "Great distraction," she agreed. "But otherwise, remember that you have to act totally normal."

"Hmm," said Jess. "Which would involve what? Going home alone at night?"

"Well." Jil smiled and pulled Jess into her arms. "Except for that."

The electric heat that buzzed constantly between them ignited as soon as they touched. Jil leaned back against the headboard and trailed her fingers up Jess's spine. She kissed the back of her neck, running her hands around the smooth contours of her waist, just holding her close.

"I don't think we have time for this," Jess murmured.

"Who's going to fire you for being late?"

Jess leaned back against her, and Jil took advantage of the position to slide her hands up Jess's ribcage and cup her breasts. Immediately, her nipples stiffened.

"Christ, I don't know how you do that," Jess muttered as Jil worked the hard pebbles between firm fingertips. She closed her eyes and sighed.

Jil didn't stop, tweaking and pinching until Jess half-turned and kissed her, thrusting her tongue deeply into her mouth as she cupped Jil's face in her hands.

Jil kissed back, biting Jess's lower lip. "I'm not done making it up to you yet," she whispered, turning Jess back around. She raked both hands from Jess's waist to her shoulders, leaving light red fingernail lines along her rib cage.

Jess smiled as fingernails scraped over her sensitive nipples. "Mmm. Do it again."

She did, and Jess shuddered. She slid her hands down and across Jess's thighs, her thumb softly brushing the sensitive flesh between her legs. Gently, she hooked her hands behind Jess's knees, and pulled her thighs apart. "Can you stay like that?"

"Let's see."

Jil dipped one finger into the hot crease, already warm and wet. She teased the soft pink lips, tugging and stroking—everywhere but the throbbing hot spot that lay ready and waiting. She used her free hand to massage Jess's neck and breasts.

"Bite me," Jess breathed.

"How would you explain the hickey?" Instead, Jil dragged her teeth across Jess's shoulder, leaving tiny red marks that would soon fade from her skin. When Jess's legs fell apart more, she slipped two fingers inside, probing the tight space.

"Fuck," Jess groaned. Her muscles clamped around Jil's fingers and she whimpered.

"Deeper?"

"God, yes."

Jil pushed her fingers in farther, pulling out slowly to ignite the sensitive areas inside. She shifted to take more of the weight of Jess's leg on her own thigh, and found her clit butted against Jess's writhing hip. As Jess moaned and pushed against her, the friction made her gasp.

"Make me come," she whispered.

Jil slipped her other hand between Jess's legs, working her fingers around the pulsing clit. She drew circles in the sensitive flesh, teasing it into a hot pebble before finally, gently, running one fingertip over it.

Jess gasped and arched her hips, grinding her head into Jil's collarbone, her hip into Jil's groin.

Jil closed her eyes and continued thrusting her fingers in and out with one hand, while circling the slippery clit with the other.

Jess moaned, her noises ricocheting off the windows in the small bedroom. She groaned deeply, lifting her hips to meet Jil's every move, almost making her come too.

Jil circled slowly inward, concentrating on the most sensitive part, and in a rush of sweat and slick juices, Jess arched her back and came.

They lay still for a moment, Jil's legs wrapped loosely around Jess's thighs, the heat between them making her even more aroused.

Jess must have noticed, because she slowly turned over between Jil's legs, and pushed her down on to the bed. She ran her hands down the length of Jil's abdomen and parted her legs wide.

Jil looked at the time but didn't argue. The way she felt right now, it wouldn't take long. When Jess's hot tongue made contact, she closed her eyes and let the waves ride over her until she screamed.

"What are you going to do today?" Jess asked when Jil finally had to roll out of bed.

"I'm going to interview some people," Jil replied vaguely.

Instantly, Jess was up and out of bed, gathering Jil's dressing gown around herself. "To think the deaths might have been linked all this time," she said. "And to think I might have known something about it…might have done something about it."

"You tried," Jil said gently. "You told your mentor, who told you not to pay attention. And you believed him."

"Did I?" Jess said, her voice almost a whisper. "Or was it just easier to go along with that because it meant not having to argue? Not having to look deeper? Jil, I'm such a coward."

Jil started. "What do you mean?"

"What kind of woman continues in a job that she's not welcome in and lies to everyone she cares about—for years—under the pretext that it's no one's business? My personal life is no one's business. What kind of disservice have I been doing to my students—to myself—all this time?"

"Jess."

"What?"

"Go forward. Not back."

Jil steered her car slowly around the suburban neighborhood, looking for a street sign that said Bone Crescent. "Turn right," said her GPS in its annoying soft British accent. To her right was a row of houses, with perfectly manicured front lawns. No street.

"At the next available street, turn right," said the GPS.

The street went straight all the way down until it curved to the left.

"What a useless piece of shit." She didn't have time to waste today. She needed information, pronto.

Jil stepped on the gas and drove to the end of the street, where she followed the curve, made a series of left turns, and finally wound up on Bone Crescent, having shut the GPS off and thrown it on the seat behind her.

She alighted at number sixty-seven. It was noon, so she couldn't tell if the lights were on in the house. But there was a car in the driveway. Good sign.

After only a moment's hesitation, she knocked on the front door.

A tired looking man answered. "Can I help you?" he asked, his voice wary.

"Yes, hello, Mr. Deloitte. My name is Jillienne Kidd. I'm a private investigator."

Mr. Deloitte frowned then stepped aside as if he'd been expecting her for some time.

"You can call me Jack. My wife will make you a cup of coffee," he said, leading the way to the kitchen. Jil didn't argue. "Marie?" said the man, his voice barely lifting. A woman looked up from where she was watering plants in the eating area. "This is Jillienne Kidd. She's a private investigator."

"Hello," Marie said, extending her hand. "Welcome."

"Thank you."

"Coffee?"

"Please."

"Cream and sugar?"

"No, thank you. Just black." Cream and sugar were a luxury on long stakeouts, and she had grown accustomed over the years to straight black tar, something even Padraig couldn't get used to.

"You're here about Tommy."

Jil turned to face him. No use tiptoeing around the topic if he was going to drive straight to the point. "I am. What can you tell me about his death?"

In the kitchen, Marie closed a cupboard door—firmly.

Jack sighed. "That depends on why you want to know."

"I'm interested in learning the truth for its own sake. And because another student has died."

"I saw the papers," Jack said heavily.

"I came across an op-ed of yours in the paper." Jil pulled out the folder she'd put together from all Elise's newspaper clippings. "You said you thought there was some sort of gang responsible for bullying your son?"

"That's what I thought at the time. Of course, we didn't really know much about gangs back then. I meant it more as a group. A collection."

"Not kids in low-rising pants carrying chains and knives."

"No. More long-sleeved preppy kids with a mean streak."

Marie set a plate of cookies on the table and handed Jil her coffee. "But that was a long time ago," she said. Shadows of worry creased her tight smile.

"A very long time ago," Jack agreed. "I was wrong about it."

"How do you know you were wrong?"

A look passed between the husband and wife—something Jil couldn't immediately read. Jack passed her the plate.

"It was a Catholic school," Marie said, sitting on the edge of the couch. "They denied it existed, and our parish priest encouraged us to let it go. Told us to find our peace in God."

Jil noticed Marie's hand shaking as she reached for a pillow that she held in her lap. Something didn't make sense.

"Tell me," she said, reaching for a cookie. "Was Tommy buried in the Catholic cemetery?"

"Well, of course," Jack said, his eyes widening. "He was a Catholic, like we are."

"We have our plots next to his," Marie said quietly.

Jil knew she had to tread lightly. She wanted the truth, but not at the price of alienating these worn down people. "The parish priest," she mused, "was he a St. Marguerite's graduate?"

Jack frowned. "Yes, as a matter of fact. He wasn't too much older than Tommy. Maybe five or six years. He graduated the year Tommy went into grade seven."

"And you said you confessed your worries to him? And that he'd told you to make peace with God?"

"Yes."

"And then what happened?" Jil pressed. "Why did you really give up your conviction that Tommy had been bullied?"

"Suicide is a sin," Marie whispered. "The priest agreed to bury him on holy ground anyway, because of his age and because he'd been baptised there."

"So you were grateful to him?"

Marie nodded.

"If he'd had any other sins against him," Jil said gently, "he might not have been buried there?"

Jack cleared his throat. Marie pressed a tissue to her eyes, which had started to leak tears. "He had no other sins against him," Jack said. His voice shook a bit.

"No," Jil whispered. "Of course he didn't."

Jack smiled wanly.

"Thank you for your time." Jil stood.

They both rose to walk her to the door.

"I wish you luck with your investigation," Jack said as he saw her to her car.

Jil glanced around his shoulder to where Marie hovered in the doorway. "The boys Tommy went to school with, the ones who are still at St. Marguerite's…"

Jack's eye twitched. "Yes?"

"The Weekly brothers, Di Tullio, Mark Genovese—was Tommy friends with them?"

"No. He used to be, but they had a falling out in grade ten or eleven. He didn't see them much after that."

"Do you know what it was about?"

Jack exhaled through his nose. "I don't think he ever said," he replied tightly.

She leaned in, her voice low. "It was those four boys—they were the ones you thought were responsible."

"I couldn't prove it," Jack muttered back. "And then after he died, one of the Weekly boys ended up in the mental hospital. Too much stress. I didn't push it after that. Please, don't say anything more."

Jil shook his hand and got into the car.

As she pulled away from the curb, she looked into her rearview mirror. Jack and Marie stood in the doorway, his arm wrapped protectively around her shoulder.

As Jil made a call to Padraig, her screen flashed a red bar. Only twenty percent battery left. Shit. Why hadn't she charged it last night? She remembered exactly what she'd been doing last night and gave herself a mental kick. How many different ways was she going to compromise her investigation for the sake of Jess?

"It's me. We'll have to be quick because my battery's low," she said when he answered.

"Okay. We'll text from now on then. What did you find out?"

"The father suspected our fab four, but couldn't prove it. Kept quiet so that Tommy would be buried on consecrated ground. Apparently, the priest had something to do with that."

Padraig swore softly, and they pieced together everything they'd learned from DiTullio and Tommy's family.

Chapter Twenty-seven

Jil and Padraig settled into the front seats of Padraig's SUV, and Jil turned on the two laptop monitors."Got sound?" Padraig squinted at the screen, which showed grainy footage, and fiddled with some settings on the keyboard.

"Barely." Jil frowned as white noise rustled in her ear. She tapped her earpiece and the sound cleared as the scene on the monitor sharpened, revealing a clear view of Mark Genovese's office.

Padraig breathed out. "I was worried for a minute." He hit another key, and the atrium showed up on the first monitor. He flipped back to Genovese's office. "All set."

"See? You're a pro." Jil adjusted the second monitor, which showed the main office, and then picked up her walkie and radioed Jess. "All clear here. Approach when ready."

"Acknowledged," came Jess's quiet reply.

Jil watched as Jess came into focus on the second monitor. She crossed the main office to Mark Genovese's open door, where he sat at his desk, his broad back rigid. She knocked twice and he turned around. "We have a bit of a problem," she said, closing the door behind her.

Jil turned up her sound, trying to catch every word.

"What is it?"

"The police have decided to reopen Alyssa's case. Turns out they don't believe it's suicide."

Mark rubbed his chin. "What do they think it is?"

Jess crossed her arms and looked concerned. "When they looked at her computer they found she'd been on a number of social media sites. They think she was cyberbullied."

"Cyberbullied?"

"They mentioned something about a suicide pact."

"A suicide pact? Is someone else dead?" Jil zeroed in to see his reaction. Mark's jaw twitched as his eyes grew wider.

"No. They think it was a fake pact. Someone encouraged her to kill herself, and she finally did it."

Mark raised his eyebrows. "Someone she knew?"

"The police think it's likely. Possibly even a student at this school. They showed me a picture of the online contact and some of their conversations." Jess shook her head. "The things he said to her were… shocking. But I don't recognize the picture."

Mark leaned back in his chair. "Maybe it was a false ID," he said. "Can they trace where it came from?"

"That's how they routed it to the school."

"Well, that could be anybody on our network."

Jess nodded. "They'll be interviewing all the Pathways kids later today. Since they live here, they have the most consistent access."

"Anyone else they'll want to interview?"

Jess shrugged. "I'll keep you posted."

"Okay. Thanks."

❖

"Moving to the atrium," Jess said over the radio.

"Make sure not to pass the door of the chapel," Jil answered. "That's where the visual cuts out."

"Got it."

Jess stood in the atrium, watching as three uniformed police officers came through the door. She nodded at Morgan as he approached. "Right in here," she said.

Morgan followed her to the main office. Jil tracked them on the monitors.

"Mark, this is Lieutenant Morgan." Jess poked her head into his office.

"Good morning." Mark extended his hand.

"Morgan needs access to a computer with all the overrides available. Can you log him on to yours?"

Mark's smile tightened. "Of course."

"Thank you. I'm going to take the other officers into the Student Services Center and start helping to conduct the interviews."

"Great."

Jess waited until Mark had logged Morgan on and then ducked out again.

Jil held her breath. If she was right, Mark would try to leave before he was caught. In a moment, she watched him exit the office and head down the hallway, past the range of the camera.

A moment later, a loud buzz sounded, followed by red flashing lights. The fire alarm had been triggered.

"Shit," Jess muttered into the walkie. "He's triggered the fire alarm. The fire department will be on their way because this wasn't a planned drill. They have to come."

Jil sprang from the car and raced toward the back of the school, clutching her walkie as staff and students swarmed through every exit. "Padraig, do you have eyes on his car?" she panted.

"Affirmative. Smart move. I don't see him yet. Kidd, are you at the back?"

❖

Jil spotted a streak of purple. "Padraig, he's headed out the back door toward the woods."

"Acknowledged. Jess, get an officer out there after her, now!"

Jil didn't have time to listen to any more. She took off running after Mark. His athletic history and long legs widened the gap between them, but she dashed behind him through the trees, determined to keep up.

Morgan's warning from earlier that morning echoed in her ears. *We need a confession, Jil. Without it, he's going to walk.*

After half a mile, she slowed down, no longer able to hear him crashing through the brush ahead. She might have missed the little cabin in the densely-packed trees if she hadn't stopped to scan the horizon.

"What the hell?" She ducked behind a tree and extracted her gun from her ankle holster. The walkie buzzed, and she quickly shut it off. Nothing like static to tip off her location.

She stalked the remaining distance to the cabin, and at the door, leaned in to listen. Someone moved around inside. What was he doing here? Did he have a weapon?

If she waited for the police to get here, she might never get a confession. After thinking again, she tucked her gun into the back of her pants and opened the door.

"Hello, Mark."

He whirled around, his head almost reaching the ceiling.

"Jil, what the hell are you doing here?"

She stared at him. "So you did know."

His jaw dropped, but he quickly recovered himself, and his mouth formed a hard line. "Yes, Julia, I did."

"How much do you know?"

He pulled himself up, his angular face cold. "Everything."

In the tiny cabin, he looked even more enormous. He could easily grab her and crush her to death with his massive bare hands. She was determined not to let him see her sweat, though. Deliberately, she took one step forward.

"You stole my notebook?"

"I did. That's when I figured out you weren't who you said you were."

"That's when you started following me?"

"I saw you with Jessica. Downtown in that restaurant."

"You started calling my house? How did you get my number?"

"I have friends everywhere, Jil. I thought you'd figure that out by now. Friends who can tap even a private line to an unlisted number. Friends who will follow people into dark tunnels."

"But those friends don't know how far you've gone, do they, GunSlinger? Or should I say, Clarisse?" Jil stepped forward again. "They don't know it goes beyond bullying and threats, do they? You're the only one who knows that."

Mark sneered. "You have nothing on me."

"Don't I? Then why are you running?" Jil looked around the cabin, at the walls strewn with newspaper clippings and photographs. On a hunch, she played her hand.

"Was this the cabin where you killed Bobby?"

Mark blanched, but said nothing.

"What are you afraid of, Mark? Ghosts from the past haunting you?"

"I have no ghosts. No regrets."

"Not even for the people you've killed?"

"You don't know anything."

"All those people: Tommy and Edward. Charleston. Regina. Bobby, Alyssa?"

"None of those deaths were my fault."

She decided to go out on a limb. "You killed those two boys from your year. Then you killed Charleston because he was going to expose you and the rest of the Sons of Adam."

Mark's jaw twitched. "What did you say?"

"Charleston? Or the Sons of Adam?"

"How do you know anything about—?"

"I'm a private eye, Mark. It's my job."

"To sniff around in things that don't concern you? Isn't it bad enough that you're corrupting a principal into your queer lifestyle? Nosing into St. Marguerite's past? You'd better watch yourself, Jil. This goes way beyond anything you can handle."

"I can handle the SoA, Mark. A group of cowards who prey on vulnerable people. Bring them to me in any dark alley and take bets on the survivor. It won't be your Sons of Adam."

Mark's jaw twitched, and he clenched his fist. "Stop saying that."

"What? The Sons of Adam?"

"Shut up."

Jil felt the cool reassurance of her handgun pressed against her lower back. The recording device swirled silently in her pocket, gathering every word. "Why should I stop, Mark? Does it bother you that your secret boys' club is no longer a secret?"

"It's not a boys' club."

"No, of course not. Because that would be too gay, wouldn't it? Too suspicious, to have a club made up only of adolescent boys. Might raise some alarms. Make people question you, right?"

"You have no idea what you're talking about."

"I think I do. I think you watched them and you liked what you saw. And I think you hated yourself for liking it and killing them was the only way to get rid of those feelings."

"I'm not gay," he rasped.

Jil lifted her chin. "Funny. You didn't say you didn't kill them."

His face contorted. "They deserved to die."

"Who did?"

"All of them!"

"Why?"

"They were at a Catholic school!"

"Doing what? Holding hands? Kissing?"

"Everything!" Mark exploded. "More than that. Right here on school grounds. I saw them!"

Jil settled back against the desk, praying that if Padraig or Morgan got there, they would stay outside until she'd heard everything. The guy was spinning out. If she didn't get the confession now, she never would.

"Tell me what they were doing."

"In the loft. Above the gym…I saw them. It's a cardinal sin what they were doing!"

"Who?"

"Those girls."

"Regina?"

"And her sick girlfriend."

Jil let the sentence hang for a moment. Out of genuine curiosity, she asked, "Why didn't you go after her?"

Mark shook his head, seeming to come out of the memory. "She left school. Went to a conversion camp." He barely seemed to realize that he'd just incriminated himself.

"So you thought your work was done?"

"I had other things to think about. And it worked. Megan came back a changed girl. She even dated one of the student council."

The student council. The SoA front. "So you moved on to other targets?"

"I never killed anyone!"

"Except those boys."

"They killed themselves."

Jil shook her head. "No, they didn't."

Mark covered his face. "I didn't mean…it wasn't supposed…"

Jil stepped closer. "What happened?"

Mark's face contorted in rage. A long moment passed, and Jil was afraid she'd pushed him too far. That he would clam up and walk free.

"They got what they deserved," she whispered. "Didn't they? You were protecting the rest of the students from being corrupted, like you were."

"That faggot kissed me," Mark growled. "That's how I knew."

"Who kissed you?"

"Edward. Then Charleston and Rocco and I, we saw him and Tommy at the movies one day. I guess they thought they were alone in the back row."

"And you figured out they were together?"

"We kept it to ourselves. Rocco figured we could use it to our advantage. You know—get a little extra spending money, some favors done."

"You mean you blackmailed them."

Genovese sneered. "Yes, Charleston and Rocco were especially good at that."

"What about Buck? He's Charleston's twin. Was he there?"

"Buck is the weaker twin by far. He thought we should leave the boys alone. Didn't agree with our 'activities.'"

"Because he actually understands the tenets of Catholic faith?"

Mark stopped. "What? That overprotective blundering fool? He's the embodiment of Christianity?"

"Yes. Love thy neighbor. Do unto others. I think he does a pretty good job."

"Strength is required of true Christians. Strength to follow the righteous path. The true path."

"Marrying someone you don't love and bearing children into a fraudulent relationship? Raising them on lies?"

"Don't you dare bring my sons into this!"

"What about your wife? How is she on the Divine path when she's married to a—"

"Don't you dare!" Mark bellowed.

She eyed him coldly. "Murderer."

"You don't understand!"

"Then tell me."

Mark ran a large hand through his thick hair. "We harassed them, it's true. We did a good job of it as well. Had them quaking in their boots every time they heard a noise in the hallway. We even got them at home in their beds by throwing rocks at their windows."

"Were you involved with the Sons of Adam then?"

"The SoA is for members only! I won't discuss it."

"Fine. So you and Charleston and Rocco followed those boys and harassed them until they couldn't face coming to school again."

"They made a pact," Mark said. "A suicide pact."

"And you saw to it that they carried it out."

"It was Tommy's idea. He was more committed. We listened to them make their plan."

"How?"

"The loft above the gym. That's where they used to meet."

"And you watched them there?"

"Yes."

"So they made a pact? And you found out when they were going to do it."

"We followed them to the gym. They tied their ropes to the rafters and were supposed to jump off the second floor balcony. Tommy did it. Edward hesitated."

"He didn't want to die."

"He had second thoughts."

"How do you mean?"

"He was just standing there, on the balcony, with the rope tied around his neck. He…he started praying to God. He was praying for us. For our souls."

Jil took a deep breath, imagining what must have been going through Edward's mind.

"He said 'Forgive them, Father, for they know not what they do. Especially Mark—'" Genovese stopped, his eyes blazing at the memory. He smashed his fist against the tabletop. "I knew what was coming next."

"What?"

"He was going to say it. He was going to say it out loud."

"That you were made like him?"

"I was not!" Mark screamed. "I wasn't anything like him!"

"But Edward saw that you were."

"He was wrong! He was a liar and a sodomist! I had to shut him up."

Jil locked eyes with him. "So you pushed him?"

Mark froze.

"C'mon, Mark. Did you have the strength to stand up for your beliefs or not? Did you let that sodomist live or did you push him?"

"All right!" Mark yelled. "I pushed the faggot. Okay? I pushed him."

"Because you were doing God's will?"

"No! It was wrong of me."

Jil shook her head. "I don't understand."

"It felt like I'd cheated. It felt incomplete. He was supposed to do it himself. He was supposed to repent his sins! That's what the Sons of Adam is all about." Mark's eyes blazed and he pounded the table when he realized what he'd said. "Damn you!"

Jil held her ground, even though every instinct told her to get out of his way. "They were supposed to repent and take their own lives?"

"Yes! Like all the others!"

All the others. "How many have there been, Mark? How many people have the Sons of Adam targeted?"

"I told you not to say that name!"

"Oh, I'm going to say it. I'm going to say it to everyone who will listen. I'm going to say it on the news, on the radio. I'm even going to sit down with a reporter and make sure it hits the front page of the paper."

Mark's face turned purple. "You have to shut up!" he roared.

Just then, the door burst open and Morgan crashed over the threshold, followed by two other uniformed policemen. "Police! Get down on the ground!" shouted Morgan.

Genovese leaped into the air, toppling the table in the middle of the room with his giant hands before he dashed for the door.

Jil rolled to the side and watched as two of the officers tackled Genovese. He snarled and tried to stand with two men on his back.

The brawnier officer took him out at the knees and slapped handcuffs on his wrists.

"Wait," Jil called, getting up.

The policemen stopped. Genovese stared at her with a peculiar look on his face.

"Bobby Hansen?"

Genovese shook his head. "Had nothing to do with me."

Jil nodded. Why would he deny that one and confess to all the others. Unless he was telling the truth?

She stared at him a moment longer, but he remained immutable. "Go ahead, take him away."

"I'm not going to jail," Genovese rasped. "I'm not!"

"Why not?" Jil retorted. "Lots of bitches there. You might even like it."

Mark lunged back into the room, but the officers had a firm grip on him and shoved him outside. Jil could hear him cursing and yelling above the crunching of leaves and twigs.

"Pig-headed," Morgan said.

"Determined," she returned.

"Foolish. Brass-balled. Stubborn as hell and impulsive."

Jil flashed him a grin. "But you love me, don't you?"

"Hell yes, baby." He winked. "If you swung my way, I'd even kiss you."

"I'd rather you didn't." Jess stood in the doorway, a wry smile playing on her lips.

Morgan put his hands up in surrender. "Wouldn't dream of it, Principal Blake."

Jil cast a quick look behind Jess to make sure nobody was listening.

"I already checked," Jess whispered.

Morgan ducked out, chuckling as he closed the door to the cabin. The old hinges creaked as the wooden door banged shut.

"This place is creepy," said Jess, looking around.

"Really creepy. I think you should have it torn down."

"I will. Right after—" And she leaned forward to lock lips in a heated kiss.

After a moment, Jil broke away.

"How did you figure it out? What made you dig more?"

Jil smiled. "Regina Francis."

"Regina? The girl who slit her wrists at school?"

"She didn't die."

"What do you mean?"

Jil lowered her voice to a whisper. "When I looked through the yearbook, the description of her didn't make sense. No outgoing girl with lots of friends is going to commit suicide. She staged her death. Her girlfriend went to a conversion camp, then finished her year at St. Marguerite's and went to university in a different province."

"That's an awful lot of trouble to go to shake the SoA."

Jil narrowed her eyes, weighing the pros and cons of telling her what she'd discovered that morning.

"What is it?" A line formed between Jess's eyebrows.

Jil sighed and blew the hair out of her face. "I wish I didn't know. I wish I hadn't gone looking."

Jess leaned into the doorway. "What did you find?"

"Suicides. Suspicious ones. High school students…."

"Where? How many?"

Jil sighed again, the weight of knowledge heavy on her shoulders. "They're everywhere. If you look hard enough, they're everywhere."

"That's why Reggie had to get out of dodge."

"She was convinced she'd be followed the rest of her life. And she probably would have. So she changed her name to Frances."

"And she and Megan?"

Jil winked. "Married. With a dog."

At home that night, with Jess sitting on her couch, drinking a large glass of Bordeaux, Jil took out her tablet.

"She's really gone?" she said to Jess.

Jess looked up, over the novel she was pretending to read. Instead, she'd mostly been staring at the fire. "I'm sorry I don't know more."

Jil sighed. "I just can't believe it. How could she disappear like that? And what about Gideon?"

"They're together still, from what I understand. In another city. With a family this time. That's all the social worker would tell me."

Jil tucked her legs up.

If she wanted to find them, she could. It wouldn't be that hard. But she wondered if it was best just to leave them alone. Let them get on with their lives.

"I know what you're thinking," Jess whispered, folding her hand tightly over Jil's. "It's hard to let go."

"I can't help wondering…if Reggie could do it…"

"Bex is just as clever, Jil. She's going to be just fine."

Jil looked past her at the crackling fire and said a little prayer for their safety. For a long time, they remained silent, just holding hands, then the phone rang, breaking their dream state.

Jil answered. "Hey, old man, how's it going?"

For a moment, he didn't say anything. Fear clutched at her stomach in his silence.

"Padraig? What is it?"

He exhaled slowly, and the hiss of his breath sent a shiver down her arms.

"I don't know how to tell you, Kidd, so I'll just come out with it."
"What? What's happened?"
"It's Elise. She's died."

END

About the Author

Stevie Mikayne was slightly shocked when a private Ottawa PI agency let her into their underground training school. For three days, she battled perpetual pregnancy nausea to learn undercover secrets, including how to use an amazing assortment of PI equipment. Although she's never gone undercover, she did work for several years with medically-fragile children at the Catholic School Board, where nothing remotely exciting ever happened to her.

Books Available from Bold Strokes Books

Venus in Love by Tina Michele. Morgan Blake can't afford any distractions and Ainsley Dencourt can't afford to lose control—but the beauty of life and art usually lies in the unpredictable strokes of the artist's brush. (978-1-62639-220-5)

Rules of Revenge by AJ Quinn. When a lethal operative on a collision course with her past agrees to help a CIA analyst on a critical assignment, the encounter proves explosive in ways neither woman anticipated. (978-1-62639-221-2)

The Romance Vote by Ali Vali. Chili Alexander is a sought-after campaign consultant who isn't prepared when her boss's daughter, Samantha Pellegrin, comes to work at the firm and shakes up Chili's life from the first day. (978-1-62639-222-9)

Advance: Exodus Book One by Gun Brooke. Admiral Dael Caydoc's mission to find a new homeworld for the Oconodian people is hazardous, but working with the infuriating Commander Aniwyn "Spinner" Seclan endangers her heart and soul. (978-1-62639-224-3)

UnCatholic Conduct by Stevie Mikayne. Jil Kidd goes undercover to investigate fraud at St. Marguerite's Catholic School, but life gets complicated when her student is killed—and she begins to fall for her prime target. (978-1-62639-304-2)

Season's Meetings by Amy Dunne. Catherine Birch reluctantly ventures on the festive road trip from hell with beautiful stranger Holly Daniels only to discover the road to true love has its own obstacles to maneuver. (978-1-62639-227-4)

Myth and Magic: Queer Fairy Tales edited by Radclyffe and Stacia Seaman. Myth, magic, and monsters—the stuff of childhood dreams (or nightmares) and adult fantasies. (978-1-62639-225-0)

Nine Nights on the Windy Tree by Martha Miller. Recovering drug addict, Bertha Brannon, is an attorney who is trying to stay clean when a murder sends her back to the bad end of town. (978-1-62639-179-6)

Driving Lessons by Annameekee Hesik. Dive into Abbey Brooks's sophomore year as she attempts to figure out the amazing, but sometimes complicated, life of a you-know-who girl at Gila High School. (978-1-62639-228-1)

Asher's Shot by Elizabeth Wheeler. Asher Price's candid photographs capture the truth, but when his success requires exposing an enemy, Asher discovers his only shot at happiness involves revealing secrets of his own. (978-1-62639-229-8)

Courtship by Carsen Taite. Love and justice—a lethal mix or a perfect match? (978-1-62639-210-6)

Against Doctor's Orders by Radclyffe. Corporate financier Presley Worth wants to shut down Argyle Community Hospital, but Dr. Harper Rivers will fight her every step of the way, if she can also fight their growing attraction. (978-1-62639-211-3)

A Spark of Heavenly Fire by Kathleen Knowles. Kerry and Beth are building their life together, but unexpected circumstances could destroy their happiness. (978-1-62639-212-0)

Never Too Late by Julie Blair. When Dr. Jamie Hammond is forced to hire a new office manager, she's shocked to come face to face with Carla Grant and memories from her past. (978-1-62639-213-7)

Widow by Martha Miller. Judge Bertha Brannon must solve the murder of her lover, a policewoman she thought she'd grow old with. As more bodies pile up, the murderer starts coming for her. (978-1-62639-214-4)

Twisted Echoes by Sheri Lewis Wohl. What's a woman to do when she realizes the voices in her head are real? (978-1-62639-215-1)

Criminal Gold by Ann Aptaker. Through a dangerous night in New York in 1949, Cantor Gold, dapper dyke-about-town, smuggler of fine art, is forced by a crime lord to be his instrument of vengeance. (978-1-62639-216-8)

The Melody of Light by M.L. Rice. After surviving abuse and loss, will Riley Gordon be able to navigate her first year of college and accept true love and family? (978-1-62639-219-9)

Because of You by Julie Cannon. What would you do for the woman you were forced to leave behind? (978-1-62639-199-4)

The Job by Jove Belle. Sera always dreamed that she would one day reunite with Tor. She just didn't think it would involve terrorists, firearms, and hostages. (978-1-62639-200-7)

Making Time by C.J. Harte. Two women going in different directions meet after fifteen years and struggle to reconnect in spite of the past that separated them. (978-1-62639-201-4)

Once The Clouds Have Gone by KE Payne. Overwhelmed by the dark clouds of her past, Tag Grainger is lost until the intriguing and spirited Freddie Metcalfe unexpectedly forces her to reevaluate her life. (978-1-62639-202-1)

The Acquittal by Anne Laughlin. Chicago private investigator Josie Harper searches for the real killer of a woman whose lover has been acquitted of the crime. (978-1-62639-203-8)

An American Queer: The Amazon Trail by Lee Lynch. Lee Lynch's heartening and heart-rending history of gay life from the turbulence of the late 1900s to the triumphs of the early 2000s are recorded in this selection of her columns. (978-1-62639-204-5)

Stick McLaughlin: The Prohibition Years by CF Frizzell. Corruption in 1918 cost Stick her lover, her freedom, and her identity, but a very special flapper and the family bond of her own gang could help win them back—even if it means outwitting the Boston Mob. (978-1-62639-205-2)

Edge of Awareness by C.A. Popovich. When Maria, a woman in the middle of her third divorce, meets Dana, an out lesbian, awareness of her feelings brings up reservations about the teachings of her church. (978-1-62639-188-8)

Taken by Storm by Kim Baldwin. Lives depend on two women when a train derails high in the remote Alps, but an unforgiving mountain, avalanches, crevasses, and other perils stand between them and safety. (978-1-62639-189-5)

The Common Thread by Jaime Maddox. Dr. Nicole Coussart's life is falling apart, but fortunately, DEA Attorney Rae Rhodes is there to pick up the pieces and help Nic put them back together. (978-1-62639-190-1)

Jolt by Kris Bryant. Mystery writer Bethany Lange wasn't prepared for the twisting emotions that left her breathless the moment she laid eyes on folk singer sensation Ali Hart. (978-1-62639-191-8)

Searching For Forever by Emily Smith. Dr. Natalie Jenner's life has always been about saving others, until young paramedic Charlie Thompson comes along and shows her maybe she's the one who needs saving. (978-1-62639-186-4)

A Queer Sort of Justice: Prison Tales Across Time by Rebecca S. Buck. When liberty is only a memory, and all seems lost, what freedoms and hopes can be found within us? (978-1-62639-195-6E)

Blue Water Dreams by Dena Hankins. Lania Marchiol keeps her wary sailor's gaze trained on the horizon until Oly Rassmussen, a wickedly handsome trans man, sends her trusty compass spinning off course. (978-1-62639-192-5)

Rest Home Runaways by Clifford Henderson. Baby boomer Morgan Ronzio's troubled marriage is the least of her worries when she gets the call that her addled, eighty-six-year-old, half-blind dad has escaped the rest home. (978-1-62639-169-7)

Charm City by Mason Dixon. Raq Overstreet's loyalty to her drug kingpin boss is put to the test when she begins to fall for Bathsheba Morris, the undercover cop assigned to bring him down. (978-1-62639-198-7)

Let the Lover Be by Sheree Greer. Kiana Lewis, a functional alcoholic on the verge of destruction, finally faces the demons of her past while finding love and earning redemption in New Orleans. (978-1-62639-077-5)

Blindsided by Karis Walsh. Blindsided by love, guide dog trainer Lenae McIntyre and media personality Cara Bradley learn to trust what they see with their hearts. (978-1-62639-078-2)

About Face by VK Powell. Forensic artist Macy Sheridan and Detective Leigh Monroe work on a case that has troubled them both for years, but they're hampered by the past and their unlikely yet undeniable attraction. (978-1-62639-079-9)

Blackstone by Shea Godfrey. For Darry and Jessa, their chance at a life of freedom is stolen by the arrival of war and an ancient prophecy that just might destroy their love. (978-1-62639-080-5)

Out of This World by Maggie Morton. Iris decided to cross an ocean to get over her ex. But instead, she ends up traveling much farther, all the way to another world. Once there, only a mysterious, sexy, and magical woman can help her return home. (978-1-62639-083-6)

Kiss The Girl by Melissa Brayden. Sleeping with the enemy has never been so complicated. Brooklyn Campbell and Jessica Lennox face off in love and advertising in fast-paced New York City. (978-1-62639-071-3)

Taking Fire: A First Responders Novel by Radclyffe. Hunted by extremists and under siege by nature's most virulent weapons, Navy medic Max de Milles and Red Cross worker Rachel Winslow join forces to survive and discover something far more lasting. (978-1-62639-072-0)

First Tango in Paris by Shelley Thrasher. When French law student Eva Laroche meets American call girl Brigitte Green in 1970s Paris, they have no idea how their pasts and futures will intersect. (978-1-62639-073-7)

The War Within by Yolanda Wallace. Army nurse Meredith Moser went to Vietnam in 1967 looking to help those in need; she didn't expect to meet the love of her life along the way. (978-1-62639-074-4)

Escapades by MJ Williamz. Two women, afraid to love again, must overcome their fears to find the happiness that awaits them. (978-1-62639-182-6)

Desire at Dawn by Fiona Zedde. For Kylie, love had always come armed with sharp teeth and claws. But with the human, Olivia, she bares her vampire heart for the very first time, sharing passion, lust, and a tenderness she'd never dared dream of before. (978-1-62639-064-5)